THE DROWNED VILLAGE

It's the summer of 1935, and eleven-year-old Stella Walker is preparing to leave her home forever. Forced to evacuate to make way for a new reservoir, the village of Brackendale Green will soon be lost. But before the water has even reached them, a dreadful event threatens to tear Stella's family apart . . . In the present day, Stella is living with her granddaughter Laura, who helps to care for her as she attempts to leave double heartache behind. A fierce summer has dried up the lake and revealed the remnants of the deserted village, and Stella is sure the place still holds answers for her. With only days until the rain returns, she begs Laura to make the journey for her — and to finally solve the mysteries of the almost forgotten past.

Books by Kathleen McGurl
Published by Ulverscroft:

THE GIRL FROM BALLYMOR

KATHLEEN McGURL

THE DROWNED VILLAGE

Complete and Unabridged

CHARNWOOD
Leicester

First published in Great Britain in 2018 by
HQ
an imprint of HarperCollins*Publishers* Ltd
London

First Charnwood Edition
published 2019
by arrangement with
HarperCollins*Publishers* Ltd
London

The moral right of the author has been asserted

Copyright © 2018 by Kathleen McGurl
All rights reserved

This novel is entirely a work of fiction. The names,
characters and incidents portrayed in it are the work
of the author's imagination. Any resemblance to
actual persons, living or dead, events or localities
is entirely coincidental.

A catalogue record for this book is available
from the British Library.

ISBN 978–1–4448–4283–8

WEST
DUNBARTONSHIRE
LIBRARIES

PRICE	SUPPLIER
£20.99	U
LOCATION	CLASS
MB	AF
INVOICE DATE	
ACCESSION NUMBER	
020425197	

Published by
F. A. Thorpe (Publishing)
Anstey, Leicestershire

Set by Words & Graphics Ltd.
Anstey, Leicestershire
Printed and bound in Great Britain by
T. J. International Ltd., Padstow, Cornwall

This book is printed on acid-free paper

For my husband Ignatius.
May there be many more Lake District
walking holidays ahead of us.

Prologue

It was the same dream. All these years, always the same dream. It was cold, snowing, and she was wearing only a thin cardigan over a cotton frock. On her feet were flimsy plimsolls. The sky was white, all colour had been sucked out of the countryside, everything was monochrome. There was mud underfoot, squelching, pulling at her shoes, threatening to claim them and never give them back. On either side of her were the walls of the houses — only half height now, reaching to her waist or shoulder at most. All the roofs were gone, doors and window shutters hung off their hinges, everywhere was rubble, the sad remains of a once happy life.

And then came the water. Icy cold, nibbling first at her toes, then sloshing around her ankles, and up to her knees. She was wading through it, struggling onwards, reaching out in front of her with both hands, stretching, leaning, grasping — but always it was just out of reach. No matter how hard she tried, she could not quite touch it, and always the water was rising higher and higher, the cold of it turning her feet and hands to stone.

Ahead, in the distance, was her father's face. Torn with anguish, saying — no, shouting — something at her. She couldn't hear his words; they were drowned by the sounds of rushing water, rising tides, a burst dam, a wall of

1

water engulfing everything around her. She knew she had to reach it — that was what he wanted. If only she could get hold of it; but still, it was tantalisingly beyond her reach.

Now the water was up to her chest, her neck, and she was trying to swim but something was pulling her under, into the icy depths, and still she couldn't reach the thing she had come here for. Her chest was tight, burning with the effort to breathe as the cold engulfed her and panic rose within her.

As always, just as the water washed over her head, filling her lungs and blurring her vision, she awoke, sweating, her heart racing, and her fingers — old and gnarled now, not the smooth youthful hands of her dream — still stretching out to try to touch the battered old tea caddy . . .

1

LAURA, PRESENT DAY

The TV was turned up so loud that Laura could hear it clearly even from the kitchen, where she was preparing the evening meal of shepherd's pie. She popped the dish into the oven and went through to the living room.

'Laura, love, you must watch this! Wait a moment, while I wind it back a bit.' Stella picked up the remote control and began stabbing randomly at buttons.

'Let me, Gran,' Laura said, gently taking the remote from her. 'What do you want me to see? Should I go back to the beginning of the news?' Thank goodness you could pause and rewind live TV, she thought. Her grandmother's hearing was not so good any more, and despite having the sound turned up so loud, she still often needed to watch snippets again, or turn on the subtitles.

'No, just this bit,' Stella said, peering intently at the screen. 'There. Play it from now.'

An image of mountains and moorlands, purple heather and dry brown bracken appeared on the TV, then the camera panned round to show a dried-up lake, where a reporter was picking his way across a bed of cracked mud. Here and there were low stone walls, an iron gate, tree stumps.

The reporter stopped beside the remains of a building.

'Usually, *if I was standing here, the water level would be over my head. But the extended drought this summer means that Bereswater Reservoir has almost completely dried up, exposing the ruins of the village of Brackendale Green, once home to a couple of hundred people before the dam was built.*'

'There! Brackendale Green!' Stella's eyes were shining.

'What about it, Gran?'

'It's — it's where I was born! Where I grew up! Until I was eleven or so, when they built the dam and then Pa was . . . Pa went . . . and we all had to move out.'

'Wow, Gran, I never knew.' Laura watched with renewed interest now. She knew her grandmother came from the Lake District originally but realised in shame that she had never asked exactly where. Stella had never talked much about her early life, although she was always happy to recount stories from her days as a young actress in London, before she'd married and had her son, Laura's father.

'That's the main street he's walking down,' Stella said, her eyes still fixed on the flickering screen. 'The pub — oh now what was it called? Oh yes, the Lost Sheep! Silly name for a pub in the fells. Sheep were always lost, but they'd find their way back, most of them. Those dear old Herdwicks, they knew their way home. What was I saying? Oh yes — the pub was there. Right about where he's standing now. Pa did like a pint of ale in there of an evening.'

'*In the 1930s, the population of Brackendale Green was approximately one hundred and fifty residents, men, women and children,*' the reporter went on. '*This number was briefly swelled when the dam-building began, but in later stages the workers were housed in prefab buildings nearer the site of the dam. The village itself was demolished just before the valley flooded, but as you can see, the lower parts of the walls are still clearly visible. Here, there's a stone bridge that crossed the stream that ran through the valley. Over there, an iron gate lies in the dried mud, presumably once the entrance to a field. In here —* ' he passed through the remains of a doorway — '*some of the floorboards survive beneath the mud. The fireplace is intact, and there's even a small stove set within it.*'

The camera panned round the room, showing the items he'd spoken about.

'Funny, seeing it again after all these years,' Stella said, her voice cracking a little. 'When you think of all that happened there . . . '

Laura glanced at her in concern. 'What happened there?'

'Oh, I mean all the people who lived and worked there, were born there and grew up. That's all I mean, love. Nothing more.' Stella watched as the news programme cut back to the studio and the presenter began talking about the state of the economy. 'Switch it off now, love, will you?'

'Sure.' Laura silenced the TV. 'Gran, you've

never mentioned this before. I'd love to know more about it. What was the village called? Bracken-something?'

'Brackendale Green. Oh, it was all so long ago.' Stella's eyes misted over and she stared at the blank TV screen, deep in thought.

'Fascinating, though. Will you tell me more about it?' Laura glanced at her watch. 'There's about twenty minutes till dinner's ready. I'll go and set the table for us now, but then I'd love you to tell me more about your childhood. Will you?'

There was a strange look on Stella's face. Laura supposed it must be a bit of a shock, seeing the ruins of the place where you'd been born, exposed to the elements after more than eighty years underwater. But there was more to it than that. Stella looked as though she was hiding something, fighting with herself over whether to confide in Laura or not.

Well, maybe she'd talk, over dinner or afterwards. Laura went back out to the kitchen to set the table. It was a Friday, and they'd begun a tradition of opening a bottle of wine together. Stella only ever drank a glass a night, so one bottle would do them both Friday and Saturday nights. Laura chose a Pinot Noir and uncorked it. Another Friday night in with her ninety-year-old grandmother. Most women of her age would be out partying, if they weren't married with small children yet. And up to a couple of months before, Laura would have been out clubbing on a weekend night too — with Stuart and Martine. She'd thought she had a perfect set-up — renting a flat with her long-term boyfriend Stuart, with her best mate Martine subletting the spare room. Lots of fun and giggles, and if sometimes Stuart had complained at her for being late back from work after a client had needed extra care, or if Martine had bitched at her for not always wanting to go clubbing every weekend, on the whole it had been good. At least, it had been good until she'd come home unwell one day, and found Stuart in bed with Martine. Laura grimaced as she remembered that day. Her life had fallen apart, and if it wasn't for Gran, and having to hold herself together for her clients, she was certain she'd have had a full breakdown.

Stella made a much better flatmate. At ninety, she needed a lot of care, but that was Laura's job anyway, and so she'd taken over most of her grandmother's needs. The agency sent other carers to cover on the days when Laura's own agency needed her elsewhere. So far it had worked out well. And Laura felt she'd done a good job keeping cheerful — on the outside at least.

The oven beeped, and Laura removed the pie from the oven and set it to rest for a few minutes on the table. She poured two glasses of wine.

'Gran? Dinner's ready.' She went back through to the sitting room where Stella was still staring at the blank television. She placed the walking frame in front of her and steadied it while Stella pushed herself to her feet and took hold of the frame.

'Ooh, my old knees,' she said with a smile. 'You'd never think I used to be able to jitterbug, when you look at me now.'

'Gran, you're doing brilliantly. Hope I'm as fit as you when I'm your age.' Laura helped the old lady to sit down at the kitchen table, and began serving the meal.

'I've had a thought, Laura, dear.' Stella put down her cutlery before she'd taken so much as a mouthful, and fixed her granddaughter with a firm stare.

'Oh-oh. What is it, Gran?'

'It's time you had a holiday. You haven't had one this summer, and after all that nastiness, you need to get away.'

'I need to look after you!' But that 'nastiness', as Gran put it, had almost swamped her, she had to admit it.

'The agency can send someone else. I managed perfectly well before you moved in. Don't get me wrong, Laura, I love having you here, but you need to live your own life as well. You've barely been out since you moved here.'

She was right, but there was no one Laura wanted to go out with. All her friends had been Stuart and Martine's friends as well, and seeing any of them would mean hearing about how loved-up they were, how they were made for each other and how great it was they were able to be together at last, as if she, Laura, had been purposefully keeping them apart! When she'd lost Stuart she'd lost the whole of her old life. And she had not done much about building herself a new life yet. It was too soon, she kept telling herself, although she knew that sooner or later she'd need to get back out there making friends again. Perhaps in time even meet a new man. Someone who wouldn't discard her like a used tissue as soon as he'd had enough. But right now she couldn't even contemplate that happening.

'Respite care, they call it — to give you a break. From me.'

'Aw, Gran, I don't need a break from you. You're easy to look after.' Laura reached across the table to take her grandmother's hand.

'Oh, I'm not really. Well, I may be easier than some of your clients, as I've still got all my marbles, but I'm under no illusions about how difficult your job is. You do it all day, then come home to more of it in the evening with me. So, as I said, I think it is time you had a holiday. And I have an idea of where you might like to go.'

'Really?' Laura raised her eyebrows in amusement. Stella wasn't usually this bossy. But it was a thought — a holiday might do her good. Stella was right that she hadn't been away anywhere since the previous summer, when she and Stuart had spent a long weekend in Barcelona, before travelling along the coast to the beach resort of Lloret de Mar where they'd met up with Martine. For all she knew, Stuart and Martine's affair had started there. Perhaps a holiday on her own would help her forget them and move on.

'The Lake District,' Stella said triumphantly. 'I know how much you love the mountains. You could do a bit of walking. And . . . '

9

'And?' Get her head together and her life sorted out?

'Maybe you'd like to visit Brackendale Green,' Stella said, looking at Laura out of the corner of her eye as if she was unsure what the reaction would be.

'The drowned village where you were born, that was on the news earlier?'

'That's the one. I mean, I know you're into family history and all that. So I thought, perhaps now's the chance to see the place. And maybe it'd help you . . . you know . . . move on. Since all the nastiness it's as though you're just treading water, living here with me, not going out at all. At your age there ought to be more in your life. A holiday might help you — what's that modern computer phrase you young people use? Reboot. Reboot your life. What do you think?'

'I think, eat your dinner before it goes cold, and let me consider it,' Laura said, smiling. Dear old Gran — always had her best interests at heart. But she was probably right in that it was time for a reboot.

Stella glared at her, then broke into a broad smile. 'Yes, you think about it, love. But don't take too long or it'll rain and the village will be underwater again.'

Laura considered Stella's proposal as she ate. Gran was right — she did love the mountains. And it would be fascinating to see the remains of the village where Gran had been born. If she could get some time off next week, perhaps, and arrange alternative care for Gran, she could pack up a rucksack, dig out her old tent and sleeping bag from pre-Stuart days, and drive up there. If she camped then the whole trip would be pretty cheap. There was a campsite in Patterdale where she'd stayed a few times years ago. Or maybe there'd be another one closer to Bereswater and Brackendale Green. She could look online. As long as there was a pub that did food nearby, she didn't mind where she stayed. She could do some hiking, think about her future and try to put the mess with Stuart and Martine fully behind her. Just a few months ago she'd thought it was only a matter of time before Stuart proposed. She'd assumed they'd marry and Martine would be her bridesmaid and hen-night organiser. Huh. How blind she'd been!

'Well?' Stella put her knife and fork neatly together on her plate. She hadn't eaten everything but these days her appetite was tiny, and Laura had learned not to try to persuade her to eat more. That worked with some of her clients but Gran would just dig her heels in.

'What?'

'Have you decided? Will you take a holiday?'

Laura smiled. 'You know, I think I might. Since you seem so eager to get rid of me! I do quite fancy a trip to the Lake District, and I've still got my old tent somewhere.'

'Good! I'm really pleased. It'll do you good. You need it and you deserve it. The dinner was delicious, by the way. I'd help you wash up, if I could, but thankfully I can't.' Stella grinned impishly, and Laura chuckled at the joke she made after every evening meal.

11

'No problem, Gran, I'll do it this time,' she said, parroting the usual response.

* * *

As she washed up, a thought came to her. Where was that old tent, and her sleeping bag? She'd brought a car full of stuff to Gran's when she'd left the flat she'd shared with Stuart, but were the tent and sleeping bag amongst it all? Not that she could remember. With a sinking feeling she remembered that she'd stored it in an eaves cupboard at the flat — the one in Martine's bedroom — and she had not checked that cupboard when she moved out. It had all been a bit of a rush.

Not for the first time, she relived that hideous day in her mind as she worked. She'd gone home early because she could feel herself coming down with a cold. In her job, it was not a good idea to battle on through bugs and germs, as it was too easy to pass them on to her frailer clients. She'd called the office, who had been able to get someone else to do her last two care visits of the day, and had gratefully driven back to the flat, picking up some Beecham's cold cures on the way. She'd let herself in, expecting the flat to be empty, but then had heard sounds coming from the bedroom she shared with Stuart. He ought to have been at work. Thinking perhaps someone had broken in, she'd grabbed a golfing umbrella from the hat stand as the nearest thing she had to a weapon, steeled herself, then burst in through the bedroom door, shouting and brandishing the umbrella. The first thing she'd seen was Stuart's bare bum thrusting up and down; the second thing was Martine's shocked face, peering over his shoulder.

Stuart looked around. 'Fuck, Lols, you gave me a fright! What's with the screaming and all?'

'Laura, oh my God!' Martine shuffled out from underneath Stuart, grabbed the nearest item to cover herself — Laura's fleecy dressing gown — and pushed past Laura, out of the room.

Laura was speechless. How long she had stood there, staring at Stuart, she didn't know. It could have been two seconds or twenty minutes. Her mind was in turmoil. Stuart? And *Martine*? Martine, who she'd considered her best friend. Stuart was scrabbling around for his clothes, which were strewn across the floor. As he stood up to pull on his underpants Laura finally found her voice. 'How long?'

'You what?'

'How long — has this been going on?'

'What?'

'You and Martine, of course! What do you think I'm talking about? How long have you been . . . *shagging* her?' She spat the word out.

'Shit, I dunno, Lols, not long, it's just . . . '

'Ten months.' Martine was standing behind her, now dressed in her own clothes. 'Sorry, Laura. You had to find out sooner or later but I guess this wasn't the best way. Stu, I said you should have told her.'

'Couldn't find the right time, hon. Well, she

13

knows now. Sorry, Lols.' Stuart reached out a hand, and Laura instinctively stepped forward to take it, then realised he was reaching for Martine. 'She's just, well, more my type, I guess. Come on, Lols, we had some good times but it hasn't been working for a while. You know that. Martine and I kind of drifted together, as you and I have drifted apart.'

Drifted apart? Had they? Well, they hadn't had as many evenings together as a couple lately, what with Laura's recent shift patterns which had meant she'd been working till ten p.m. five nights a week. The other two nights if they went out Martine had always come with them. And — ten months? *Ten!* Laura could not seem to form any sentences to respond. It was all too much to take in at once. She'd been living a lie for nearly a year!

'Lols? I guess maybe you and Martine should swap rooms. I mean, now it's all out in the open . . . ' Stuart said, with a shrug.

That did it. 'Swap rooms? You think you just move me into the spare room now you're bored of me, and Martine into our room? It's as easy as that? You bastard, Stuart. You are a complete and utter GIT! And you — ' Laura turned to Martine — 'how even could you? I thought you were my friend. My *best* friend. Well, fuck you.' She picked up the nearest object to hand — a ring-binder folder of Stuart's containing details of his work projects — and flung it across the room at them both. Satisfyingly, it popped open in mid-air, showering papers everywhere.

'Laura, for fuck's sake, that stuff's important!'

14

Stuart began gathering up the loose papers.

'More important than me, clearly.' Laura crossed the room, trampling across the papers, and flung open the wardrobe. She grabbed a holdall and began throwing her clothes into it.

'What are you doing?'

'Leaving you two lovebirds — what does it look like? You can refund me the rent I've paid for this month. I'll collect the rest of my stuff tomorrow when you're out.' She tried to close the bag but the zip got caught in a woolly jumper she'd rammed in the top.

'Where will you go?' asked Martine. She at least had the grace to look mortified, unlike Stuart who seemed merely annoyed that he'd been found out.

'Why the fuck should you even care?' Laura swept an assortment of toiletries, make-up and jewellery from the top of the chest of drawers into a carrier bag. She leaned over the bed to grab her half-read book from the top of the bedside cabinet and Stuart cringed as though he thought she was about to hit him. 'I'm going. You can move your stuff in tomorrow when I've cleared it out properly.' And with that, she'd stormed out of the flat, banging the door so hard that their downstairs neighbour stuck his head out to see what was going on.

In her car, she'd sat breathing deeply for a few minutes. She'd left the cold and flu remedies she'd bought in the flat, and was feeling worse. Not surprising, really, she told herself. It's not every day you lose your boyfriend, your best mate and your home all while trying to battle the

15

onset of a cold. Where *would* she go? And then the tears had come.

★   ★   ★

Now, finishing drying up the dinner things and with unbidden tears trailing down her cheeks at the painful memories, she recalled it was at that moment, her lowest, most despairing point, that a text had arrived, from her gran. Dear Laura, the text read, Stella being of the generation that felt all written communication should be properly spelt and punctuated, if you get the chance could you pick up a pint of milk for me and drop it round? Clumsy old thing that I am, I dropped the carton all over the floor, and now there's none for my bedtime Ovaltine. Thank you, with love from Gran.

And that was when she'd worked out her plan. She would ask if she could stay with Stella until she could work something else out. What that something else would be she had no idea. In return she could help with Gran's care, reducing her costs. She'd bought more cold remedies and the milk, and turned up on her grandmother's doorstep, her eyes red and her nose streaming. Stella had been horrified by what had happened but delighted by the idea of having Laura to live with her, telling her she could stay for as long as she wanted.

Laura put away the last of the dishes, splashed water on her face and dried her eyes, then picked up her wine glass and went through to the sitting room where Stella was quietly knitting squares for a blanket. The cat, Jasper, was curled up beside her, battling with himself. He knew he was not allowed to play with the knitting wool but oh, how he wanted to! His eyes watched the yarn dancing across Stella's lap, and every now and then he would twitch as though he was about to go for it.

'Do you realise I've been living here with you for two months now?' Laura said, as she gave Jasper a stroke and sat down.

'Nearly three months, dear. You arrived on June the sixth — I remember because it was the D-Day anniversary — and now it is August the twenty-eighth. Are you fed up with your old gran yet?'

'Not at all — I love being here!' Laura wasn't lying. It had all worked out better than she could have hoped. Gran had offered a sympathetic ear, some gently given advice, a comfortable room to sleep in, and was great company when Laura wasn't working. No matter that her parents lived in Australia — when you had a gran like Stella! And although Laura had not yet done much about rebuilding her life, she knew that her sojourn with Gran had at least given her time to get over Stuart. Was she over him? She hoped so, but did still find herself crying herself to sleep sometimes, even though she knew he wasn't worth it.

'But you do need a holiday,' prompted Stella, with a questioning glance at Laura.

Laura smiled. 'Yes, I am owed loads of leave, and it would be lovely to see where you lived. I'll call round to the flat tomorrow and try to retrieve my tent and sleeping bag that I left there, and I'll talk to Ewan in the office about booking the time off, and getting someone to cover your care. Ewan's a mate of mine. He'll sort it out for me, even though it's short notice. Thanks for the suggestion, Gran!' And while she was away she'd have a good long think about her future and make sure she was fully over Stuart, she decided.

She held up her wine glass and Stella clinked it with her knitting needles. The old lady's expression held something that Laura couldn't quite read. She seemed pleased Laura had decided to go to Brackendale Green but at the same time, it was as though she was fighting an internal battle. She was definitely hiding something.

2

JED, APRIL 1935

Jed held tightly to his daughter Stella's hand as they walked up the steep track that led up on to the fells behind the village. Three dozen mourners followed behind them. The coffin containing his beloved Edie had been taken by road, in the hearse, to Glydesdale in the next valley where she would be buried, but Jed had chosen to walk the old way, the traditional route over the hills, to reach the church.

'All right, lass?' he asked Stella, and received a mute nod in reply. The poor mite, of course she was missing her ma. No child of ten years old ought to be left motherless. No child of two, either, Jed thought, thinking of little Jessie whom he'd left behind in Brackendale Green being cared for by a neighbour. But Edie had died, of cancer, leaving Jed and the two girls alone.

It broke his heart that they could not bury her in St Isidore's Church in Brackendale Green, where generations of his family had been buried. But the dam-building had begun, there were compulsory purchase orders on every house in Brackendale, and the village's days were numbered. In another year or maybe even less everyone would have to move out. Where he, Stella and Jessie would go or what he would do for a living Jed had no idea. He could not think

19

that far ahead. The last year had been taken up with caring for Edie, and now she was gone he would need to figure out how he could manage to look after the girls and still work. And then there was his father, Isaac, who was increasingly frail and also dependent on Jed for support.

Well, all those worries would have to wait until Edie was safe underground in Glydesdale churchyard. He took a deep breath. At least the weather was fine for her burial. It was the kind of day Edie had always loved — springtime, with blue skies, clear air, bright green foliage on the trees and bushes, and down in the valleys, an abundance of fluffy black Herdwick lambs on their spindly legs. A time of rebirth and hope for the future. But not this year. This year it was a time of death and fear of what was to come.

'Is it much further?' Stella asked. She was usually a good little walker, but the past few weeks had been hard on her. Jed had relied on her to prepare food and look after her sister, while he sat at Edie's side.

'Not so far now,' he replied with a reassuring smile. They walked on in silence, but a moment later when Stella stumbled on a rough section of the track, he scooped her up onto his broad shoulders. 'I'll carry you for a bit, lass, to give you a rest.'

'Thanks, Pa,' she said, as she tucked her feet under his arms and held his upraised hands for balance. He gritted his teeth with the effort of walking uphill with her weight on his shoulders. He'd not carried her like this since she was smaller, and it was tough going, but she was his daughter so she could not be a burden. He could do this.

'Stella, get down, you're a big enough girl to walk it yourself without making your father carry you.' It was Maggie, Jed's neighbour, who'd caught up alongside them.

'Ah, she's all right up there, Maggie. The poor lass is exhausted so I don't mind carrying her a while.' Maggie had been a good friend throughout Edie's illness. She'd helped nurse her, she'd brought in pots of mutton stew for their dinner, and once, she'd cared for Jessie while Stella was at school, to allow Jed to stay with Edie.

'She looks so heavy, such a burden for you. Well, we're almost at the top — then perhaps she can walk by herself. You can't be carried all the way to your own mother's funeral, now can you?'

'Pa, I'll walk now,' Stella said wearily, and Jed hoisted her down again. The child hung back behind him with some of the other mourners, as Maggie fell into step alongside him. Stella didn't much like Maggie, he knew.

'That's better,' Maggie said. 'Now we can talk as adults. Jed, you'll need help managing the girls, won't you? I mean, I'll do what I can for you, but long term, you'll need someone living in. You'll need to take another wife.'

'For the Lord's sake, Maggie, I've not yet buried my first wife!' Jed could not help blurting out the words. 'Give me a chance, woman.'

Maggie had the grace to hang her head. 'I'm sorry. You know me, Jed. Sometimes I speak my mind before I think it through properly.' She

21

reached out to touch his arm. 'I want only the best for you, never forget that.'

Jed softened his expression. 'Aye, Maggie, I know that.'

They walked on. Maggie paused to flick a stone out of her shoe, and Stella then ran up to take her place beside Jed once more, slipping her little hand into his roughened one.

'I was thinking, Pa, that Ma would have liked this walk, and with all the village coming too. Perhaps we should have carried her over this way to the church.'

'It'd have been a struggle, lass. But you know, a hundred years ago that's what the people of Brackendale did with their dead. Before St Isidore's graveyard was consecrated, coffins were carried over here all the way to Glydesdale for burial. That's why it's called the Old Corpse Road. See that flat stone, there?'

Stella looked where he was pointing, at a large flat-topped stone just off the path.

'It's a lych-stone. The men would have placed the coffin there for a rest. There are a few of them on this route, and then the final one in the lych-gate of the Glydesdale church.'

Stella shuddered. 'Are there ghosts up here, then? If so many dead bodies were carried along this path?'

Jed smiled sadly at her. 'Who knows, lass? Perhaps there are. Well, we need to walk a bit faster if we're to get to Glydesdale in time to meet your ma's coffin there. Can you manage it?'

She nodded solemnly, and quickened her pace. Jed matched it, and the crowd behind did too. So many from the village were coming to the funeral. Everyone except Janie Earnshaw, Maggie's mother, who'd offered to stay behind and take care of little Jessie as she had to stay to look after her sister Susie anyway. A funeral was no place for someone like poor Susie.

The sun was climbing higher and the day was warming up from its frosty start. Jed checked his pocket watch — the one that his father, Isaac, had passed on to him. They would be on time, as long as they didn't slow up at all. In any case, the vicar would surely not start the service without them. Jed was still glad he had chosen to walk rather than ride in the hearse with Edie, or in a motorcar following it. The fresh air and exercise after the days stuck indoors at Edie's sickbed were doing him good, helping him to realise that life would still go on and it was up to him, for the sake of the girls, to make the best of it. Though how he would manage it he didn't know. He'd lost his wife and soon he would lose his home, his workshop, his business as a mechanic, and indeed his whole community, the village where he was born and had lived all his life. Times were tough. But he'd promised Edie, as she lay dying, that he would give the girls a good life. They'd want for nothing, if it was within his power to provide it.

Stella tugged on his hand. 'Look!' She was pointing high above them, where a skylark was singing its heart out. 'It's Ma. She's telling us she's all right, and that it doesn't hurt any more, and that she wants us to be happy.'

Jed looked up, and blinked against the bright

23

sunlight. 'Yes, lass, perhaps it is your ma. We'll do our best to be happy, eh, after today at any rate.' His voice broke a little as he spoke. He hadn't yet told Stella that they would have to move out of their home in a year. She knew about the dam, of course — she'd seen the land where it was to be sited being prepared, the new road being built for the workmen to use. And it had been impossible to prevent her from hearing the talk in the village. It had been almost the only topic of conversation for months, ever since that first meeting when officials from the water board had called the villagers together in the Lost Sheep and told them their valley was to be flooded to build a reservoir. The water would be piped all the way to Manchester. So Stella knew, but whether she had worked out that they would not have long left in the village Jed didn't know. And now was not the time to talk about it.

They were descending now, into the Glydesdale valley. The familiar mountains surrounding Brackendale were out of sight, and instead there was a new vista — steep screes tumbling down to meet the lush fields of Glydesdale, a few farms dotted through the valley and a little cluster of cottages surrounding the church. Soon they would join the road at the bottom that followed the stream through the dale to the village and the church where Jed would be reunited with Edie's coffin, before it was put into the ground. He'd be walking this route many more times over the next year, he knew, coming to visit her grave. And after that, when Brackendale was evacuated, who knew where he'd be living. He could only hope that he would still be within easy reach of the Glydesdale church so he'd be able to continue paying his respects.

★ ★ ★

Edie's older sister, Winnie, a spinster who lived in the nearby town of Penrith, met them by the church lych-gate. Her eyes were red-rimmed. 'One so young as Edie should never have to be buried,' she said, between her sobs, and Jed nodded in reply, swallowing hard, not trusting himself to say anything. He did not want to break down in front of Stella, whose hand he held tightly throughout the quiet and sombre service. The girl was so brave, he thought. Only a few gentle sniffs gave away the fact that she was weeping. She held her head high throughout, and stepped forward to throw a handful of dirt into the grave when he nudged her. Only then did she have to dash away a tear.

As they walked away from the grave and people started heading back up the track that led over the fells and back to Brackendale, Jed began to regret his decision to walk. Poor Stella — the child had had enough. How could he have expected her to walk all the way here and back again? She was exhausted. He looked around for someone who might have driven the long way round from Brackendale. Perhaps someone would be able to give her a lift. But almost the whole village had walked with him, as a sign of solidarity. He had welcomed it, but right now he could do with someone who had a motor car, or at least a pony and trap. Winnie had travelled by bus, and hurried off after the service to catch the one back to Penrith, after pressing Jed's hand and urging him to stay in touch.

'Jed Walker, isn't it? I am sorry for your loss.'

He spun around to see who was speaking. She was a well-dressed woman of perhaps forty, wearing a tailored black coat and a neat hat, and carrying a shiny black handbag.

'Aye, I'm Jed Walker,' he answered.

She held out a black-gloved hand. 'Alexandria Pendleton. Your wife used to be my housemaid, before she married. I live up at the manor.'

Of course, he recognised her now. She was from the 'big house' as the village folk liked to call it. In days gone by, before the Great War, the Pendletons had owned most of the land around here. But now there was just the manor house and one farm. The current squire of the manor worked in government and spent most of the week in London, travelling up and down the country each week by rail. Jed shook her hand, ashamed of his rough workman's hands against her soft leather. 'Pleased to meet you, ma'am.'

'Edie was a good worker. We missed her when she left us to get married. So tragic that she has died so young. Oh, is this your daughter?'

Stella had sidled up to Jed and once again slipped her hand into his.

'Aye, this is my eldest. Stella, say hello to the lady.'

Stella bent her knees in an approximation of a curtsey, then stepped back so she was partly behind Jed. She was hiding her tear-stained face, he realised.

'Sorry about the lass. It's been a hard time for her, and we had a long walk over the fells from Brackendale.'

'Surely you're not going to make her walk back as well?' Mrs Pendleton looked shocked. 'Wait there a moment.' She trotted off across the churchyard in her high-heeled shoes, and caught the arm of a man in a chauffeur's cap and jacket. Jed watched as she spoke to him; he nodded, and then she returned to Jed and Stella.

'You shall ride back to Brackendale in my motorcar. Thomas will take me home first for I have much to do, and then he will return here to take you and the child home.' She nodded curtly, a woman who was clearly used to being obeyed.

'Thank you. That is very kind,' Jed replied.

'It is nothing. You can wait by the lych-gate.' Mrs Pendleton took her leave, and walked over to the front of the church where her Bentley was waiting.

'Come on, lass. We'll wait where she said, and then we'll get a ride in a big, powerful motorcar.' Jed took Stella's hand and began to walk over to the lych-gate. But before they had got very far, Maggie approached.

'What was all that about? Hobnobbing with the gentry now, are you?' She gave him a quirky smile as if to show she was teasing. Jed felt irritated. Why couldn't the woman see that today, the day he buried his wife, was no time to be fending off flirtatious neighbours?

'Stella's tired. Mrs Pendleton has offered her

27

motorcar to take us home.'

'Ooh, exciting! Is there space for me, do you think?'

Jed shook his head. 'She offered the ride to me and Stella. I wouldn't dare take anyone else. The word'll get back to her and she'll think I was taking advantage. Sorry, Maggie.'

'Hmph. I suppose I'll have to walk, then.' Maggie turned on her heel and marched away, leaving Jed breathing a sigh of relief. They had history, he and Maggie. Way back when they were young, just in their twenties, he'd stepped out with her once or twice. There'd been a couple of bus rides into Penrith, and visits to the cinema. A dance or two, and a Christmas kiss under the mistletoe in the Lost Sheep. But then he'd met Edie and had fallen head over heels in love with her — her easy laugh, her endless optimism and kindness, her soft grey eyes and capable hands. He'd had to let Maggie down gently, and although she'd come to his and Edie's wedding and congratulated them, she'd never married herself, and he'd always suspected she had never quite got over losing him. Well, it couldn't be helped. A man couldn't influence who he fell in love with, could he? And he would never regret a second of the time he'd spent with Edie.

He sat beside Stella, inside the lych-gate, and took her hand. 'We'll be all right, lass. You, me and little Jessie. We've still got each other, and your ma'll be watching over us from up above, like that skylark you saw.'

She turned to him and offered up a sad smile.

His heart melted. She was the spit of Edie, and like her in temperament too. Jessie, in contrast, was shaping up to be more like him — impetuous, contrary, and a bit of a handful at two years old. But Stella was a darling, a good girl, a real asset. Just as well. She'd had to grow up quickly when her mother became ill, and now she'd have even more responsibilities if they were to stay together as a family, the three of them. He sighed. The future would be tough, and he had no idea how they would manage. His only consolation was that his love for his daughters was surely powerful enough to pull them through.

A crunch of gravel made him look up. The Bentley was back. The chauffeur remained sitting in the driving seat, gesturing to Jed to open the back door. He'd have got out and opened it for Mrs Pendleton, Jed thought wryly, but he was grateful enough that Stella was not having to walk. He tugged open the door, and Stella climbed in first, then he followed. Inside, the car smelt of leather and polish. If it hadn't been the day of Edie's funeral Jed felt he'd have enjoyed the experience. It wasn't every day you had a ride in an expensive motorcar like this one. Usually his transport would be the bus to Penrith or a ride in a trailer towed by one of his neighbours' tractors.

The road route back to Brackendale took them to the bottom end of the Glydesdale valley, following the stream, before turning northwards in the direction of Penrith. A little further along there was a left turn, heading westwards into the

Brackendale valley. This was the new road, built by the waterworks to allow easy access for the construction traffic. It was smoothly surfaced and wide enough for two tipper trucks to pass each other. A far cry, Jed thought, from the rutted old track, more potholes than tarmac, that they'd had to use before. The new road continued past the dam worksite and as far as Brackendale Green, along the side of the valley. It marked, Jed supposed, where the new waterline was expected to be, once the valley was flooded.

'Pa, look,' Stella said, tugging his arm and pointing out of the window. The site of the dam had come into view as they'd rounded a corner. It had been a few months since he'd last come this way, and it was clear much progress had been made. Whereas before there'd been just a scar across the valley where the land had been cleared and dug out to house the huge foundations for the dam, now there were massive concrete structures rising up. Fifty feet wide at the base, and tapering towards the top. The highest sections were over fifty feet high but Jed had heard the dam would be up to a hundred feet above the level of the Bere beck that flowed through the valley.

'It's coming on,' he said to Stella.

'What will happen when the dam goes all the way across?' she asked, turning to him with her wide, sad eyes. So like Edie's, he thought, with a stab of pain at her loss.

'Then the water will rise up on the upper side, and the little lake we already have will grow very much bigger, lass. And they'll control how much water flows through into the pipes that will lead all the way to Manchester.'

'What about our village? Will the water reach there?'

'It will eventually, lass.'

'What will we do?'

Was this really the best time for such a conversation? On the very day they'd buried her poor mother? Jed sighed. She had to know, sooner or later. 'We'll have to go and live somewhere else. Everyone will.'

'Where?'

'That I don't know, lass. I really don't know.'

3

LAURA

It was late afternoon by the time Laura arrived at her destination. She'd researched on the internet for campsites near to Bereswater, the lake that occupied the valley where Brackendale Green had once stood. There was one in the next valley, Glydesdale, and she'd been able to book a pitch online. And finally, after a long and tedious drive up the M6, here she was, with a full week ahead to climb some mountains, relax in the sunshine, have a long hard think about her future and of course, explore Gran's birthplace. The weather forecast predicted that the dry, sunny weather would continue for a few more days yet.

The scenery, as she'd left the main roads, entered the Lake District and driven along the narrow twisting road that led into Glydesdale, had been breathtaking. Dry stone walls lined the lane, beyond which were fields in which the year's lambs, now four or five months old, still bleated for their mothers and tried to suckle. A pretty stream ran along the valley bottom. Either side of the valley, beyond the fertile low-lying fields, were the slopes of the mountains, or 'fells' as they were more usually known in this part of the country. Bracken gave way to heather higher up, then craggy rocks. Here and there scree runs tumbled down the mountainsides. A waterfall, now only a trickle after the prolonged drought, made its way down over rocks and through a ravine lined with stumpy trees. It was beautiful. Laura couldn't wait to get her walking boots on, her rucksack on her back, and start exploring. She felt as though the countryside was already working wonders and washing away her problems. What a great idea of Gran's it had been, to have a holiday now before the good weather ended!

At the campsite she parked outside the wooden building which served as an office and small shop, and went inside to check in.

'You've come at a good time,' the girl who was manning the desk and cash register told her. 'The kids go back to school this week, so all the families left at the weekend. We're half empty so you can pick your pitch. Down beside the stream is nice, and there are a few trees for shade if it gets too hot.'

'Sounds lovely!' Laura said, accepting a map of the campsite which showed where the amenities — shower block, toilets, launderette — were sited.

'We open the shop at eight each morning, and there'll be fresh bread and croissants, plus bacon butties, coffee and tea if you don't want to cook your own breakfast. We can do packed lunches too, if you're off up the fells.'

Laura grinned. 'Perfect. What more could a camper want?'

The girl smiled back. 'We aim to please. A detailed weather forecast for the next day is pinned on the door each afternoon. Worth checking before you set out, but I can tell you there's no danger of rain until at least Friday. So, there's your tag to hang on your tent, and a sticker for your car windscreen. As I said, take any pitch you want.'

'Thanks so much. I think I'm going to enjoy camping here,' Laura said. She turned to leave, and almost bumped into a sandy-haired man who she hadn't noticed was standing behind her, waiting to pay for a pint of milk and a pack of sausages. 'Whoops! Sorry.'

'No problem,' he said. 'You missed standing on my foot, so that's OK.' He smiled, an attractive, slightly lopsided smile that made his grey eyes crinkle at the edges. 'You've just arrived? I can recommend those pitches beside the river. Perfect to cool your feet after a hot day walking in the hills.'

'Thanks, I'll go and check it out,' Laura replied, as she left the office.

'Enjoy your stay.' He waved, then turned to pay for his shopping.

★   ★   ★

That bloke was right, Laura thought, as she drove slowly around the campsite, checking out the available pitches. The area beside the stream was definitely the most inviting, and there was a large pitch free beside a spreading oak tree. She pulled out her compass to check which way was east. Always good to have some shade in the mornings, or the heat of the morning sun could drive you out of your tent before you'd had a chance to have a decent lie-in. Looked like the tree would do the job, so she parked her car, opened the boot and began setting up camp.

The tent was brand new. As was her sleeping bag. In the end, she'd avoided a possible confrontation with Stuart by treating herself to new kit. For summer camping, cheap festival gear was good enough. It only took her half an hour to get everything set up, and her little camping gas stove (also new) up and running to make a cup of tea. She unfolded a deckchair she'd found in Gran's shed, set it in the sunshine and sat down to wait for her pot to boil. Behind her, the little stream was chuckling to itself like a giggling child as it bubbled over stones down the valley. Ahead of her was the most amazing view, framed by branches of the oak, across the valley to the fells. She'd need to pull out her detailed map of the area to work out which ones they were, but already she could see an enticing-looking path zigzagging its way up one of them. But that would have to wait — tomorrow she wanted to go to Brackendale. She sighed with contentment. It was shaping up to be a very good week.

It was years since she'd last been camping. Stuart's style was more suited to package holidays in Ibiza — sunshine, booze and partying. She'd gone along with it because she loved him and loved being with him. And they'd had fun. At least, she'd thought it was fun at the time. Looking back, she wondered why she'd never pushed for them to try a different type of holiday. One that didn't involve daily hangovers.

Would he have agreed? Who knew? If he had, it might have left them with a healthier relationship — one in which they were more of a partnership. She could see it more clearly now they'd been apart a few months — theirs had not been a relationship of equals. She'd always done whatever Stuart wanted, as though she was his pet lapdog. Perhaps it was as well it had finished the way it had, allowing no way back, although she did miss the intimacy. She missed having a best friend, too, and knew it would be ages before she could trust anyone fully again.

She spent the evening lounging outside her tent, cooking a simple meal of pasta with grated cheese, which tasted amazing when accompanied by a glass of Pinot Noir. She read books until the sun went down behind the mountains, took an evening walk around the campsite, called Gran to check she was all right, then put herself to bed early, just as it was getting dark, tired after the long drive north. Maybe the Lake District was already working its magic, as she managed to doze off without crying herself to sleep.

★　★　★

The following morning dawned bright and clear, but despite the shade of the oak the inside of the little tent was stifling hot by eight o'clock. Laura dressed quickly in shorts and a T-shirt, and bought coffee and a bacon butty from the campsite shop. As she ate them she studied her map, and realised the zigzag path she could see going up the fells on the other side of the valley led into Brackendale. It was marked on the map as the Old Corpse Road. 'Interesting name for a footpath,' she muttered to herself, making a mental note to google it at the next opportunity. It looked to be about three kilometres to walk, with four hundred metres of ascent, from the campsite to Brackendale, and on a day like this why not walk it rather than drive around? She packed her rucksack with a bottle of water, a hastily made sandwich and some snacks, donned her walking boots and set off.

To begin with her route took her along the lane going further up the valley, past a church with its overgrown graveyard, full of lopsided lichen-clad gravestones. A little further on, a public footpath sign pointed the way to 'Brackendale via Old Corpse Road'.

The track wound its way between acres of waist-high dried-out bracken, then began the zigzags she could see from the campsite, where heather and outcrops of rock flanked the path. As she climbed higher the temperature seemed to increase as there was no shade and very little breeze. The land smelt dry and dusty. She sat to rest on a flat-topped rock that was just to the side of the path, wondering whether it was natural or had been placed there for some reason. She took a gulp of water from her bottle, wishing she'd brought more than one as she was not at the top of this climb and it was half gone already.

As she walked she found herself thinking about her clients, and wondering how they were getting on without her. Of course the agency would be sending alternative carers, but some clients always told her how much they looked forward to Laura's visits. Like dear old Bert Williamson, who always had a joke ready for her every time she came. As often as not it'd be one she'd heard before — usually from Bert himself the previous week, as his memory was not the best — but she'd chuckle anyway and tell him he was such a card, as she got him washed, dressed and ready for the day. And lovely Ada, where her morning calls would always include helping the old lady pick out earrings and a necklace to match her outfit for the day. Her job paid poorly but it was so meaningful and worthwhile, and people like Bert and Ada made it enjoyable. The worst moments were when she arrived at a client's home to find them very sick, and she'd need to call an ambulance and send them off to hospital, knowing there was a strong chance they wouldn't come home again. Her training had taught her not to get too involved with clients, but sometimes she couldn't help it.

At last the gradient levelled out and she found herself crossing a rounded hilltop, land that might be boggy in a wet season but currently was formed of hardened mud, with the path winding its way through. The view changed — now she could see a new range of higher hills that must be on the far side of Brackendale looming on the horizon. Eventually the path began to lose height and then suddenly, as it turned a corner, there it was — the whole valley of Brackendale laid out before her. She gasped at the sight. Away over to her right she could just see the dam, and a small lake, not much more than a pond, this side of it. A huge expanse of muddy lake-bed covered the rest of the valley floor, just as she'd seen on the TV news report. Around the edges was a fringe of pebbles, as though normally the reservoir had a bit of pebble beach. The valley sides were lined with trees. She squinted, trying to pick out the ruins of the village amongst the dried mud, but from this height it was difficult to be sure what she was seeing. It would be nice to have a companion, someone to talk to about what they could see, but of course there was no one. Stuart would never have come on this type of holiday. Neither would Martine. With a jolt Laura realised those two were probably well matched after all. She sniffed back the tears that threatened to fall, pushed all thoughts of Stuart out of her mind and picked up her pace on the descent, desperate to get down to the lakeside and start exploring.

The bottom of the track led into a car park, after crossing a stile. There were a number of cars parked there, presumably either hikers or tourists who'd come to see the empty reservoir. An information board beside the car park gave a few sketchy details about the history of the valley and the building of the dam, complete with a grainy photo of what the village of Brackendale Green looked like in the early 1930s. Laura peered closely at this, noting the church, a pub, a bridge over a stream, a group of cottages tightly packed in what was presumably the village centre, and then some more scattered cottages and farm buildings further out. She lifted her head to look at the dried lake-bed, where she could now clearly see the low, broken walls that the TV reporter had pointed out. She tried to map buildings shown on the photo against the ruins but from where she was standing it wasn't possible. Time to venture onto the dried mud and explore it properly.

She crossed the car park, walked a little way along the lane that would normally hug the shores of the lake, then when she was near to some of the ruins she left the road, crossed the band of pebbles and tentatively set foot on the grey mud. It was rock solid, criss-crossed with cracks from the weeks of sunshine, and smelt a little of rotting vegetation, as any aquatic plants the lake had hosted had long since perished in the dry heat. More confident now that she'd discovered how firm the mud's surface was, she set out across it to the nearest piece of wall. It was about waist high, with mounds of rubble inside, and a clear doorway. On the opposite side to the door were the remains of a window, complete with some green-glazed tiles on the inside ledge. Laura entered the cottage, and immediately felt the surface beneath her feet change, as though there were only a couple of inches of dried mud on top of a more solid base — stone flags, she presumed.

The next cottage felt different underfoot. She knelt down and rubbed at the dried mud with her fingertips, discovering wooden floorboards beneath. Presumably pretty rotten after eighty years underwater, so she left that cottage quickly.

There was someone else crossing the lake-bed towards the ruins. As he approached she recognised the sandy-haired man from the campsite. He was heading directly for her, and raised a hand in greeting.

'Amazing, isn't it?' she said, when he was within earshot.

He smiled, and pushed a hand through his hair. 'Certainly is. To think people once lived here, walked up this street, went into their homes or shops or pubs.' He turned and gazed across the remains of the village, then pulled a bottle of water out of his rucksack and offered it to her. 'I can't believe how hot it is, either.'

'I know. Boiling. But I've got my own water, thanks.'

They began walking along what must once have been the main street through the village, with remains of buildings tightly packed on both sides. 'I'm Tom, by the way,' he said, holding out his hand for her to shake.

'Laura. Pleased to meet you.'

'So did you come here especially to see the remains of the village?' he asked.

She nodded. 'Well, yes, but also to have a holiday and do some walking. I adore the Lake District.'

'Me too. I've been here a week already, climbing with a mate. He's a teacher so he had to leave at the weekend and go back to work today. But the weather's so amazing I decided to stay for a few more days on my own as I'm not due back in the office till next week.' He stopped and once more looked around at the ruins, then spoke quietly, almost to himself. 'I wonder which one it was.'

'Sorry?'

He shook his head slightly as though coming out of a daydream. 'Sorry. Just musing. I've researched my family tree, you see, and one branch of my ancestors came from here.'

'Wow, that's amazing! My grandmother was born here, too. That's one reason why I came. We saw an item on the news about it, and she told me then she was born here. I hadn't known. She's a bit too frail to make the trip up here herself, though.'

'Do you know which house she lived in?'

Laura shook her head. 'No, I've no idea.' She looked up at him and smiled. 'Weird to think our ancestors might have known each other. Who was it in your family tree who lived here? How long ago?'

'My dad's maternal grandmother. That's my great-grandmother — she was the last of the family to live here. Her daughter, my grand-mother, was born elsewhere, during the war. My great-grandmother married, had her daughter and was widowed all during the war years. Your grandmother must be quite a bit older than mine, if she was born here.'

'She's over ninety.'

'A great age. Does she have any memories of being here?'

'Yes, some, I think, though she hasn't spoken much about it.'

'You should ask her.'

'Yes. I could ask her too for names of anyone

she remembers from those days. But she was only about ten or eleven when the village was abandoned so she might not remember anyone. What was your great-grandmother's name?'

'Margaret Earnshaw.'

'My gran is Stella Braithwaite. But that's her married name. I'm not sure what her maiden name was. I need to make a list of all these questions to ask her!' Laura grinned. It was great to have someone to talk to about all this, and Tom certainly seemed interested.

'It's fabulous that she's still around to ask. My grandmother died a few years back so most of what I know is from online research. In fact, it was when she was diagnosed with cancer that I began researching my family tree. I recorded her speaking about the past, everything she could remember, to give me a start. But she never lived here, and she said her mother, Margaret — though everyone knew her as Maggie — never spoke about her early life.' Tom sighed. 'So I've no one to ask. The people who lived here are all just names and dates to me.'

They'd reached the end of the main village street, and come to a small stone bridge. It looked incongruous sitting there in the middle of the lake-bed, a bridge crossing nothing. 'This must have been the footbridge over the stream that flowed through the valley to the original small lake. It's marked on the old maps of the village,' Tom said. 'Amazing that it's still in such good condition.' He ran a hand over the stonework. He was right — the mortar between the stones appeared solid, the surface of the

43

bridge looked as though a quick sweep would restore it to perfect condition.

They turned and looked back at the village. 'I really want to know more about it now,' said Laura. 'Coming here has made it all very real. I can't wait to ask Gran to tell me more about it.'

'Why don't you ask her now? You could ring her, perhaps? Maybe she could describe whereabouts her house was. And I'd love to know if she remembers any Earnshaws.'

Laura looked at her watch. Monday, midday. Gran would be at home, pottering around the house, perhaps thinking about making herself a light lunch. She had no lunchtime carer visit, so unless one of her many friends had come to call, she'd be on her own, and hopefully the phone would be within reach. 'OK, I'll try her now.' She pulled out her mobile and punched in Gran's number. Thankfully, standing out here in the middle of the valley there was some reception. She felt a quiver of excitement as she waited for Stella to answer. Would she be able to pick out the right house? What a shame Gran was not fit enough to be able to come here herself.

4

JED

'Stella, watch Jessie for me, will you?' Jed called from the workshop, where he was trying to file down a piece of metal to make a replacement bracket for the seat of old Sam Wrightson's tractor. Jessie, now that she could walk, was becoming difficult to look after when he was trying to work. While she'd been a baby he could put her in the playpen he'd made from chicken mesh, with a few toys, and she'd amuse herself. She'd always seemed happy enough as long as she could see him. But now, she refused to go in the playpen and if he put her in it she simply lifted one side of it up and crawled out underneath, giggling in that infectious yet infuriating way she had. And then she'd stand too close while he was welding, or start lifting tools off his bench to play with, or try to play hide-and-seek under the workbench. It was really not a suitable place for a small child to be.

'Yes, Pa, coming.' Stella was just home from school, thank goodness, and if she could keep an eye on Jessie for a couple of hours Jed would be able to get on with some work, until the light failed. He had electric light in the workshop, but was short of oil for the generator — what little he had needed to be conserved.

'Come on, Jessie. Let's go and look for

tadpoles. Pa, we'll be down by the lake. I won't let Jessie get wet.' Stella retrieved Jessie from the pile of oily dust sheets she'd been hiding in, and took her by the hand.

'Be back in time for tea,' Jed said.

'All right.' Stella and Jessie left the workshop, and Jed heaved a sigh of relief. He could get on uninterrupted at last. And he needed to. If he didn't get some of his backlog of jobs finished he wouldn't be paid. That would mean no more oil for the generator, no new clothes for Stella who was rapidly growing out of her school uniform, and no food on the table. Life was indeed hard. He still missed Edie with a pain that felt like an iron fist punching him in the gut. He'd promised her the girls would want for nothing. He would provide for them, no matter what it took.

'Jed? Hello! I saw Stella go out with your little one, so I guessed you'd be on your own now. Let me make you some tea — I'm sure it's about time you sat down for a rest.' It was Maggie.

Jed sighed, and put down his tools. 'I could do with a cuppa, it's true, but I've not the time to sit down to drink it.'

'Oh, you will. It'll only be a few minutes. I'll pop into your kitchen and make the tea then, shall I?' Maggie didn't wait for an answer, but went through to his cottage straight away. He continued working while she was there, feeling vaguely uncomfortable about her being in his home on her own, poking about in what he still thought of as Edie's kitchen. But, he berated himself, she was only being kind and neighbourly. And he could certainly do with the tea.

46

She was back a minute later with a steaming mug, and a slice of fruit cake. He pressed his lips together. That cake had been a gift from Mrs Perkins at the village shop, and he'd been saving it for the girls' tea. But if he told Maggie that, it would be admitting how much he was struggling.

'Thank you.' He took the mug and sat on a stool beside his workbench.

Maggie pulled a battered chair forward, brushed it off, and sat tentatively on the edge of it. 'Any time. I'm here for you, you know. Anything I can do to help.'

Take Jessie for a few hours each day, Jed thought, but he'd tried that once when Edie was sick and it hadn't worked out. Jessie hadn't taken to Maggie, and she'd ended up bringing the tantrumming child back to him after only an hour, saying she was uncontrollable. 'Thanks, Maggie.'

She smiled, patted her hair, and pulled her chair a little nearer him. 'Remember, any time you need anything, anything at all, you know where I am.'

'Thanks,' said, again. 'Actually, Maggie . . . '

'Yes?'

'I just need some time to get on with my work. Stella's taken Jessie out for an hour or so, and I need to get this piece finished for Sam Wrightson's tractor seat, and at least one of those bicycle repairs done, and the knife-sharpening for Mrs Perkins, before they come back.'

'But it's already five o'clock. Surely it's time to

stop work for the day? We could go across to the Lost Sheep for a drink while they're out.'

He shook his head. 'No, Maggie, I really must get this work done now.'

'Oh, well. Later, perhaps? When the little one's in bed? Your Stella can babysit.'

'I might be in the Sheep for a pint later,' he said. It was Friday after all, and it had been a tough week. With Stella home all weekend he could catch up on his work then.

Maggie smiled wolfishly, and once more patted her neatly waved blonde hair. 'I shall see you there, then,' she said. She stood up, brushed down the back of her skirt, and leaned over Jed to kiss his cheek. Her blouse had a couple of buttons undone, and he averted his eyes to avoid seeing straight down the front of it.

'You're blushing!' she said, with delight. 'It was only a peck on the cheek, you silly man!' She flounced out of the workshop, stopping at the door to waggle her fingers at him. 'See you later!'

He let out a huge sigh. Well, at least now he could get on at last. He finished his tea, took the uneaten slice of cake back through to the cottage, and continued working until Stella came home with a tired but happy Jessie.

* * *

After tea, when Jessie was fast asleep and Stella ready for bed but snuggled with a book beside the kitchen stove, Jed fetched his cap and jacket. He was tired, but a pint would help him sleep. Too often these days he lay awake for hours fretting over the future. 'I'll be off to the pub then, lass. You know where I am if you need me.' The pub was less than fifty yards up the lane from the cottage, so he had no qualms about leaving the girls on their own.

'We'll be fine, Pa. I'll be off to bed at the end of this chapter anyway.' Stella yawned, then reached up to kiss his cheek. 'Night-night.'

He gave her a squeeze and kissed the top of her head. What a good daughter he had! She'd taken on so many responsibilities since Edie's death, and yet nothing seemed to faze her. She was so grown up, and yet still able to play as a child should, with Jessie or her schoolmates.

Before going to the pub he walked to the other end of the lane, where, on the edge of the village, was his father's tiny cottage. He tapped on the door but did not wait for an answer — Isaac was a little deaf and more often than not, asleep beside his fireplace. The door led straight from the lane into the front room, which was both kitchen and sitting room. Behind it, at the back of the cottage, was a bedroom, and outside in the yard, a privy.

As usual, Isaac was sitting in his armchair, head tilted back, snoring loudly when Jed entered. He gently shook the old man awake, then banked up the fire.

'All right there, Pa? Have you had your dinner?'

'Aye, nice bit of lamb stew. Maggie brought it, bless her.'

Jed raised his eyebrows at this. Was this another of Maggie's attempts to get into his

49

good books, or just an example of neighbourly kindness to an old man? 'Good of her. Was it nice?'

'Aye. Could have done with a pudding, after. You're not looking after me enough, lad. All day here, on my own, and only for Maggie coming in I'd be starving by now.'

'I'm here now, aren't I? And if you hadn't eaten already I'd have fetched you something.'

Isaac grunted. 'Nowt but a crust of bread and cold mutton, no doubt. Ah well, 'tis the lot of the old to be neglected. Suppose you're off to the pub now. Never mind me. I'll sit here a while and smoke my pipe afore I haul myself into my bed.'

Jed ignored the grumbling. Isaac had been a long-time widower, and as he'd aged he'd become more and more grumpy. No matter what people did for him, he'd always complain it wasn't enough. Jed finished banking up the fire, made his father a cup of tea and fetched him his pipe and tobacco. 'There, now. You have all you need. I'll look in on you tomorrow — I'll bring little Jessie up to see you at lunchtime.'

Isaac smiled toothlessly. 'Ah, the little pet. Yes, you bring her. She loves her old grandpa, does that one. Well, if the Lord spares me till the morning, I'll have her bonny face to look forward to.'

At least that had cheered Isaac up a little. And Jessie did seem to like him — she'd always climb onto the old man's lap and cuddle up, stroking his beard. Jed checked there was nothing else he could do, then bade his farewell. Time to get himself on the outside of a good pint, he thought. He knew that sooner rather than later, Isaac would have to give up living alone in his little cottage. He'd have to come to live with Jed and the girls. They could turn the little parlour, rarely used since Edie's demise, into a bedroom, as Isaac would not be able to manage the stairs. Then Jed would be at his father's beck and call, and there'd be even fewer opportunities to get his work done. But Isaac was his father, and he'd take care of him, no matter what. God, how he needed that pint now!

★ ★ ★

The Lost Sheep was busy that evening. Good, Jed thought. Less chance of Maggie cornering him, if there were plenty of other people about. He was more than happy to spend time with her in a group, but on her own she was just too pushy for his liking. It was only a month since Edie had been buried. It wasn't right to be seen with another woman. Especially one that he wasn't even the slightest bit interested in.

Sam Wrightson was standing near the bar, and Jed went straight over to join him, ordering himself a pint of ale from the landlord, John Teesdale. 'Evening, Sam. Busy tonight, isn't it?'

'Aye. Some of the navvies from the dam-building are in. That lot, over there — ' Sam jerked his head backwards to indicate a group of men who'd clearly already had a few pints. 'You fixed my tractor seat yet?'

'Yes, the part's all ready for you. Bring your

tractor to me tomorrow and I'll fit it for you.'

'Good. Fed up of that seat swivelling round. Tricky to drive forward when you find yourself facing backwards. Well, cheers.' Sam held his glass aloft. Jed chinked his own against it, then took a long pull of it. In the corner, the dam-workmen were beginning to sing raucously, one of them standing on a stool to conduct the others.

'They're having a fine time,' Jed commented.

'Aye. Teesdale's keeping an eye on them, though. Word is they caused trouble the other night, up at the King's Head. Landlord there threw them out and banned them for a fortnight. That's why they've come down here.' Sam eyed the gang warily. 'They've a cheek, though, turning up here, when it's their work that's going to be the death of our village.'

'They're just doing their job,' Jed replied.

'That's as maybe, but they should do their drinking elsewhere.'

Jed nodded vaguely. 'Aye, maybe so.' Sam wasn't letting go of his theme. 'Pub feels different with them here, too. Doesn't feel right. Listen to that singing, if you can call it that. Caterwauling, more like. Not what we normally have in the Lost Sheep.'

'Everything's changing, Sam. We've only to get used to it. 'Tis all we can do.'

Sam snorted. 'I'll not get used to it. I'll be moved out of Brackendale afore I'm used to it.'

'You got somewhere to go?' Jed raised his eyebrows. People were beginning to move out, and he knew he should start looking for jobs and accommodation elsewhere, but his heart hadn't been in it. Not since Edie died.

'Fingers in pies, Jed. Fingers in pies. Nothing definite.' Sam sighed and looked around him. 'Just hope Teesdale stays till the end, and keeps this place open.' He stepped smartly sideways to avoid being jostled by one of the dam-workers. 'Hope he bans this lot before then, any road.'

'Hard to believe though, isn't it? That all this will be gone? I were born here. So were you, Sam. So was my pa. Generations of us Walkers, in Isidore's churchyard. Only my Edie over in Glydesdale. But all our history, our community, everything, will be gone, underwater, just so the people of Manchester can run their taps.' Jed shook his head sadly. 'Hard to believe.'

'Ah, Jed, lad. You'll find someplace else. And in time, some new lass to take Edie's place.'

'No one'll take Edie's place, ever,' Jed said firmly.

Sam put a hand on his shoulder. 'Aye, I know, I don't mean like that. But you'll move on, marry again, find someone to help take care of those girls of yours. You'll be all right, in the end.'

''Tis true I need help with the girls. With Jessie, anyway. She's a right handful. Sometimes I don't know . . . ' Jed broke off from what he was saying as the door opened and Maggie arrived. She'd obviously taken pains with her appearance — wearing a silky pink dress that swished about her legs as she moved, a matching silk flower tucked in her hair over her ear, and bright red lipstick. He stood to welcome her, to

53

usher her over to where he and Sam were sitting, but before she spotted him in the throng one of the dam-workers called out.

'Well, look what we have here, boys! Nice! Very nice indeed!' The man's companions joined in with catcalls and whistles. Maggie blushed, smiled, and sashayed over to the bar.

Jed stepped forward to offer to buy her a drink and thank her for having taken Isaac a meal, but the dam-worker was there first. He was shorter than Jed, but stocky and muscular. 'Well, darling, what'll you have? I'm buying.' He didn't wait for an answer but beckoned John Teesdale over. 'Gin for the lady, here!'

'Maggie, are you all right?' Jed asked.

'Course I am. Just fine. This gentleman's buying me a drink, aren't you?' She patted the man's arm and smiled coquettishly up at him.

'I'm right here if you need me,' Jed said quietly.

'Didn't you hear the lady? She said she's just fine. So leave her be. She's with me, ain't you, Maggie?'

She giggled. 'For the moment. What's your name, handsome?'

'Donald. But the lads all call me Donkey.'

'Donkey? Why?'

'Wouldn't you like to know, darling, wouldn't you like to know!' The man threw his head back and guffawed. Jed had stepped back out of his line of sight, but was staying close by. He caught John Teesdale's eye, who gave him a tiny shake of the head, as if to say, don't be starting a fight in my bar. Sam Wrightson was watching him too,

54

but Sam, he knew, would be the first to back him up if it came to it. Well, Jed was no troublemaker but Maggie was a neighbour, and a good one even if she was a little pushy at times, and he'd not stand by and see her get into trouble. If it was just harmless high spirits from the navvies that was one thing, but he was ready if any of them went too far.

'Ooh, you naughty thing!' Maggie said, giggling, as she gave the man a playful slap on his arm.

In retaliation he caught hold of her by both arms. 'The lady likes it rough, does she?'

Maggie twisted herself free and took her drink from Teesdale. 'Thanks, John.' She turned back to the man. 'Now, now, Mr Donkey, not *that* rough.'

It was enough for Jed. 'You leave the lady alone,' he snarled at the man.

'Spoken for, is she? You never said.' The man smiled slyly, and turned back to Maggie. 'But I've paid for her drink, now. Which means she owes me. Come on, darling, how about a little cuddle, eh? Just a little cuddle for a hard-working man, eh?' He pulled her towards him with one hand on her back and the other on her bottom.

'Hey! Let go!' she said, twisting to get herself free but he was holding her tight.

That was it. Jed tapped the man on the shoulder, and when he looked round swung a hefty right hook at him. The man's head snapped backwards and blood began pouring from his mouth. He immediately hit back, but Jed was too quick for him and the blow merely glanced off his shoulder.

At once the other dam-workers were on their feet, piling in to their friend's aid. Sam was on his feet too, and John Teesdale, six feet tall and muscly with it, lifted the flap on the bar, ushered Maggie behind it where she was safe, and stepped out to separate the fighters. 'Come on now, gents, not in my bar.' Between him and Sam Wrightson they pulled Jed away from the man, and the other dam-workers got their friend under control, with much jeering and shouting.

'It's all right, John,' Jed said. 'I've no wish to wreck your bar. Just want to keep Maggie safe, is all. Come on, Maggie. I'll take you home. We'll not be back here again unless John bans those navvies. Come on, lass.' He put a protective arm around her shoulders as he led her out of the pub, to more jeering from the workmen.

As soon as they were outside and in the street Maggie turned to him and flung her arms around his neck. 'Oh Jed, thank you! I shouldn't have flirted, but he seemed nice to start with. And — ' she sighed and looked away for a moment before returning her gaze to his — 'I suppose I thought if I made you jealous you'd take more notice of me. Well, that worked! But I hope you aren't hurt?'

He peeled her off him, and flexed the fingers of his right hand. The knuckles were red and swollen. 'No, I'm not hurt. Nothing that won't heal, any road.'

She leaned in towards him, once more reaching up to put her arms around him, but he took a step backwards. 'Maggie, don't. I mean, I'll walk you home, see you're safe, but it doesn't mean anything.'

She stepped away and glared at him. 'Why did you fight for me, then?'

He shrugged. 'I'd defend any woman against a thug like that.'

'So I'm nothing special to you?'

'You are a beautiful woman, a kind neighbour, and I am proud to call you my friend,' he replied, speaking softly. He sighed. 'You're a good woman, Maggie Earnshaw. You'll make someone a fine wife some day. But not me, Maggie. My heart belongs to Edie, and always will. I'm sorry.'

She drew in her breath sharply, and gave him a look that would sour milk. 'There's no need to walk me home,' she said, turning away from him, her head held high. He watched her walking away, up the lane, towards her home on the edge of the village. He followed at a discreet distance, in case any of the men came out of the pub, until he saw her enter the door of her cottage. With a sigh he walked back to his own home, avoiding passing the pub. With luck, Teesdale would ban the dam-workers and stick to custom from the village. It had always been enough for him in the past. But the past was gone, and everything was changing now.

5

LAURA

Stella answered the phone after just a couple of rings.

'Hello? Mrs Braithwaite speaking,' she said, and as always Laura was mildly amused by the posh-sounding 'telephone voice' Gran always put on when answering the phone.

'Gran, it's me, Laura. I'm at Brackendale Green now, and it's just like you saw on the TV — you can walk right across the lake-bed and in and out of the old buildings.'

'Oh my goodness! How very strange!'

'It's a shame you aren't here too. Perhaps I should have brought you.'

'Oh no, dear. I'm too old to be gallivanting all the way up to the Lake District. My holidaying days are over. So, tell me, what can you see?'

'Well, right now, I'm standing on a little stone bridge that looks like it used to be at the end of the main village street.' Laura glanced at Tom who was listening in, smiling broadly. She decided not to mention to Gran that she was with someone. Gran would only try to matchmake. She'd said many times that Laura was too lovely a girl to be on her own for long and that it was time she started dating again, or 'stepping out' as Gran put it.

'I remember that bridge. It was very near my father's workshop.'

'Really?' Laura looked back towards the village, trying to visualise how it might have been. She realised she did not know anything about Stella's father, her great-grandfather. 'What kind of workshop? What did he do for a living?'

'He was a mechanic,' Gran replied, her tone low and wistful. 'He had a workshop where he mended people's cars, tractors, generators, anything, really. Bicycles, too.'

'I suppose he had to move his business when the village was abandoned,' Laura said. There was a silence at the other end of the phone, and a little gasp, as though Stella was stifling a sob. 'Gran? Are you all right?'

'Yes, dear, of course I am. Never mind your silly old gran. It's just bringing back memories, you being there.'

'Which house did you live in? Can you direct me to it, from the bridge?' Tom perked up at this question. Laura knew he was longing for her to ask if Gran had known his ancestor Maggie Earnshaw.

'Well now, let's see if I can remember. If you walk into the village, on the left there were three cottages, then a gap. Then opposite that gap was a huge tree. An oak. That wouldn't be there now, would it?'

Laura walked along the village's main street, counting those first three cottage ruins. 'There's a tree stump, Gran.'

'Oh yes, they did chop all the trees down, I

remember now. Next to the tree there's a building — that was my father's workshop. And our cottage was right behind it, with the door opening onto Church Street. Opposite but a bit up the road to the right of our front door was the pub — the Lost Sheep. Pa often used to go in there of an evening.'

'Leaving your mother looking after you?'

'Yes, me and . . . well. Until Ma died. She died when I was ten, you know. Not long before the dam was built. Pa was glad she never had to see the village being demolished.'

Laura suddenly realised how little she knew of her grandmother's early life. But now wasn't the time to go into all of it. She had followed Stella's directions and was now standing in front of the remains of Gran's cottage. 'Well, I'm here now. The walls of your cottage are about waist-high — the top parts have been demolished. There's a window to the left of the door. I'm going in . . . there's a fireplace opposite, quite large, like an inglenook fireplace. There's . . . '

'I wonder if they can find it?' Gran's voice sounded faint and tremulous.

'Find what? And who do you mean by 'they'?' Laura asked.

'It might still be there. After all this time. Too late, of course, but perhaps they can get it . . . '

'Gran? Are you all right? Get what?'

'The box. It might still be there, after all this time.'

'What box? Where?'

'Oh, the old tea caddy. It's probably not still there. Not after being underwater all this time.'

Gran gave a huge sigh, and when she spoke again she sounded more like her usual self, to Laura's relief. 'Don't mind me, Laura. I'm just a silly old woman, talking about a silly old thing that used to be in the cottage.'

'Well, there's nothing here now,' Laura said, looking around her at the interior of the cottage. 'Just some rubble, dried-out mud, a bit of driftwood. I'll take some photos, then when I'm home we can look through them, if you'd like.'

'Yes, that would be lovely, dear. Well, I'll let you go now and you enjoy your holiday. I've got Sophia coming tonight to help me get ready for bed, so don't you worry about me at all.'

'Sophia's lovely. I'm glad they've assigned her to you. I'll ring again tomorrow.'

'No need to ring every day, love. I'm perfectly all right.'

'OK Gran, I won't. Bye then. Love you.'

As she ended the call, Tom stepped forward into the cottage. He'd been hanging back, presumably so he didn't overhear all of her conversation. He looked at her questioningly. 'Was this where your grandmother lived?'

'Yes, from what she said, she lived here. The building behind was her father's workshop. And that one over there,' Laura pointed out of the door, 'was the pub. The Lost Sheep, it was called.'

'Yes, I've seen some old photos of it. Had your gran ever heard of any Earnshaws?'

Laura shook her head. 'I'm so sorry, I didn't ask. I'll ring her again tomorrow. Thing is, she was acting a little strangely so I didn't want to

61

bombard her with too many questions. It must be so weird for her, knowing that people are walking around the village, and in and out of her old home, for the first time in so many years.' She decided not to mention Stella's ramblings about a tea caddy.

Suddenly, Laura felt overheated and a little dizzy. The sun had been beating down on her head for hours, and there was no shelter out here in the middle of the lake. She sat on a low part of one of the cottage walls, pulled out a water bottle and drank, realising she was probably a little dehydrated.

'You OK?' Tom asked.

'Too hot. I think I need to get into some shade.'

'Come on. There are trees beside the car park. Do you have a hat you can put on, to keep the sun off your head?'

'Yep. Back in my tent,' Laura replied, with a rueful smile at him.

Tom shook his head in mock exasperation, then held out a hand to haul her to her feet. She took it gratefully. Unlike her own, hot, dry hand, his felt strong and cool.

'Steady now,' he said, as she stumbled slightly, her head spinning. He caught hold of her upper arms and held her until she got her balance.

'Sorry. I'm all right now. Best get into that shade, though.'

He let go of her, but walked close beside her all the way back across the lake-bed to the car park. She noticed him taking little worried glances at her, and was grateful for his concern.

She'd been stupid not to wear a hat. It might be September but the sun was still so strong.

At last they reached the car park, and found a bench hewn out of a tree trunk that was under the shade of a spreading oak, rather like the one Laura had pitched her tent beneath. She sat down, immediately feeling better now that she was in shade.

'Can't believe how hot it is, this late in the summer,' Tom said.

She nodded. 'I'm beginning to regret having walked here from the campsite. Obviously I'm not as fit as I'd thought.'

'You walked?' Tom looked back towards the Old Corpse Road. 'I drove. I'd planned to have a quick look at Brackendale and then go for a walk up that ridge there, that leads onto Bracken Fell. But now I'm thinking I should drive you back to the campsite. That's my car, over there.' He pointed at an elderly, beaten-up estate car. 'Come on. Let's take you back to the campsite for a rest and get some liquid into you.'

It was a very tempting offer. Laura looked at him gratefully. She might have only just met the man but there was something about him that she liked. 'Are you sure? I don't want you to miss out on your walk.'

'It's too hot, anyway. I can do it some other day — I'm here all week.' He stood, rummaged in a pocket for his car keys and clicked the unlock button. The car's indicators flashed in response, and he crossed the car park to it and opened all the doors. 'Wait a minute until some air's blown through.'

The car was still stiflingly hot when Laura got in, but once they'd got going, with the windows wound right down, it cooled quickly. 'Sorry the air conditioning doesn't work,' Tom said, as they drove past the dried-up lake. 'Hey, in a minute we'll pass the dam. Want to stop for a moment and take a look? I've a spare hat in here somewhere you can wear to keep the sun off.'

'Sure, I'd love to see it,' Laura replied. She was feeling better already from the breeze through the car and the water she'd drunk. A few moments later, Tom pulled into a small car park beside the dam. He rummaged around in the clutter strewn across the back seat of the car and retrieved a baseball cap, which proudly displayed the Munster Rugby club logo. 'Sorry, best I can do, but it'll help.'

'It's perfect,' she said with a smile, and pulled it on. They walked over to where a low wall marked the edge of the car park, from where there was a view along the length of the dam on the lakeside. 'Look, you can see how high the water level normally is,' Laura said, pointing to marks near the top of the structure, a change of colour of the concrete. 'Amazing to think how much water is normally held back by this.'

'Yes, well, of course, all of the area we were walking around is normally well underwater,' Tom replied. 'Shame they don't let the public walk across the top of the dam.'

Laura looked where he was pointing. There was a narrow walkway that led across the top of the dam to the far side of the valley. But a hefty

64

locked iron gate barred access to it. 'I suppose it's not safe.'

'Probably safer than some of the more hairy ridges up the mountains,' Tom laughed. 'Want to have a look at the information board over there?' They walked over to it, and read the brief history and technical details of the dam. 'Fifteen hundred feet long, fifty feet wide at the base, ninety feet high. Ugh. Don't you wish it was all in metric?'

'Yep. Good grief, what a lot of concrete they used.' Laura peered closely at the pictures of the dam under construction — men precariously balanced on scaffolding while they poured concrete; men in waders, thigh-deep in wet concrete; men sitting high up on the top of the structure eating their lunches. 'No health-and-safety regulations back then, by the look of things.'

'No. Two men died, it says here.'

'That's so sad.' Laura was silent and thoughtful for a moment. 'I understand the need for the reservoir, but it does seem a shame that a village had to be destroyed and men lost their lives to achieve it.'

'I guess there's always some risk to the workmen building something of this scale. And as for the village, I'd like to think that if there had been a suitable uninhabited valley they'd have used that instead. It'd have cost less for a start.'

'I suppose so.' Laura gazed at the view down the valley, below the dam. The river was barely more than a trickle, winding its way between fields and woods, similar to the landscape in Glydesdale. To the left and across the valley was a collection of unattractive boxy houses, at odds with the traditional Lakeland stone cottages. 'What's that place over there?'

Tom consulted the map on the information board. 'It's called New Brackendale. It was built to house the dam-workers, and then some of the people from Brackendale Green moved here after the valley was flooded. Ugly-looking place, isn't it?'

Laura nodded. Compared with the photos of the old village that she'd seen on the other information board, this one was certainly much less appealing. 'I wonder if any of our ancestors moved there?'

'My family didn't. They went to Keswick,' Tom replied.

'I don't know about Gran. All I know is she moved to London as a young woman, when she became an actress. She was in a few plays in the West End, then she met my grandfather and gave up acting but stayed living in the south. I must ask her where she moved to after the dam was built. Yet more questions for her!'

'You need to write that list,' Tom said, with a smile. 'Shall we go?'

They got back in the car, and continued along the road out of the valley. From the dam onwards it was much wider, clearly built for much more traffic than the narrow lane beside the lake that only led to a walkers' car park. On either side of the road, the fells became lower and the valley wider as they continued. Laura felt a pang of regret as they left the mountains behind — daft, she thought, as it was only temporary and as soon as they took the turn that led into Glydesdale they'd be heading deeper into the mountains once again. There was something about being surrounded by lofty peaks that she loved. It healed her soul, she thought. And her soul certainly needed some healing after what Stuart and Martine had done.

At the next junction, there was a small road leading off to the right, signposted 'Brackendale House Museum'. 'Ooh, I wonder what's there?' Laura said.

'Don't know. Perhaps some local history? Sounds like it could be worth a visit.'

Laura was silent for a moment, debating with herself whether to ask him if he'd like to go there, in the next day or two, with her. If she did, how would he respond? Would he consider it just a friendly request to follow up on their shared interest in the drowned village, or would he read more into it? She liked Tom. She'd only known him an hour or so, but she felt comfortable in his company and already she was beginning to feel she knew him. They'd clicked, somehow. As an experiment, she made a mental comparison of Tom with Stuart. He was kind — the way he'd treated her when she felt dizzy was testament to that. Stuart would have scoffed and told her to 'man up'. Tom was interested in some of the same things as her — history, mountains — whereas Stuart was more into video games and nightclubs. Tom was tall, broad-shouldered, strongly built, with soft grey eyes that crinkled when he smiled. Stuart was good-looking, sure, but in a cold, chiselled way. His eyes were dark and brooding, and his smiles did not always reach them. But however nice Tom was, Laura knew she was not ready for any kind of new relationship yet, and she'd hate him to think she was interested in him.

The moment passed, and she realised it was too late to sound spontaneous if she asked Tom if he'd like to go to the museum with her. She felt a pang of regret. She shouldn't have been overthinking things. The rest of the journey passed more or less in silence, with each of them making only a few comments about the scenery they passed through.

★ ★ ★

Back at the campsite, Tom dropped Laura off beside the shop, with a cheery 'See you later, drink more water!' as she needed to buy something for the next day's breakfast. She did not see where he drove off to.

She spent the rest of the afternoon resting and rehydrating, paddling in the stream, lying in the shade of the oak with a book. Bliss. She decided to go to the pub for an evening meal rather than cook again on her little gas stove, so just before darkness fell she stuffed her purse into a pocket, closed up her tent, and walked across the campsite and down the lane the short distance to the pub. It was a converted farmhouse, with a few rooms used for B&B, and a side extension that was open as a cafe in the daytime. The bar itself was in a low-ceilinged, stone-flagged room, with an assortment of small wooden tables and chairs dotted around. A large fireplace suggested it would be delightfully cosy in the winter months. A sign over the door announced that walkers and dogs were welcome, no need to remove muddy boots. She grinned at this. Her kind of pub, and the last place she could imagine Stuart fitting in.

She ordered a pint of the local bitter and a dinner of pie and chips, and noted the WiFi network name and password that was written on a note pinned above the till. Free WiFi. Perfect. She found a small table tucked in a corner, pulled out her phone, connected to the internet and began searching for information about Brackendale Green, the dam and the Old Corpse Road. Now that she'd seen it, it was all so much more exciting and interesting.

She was so absorbed in reading the web pages she'd found that she didn't immediately notice Tom sit down next to her. 'Room for a little one?' he said.

She looked up and smiled. 'Of course. Can I get you a drink? As a thank-you for looking after me today.'

'Later, perhaps. I'm all right at the moment.' He held up a nearly-full pint. 'Are you eating? I can recommend the pies here. I've ordered one myself.'

'That's exactly what I've ordered, too. Want to look at the pictures of Brackendale I've found?' She passed him her phone, and he peered at the images she'd been scrolling through. 'Having been there brings it all to life, doesn't it?'

'Certainly does.'

Their food soon arrived, and after eating they resumed searching websites and exchanging the titbits of information they'd found.

'Hey, here's the website for Brackendale House Museum,' Tom said, handing his phone over to her.

'Oh yes, that place we passed,' Laura replied. 'I definitely want to visit that.'

'Me too,' Tom said. 'I want to go up Bracken Fell tomorrow, but maybe we could do the museum the day after? Actually, do you fancy climbing the mountain with me as well?'

'If you're sure. I mean, I don't want you to change your plans for me,' Laura said, allowing a tone of wariness into her voice. It wouldn't do to let him think she was available. She'd need to make it clear she wasn't interested.

'Well, I'm definitely going, and it'd be good to have some company,' Tom replied.

'Well then, why not?' Laura smiled and Tom grinned back.

6

JED

Thankfully, John Teesdale had decided to remain loyal to his long-term, village customers and had sent a message to the dam-works to say that their workmen were no longer welcome in his pub. Jed was able to go for a drink once or twice a week without fear of running into the man whose lip he had split.

It was harder, however, to steer clear of Maggie, but since that night she seemed to have cooled off towards him. Jed hoped that meant she had got the message, and would leave him in peace now. She was undoubtedly an attractive woman, but he was not interested. Not now, and probably not ever. There was enough for him to worry about without the added complication of a woman.

'Heard the latest?' John Teesdale said, as he poured Jed's pint of bitter. 'They're going to move all the graves. Everyone in St Isidore's churchyard — they're going to dig them up and rebury them in Glydesdale. Well, I suppose better that than have them under twenty feet of water.'

'My Edie will be reunited with her parents, then.' Jed nodded. It was a macabre thought — that all those graves would be exhumed — but it was the right thing. People would still

71

want to be able to pay their respects at the graves of their loved ones, and once the valley was flooded that would no longer be possible if they were left in St Isidore's. He was glad that Edie herself was already over in Glydesdale, and would not have to be disturbed.

'Aye. Though they'll put the folk from St Isidore's in a new part of the Glydesdale churchyard. Bishop's been up to consecrate an extra field — they'll need a lot of room.' Teesdale handed Jed his pint, and took payment for it.

'Any idea when they're going to start?' Jed asked.

'This week, as I understand it. There's a notice gone up on the church door. It'll all be done under a tarpaulin, behind screens. Each set of remains will go into a new coffin and there'll be a hearse waiting to drive them around to Glydesdale where they'll be reburied.' Teesdale leaned on the bar, and shook his head. 'There's a schedule up telling you which graves will be dug up on which day. It's to be my ma and pa's grave on Wednesday. I'll have to shut up shop here, and be standing by. They don't want you watching, but you're allowed to stand behind the screens, and go with the new coffin to Glydesdale, see it's all done properly.'

'I'd better go and read that notice, then,' Jed said. He hadn't been to church much lately. Not since Edie had died. But his mother was in St Isidore's churchyard, and perhaps he should be at hand when her grave was exhumed. Perhaps he should bring Isaac along, too. Teesdale had turned away to serve another customer, so Jed took his pint to a seat near the window that faced up the lane towards the church, and contemplated what was happening to the village. If it was time to start moving the dead out, it wouldn't be much longer before it was time to move the living.

Teesdale passed by, collecting empty glasses, and sighed. 'Ah, 'tis all changing. Nowt'll ever be the same again, once we're all spread to the four winds. You found somewhere to go yet, Jed?'

He shook his head. Why did people keep asking him that? The future was hanging over him like a sword suspended by a thread. It terrified him just to contemplate it. But soon he'd have to do something about it, he knew. 'Not yet, John, not yet.'

'Time's running out. Don't leave it too long. Reckon this village'll be a sad place for the last few to leave. That'll no doubt be me and the missus, any road.'

'Aye.' Jed tried to imagine the houses standing empty, but it was a painful image and not one he could dwell on. He made a decision. He'd buy the *Westmorland Gazette* and start looking for work and accommodation. Tomorrow he'd do it. Or the day after.

★   ★   ★

Jed finished his pint and decided to call in on his father before going home. The children would be all right — Jessie had been fast asleep before he'd even left, and Stella had been reading in her bed, promising to snuggle down to sleep when it

73

became too dark. The thought of his ma's grave being exhumed was preying on his mind, and the sooner he told Isaac the better. He walked quickly to the far end of the village and pushed open the door to Isaac's little cottage.

'Pa?' he called as he entered. It was only around nine o'clock but the old man had already got himself into bed.

'That you, Jed? I were almost asleep.'

'Sorry, Pa.' He walked through to the back room and sat on the end of the bed. 'Something I need to talk to you about. But if you want to sleep, I'll come back tomorrow.'

'No, lad, now's as good a time as any. Put the kettle on first, though.' Isaac shuffled himself into a sitting position, and lit the paraffin lamp beside his bed. His was one of several small cottages in the village that did not have electricity. There was no mains electricity at all but the larger buildings all ran their own generators.

Jed went back through to the kitchen and popped the already half-full kettle on the stove. He cleared up the remains of Isaac's dinner, washing the plates and cutlery he'd used, while he waited for the kettle to boil. The place was filthy, he realised; even in the gloomy light of the paraffin lamp he could see the thick dirt. He'd have to find some time to come up here and do some cleaning. Isaac clearly wasn't coping.

With the tea made, and poured into two chipped enamel mugs, Jed took them through to the bedroom and handed one to his father.

'Cheers, lad. Now, what was it worth

disturbing my sleep for? Your little Jessie all right, is she? Who's looking after her?'

'She's at home with Stella,' Jed replied. 'Pa, it's about Ma. Her grave.'

'What about it? Need tending, does it?, I used to keep that graveyard so tidy, back in the day. 'Spect it's gone to rack and ruin now.'

'No, Pa. Something else.' Jed took a deep breath. 'They're exhuming the graves. Going to move them all to Glydesdale. It starts next week, John Teesdale says. There's a schedule, so I'll call in to the church tomorrow and find out when Ma's will be done. I'll take you, if you want to be there.'

'Exhuming? You mean, digging up?' Isaac caught hold of Jed's arm in a tight grip.

'Aye. But it'll all be done properly — behind screens, with dignity. They're to be reburied in Glydesdale in smart new coffins. We can be there for Ma, go with her to Glydesdale and see it's done properly.' Jed looked at his father and frowned. Isaac was white and shaking. 'What is it, Pa? What's wrong? It'll be hard, seeing Ma's grave disturbed, but it'll mean we can still visit . . . '

But Isaac was shaking his head. 'They can't dig them up. They can't. 'S'not right. I'll not dig it up again.' Isaac thumped the mattress defiantly.

Jed remembered that Isaac had once been the gravedigger at St Isidore's, long ago, before Jed had even been born. Perhaps it was that he was referring to? All his hard work to bury the poor souls, all to be undone.

He patted his father's arm. 'Aye, I know, Pa. All your work. You did a good job back then, but now it's someone else's turn to do the digging. You won't have to.'

Isaac was still shaking his head, and screwing up the corners of his bedcovers in his hands. 'It'll all be bad, all be uncovered. And at my time of life and all. 'S'not right, 's'not fair.'

'It'll be hard for all of us who've loved ones in that graveyard. But it's for the best, you'll see. Come on now, Pa. Drink your tea. Stop fretting. If you think it'll be too hard to see Ma's grave dug up, I'll go by myself. You don't need to if you don't want to.'

''S'not fair, after all these years,' Isaac muttered.

'Shh, now. Drink your tea.' So this was it. Jed had always worried that his father might lose his mind, and here it was happening, far too quickly. There was no putting it off any longer. Pa would have to move in with him and the girls, as soon as possible, so Jed could keep an eye on him. How Jed would cope he had no idea, but Isaac was his father and it was his duty to care for him.

★ ★ ★

Jed's mother's grave was exhumed on a grey, drizzly morning just a few days later, with Jed in attendance, a protesting Jessie on reins at his side. Stella was at school. Jed had decided it was best if Isaac didn't attend the exhumation and had not mentioned it again. His Pa seemed to have withdrawn into himself, and kept muttering about not wanting the graves dug up, and it being unfair. Who knew what he was saying. It must be something related to his time as a gravedigger, Jed thought.

It was a solemn and strangely surreal moment — although Jessie didn't give the occasion the respect it deserved, choosing that moment to fling herself to the ground, covering herself with mud and throwing a full-blown tantrum when Jed scolded her — to see the new, plain casket that contained his mother's remains brought out from behind the screens and loaded into the hearse. Jed followed behind, in a black car paid for by the water company and driven by a uniformed chauffeur, with Jessie on his lap. It was the second time he'd been driven this route by a chauffeur, he thought, remembering the journey back from Edie's funeral in Mrs Pendleton's motorcar. A different daughter accompanied him this time.

At Glydesdale Church, the reburial was quick and no-nonsense, with the vicar saying a few simple prayers as the coffin was lowered into the newly dug grave. Afterwards, Jed took Jessie to visit Edie's grave, in the older graveyard beside the church. He pulled up some weeds from around the headstone and laid a bunch of bluebells beside it.

'Look, Jessie. Mama's there,' he said.

The child stared at the gravestone and shrugged. 'Mama gone to heaven,' she said, parroting the words Jed and Stella had used to explain her mother's absence. She ran off to hide behind another gravestone, giggling. Jed sighed.

So soon after Edie's death and it seemed that already Jessie was forgetting her. He supposed that in time, she'd forget her completely. But he couldn't help but smile too. That giggle of Jessie's was an infectious sound that always gladdened his heart. So much better to hear than the tantrums she'd had earlier in Brackendale!

'What a simply adorable child. Is she yours, Mr Walker?'

Jed stood, startled by the voice, and found himself once more facing Alexandria Pendleton. He removed his cap. 'Yes, ma'am. She's my youngest. Jessie, come here. This isn't a place for playing.'

In response, Jessie just giggled again and climbed upon a full-length tomb, which to Jed's horror bore the name Pendleton on the side.

'Jessie, get down off there! It isn't for playing on. Ma'am, I apologise. She's not quite three years old and knows no better.'

But Mrs Pendleton was smiling, and waved her hand dismissively. 'It's perfectly all right. A child of that age does not understand death, and she's within her rights to play when she gets the chance to.'

'Thank you, ma'am,' Jed replied.

'Are you here to pay your respects to Edie?' Mrs Pendleton asked. 'It's a long way to come, especially with your little one.' She was still watching Jessie play.

'Yes, but also to see my ma's remains reinterred,' Jed replied. 'They're moving all the graves from Brackendale Green to here, before the valley is flooded.'

Mrs Pendleton nodded. 'Ah, yes. I was part of the church committee, agreeing to have the graves moved here. I've been here today to oversee the process. I am sorry one of them is your mother's. It must be very difficult for you.'

'Aye, but if she's here along with Edie I can visit them both together.' Jed realised that throughout their conversation, Mrs Pendleton had not taken her eyes off Jessie once. He squirmed a little. The child's coat was covered with mud from having rolled on the ground at St Isidore's. 'Jessie, come here and say hello to the lady.'

The little girl for once did as she was told and skipped over, slipping her hand into her father's. 'Hello, lady,' she said.

'Hello to you too, little miss,' Mrs Pendleton said, crouching down to speak to Jessie at her own level. 'What a pretty child you are.'

Jessie's response was just to giggle and run away again, leaving Mrs Pendleton smiling indulgently after her. 'What a lovely sound a child's laughter is,' she said, almost in a whisper.

There was a gentle beep on a car's horn, and Jed realised it was the black car, ready to return to Brackendale Green. The hearse had already made its return journey. The schedule was for four exhumations and reburials each day, and it was time they went back, or he'd be left with no lift.

'Beg pardon, ma'am, but we must go now, the motorcar's waiting.'

She nodded, still watching Jessie, as he fetched the child and took her back to the car. There was something odd about her gaze. It was full of longing, and something else he couldn't quite put his finger on. Perhaps she was simply disapproving of Jessie's muddy clothes. He held Jessie tightly in the car on the way back to Brackendale. She was a handful, but such a precious little thing.

★   ★   ★

It was two days later that the discovery was made. The exhumations were about a quarter done, when the grave-diggers reached the not-quite-final resting place of Martha Atkins. There was quite a crowd waiting behind the screens for Martha's remains to be brought out and loaded into the hearse, for she had been the grandmother of Maggie Earnshaw, and mother of Janie Earnshaw and also of Janie's simpleton sister, Susie. All were standing solemnly waiting for the moment when the new casket would be carried out from behind the screen. Even Susie was to go with them to Glydesdale — Martha was her mother too, Janie had said, and besides, there was no one else available to keep an eye on her.

Jed passed by with Jessie as they stood waiting, and although Maggie glared at him he felt he should stop and pay his respects. He knew how emotional an occasion it was. Stella was at school and Jessie was, for once, behaving herself, so he decided to wait a while until the hearse left.

'How do, Janie. Hello, Susie,' he said, and

nodded at Maggie who turned her face away. 'It's not easy, is it, this?'

'No. But it's got to be done,' Janie replied. 'I'm glad for you that Edie did not have to be moved.'

'They're moving Ma,' Susie said, her round face gazing up at him, her eyes sad and worried.

'They are, Susie, lass, you're right.' She was looking old these days, and indeed must be well past fifty, though he always thought of her as a child. He always had done, even though she was a generation older than him. She had that simple, childlike face and way of speaking. Even now, she was holding Janie's hand, and shuffling her feet in the dirt.

'Don't want them to move her,' she said, pushing her bottom lip outwards.

'They have to, Susie. I told you, it's so we'll still be able to visit her, even after the village is gone,' Janie told her sister gently.

'Don't want the village to go,' Susie replied.

'Oh no, please don't let her start a tantrum, not now,' Janie whispered, raising her eyes to the heavens.

Jed thought quickly, trying to come up with something to distract Susie, but Maggie was quicker. 'Don't worry, Aunty Susie. Remember what I told you about the cake we're going to make for tea? With jam inside, and buttercream as well, and you can sprinkle the icing sugar on the top.'

'And the first slice for me?' Susie said, raising her round eyes to Maggie's.

'Of course. And we are going to do this as soon as we get back from moving your ma.'

Susie looked conflicted for a moment, as though deciding whether to protest against the moving of her mother, or continue to be happy about the prospect of cake for tea. But as Jed had seen so many times before, her natural happy nature won out and she smiled broadly. 'We're having cake for tea,' she announced.

'Cake for me too?' asked Jessie, slipping her small hand into Susie's chubby one.

'If you like,' Susie said, beaming down at Jessie, and the crisis was over.

There was some commotion going on behind the screens. Janie frowned. 'What are they shouting about now?'

'I'll look,' Jed said, and he pushed through a gap in the screens, leaving Jessie still holding Susie's hand. He expected to be told to get back, but the three men — two gravediggers and an overseer — were all crouched on the ground, peering at something they'd dug up. The new coffin stood empty beside them — they had not yet dug deep enough to reach Martha's remains. 'What is it?' he asked.

'Something odd in the grave,' the overseer said. 'We weren't expecting this.'

'Course we weren't,' one of the gravediggers said. 'How could we be expecting to dig up treasure? Ay-up, is it finders, keepers?'

'No, it is not. We'll have to inform the police. This looks very valuable, and it's probably no accident that it's in the grave.'

'Maybe the relatives know something?' the gravedigger said.

'They're standing just back, behind the

screens,' Jed said. 'What have you found?'

The overseer stood up and took a step back, gesturing at a dirty package on the ground. Jed moved forward for a better look and gasped. Wrapped in oilcloth was an old tin box, and spilling out of that was a fistful of jewellery, gold, rubies, diamonds, necklaces, earrings, bracelets — all jumbled together. 'Is it real? Or paste?'

'Looks real to me, but that's to be discovered, I suppose. So, let's ask the relatives if they have any idea about this.' The overseer stepped out from behind the screens, holding the tarpaulin bundle. 'Ladies, sorry to intrude, but, ahem, this was found in the grave, on top of the coffin. Does anyone recognise it? Looks too valuable to stay buried in the ground.'

Jed watched as Janie and Maggie stepped forward to look. Both women gasped as they saw what was wrapped inside the tarpaulin. Susie hung back a little, her mouth open and her eyes wide.

'No, sir, never seen that before. What's it doing in my mother's grave? She never had anything like that — I'd know if she had,' Janie said, her hand over her mouth.

Maggie glared at her, and gave her a little kick as if to shut her up. She wanted to lie and say the jewels were her grandmother's so they could keep them, Jed realised, but it was too late — Janie had told the truth.

'I seen it before,' Susie said quietly. Then, louder, 'I seen that bundle.'

'What? What are you talking about, Susie?' Janie said. 'How can you have seen it?'

'When Ma were put in the hole. I seen it then.'

'Don't be daft, Susie, love. You weren't at Ma's funeral. Old Mrs Eastbrook looked after you, as Pa didn't think you'd cope with it all.'

Susie was shaking her head. 'It were later.' She bit her lip, in a gesture that Jed knew meant she was scared she would get in trouble for what she was about to say.

'Later?' Janie frowned at her sister. 'Ah, you're talking rot.' She turned back to the overseer Mr Banks and shook her head. 'I'm sorry. Ignore her. The jewels are nothing to do with us, sadly. I hope you can find their owner.'

'It were his pa,' Susie shouted. She was pointing at Jed. 'His pa. He put them in the hole with my ma. I seen him do it. I come out the house when I were supposed to be in bed, 'cause I wanted to say bye-bye to Ma and I knew she were in the hole. It were dark. I hid over there.' She pointed to a large yew tree. 'He never seen me but I seen him, and he dropped that in the hole with Ma and then spaded in the soil on top. I seen him. I seen it all.'

'His pa?' Maggie approached Susie and bent to look her in the eye. 'Aunty Susie, do you mean Isaac Walker put the tin in the grave?'

Susie nodded solemnly and pointed again at Jed. 'His pa done it. He looked all around to make sure no one seen him, then he dropped them in. But I seen him. I were over there.'

'Why didn't you tell anyone about it?'

Susie shrugged. 'No one asked me.'

'Well, this is a rum situation,' the overseer said. 'I shall have to inform the police who will

84

try to track down the rightful owners. Looks to me like the proceeds from a robbery, I dare say. And the police, I am sure, will be most interested in this person's evidence.' He nodded to Jed and the women, dropped the jewels back in the tin and walked away.

7

LAURA

The evening in the pub with Tom passed quickly. She found herself telling him about her job as a carer, her lifestyle living with Gran, and her previous trips to the Lake District, years ago. They swapped stories of the mountains they'd climbed. She told him of an epic day on Pillar when she'd rounded a shoulder of the mountain to be faced with wind so strong it almost blew her off. After battling on for a few more minutes she'd had to give up and retrace her steps, back to the sheltered side of the mountain. Tom for his part told her of a winter climb up Helvellyn via the notorious knife-edge ridge of Striding Edge. The weather had been perfect but very cold, and the ridge was icy in places. 'One slip up there and you fall five hundred metres,' he said. 'We probably shouldn't have attempted it, but hey. We survived.'

'I love Striding Edge,' she said. 'Definitely the best route up Helvellyn.'

He stared at her, clearly impressed that she had accomplished that climb. She decided to keep quiet about the fact that some sections of it had scared her witless, and it was only because she'd been with her dad and brother that she had been able to complete the climb.

'It certainly is,' he agreed.

They talked until closing time about mountains, walks, expeditions, plans for the week, places they'd like to travel to, experiences they'd like to have. Laura discovered they appeared to have a lot in common — not least their love of wild places. Stuart's idea of a wild place was a packed nightclub playing pounding dance music, she thought wryly, and realised the one thing she had not mentioned to Tom at all was her relationship with Stuart. Her ex-relationship, that was. Her ex-best friend, ex-boyfriend, ex-flat, ex-lifestyle. She missed it all still, but knew she could never have it back. She'd told Tom lots about her teens and early twenties, the pre-Stuart days, and about the last three months living with Stella, and nothing at all about that yawning void in her past that was the four years with Stuart. That was all too complicated to go into, bearing in mind she'd only really met Tom that morning.

For his part, he'd mentioned a woman called Sarah a few times, as someone he'd been to the Lake District with many times, someone he'd climbed and hiked with.

'Your girlfriend?' Laura asked.

'Ex. She moved on,' he replied, and his closed expression told her it was not a welcome topic. Fair enough — Laura didn't want to talk about Stuart either.

Finally, when the pub called time and the lights went up, they left and walked back to the campsite in the warm night air. It was sweetly scented with honeysuckle overgrown from a cottage garden, which wound its way through the hedgerows that lined the lane. The sky was clear with a half-moon just rising above the hills, and Laura found herself wishing the evening would never end. It was good to have met someone she could talk to, a new friend. That was all Tom could be — she wasn't looking for another relationship. It was too soon after Stuart, and she was too badly scarred. She needed a good long time alone.

When they reached her tent, he turned to her and raised a hand. 'Night, then. See you around nine in the morning for that walk?'

'Sure.' She watched him walk away, then pulled out her sleeping mat and lay on it outside her tent for a while, staring up at the stars, trying and failing to empty her mind. Her thoughts swam amongst Stuart, Martine, Tom, and her gran's ramblings about a missing tea caddy in the ruins of Brackendale Green. Eventually she decided enough was enough and it was time to get some sleep.

In her tent, she retrieved her head torch from her rucksack, switched it on and began the process of getting ready for bed. She'd barely begun when her phone beeped — a text had arrived. Who'd be texting her this late? She pulled it out and frowned. Stuart.

Hey, Lols. I hear you are on holiday. Hope you are having fun. Xxx

What on earth? It had been three months since they'd split up, and in that whole time they had only exchanged a couple of texts about practicalities such as picking up her gear, transferring the flat's utility bills into Stuart's name rather than hers, retrieving her share of the flat's damages deposit. What should she do — text back? Ignore it?

She was still staring at her phone, pondering what to do, when another one arrived.

Was thinking about you a lot today. Miss you. Think I made a mistake.

A mistake? Her heart began pounding. Did he want her back? Did she want him back? Could she even take him back, after all that had happened? It was true that despite everything, she missed him. She missed the camaraderie of living in the flat, the closeness of snuggling up to some-one every night, the feeling that her future was mapped out. But — what he and Martine had done — no. There was no way back from that.

The phone rang, making her jump. It was Stuart. She held it, staring at it as it rang, unable either to answer it or to decline the call. Let it go to voicemail. She could listen to the message, if he left one, later, and decide how to respond. How many times would it ring before it stopped? Would it ever stop? Half the Lake District had no mobile reception, with the mountains blocking all signals. Why couldn't this campsite be the same? She'd been pleased to find she had reception here when she arrived and could call Gran, but now she'd rather not know that Stuart was trying to contact her.

At last the phone stopped ringing. She put it down, with sweaty palms, and waited for it to ring again as it surely would if he'd left a voicemail. Five minutes passed but there were no more calls. No message; just those two texts. No, she wouldn't reply. Not now. Maybe in the morning. Let Stuart think she had no reception, or her phone was on silent. Let him think what he liked. She owed him nothing. Maybe she should block his number. She must be strong. She took a deep, steadying breath, and switched her phone off for the night. It was low on charge anyway. She'd need to plug it in at the campsite office for an hour or so in the morning.

Laura had a restless night. She was too hot, she'd had a bit too much to drink, and then Stuart's texts and call kept her awake and fretting. What did he want? What did he mean by saying he thought he'd made a mistake? How should she respond? At last she fell asleep only to dream of Stuart shouting at her, his mouth huge, red and ugly, and then Tom, stepping between them, pulling her away, and then a dried-up lake-bed, broken walls and her grandmother stumbling towards her across the mud, muttering about something hidden, something lost, something wrong. She woke in the early hours sweating, her mouth parched, her heart racing, but a decision made: she would ignore Stuart's texts and calls. He'd probably made them when he was drunk. He wouldn't send any more. And she was certain she did not want him back, not now, or ever. That chapter of her life was most definitely over.

★ ★ ★

Thankfully she did manage to sleep again, and woke at seven feeling much better than she had felt at three. She switched on her phone and checked her voicemail — no messages. What a relief. She did not want to even hear Stuart's voice, not here, on holiday.

She picked up a book to read for an hour. No need to get up just yet — there was plenty of time to have breakfast before meeting Tom for the planned climb up Bracken Fell. This early in the morning the air was a little cooler and it was pleasant to lie in her sleeping bag reading.

When the phone rang again her stomach lurched. No, please, not Stuart. She looked at the display and discovered with relief that it was Stella. The relief was quickly replaced by worry — why was Gran phoning so early in the morning? What had happened? Or was it Gran's carer, phoning with bad news? She answered quickly, her palms sweating.

'Gran? Are you all right?'

'Laura, dear. Yes, I am all right. Is it too early? I had trouble sleeping.'

'Oh dear. So did I.' Laura fleetingly debated telling Gran that Stuart had called but immediately dismissed the idea. No point worrying her. 'It's just so hot, isn't it? Is that what kept you awake?'

'What dear? The heat? Oh no. It was my silly old head, going round and round, thinking about the old tea caddy and whether it would still be there after all these years, and whether . . . oh, I don't know. Whether you'd be able to find it, after all this time.'

Laura felt a pang of worry. Stella was rambling again. Perhaps she should never have gone away and left her — not if she was beginning to show signs of dementia. 'Gran, what are you talking about?' she said gently.

'Oh, my dear. You probably think I'm making no sense. There was a tin box — an old tea caddy — in our house in Brackendale Green. Pa wanted me to fetch it, but I couldn't. He wanted it so much, but I couldn't get to it.'

'Why couldn't he get it himself?'

'He . . . he wasn't able to come back. He was . . . well. He was somewhere else. He'd asked me to fetch it for him. But the water was . . . there was water everywhere.'

Laura frowned, trying to make sense of what her grandmother was saying. 'Are you talking about after the village was flooded? You came back for something?'

'Yes, that's right. It was because of Jessie. That's why I had to go back.'

'Who's Jessie?'

There was silence on the other end.

'Gran? Who's Jessie — you said you had to go back because of her?'

Stella sighed. 'Dear, sweet little Jessie. My sister.'

'I never knew you had a sister?'

'No, dear. I have never spoken about her. It was all so long ago.'

'Gran, what happened to her?'

'She was only just three. It was in the last few months before we had to leave the village. Ma was dead, and I know Pa had been struggling to look after us both. Jessie was a lively little thing, you see, a bit of a handful and for a man on his own looking after two children . . . well, I'm sure whatever happened he never meant it to.'

What was Gran trying to tell her? Laura wished she was with Stella now, holding her hand, coaxing the story out of her. It was so much harder by phone. 'What happened?' she asked again gently.

'She . . . she died. I saw her for the last time in the morning, before school. I dressed her that day, in her favourite pink frock that was too small for her but she did like to wear it. And a cardigan that Ma had knitted for her when she was sick. Poor Ma, lying there on her deathbed, determined to finish off that cardigan so that her little daughter would have something new to wear. And she managed it. All but the buttons, which I sewed on for her. But anyway. Jessie was wearing the pink dress and the cardigan, and I had tied her hair with a ribbon bow on top. I can picture her now, so clearly, after all these years. Must be eighty years ago now, or more, and she's fresh as a daisy in my mind. Oh, dear me.'

'That was the last time you saw her?' Laura prompted.

'Yes. I dressed her, and we had breakfast, and then I went off to school. The schoolhouse was down the valley, at Beresford, below where they built the dam, and the children went there from both villages and from farms all around. It was a two-mile walk from Brackendale Green. Tough going in winter if it snowed, I can tell you.' Stella took a deep breath before continuing. 'When I got home that afternoon, Jessie was . . . she was gone. My poor little sister! Hardly more than a baby she was. Such a lovely child when she was behaving. You know, I can still hear her giggle clear as anything, as though she was right here in the room with me.'

Laura asked gently, 'Gran, how did she die?'

'Oh Laura, love. It must have been an accident. They said it was murder but he wouldn't . . . he could never have . . . and they never found . . . ' Gran's voice trailed away beneath shuddering sobs.

'Gran, please, don't upset yourself. I shouldn't have asked. We can talk about it when I'm back home, if you want to.' Laura was cursing herself, wishing she was there to wrap her arms around her grandmother and comfort her.

'No, no. I must tell you now, while you're there.' Stella took a deep steadying breath. 'You might be able to find it.'

'Find what?'

'The tin. I couldn't reach it. But now, well maybe, if it's still there . . . Of course, it might not be. I never knew why Pa didn't just . . . but he asked me to fetch it, and I tried. Oh Laura, I tried so hard to get to it but I couldn't. And then . . . it was all my fault, you see? All my fault, what happened after that.'

'What's in the tin?'

Another silence, and sounds of eye-wiping and nose-blowing. When Stella spoke again her voice was very quiet, barely above a whisper. 'I don't know, love. I just know it was important, and Pa wanted me to fetch it.' She was quiet again for a moment. 'I failed him. It was all my fault.'

At that moment Laura's phone bleeped,

94

warning her its battery was critically low.

'Gran, my phone's almost out of charge. It'll cut me off any moment. But what do you think was your fault, Gran?'

'All of it, all of it.'

'So, this tin — of course I will look for it, but where do you think it is?'

'In the — '

Stella was cut off. Laura stared at her phone. Its screen was black, dead, completely out of charge. She tried to make sense of all that Stella had said. What had happened to her little sister? What was this tea caddy she kept talking about, and what was in it? Why was it so important? Well, she would have to wait now until she could speak to Gran again.

8

JED

Jed stared after the overseer as he walked away with the bundle of jewels in his hand. Then he turned to look at Susie Atkins. 'Are you sure, Susie, love? What you said about seeing my pa drop that bundle in the grave?'

She nodded solemnly.

'It was a long time ago. How can you remember it?'

'I were there, I seen it, I seen it all,' she said stubbornly, and pushed out her lower lip.

'Jed, please. She'll have a tantrum. Can we not just leave it at that?' Janie Earnshaw said, as she took her sister's hand.

'Susie, remember what Maggie said about making a cake, as soon as we've finished seeing Ma reburied?'

Susie grinned and nodded. Jed realised it was not the right time to ask any more questions. He picked up Jessie, sitting her on his hip, took his leave of the women and went on his way, his mind churning. If Susie had seen Isaac drop the bundle of jewels into the grave then presumably Isaac knew what was inside it. Which meant, assuming the jewels were stolen, that he must be involved in some way. But why hide them in a grave that was then filled in? It made no sense. Jed would have to ask him about it. And judging by what Mr Banks the overseer had said, he should ask him before the police followed it up. One more thing to worry about, as if there wasn't enough on his plate already.

Jed called at the village shop, buying milk, bread and a pound of beef mince for their dinner from Mrs Perkins. There were some homemade pies on the counter, and he bought one of those as well, for Isaac's dinner. This left him with very few coins in his pocket, but Sam Wrightson owed him a few bob, and John Teesdale had mentioned needing him to fix his boiler, so there was work lined up and money coming in, for the moment. They were surviving, and as long as he could find ways of keeping Jessie out of trouble while he worked, his little family would be all right for now. Who knew what would happen in the longer term. He could not think more than a few days ahead. But what of Isaac? What would become of him?

'Come on, Jessie, lass, let's go and visit your grandpa, shall we?'

'Grandpa, Grandpa!' the little girl squealed, as she instantly began running up the lane towards Isaac's house.

Jed laughed. 'Wait for me! I've all this shopping to carry!' He ran after her, and scooped her up under one arm. It wouldn't do to let her walk. She had a habit of darting off into people's front rooms or backyards; if he didn't watch her he was in danger of losing sight of her. Once he'd spent a whole afternoon searching the village for her, only to finally discover her curled up asleep under a table in Sam Wrightson's kitchen. No one locked their doors in this village.

He set her down on Isaac's doorstep, and let her open the door herself. 'Grandpa!' she squealed again, as she ran inside. Isaac was in his rocking chair beside his stove, and Jed was worried to see that he looked grey and ill. Was it really a good time to ask him about the jewels found in Martha Atkins' grave? A sudden thought came to him. When he'd spoken to Isaac about Ma's exhumation, Isaac had seemed agitated about the idea of digging up the graves. Was it because he was frightened of what might be found? Was it possible Susie was right, and Pa did know something about the jewels?

'Hello, little monkey,' Isaac said, grinning toothlessly at his granddaughter. 'Climb up for a cuddle, will you?' He reached down and helped Jessie clamber onto his lap. She immediately wrapped her arms about his neck and began plastering his grizzled old face with kisses.

'Pa, I brought you a pie from Mrs Perkins for your dinner. You can heat it up later. I'll make a cuppa now, shall I?'

'Aye, lad. I'd like a cuppa. Been sitting here a long time.'

Jed filled the kettle and put it on the stove top. 'Not good for you to sit still so long, Pa. You should get up and move around a bit more.'

Isaac shook his head. 'It's getting hard to move around, lad. My old knees. And hips. Stiff as old leather, I am. All I can do to get myself in and out of bed each day.'

Jed put a spoonful of tea in the pot. He knew

it wouldn't be long now till Isaac needed to move in with him and the girls. One more responsibility to fall on his shoulders, but not one he would shirk. Family was family. You did what you had to, however hard it was. However much it wore you down and left you feeling exhausted and despairing. He pottered about, preparing the tea, listening to Jessie chatter nonsense to her grandpa, and wondering how to bring up the subject of the jewels found in the grave.

'Pa? They were digging up old Martha Atkins today, to rebury her in Glydesdale along with Ma and the others.'

'Martha Atkins, eh? I remember her. Died of pneumonia. Her poor little lass Susie left all alone but Janie did a good job mothering her all these years.'

'Did you dig Martha's grave? Can you remember?'

Isaac looked at him sharply. 'Might have done. Can't recall all the graves I dug. Why do you ask?'

This was the moment. Jed lifted Jessie off Isaac's knee and sat her in a corner with a biscuit to keep her quiet. He turned back to his father. 'They found something in Martha's grave. A tin, wrapped in oilcloth. And inside . . . ' He watched Isaac carefully, looking for a reaction, but none came. Susie, surely, was mistaken then.

'Inside?' prompted Isaac, raising his watery eyes to Jed's.

'Inside was some jewellery. Diamonds, rubies, all sorts. Good stuff. Buried along with Martha.'

Isaac had become very still, staring down at his lap. 'Jewels, you say?'

'Pa, as you were the gravedigger around the time when Martha died, they're going to come and ask you about it,' Jed said gently.

'Who's asking me?'

'The police, Pa. They think whoever dug the grave must have put the jewels in it.'

'I didn't dig all the graves. I don't know nothing about any jewels,' Isaac said, pinching his lips together and shaking his head. Just the way Jessie did when she was denying some misdemeanour, Jed thought.

'They're going to ask you about it anyway,' Jed replied. 'Make sure you have your story straight.'

'It were Fred Thomas,' Isaac suddenly blurted out, making Jessie look up at him, her eyes wide. 'He were the one that took them, not me. It were nowt to do with me. He were going to go back and dig them up, once the police had searched his lodgings and left him alone.'

'Frederick Thomas?' Jed knew the name. Mr Thomas ran a plant nursery in Penrith. He was a wealthy and successful man who had been a friend of Isaac's when they were young. Jed had often heard his father mention him.

'Aye. It were him, and I had nowt to do with it.'

'Grandpa, more biscuit!' Jessie ran across from the corner where Jed had put her, and clambered back onto Isaac's lap. The old man instinctively put his arms around her but his eyes remained fixed on something in the middle distance, or perhaps in the past. Jed shook his head sadly, as

100

he got up to finish making the tea. It was clear that Isaac did have something to do with the burying of the jewels, and quite possibly their theft, too. Well, Jed would have to get the truth out of him, and then work out how to keep it away from the authorities. Isaac was too old and frail to handle being interrogated by the police.

'Help me use the privy, would you, lad?'

Jed looked in surprise at his father. This was a new development. Isaac had never asked him this before. The old man's eyes were sad, pleading, and there was a touch of embarrassment in them. 'Of course, Pa. Come on, off you get, Jessie. Grandpa needs to get up.'

'No! Want to stay with Grandpa!' Jessie clasped her little arms around Isaac's neck and he had to pry her off, despite the screams of protest. 'Now then, behave, or I won't bring you to see Grandpa,' he admonished.

He helped Isaac stand on shaky legs, fetching a stick for him. It was too late, he realised, noticing the dark stain spreading across the front of his trousers. 'Come on, Pa. I'll get you cleaned up and in some fresh trousers.'

Isaac shook his head. 'There's none that's clean,' he said quietly.

'I'll wash some, then.' Jed led his father out the back door of the cottage and across the yard to the outside privy, and helped him get seated. While he did his business Jed searched for something to dress him in, and found only an old pair of underpants. They would have to do. Isaac could put a rug over his knees. Or . . . and with a sigh Jed knew there was only really one option — it was finally time for Isaac to move in with him. Another worry, another responsibility. Maybe it'd be easier all round if he did. He hoped so. There wasn't much more he could cope with,

He helped the old man into the clean underpants and led him back inside, to sit down again on the chair he'd quickly wiped clean. Jessie had amused herself in the meantime by wrapping herself in a blanket and rolling around the kitchen floor, pretending to be a caterpillar. 'Pa, I'll take your washing back home and get it done with mine. I'll bring you a pair of my trousers, and then, Pa . . . '

Isaac looked up at him with watery eyes.

'Then, Pa, I'll help you up the road to my house. It's time you moved in with me and the girls.'

'Ah, no, lad. I'll not be doing that. I'll be too much a burden on you. You've enough to do since your Edie died.'

'Pa, it'll be easier for me having you in the house, rather than up the other end of the village. I can make sure you get your meals, get you to the privy on time. Besides,' he said quickly, as his father shook his head stubbornly, 'you'll be able to help look after Jessie. She's a bit of a handful when I'm working. If you're there, you can watch her. She's better behaved around you. You'll be a real help.'

'Aye, it'd be good to spend more time with the little one,' Isaac said thoughtfully. 'Well, if you're sure, lad. I admit I need a bit more help these days. My old knees aren't what they were.'

'I'll make you a bed in our front room. You won't need to go climbing our stairs. I'll leave Jessie here while I fetch those trousers, then.'

★   ★   ★

Outside, Jed sighed heavily. It did make sense to have Isaac move in, but he could see that life was going to become yet more difficult. If only Edie hadn't died when she did. He needed her. They all needed her. But now, they only had him — Jessie, Stella and Isaac, all dependent on him, to earn enough to live on, to cook, clean and care for them. Soon they'd be homeless. And before that, he realised with a jolt, Isaac might be accused and perhaps convicted of a long-ago robbery.

It was a tough job getting Isaac from his cottage at one end of the village to Jed's, at the other end. Isaac used two sticks, and Jed carried his chair — which they needed, anyway. Although the distance was only a couple of hundred yards, Isaac had to sit and rest several times. ''Tis the longest I've walked in a while, lad,' he said, with an apologetic look.

'No matter, we can take all day if we have to. And once you're with me, the furthest you'll need to walk is to the privy. Unless you fancied a pint in the Lost Sheep of an evening, of course.' Jed winked at his father. It had been a long while since Isaac had been able to enjoy a drink in the pub, but now perhaps he would, occasionally. 'Jessie, pet, come here and walk beside your grandpa.' The child was scampering back and forth like a puppy, poking around in puddles, finding things to pick up and put in her mouth, banging on doors and giggling as she ran.

Halfway along the lane, Isaac stopped again.

'Need more rest, Pa?'

'No. It's just something I've recalled. Something in my home I can't leave there. We have to go back.' Isaac tried to turn, but Jed held his arm.

'Pa, it's all right. I'll fetch your things later, and bring them to my cottage. I'll bring everything you need, and if there's anything I miss you can tell me and I'll go back and fetch it.'

'Something important, got to keep it hidden,' Isaac muttered.

'What is it, Pa?' Isaac certainly seemed agitated about this thing, whatever it was.

'A tin. Got precious things in it.'

'Ah, Pa. You're muddled about the tin in Martha Atkins' grave I was telling you about. That's been taken off to the police. It's not in your cottage.'

But Isaac was shaking his head. 'Not that tin. 'T'other one. Tea caddy, it is. Got to keep it safe. Where's safe in your house? Hidden, I mean. Got to keep it hidden.'

'I'm sure we can find a hiding place, Pa.' Jed tried to make Isaac walk on. What on earth was he talking about? Jessie was out of sight down the lane, probably already back at their home. At least he hoped she was, and not hiding in some other cottage, playing a trick on him. Now really wasn't the time for those kinds of games.

'Go back, fetch it now, lad. 'Tis under my bed,

there's a loose floorboard, and 'tis hidden under there. Fetch it now. I won't rest easy till it's with me again.'

Jed shook his head. 'Right now, Pa, I need to get you safely back to my house, and then I need to find Jessie, and *then* I can go back and fetch your things. I don't know what this tea caddy is you're talking about. I don't remember ever seeing it.'

'Kept it hid, didn't I? Kept it hid from you and your ma. Not something I'm proud of.'

'What's in the tin, Pa?'

Isaac set his mouth in a tight line. 'Nowt you need to know about, lad.'

Jed sighed. He clearly wasn't going to get any sense out of Isaac now. Well, one thing at a time, and the priority now was to get everyone safe inside his cottage. 'Come on, Pa. Nearly there. Sooner we're there the sooner I can go back for your things.'

Thankfully at that moment Stella appeared, walking up the lane from the direction of their house, home from school, leading a dripping-wet Jessie by the hand.

'Hello Pa, hello Grandpa. Found Jessie sitting in a puddle. Everything all right?'

'It is now you're home, lass,' Jed said with a smile. 'Take care of Jessie while I help Grandpa, will you? He's moving in with us.'

* * *

It was two days later that the police called on Jed in his workshop. There were two — a detective

105

sergeant, a red-faced man in his middle years, and a constable, young and fresh-faced. The sergeant introduced himself as DS Theakston. 'Mr Walker? We are enquiring as to the whereabouts of your father, one Isaac Walker. He's not at his home.'

'No, he doesn't live there any more,' Jed replied warily, although he knew only too well what it was they wanted Isaac for.

'Do you happen to know where he lives now?' Theakston said, pulling out a notebook and pencil.

'Aye, I moved him in here with me a few days ago. He's old and frail, and needs help with day-to-day things — getting dressed, eating, going to the privy. Poor old Pa.' Jed shook his head sadly. It wouldn't hurt to have the police feel pity for Isaac before they began questioning him. The constable gave him a half-smile as though he sympathised but Theakston gave him a sharp look in return.

'Is he here now? We need to speak with him.'

'Wait here. I'll see if he's available.' Jed hurried through from the workshop to his cottage, closing the door behind him. He did not want the police to follow. Better to have a few moments with Isaac to prepare him.

The old man was sitting where Jed had left him that morning — dozing on the chair brought from his cottage, by the kitchen stove. Jessie was playing at his feet, her toys strewn across the floor. Stella was at school. 'Pa? The police are here to see you.' Jed spoke urgently.

Isaac awoke with a start. 'The police? What are

they wanting with me?'

'It'll be about those jewels found in Martha Atkins' grave. Remember I told you about them. You dug the grave, so they'll want to ask how the jewels got in there.'

Isaac looked confused for a moment, then nodded. 'Aye. I remember. You told me to say it were Fred Thomas.'

'I didn't tell you to say that! You said it was him, and I advised you to get your story straight before they came. They're here now.'

There was a tap on the door before Jed could say anything more. He wondered whether Theakston and the constable had overheard anything. Well, if they had, there was not much he could do about it. He opened the door and the policemen entered, looking all around them as they came in, fingering the pans and plates on his dresser, running their fingers across the table surface. Jed felt oddly violated.

'Mr Isaac Walker?' Theakston addressed the old man, while the constable took a seat, uninvited, at Jed's table and pulled out his notebook.

'Aye. Who's asking?'

'Detective Sergeant Theakston, of the Westmorland police. You were, I understand, the principal gravedigger at St Isidore's Church, Brackendale Green, around the year 1895?'

'Aye.' Jed watched as Isaac's mouth set into a firm line.

'And you'd have dug the grave of — ' Theakston consulted his notes — 'one Martha Atkins who died in July of that year?'

'Mebbe. I can't remember.'

'Mr Walker, in early July of that year, a robbery at Brackendale House was committed. Mr Edward Pendleton reported a break-in while he and his wife were away. The thieves knew exactly what they were looking for and took some very valuable jewellery. Perhaps you remember this event?'

'Can't say as I do,' Isaac said, shaking his head. 'Were a long time ago.'

'Really?' Theakston said, raising his eyebrows. 'But our records say that you were questioned about it. Besides being the gravedigger here, you also worked as a part-time gardener up at Brackendale House. All the staff there were questioned, including you, and their lodgings searched, as the assumption was that it must have been someone with access to the house who knew it would be empty on that night.'

'Excuse me, sergeant,' Jed interrupted, 'but if my father was questioned and eliminated from inquiries back in '95, why are you asking him about it again now?'

'No one was convicted of that theft and the jewels were never found.' Theakston puffed out his chest as he continued speaking. 'Until now. A box containing the jewels was found in Martha Atkins' grave. You, Mr Walker, had firstly the opportunity to commit the robbery and sec- ondly — ' he counted off on his fingers — 'the means to hide the proceeds of the theft in the open grave you'd dug.'

Jed shook his head. 'Daft place to hide something.'

Theakston glared at him. 'I assume there'd been an intention to go back and dig them up again, once enough time had passed.' He turned to Isaac. 'Is that right?'

The old man folded his lower lip over his upper one, as though buttoning his mouth.

Theakston sighed theatrically. 'Well, the jewels have been identified as those belonging to the Pendleton family, and you have been identified by an eyewitness as having dropped the bundle into the open grave on the night following Martha Atkins' funeral . . . '

'Who saw me?' Isaac blurted out. Jed rolled his eyes at this — it was as good as an admission of guilt.

'Susan Atkins. So you're admitting you threw the bundle in the grave?'

'That Susie's a simpleton. You can't take her word for owt,' Isaac said.

'She knows what she saw. She's completely certain of it. Did you throw the bundle in? Mr Walker, we can arrest you on suspicion of the theft and continue this conversation at the police station in Penrith, if you'd prefer. Tomorrow, after a night in the cells. Maybe that would help you to remember.'

Jed gasped. 'You can't threaten him like that. He's an old man, infirm, as you can see. Barely able to walk.'

'Able to remember though, I'll warrant.' Theakston folded his arms.

Jed stared at his father. Now was the time, if he wanted to save himself, to mention Fred Thomas's name. But would he? Or would he remain loyal to his old friend, even if it meant taking the blame himself? Jed realised he could not guess what Isaac would do. You can know a man all your life, and yet not be able to predict what he'll do when put to the test.

'So, Mr Walker, you put the jewels in the grave, but was it also you who stole them from Brackendale House? This is your last chance to tell us the truth, before I have you taken to the station at Penrith.'

Isaac opened his mouth to speak, and Jed found himself holding his breath. Whatever he said, this was going to change everything.

9

LAURA

There was no way she could call Gran back until she'd charged her phone. Gran had sounded so upset. Perhaps it was better not to ask her any more about her lost sister just yet. Give her a chance to calm down a little. Laura looked at her watch. The campsite reception opened in half an hour so she could leave her phone there to charge. And Gran's carer, Sophia, would be due to call on her about now anyway.

It was yet another glorious day, with not a cloud in the sky. Laura smiled as she stuck her head out of her tent and looked around. The perfect day for a climb up to a summit or two. And better still, she would not be by herself, but was going with Tom. As long as she remembered to drink enough water to cope with the heat, it promised to be one amazing day. In any case, it wouldn't be as hot on the tops of the fells.

She hummed to herself as she dressed, and on an impulse decided to go and buy a cup of tea and a bacon sandwich from the campsite office rather than bother firing up her camping gas stove. She had to go over there anyway to put her phone on charge, and to order a round of sandwiches for her lunch.

Tom'd had the same idea, it seemed, for he

was also in the campsite office ordering a breakfast bun.

'Morning! Did you sleep well? Great day for our walk up the ridge, isn't it?' he said.

'Fabulous day. You'll have to show me on the map what route you're suggesting.' She loved maps — following the contours, trying to visualise the lie of the land from its two-dimensional representation.

'Will do. Bring your breakfast over to my tent and I can show you while we eat?'

She smiled. 'OK, you're on.'

★ ★ ★

Tom's tent was twice the size of hers, and much better quality. She felt almost ashamed of her cheap festival tent, but after all she had bought it in a hurry. She'd carried over her tea and sandwich, and he pulled out a sleep mat for her to sit on to eat, while he spread the map on the ground.

'So, we'll start by driving round to the car park at the head of Brackendale, then we'll take this path around the end of the lake and up that ridge. Should be great views looking back, of the dried-up reservoir and remains of the village. That path brings us to the top of Bracken Fell, and then we can stay high and follow the path over Brown Pike and Berefell and then down via this gully.' He pointed it out on the map. 'There's normally a gushing waterfall here, flowing into the Bere River that feeds the reservoir, but it'll be only a trickle at the moment. We can then follow the stream right back to the car park.'

'Sounds like a great walk,' Laura said, peering closely at the map. A long one, she thought, but she was up for it.

'We could, I suppose, start from here by going over the fells via the Old Corpse Road and down to the Brackendale car park from there, but we'd have to do that climb in both directions.'

'No, let's drive round to the start. I don't want to be worn out before we even get to the track we've planned to do!'

'OK.' Tom was thoughtful for a moment. 'Weird name for a footpath, isn't it — the Old Corpse Road? Wonder why it got that name?'

Laura grinned, happy to be able to answer this one, as she'd wondered the same thing after her first walk and had looked it up online. 'Centuries ago, before there was a church in Brackendale Green, they used to carry their dead via that track down to the church in this valley for burial. There are flat stones set along the way where they used to rest the coffins.'

'So we've both probably got some earlier ancestors in the churchyard here in Glydesdale then?'

Laura nodded. 'Yes, I reckon so. I quite fancy poking around there some time and seeing if I can spot any Walker graves. That was Gran's maiden name, by the way.'

'Well, let's do it. Later today if we have the energy? Or tomorrow. I'll look for Earnshaw and Atkins graves. I like old graveyards. There's something so peaceful and timeless about them.

All those souls, sleeping for ever. Have you finished your tea? We should get going — try to get up onto the ridge before the day gets too hot.'

Laura gulped the last of her tea and nodded. 'Yep, give me a couple of minutes to pack my rucksack and close up my tent, and I'll be ready.' She jogged over to her own tent and gathered together the things she'd need for a day in the mountains. With not a cloud in the sky it seemed mad to pack a mac and a survival bag but you never knew what might happen and her years of experience wouldn't let her set foot on the hills without being well equipped. She tugged on her walking boots, tied her hair in a ponytail and at the last minute remembered to ram a sunhat firmly on her head. With two large water bottles filled, her sandwiches packed and phone collected from the office, she zipped up her tent and walked back over to Tom.

★   ★   ★

The car park round at Brackendale was almost full, as more and more people had come to explore the ruins of the village. An enterprising ice-cream van had set up at the end of the car park and was doing a roaring trade already, even though it was not yet ten o'clock. Laura fought off the urge to suggest they buy one, and followed Tom as he set off on a path that would normally be hugging the lakeside. It was already hot, and she fervently hoped there'd be a bit of breeze when they reached the ridge. After a little while the path turned away from the lakeside and began to climb, up through thigh-high bracken which was prematurely brown and withered due to the drought. The path underfoot was rock-hard, and the air smelt of dried earth. The land was crying out for rain, Laura thought. The weather forecast was predicting a few more days of sunshine, then an area of low pressure would bring rain. Well, she'd enjoy the weather while it lasted. And enjoy present company, she thought, enjoying the sight of Tom's broad shoulders and taut buttocks climbing the path ahead of her. He was definitely a well-built man.

Tom didn't stop until the path reached a rocky outcrop which they had to scramble up. He paused at the foot of the crag and pulled out his water bottle. She was sweating and panting as she reached him, but exhilarated by the physical activity and enjoying every moment. She took a long drink from her own bottle, and he watched approvingly. 'It's all right,' she said. 'I'm not going to make the mistake of not drinking enough again.'

'Good. You all right with a bit of scrambling? If not, there's another path going round that avoids this bit.'

'I love a bit of scrambling,' Laura replied.

'Right then! Onwards and upwards.' He grinned, tucked his water bottle back into a side pocket of his rucksack and led the way. The first few moves on the crag needed hands on — a big step up, pulling on a jutting-out piece of rock that was just the right height to make a perfect handhold. Then a shuffle along a ledge, a short

115

clamber, and a shimmy up a little gully. It was hard work but hugely enjoyable, and Laura felt almost disappointed when she came out at the top of the gully to realise that was the top of the crag, and from there they would rejoin an easy path across a patch of dried-up marshland, before reaching the main part of the ridge.

'Worth having a look at the view back to the valley from here,' Tom said, nodding in the direction of the lake behind them.

Laura turned to take it in. The whole of Bereswater Reservoir was laid below them, two-thirds of it completely dried out, with only a small lake remaining behind the dam. From here, as with the view from the other side on the Old Corpse Road, you could see the layout of the whole village and the old road that ran through the valley. A small stream trickled though the middle, joining the remains of the lake.

'It must have been so beautiful before it was flooded,' she said.

'Yes, but now, when the reservoir is full, it is just as gorgeous. Possibly more so,' Tom replied. 'It's definitely one of my favourite valleys. This and Wasdale.'

'I love Wasdale too.'

'Your favourite?'

She thought about it for a moment. Dramatic Wasdale, with its deep lake, steep screes and imposing mountains — was it her favourite? 'Actually, I think I like Ennerdale best because it's so unspoiled. You have to walk or bike into it, and you really feel you've got away from it all.'

She fell silent, enjoying the peace of the mountains, and thinking about how good it had been to get away this week. Gran had been right. She'd badly needed a holiday, and now that she'd been away a few days and was relaxing into it, she was beginning to realise how tautly wound up she had been. This holiday was healing her, and could be the start of a new, Stuart-free phase of her life. Although receiving those darned texts from him the previous night had not helped.

Tom was looking at her quizzically. 'What do you need to get away from, Laura? You're looking thoughtful.'

'Ah, the usual. An ex,' she replied, as she began walking along the path. If she was going to talk about Stuart she'd rather do it as she walked than while looking into Tom's eyes in a crowded pub.

'Oh. Who ended it, him or you?'

'Me.' Laura walked a few steps further before continuing.

'I found him in bed with someone else.'

'That's shit.'

'Yes. It was my bed. And my best friend he was with.'

'What a bastard.' Tom shook his head.

Laura found she appreciated his solidarity. 'Well, that's what I thought. So I dumped him, dumped my friend who happened to be our flatmate as well, packed a bag and moved out. That's why I live with my gran now. There was nowhere else to go at short notice.'

'Good old Gran, eh?'

Laura smiled. 'Absolutely. And it's worked out really well for both of us. She saves on her care costs and I live rent-free. Actually, it was her idea I came up here for a holiday. She thought I needed one, and she was right, I did. I'd had no time off since ending things with Stuart. I'd thought it would be best to throw myself into my job but my work can be stressful at times.'

'You needed the healing power of the fells.' Tom nodded sagely, and paused a moment to gaze around him at the magnificent view. 'It works wonders, doesn't it?'

'Certainly does.'

They were on the ridge now, following a path that wound its way over the rocks, sometimes requiring them to use hands as well as feet. There were views to both left and right into side valleys that branched off Brackendale. The one on the left held a small tarn, its waters seriously depleted. A waterfall trickled pathetically into it, and Laura recognised the path beside it as the descent route they were planning to take. The valley on the right was filled with shrubs and bracken, its sides steep, rocky and inaccessible.

'You wouldn't want to fall down that side,' Laura commented.

'No. Looks pretty steep, doesn't it?'

As they stood gazing at the view, Laura noticed a large bird of prey wheeling around in the thermal updraughts. 'Look! What's that?'

Tom shaded his eyes and looked where she was pointing. 'Apparently there are a pair of golden eagles that nest somewhere around here.

Wonder if that's one of them?'

'Eagles? Really? In the Lake District?' Laura knew there were eagles in Scotland, rare but monitored and protected. But here in England? She watched the bird as it circled, coming lower and lower and finally landing on a crag halfway up the right-hand valley side. Once it was amongst the rocks and heather she could no longer pick it out.

'That must be where its nest is. Either that or it spotted some poor creature who's destined to be dinner,' Tom commented.

'I had no idea there were eagles here. I feel so privileged to have seen it.' Laura was still staring across the valley to where she'd seen it last, wishing she had some binoculars.

'There's only this one pair, here. And I believe they're quite elderly so who knows how long they'll last.' Tom looked at his watch and pulled out his phone to make a note. 'There's a website where you can report sightings of them. I'll do that later, when we're in the pub.'

Laura smiled to herself at that mention of 'we' and the assumption that they'd spend the evening together in the pub again. After a tough walk she'd want a big pub dinner rather than something cooked on her little stove, and his company was definitely a big draw. She pulled her own phone out to take a few photos, although the eagle could no longer be seen. There was a little envelope icon showing she had two new texts. She opened up the first and sighed — another one from Stuart. Where are you, babe? Called round to your Gran's but she said you were away and wouldn't tell me where. Want to see you & apologise.

Apologise? Like a simple 'Sorry, love' would put it all right? Martine must have dumped him. It was the only explanation for him to want her back. Well, he wasn't going to get her back. Not now, or ever.

The second text was from Martine. It's all over now between me and Stuart. Can't believe I did that to you. So sorry, hon. Will understand if you never forgive me. M.

'Bloody hell.' Laura shook her head. Could she ever forgive Martine? She would never be able to fully trust her again, and surely that was the point of friendships? She missed Martine but knew they'd never again be close. It'd take her some time to think about how or even if to respond.

'Everything all right?' Tom asked.

'Yes, all OK. Just heard that my ex and my friend have split up. Both are asking my forgiveness. Not quite sure how I feel about it.'

'Hmm. Tricky. Do you want either of them back in your life?' Tom's expression was one of sympathy.

'I don't know.' She shook her head. 'I'll need some time to think about it all.'

'Yes, it takes a long time to get over that kind of betrayal.' He stared into the distance, then turned towards her as though he'd made a decision. 'Something like that once happened to me, too. About three years ago, I was engaged. We lived together.' He broke off and gazed across the valley where they'd seen the eagle.

'What happened?' Laura asked gently.

'One day, she — Sarah — picked an argument. About nothing, really. I'd vacuumed the house, and that had meant picking up some of her stuff from the floor. Papers, books, some work stuff. I just stacked it up and put it on the table. When she found I'd moved it, she went ballistic. There was nothing important there that I'd noticed — some junkmail, the novel she was reading. But she shouted and ranted, how dare I touch her stuff, was I spying on her, who did I think I was to control her life like that.' Tom took a deep, shuddering breath before continuing. 'I mean, she was acting as though I was some sort of monster. My mouth was hanging open. I'd done nothing — except clean the bloody house. Anyway, to cut a long story short, she escalated it out of control, then went upstairs, pulled a suitcase out of the wardrobe and left. And that was it. She was gone.'

'Oh my God.' Laura couldn't quite think what to say. His words brought back uncomfortable memories of the day she'd had to pull a bag from the wardrobe and hastily pack it, while Stuart and Martine. watched.

'The thing is, the case was already packed. She'd planned to leave me. She engineered that row, from start to finish. And that wasn't the end of it.'

'No?'

'Next day, she emptied our joint bank account and maxed out a credit card that was in my name.' The eagle was wheeling around in the thermals again, and Tom watched it for a moment before continuing. 'I got the stuff on the card stopped, but couldn't do anything about the bank account. We'd been saving for our wedding.'

'Bloody hell.'

'I know. Anyway, there's been no one in my life since. A therapist would say I've been finding it hard to trust. Sarah moved away. Last I heard she was living with some rich banker in Dubai.'

'Must have hurt, though.'

'Oh yes, it did at the time. But after a few months when I was able to look back on it with the perspective of distance, I realised that things hadn't been right between us for a long time. We'd got engaged because everyone else seemed to be doing it, and because our families kept asking us when we were going to marry. All the wrong reasons. She was spending more and more time out with her friends, clubbing till all hours. I was finding any excuse to go climbing or walking, with my own mates. We had nothing in common. We'd met at a mutual friend's party, hit it off, and somehow found ourselves going out together. She moved into my house when her landlord sold the flat she was renting. Our relationship became a habit. A few months after she'd gone all I felt was relief.' Tom pulled out his water bottle and took a swig from it.

Laura smiled sympathetically at him. That sounded very similar to her own story. She realised now she had very little in common with Stuart, and they'd just fallen into living together because everyone else was doing it and it had made financial sense. She'd assumed they'd stay together, but now it was over, if she scrutinised her feelings properly, the overwhelming one was of relief, just as Tom had described.

So Tom had trust issues? Well, so did she. Another thing they had in common.

'Yes, I think I feel more relieved than anything else as well,' she said.

Tom replaced his water bottle. 'Still, there's been no one else since. It's left me reluctant to start any new relationship.'

'Me too,' she replied, ignoring the pang of regret she felt at his words.

He gestured up the mountain. 'Well. Enough of all that. Shall we continue?'

Laura nodded, and set off walking again. Now they were higher up it was cooler, the perfect day for a mountain climb. Everything felt good. Except for Stuart bugging her. But he was miles away and good old Gran was not telling him where. Neither would she herself, and she certainly wouldn't reply to his texts. She couldn't right now anyway — she no longer had a signal on her phone. 'I should phone Gran again today at some point, when we've got reception.'

'Yes. Find out more about this mysterious box she wants you to look for. It's got me intrigued. I'll help you look, or do whatever it is she wants. That's — ' he suddenly looked uncertain — 'that's if you want me to, of course. Tell me if I should butt out.'

Laura regarded him solemnly for a moment, and came to a decision. He was keen to help, and she wanted him to, so he needed to know all that Gran had told her. As they walked she related everything Gran had said on the phone.

'Oh Christ. That's terrible about her little sister! So this tea caddy she wants you to find, that's related to this somehow? I definitely want to help you look for it, then.'

'I'd love you to help. But I can't see how we could possibly find something that dates from her time in the valley.'

. 'Presumably it was well hidden somewhere. Seems important to her, from what you told me she said.'

Laura nodded. 'Yes. I don't understand the connection between her sister and this box she wants to find. I don't think she knows either. Maybe there is no connection at all.'

'But if it is important to her, we should at least have a go at finding it, while we have the chance. Once the weather changes and the reservoir refills, there could be no more opportunity for many years.'

He was right, Laura realised, and berated herself for not going back to the village today to look for it. The mountain-walking could have waited. Maybe they'd have time when they came down, to go and have a look in Gran's old cottage. She could phone and ask her to direct them to exactly where she thought it would be — there was phone signal out in the middle of the dried-up lake. Whatever it was, Gran's mind needed to be set at rest.

They walked on for a while, the path along the ridge taking them higher and higher. Laura barely noticed the scenery — her thoughts were bound up with Gran and the mystery of this tea caddy, with the occasional unwelcome intrusion of worries about whether Stuart would try to phone again. She really should block his number. She wanted no further contact with him.

At last they reached the end of the ridge and after a short scramble found themselves on the summit of the mountain — Bracken Fell. There was a triangulation point and a dry stone shelter that would no doubt be very useful if you arrived here on a windy day, but today the little breeze there was, from the south, was very welcome.

'This looks like a lunch spot,' Tom said. 'But first, come here for a summit selfie.'

Laura grinned and stood beside him, leaning on the trig point, as he held up his phone and took a photo of the two of them. He'd put his other arm about her shoulders, and for a brief moment she had snuggled up against him, enjoying the feel of his muscular body against hers.

He tucked his phone back in his pocket and looked down at her, his arm still around her shoulders. 'Thanks for coming up here with me. Always better to have company on a hike.'

'Thanks for bringing me up here too.' She smiled up at him. For a moment she thought he was going to kiss her, and before she realised what she was doing, she pulled away a little. Stuart had hurt her so much. It was too soon. Anyway, Tom had said he didn't want a new relationship.

But Tom just gave her a squeeze and then let go, turning away from her to find a suitable spot to sit down and eat his lunch. Laura found a flat stone opposite him to sit on and took out her sandwiches. They ate in companionable silence; Laura thinking about all that Tom had told her about himself, as well as about the texts from Stuart and Martine, and how she felt about it all.

★   ★   ★

By the time they'd completed the walk, over several summits and down via the tiny trickle that was all that was left of the Bere Force waterfall, Laura was exhausted. She'd run out of water and the heat of the day had intensified. All that kept her going on the final part of the descent was the hope that the ice-cream van might still be in the car park. She would buy a bottle of water and the largest-size soft ice-cream cone with at least two flakes. All thoughts of going searching in Brackendale Green for Gran's box had evaporated in the heat — she was too tired and hot to spend time in the baking middle of the reservoir. That would have to wait for another day.

She and Tom had talked non-stop after the initial ascent, when they'd got their breath back. They'd fallen silent on the way down. He must be as tired as she was, she guessed, as she plodded on, one foot in front of the other, a tingling on her right heel warning her of a blister in the making. Just don't stop, she told herself. Keep going, and hope the ice-cream van is there. After the last turn in the track the car park came into view.

'The van's still there,' Tom said with a grin, and she realised he'd been having the same fantasies as her.

'Thank the good Lord for that!' They both sped up a little, and Laura twisted her rucksack round to the front so she would waste no time and could get her money out before reaching the van.

It was the best ice-cream she had ever tasted.

10

JED

'It were Fred Thomas. He stole the jewellery tin and told me to hide it. The police were going to search the homes of all us workers up at the big house.' Isaac spoke quickly, shaking his head. 'I were scared. I hid it the first place I could think of. I meant to go back and dig it up some dark night and give it back to him. I never wanted nothing of it.'

'Fred Thomas?' DS Theakston made a note. 'And who is he?'

'Lives up at Penrith now. Runs the plant nursery. Back then he were a gardener along with me.'

'*Councillor* Frederick Thomas?' Theakston said in surprise.

Isaac nodded. 'Aye. Done well for himself.'

'Do you have proof?'

This was where it would all come undone, Jed realised. Isaac had no proof. It was only his word, set against that of a respected man, and with an eyewitness who'd confirmed that Isaac was involved. But to his astonishment Isaac nodded.

'He kept one piece. It were a ring. Ruby stone. He told me he were going to give it to the woman he loved, and a year later he was wed. Check his wife's finger. See if that matches up with the description of any of the stolen pieces. It's engraved on the inside — 'Love always' or some such muck.'

Theakston looked satisfied with himself as he noted this down. 'Thank you, Mr Walker. You have been very helpful. You may be granted immunity from prosecution if what you say turns out to be true and it was Thomas who committed the theft and put pressure on you to do his bidding and hide the proceeds. We shall see. Good day for now. I expect we may need to speak with you again.'

Jed showed them out, and returned to sit beside his father. 'Is that true, Pa? About the ring?'

Isaac regarded Jed with rheumy eyes. 'Aye. We'd agreed who would keep what, wrote it all down. I kept my copy of the paper with our agreement on, in the tea caddy. But then when they threatened to search our lodgings we put it all back in the tin to hide — except the ring, which Fred said was small enough to hide elsewhere until the hue and cry died down.'

Jed gasped. 'You'd agreed to divide it up? So you were involved in the robbery as well? Oh Pa!'

Isaac shrugged. 'Not fair when the likes of the Pendletons had so much and the likes of me had so little. We were just evening things up a bit. But look at us now — Fred Thomas in his big house in Penrith and me with only the clothes on my back sitting in your kitchen. If he gets done for this and not me that's just payback. I took the risks, hid them jewels, or most of 'em, anyway, and never had any benefit from them, all my life. Fred moved to Penrith, went up in the world. He became 'respectable', so he said. Told me not to dig them jewels up. Told me we'd made a mistake and to let them lie. 'T'isn't fair, it isn't.'

Jed could only stare at him. He'd always thought of his father as an honourable man. But it seems he was a thief, and not only that, a bitter one who would betray an old friend to save himself. Even so, Isaac was his father, and Jed knew he would do everything in his power to protect him and ensure the last part of his life was as comfortable as it could be. Family was family, after all.

'Where's that tea caddy now? Where you put your agreement with Fred?' Jed realised that document needed to be destroyed or at least well hidden, in case the police came searching.

'I told you, lad. Under a loose floorboard in my bedroom, in my own cottage. Asked you to fetch it, I did, but you wouldn't listen.'

'I'll fetch it now, Pa.' Jed made sure the police had left the village, then walked up to Isaac's old cottage. In the bedroom, he shoved the bed away from the wall and found the loose floorboard, just as Isaac had said. Underneath was an old Victorian tea caddy, decorated with pictures of Indian women picking tea. Jed prised off the lid and tipped out the contents. There was a document, as Isaac had said, but that was not the only thing inside. Clearly Pa was still not being entirely truthful. Well, the only course of action was to hide this tea caddy, and make sure the police never found it or its contents. It would be safer in his own cottage. Jed tucked it under his jacket and took it home.

* * *

There were no further visits from the police for the following week. Jed kept his ears open in the Lost Sheep for any news while keeping quiet about his Pa's involvement, and scanned copies of the local newspaper in Mrs Perkins' shop, but there'd been nothing printed about the case since the news of the discovery of the jewels. He avoided Susie Atkins in case seeing him made her say anything more about what she'd seen all those years ago. The exhumations came to an end, with everyone from St Isidore's churchyard moved to Glydesdale Church. The graveyard was a forlorn place now, Jed thought, with its bare earth and empty graves that had only been roughly filled in. He'd had to keep Jessie away, frightened that she might play in the mounds of loose earth and be buried herself.

The dam-building was almost complete now. Jed had not been able to travel down the valley to see it, but word was that it was at full height for the width of the valley, and that now the workmen were completing the towers at either end that would house the mechanism for opening and closing the valves at the bottom of the dam, allowing water to flow through or not. When the day came that the valves were closed, water would begin to back up behind the dam, causing the existing little lake to overflow its banks. Soon afterwards water would flood into

131

the village, and it would have to be evacuated. Already some people had left, finding homes and jobs in other valleys. Brackendale farmers were preparing for their last season in the valley. Jed still had no idea where he would go. He had no family nearby. There was Edie's sister Winnie in Penrith, but she did not have enough space for Jed, Isaac and the girls. In any case he could not throw himself upon her. She had her own life. He was, he realised, still putting off the moment when he'd have to actually come up with a plan for their future. There was enough to worry about at the present time. Isaac was not proving to be an easy housemate.

It was when he was in the Lost Sheep one night, unwinding after a day in which Isaac had got through three pairs of trousers, and in which Jessie had managed to burn her hand on the stove, that he heard the news. He'd felt guilty going out that night, but with Jessie asleep at last, her hand bandaged, Isaac in bed and already snoring, and Stella promising to go to bed as soon as she'd completed her homework, he'd felt the need for a pint or two. He deserved it, he told himself. Life was tough.

Maggie was in the pub that night, but she turned her back as soon as she saw him walk in. He ignored the snub and went to the bar, ordering a pint of best bitter from John Teesdale.

'Heard the news from Penrith?' Teesdale asked him as he poured the pint. 'That Frederick Thomas, him that runs the plant nursery and sits on the council, he's been arrested. Apparently that loot found in Martha Atkins' grave was something to do with him — he stole it forty years back. Must have thought he'd got away with it, though it can't have done him any good being buried all these years.'

'Has he confessed?' More to the point, Jed thought, would he tell the police that Isaac had been an accomplice in stealing the jewels, not just in hiding them?

'Aye, I believe so. He's in custody. They'll sentence him, he'll go down, and he'll lose his business and his standing. All for a youthful mistake that brought him nowt. Makes you think, doesn't it?' Teesdale handed Jed his drink.

Jed took the pint and nodded. 'It does, that. What's happening to the jewels?'

'Being returned to their rightful owner, I believe. At least, their rightful owner's heir. They belonged to the old Mrs Pendleton, but she's long gone. So they'll go to her son, what's his name, Sebastian Pendleton. Expect he'll make a present of them to his wife, Alexandria, I think her name is.'

Alexandria Pendleton. The woman Jed had met twice over at Glydesdale Church — first at Edie's funeral when she'd loaned her motorcar and chauffeur so that Stella wouldn't have to walk back, and the second time when he'd gone to see the reburial of his ma.

He took his pint and sat at an empty table, alone. Maybe Sam Wrightson would be in later. If not, he'd just enjoy the peace and quiet, and the feeling of not having to do anything to look after others for a little while. The good Lord knew he needed that.

But his peace was not to last. Maggie passed by on her way to the bar, and stood before him. She was dressed in that swishy silk dress again, the one she'd worn on the night there was trouble with the dam-builders. She leaned over the table towards him, seemingly to ensure he had a good view of her cleavage. 'I hear your pa got off, then. You must be very relieved.' Her tone was one of vindictiveness, but he would not rise to it.

'Pa admitted to putting the jewels in the grave but that's all,' he said.

'Your pa's a decent man. Not like his son,' she said. 'Leading a woman on and then dropping her like a stone. I haven't forgotten what you did. I won't forget. You'll be sorry, some day, that you didn't accept me. I could have been good for you.' The last words were hissed out, as she straightened up and continued on her way to the bar.

He sighed and slumped in his seat. So much for his quiet drink, unwinding after a hard day. Maggie had just made it worse. One good thing about leaving the village would be that he would no longer be her neighbour, at risk of seeing her daily in the street or pub. If only Maggie could forget him she might have a chance with someone else, and that would be better for both of them. He wondered where she, Janie and Susie would be moving to. He should find out, he thought, so he could be certain to move his family somewhere entirely different. When he finally got around to doing something about their move, that is. It was all he could do to manage his chores from day to day. There was never any time or energy left to consider the long-term future. And he couldn't see how this could change, while there was still Isaac to look after, and Jessie being such a handful. Things were becoming worse not better, in these months since Edie's death.

'All right, Jed?' Sam Wrightson's voice shook him out of his morbid thoughts.

'Aye, I'm as right as I ever am, these days,' he replied.

'Life being tough on you, is it?' Sam's eyes were full of sympathy as he sat down with his pint, next to Jed. 'Losing Edie so young.'

Jed nodded, not trusting himself to speak.

'And those girls. Stella's growing up fast, isn't she? Spit of her mother she'll be when she's older. I saw her out with Jessie the other day. Little one was giving her a right run-around. She's a bit of a wild one, I'd say;'

'Aye, she can be. An angel at times, a devil at others. Love her to pieces, though. Wish I had more time to spend with her, play with her the way I used to, when Edie was around.'

Sam looked at him quizzically. 'Coping all right, are you? With your pa moving in and everything?'

Jed breathed out heavily and took a long pull at his pint before answering. Sam was a good friend, and he needed someone to confide in. 'To tell the truth, Sam, I'm barely keeping my head above water. Working, keeping house, looking after the girls and Pa — it's difficult. I'm not one to complain, but sometimes I lie in bed at night and wonder what'll become of us all. I've no spare time to search for new work or anywhere to live. Barely enough time to work to earn enough to put food on the table. Can't see where it'll all end.' He shook his head as if to correct himself. 'Actually, I do know where it'll end. With my home, this pub and this village being submerged underwater, leaving me and my family homeless.'

'Won't come to that, Jed. Something'll turn up. Some way out of this mess, you just wait and see.'

'Can't see what. Not while there's Pa and the girls to care for. Not Stella, like — she's no bother. But Jessie. She's a full-time job by herself.' Jed didn't know how Edie had managed, especially when she was ill. Perhaps he just wasn't as good a parent as she had been. Or perhaps Jessie was becoming harder work as she grew older.

'Aye, aren't all children when they're little? Which reminds me, I got to tell you summat odd. I saw young Jessie and Stella up at the lake t'other day. Having a fine old time they were. Jessie went balancing along a fallen tree trunk that stretched into the lake. Stella tried to stop her but you know your Jessie, mind of her own, that one. Anyway, she fell, landed face down in the water. Your Stella had to kick off her shoes, wade in and save her. Funny thing was though, that Pendleton woman from the big house was standing there, up on the lane, watching it all. She didn't do owt to help, just stood staring at the two of them.'

Sam drained his glass. 'At any rate, before you know it Jessie'll be grown and as easy to handle as your Stella. Another pint?' He rose to go to the bar.

'Aye, I will. Thanks.' Jed slumped back again. It'd be years before Jessie became easier to handle. And meanwhile there were all the other problems he had to deal with. He could see no end in sight.

★   ★   ★

Two days later was a Saturday so thankfully Stella was at home to help look after Jessie and Isaac. Jed was taking advantage of the extra help to get on with some work. He was in his workshop when he heard the sound of a motorcar coming closer, and then stopping somewhere nearby. He put down his tools, wiped his oily hands on a rag and went out to see who it was. It was the Pendletons' Bentley — the same one he'd had a lift in after Edie's funeral, parked outside the Lost Sheep. The chauffeur was sitting in the driving seat, his leather-gloved hands still on the wheel. As he watched, a rear door opened and a smartly dressed man who he guessed was Sebastian Pendleton climbed out, followed by Mrs Pendleton. They looked around, then stepped inside the pub. Long way to come for a pint, Jed thought, but each to their own. A gaggle of small boys were crowded around the Bentley, exclaiming over its shiny paintwork and smooth lines. The chauffeur got out of the car and shooed them away irritably, pulling out a white handkerchief to polish off their finger-prints. Jed laughed and went back into his workshop to continue working.

Not for long though. A moment later there was a tap on the door which then swung open. It was the Pendletons. Once more Jed downed tools and wiped his hands on his overalls, but realised with dismay they were still filthy, and he would not be able to shake hands.

'Mr Walker. We have met before, haven't we?' Mrs Pendleton raised her chin, clasping her gloved hands in front of her.

'Yes, ma'am. Over at Glydesdale, and you very kindly had your chauffeur drive me and my Stella home after my wife's funeral. I was — still am — so grateful. Please, come through.' He showed them through to the cottage kitchen, that now doubled as a sitting room since Isaac had moved in.

'Kind of you, Alex,' the man said, nodding at her. He turned back to Jed. 'I'm Sebastian Pendleton. We're actually here on a rather delicate mission. There's another Mr Walker, I believe, a Mr Isaac Walker?'

'My father, yes,' Jed said warily. What did they want with Pa? Surely not about the jewellery theft. They'd got the jewels back, Teesdale had told him. Mrs Pendleton had removed her gloves and was wearing, he noticed, a large ruby ring on her right hand. And Fred Thomas was in custody for the crime.

'He's infirm, as I understand it from Detective Sergeant Theakston?' Mr Pendleton said, with a frown.

'Aye, he is that,' Jed replied. 'He can't fend for himself any more. I do my best by him.' He wondered if Isaac, in the next room, could hear them.

'I'm sure you do. We understand that he was involved in the theft of my mother's jewels, back in '95. He hid them, did he not?'

Jed nodded slowly. No point denying it. Presumably they'd heard from the police everything Isaac had said.

'An accessory to the crime. Receiving stolen goods. Perverting the course of justice, perhaps.'

Jed could not believe what he was hearing. 'What?'

This time it was Mrs Pendleton who spoke. 'Your father is guilty, as guilty as Frederick Thomas, in all likelihood. Sergeant Theakston advised us not to pursue the case any further, now that we have the jewels back and Thomas has admitted his guilt, but don't you see, Mr Walker, justice must be done. Your father should pay the price for his crime too. We are here today to warn you that we wish to press charges. We'll bring a private prosecution if need be. Mr Isaac Walker will be arrested and brought to trial, as is right and proper.'

'No! You can't do this! He is old and frail. He does not deserve this.' Jed sat down heavily.

'On the contrary, Mr Walker, he *does* deserve this, if he is guilty. Age is no excuse.' Mrs Pendleton folded her hands in front of her and set her mouth in a grim line.

'Please ma'am. He wouldn't survive a trial. He — ' Jed took a deep breath to steady himself

— 'he's going downhill rapidly. He may not live much longer, as it is. This would just speed his end, I'm sure of it. Please, ma'am, sir. Have a heart. Leave him be. What benefit can it bring you?'

Mr Pendleton stared straight at Jed, unblinking. 'Justice, Mr Walker. Justice must be done.'

11

LAURA

Laura awoke the day after the hike up Bracken Fell to another glorious sunny morning, forecast to be even hotter than the previous day. Laura dressed quickly inside her tent, wearing a loose white shirt and long cotton skirt, for the trip to Brackendale House Museum that they'd planned on the way down the mountain. The skirt was one she'd brought to wear to pubs in the evenings but would be the coolest thing on what promised to be a scorcher. Remembering her reaction to the sun the first day she rummaged at the bottom of her holdall and found a floppy cream sunhat. Not pretty, but practical. She smiled as she imagined Tom's approval of her headgear.

She fried herself a couple of sausages for breakfast, and sat in the shade of the oak tree to eat them and wait for Tom. Her mind was running over what Gran had said, about her little sister. Dying so young! And why had Gran said it was all her fault? What was she blaming herself for after all these years? She wondered if she should call Gran again now but she remembered Gran's insistence that she didn't want a phone call every day.

And then there were Stuart's texts. Something else to ponder on.

Tom arrived on foot on the dot of ten o'clock as they'd agreed, and they walked together to his car, parked beside his tent, which was further along the campsite track but just as near to the stream as Laura's pitch. 'Wish the stream was deep enough for swimming in, don't you?' Laura said.

'Yes, it'd be lovely at the end of a hot day. There are safe places to swim in some of the lakes though. Do you fancy that, later on?'

'Definitely!' Laura could think of nothing she'd like more. But had she packed a swimsuit? Well, she could always swim in a T-shirt and shorts, if need be.

They got in Tom's car and drove along the now-familiar road out of the Glydesdale valley. It was still early but already the tarmac shimmered in a heat-haze ahead of them. Tom chatted about the weather, his plans for more walks, and what they might find in the museum as they drove.

They headed towards Brackendale valley, but this time took the turn marked Brackendale House Museum. It was a National Trust property. Laura smiled to herself to discover Tom was a member. She had always wanted to join too, but Stuart of course had had no interest in going round old houses, museums or visiting beautiful countryside.

Tom parked in the gravel car park to the side of the house, and they walked through its grounds, beneath mature beech and oak trees, towards the main building. To the side was a wooden hut selling refreshments, and picnic benches were dotted around on the grass.

Brackendale House itself was not particularly large — more of a manor house than a stately home. It looked to be part Tudor with some more recent additions — a Gothic wing suggested Victorian tastes and a colonnaded portico Regency influence.

'Bit of a mishmash of styles, isn't it?' Tom commented, echoing Laura's thoughts.

'I rather like it. It wears its history on its sleeve. Why stick to one style when you can have a bit of them all?'

Tom laughed. 'Well, shall we go in?'

They entered the house through its main door, and bought entrance tickets from a guide sitting at a huge, ancient desk. In the dark wood-panelled hallway the temperature was much cooler than outside. Laura removed her hat, and found herself half-wishing she'd brought a cardigan.

'What a relief to be somewhere cool!' Tom said. 'Must be the thick stone walls, keeping the heat out. Bet it's cold here in winter though. Must be, to need that.' He nodded at a huge stone fireplace that took up most of one wall in the hallway.

Laura consulted the leaflet she'd picked up at the entrance. 'So, there are a few rooms furnished as they would have been in late Victorian times, and some other rooms in use as a museum, telling the story of the house and Brackendale valley. What do you fancy looking at first?'

'The furnished rooms,' Tom said, and they went through to view those. Much of the

143

furniture had been in the house for over 150 years, bought by a family named Pendleton who had owned the house for many generations, according to the information boards which stood inside each room. The rooms were cool and a little gloomy, with heavy dark oak panelling and too much furniture filling every inch of available space, in true Victorian style. On the walls were portraits of various members of the family. One, of a woman in late Victorian evening dress, showed her adorned with jewels — a small diamond tiara, a choker set with emeralds, a large ruby ring and a butterfly-shaped brooch.

'They were well off, then, for country gentry,' Laura said, nodding towards the portrait. 'Or did she put on every piece of jewellery she owned for that portrait?'

'Certainly looks like an advertisement for the wealth of the family,' Tom agreed, as he bent over to read the typewritten note displayed beside the portrait. 'Oh, look at this. The portrait is of a Mrs Amelia Pendleton, and shows her wearing the jewellery that was stolen from this house in an infamous burglary in 1895. It says, 'See museum for the full story.''

'Sounds interesting!' Laura looked around the rest of the room, then led the way through to what had once been the manor house's dining room and which was now one of the rooms used for the museum. There were various displays, covering the geology and history of the Brackendale valley from its beginnings in the last ice age, through to its popularity with fell walkers in the current day. Of course the abandonment of Brackendale Green and the building of the dam were covered in some detail, with plenty of photos of the dam under construction, and of the village as it had been during the early part of the twentieth century. Laura looked closely at these photos, picking out the Lost Sheep pub, and trying to identify her grandmother's cottage and great-grandfather's mechanics workshop. One photo showed what could be a workshop, with a tractor half in and half out, and a man, pipe in mouth, standing beside it. 'Look, Tom, that might be my gran's dad,' she said, pointing it out.

'Cool! Take a photo of it to show her.'

'Good idea.' Laura pulled out her phone and took a snap.

'Here's the bit about that jewellery burglary,' Tom said, and Laura crossed over to where he stood, beside a display board. There were several photos, of the manor house, the jewels, the portrait they'd already seen, and the Brackendale Green churchyard. And there was also a photo of a white-haired man in prison garb, captioned *Frederick Thomas — convicted of the theft over 40 years later*. Tom was reading the text that accompanied the photos silently, and as he did so he gasped.

'What is it?' Laura asked. She had not yet begun reading.

'One of the names mentioned here is in my family tree,' he said. 'Here — Martha Atkins. She was my great-great-great-grandmother, if I remember correctly.'

145

Laura raised her eyebrows in surprise and began reading aloud from the top of the board.

'On a dark night in July 1895, an audacious burglary took place here at Brackendale House. The owners were visiting friends in London at the time, and the housekeeper had been called away to a funeral, leaving the house empty overnight. The thieves were apparently aware that the house was empty, and were able to gain entry simply by breaking a window at the back. With no one in the house to hear them, they could have stripped it bare of valuables, but instead they took only Amelia Pendleton's jewellery, which had been kept in a tin box in a drawer in her bedroom. The housekeeper discovered the break-in when she returned the following day, and called the police.

Because 'inside knowledge' was suspected, everyone who worked for the Pendletons or on any of their farms was questioned. The homes of Frederick Thomas and Isaac Walker, both employed as gardeners at Brackendale House, and who had been at work on the day of the robbery, were searched, but no trace of the jewels was ever found . . .

. . . until 1935, when work began to exhume graves from St Isidore's churchyard in Brackendale Green, prior to the flooding of the valley. In the grave of a woman named Martha Atkins who had been buried in July 1895, workers discovered a tarpaulin bundle containing the jewels in their tin. None of Martha Atkins' living relatives recognised the jewels, and the police were brought in.

In a bizarre twist, one of Martha Atkins' daughters, Susie Atkins, who had Down's Syndrome, said that she had seen Isaac Walker — who as well as being a gardener here at Brackendale House was also the gravedigger for St Isidore's Church — drop the bundle into the open grave on the night after her mother's funeral. Walker was questioned, but said he had had nothing to do with the robbery but had been given the bundle by Frederick Thomas, who pleaded with him to hide it. Walker was given immunity from prosecution for his information.

Frederick Thomas was by 1935 a prominent businessman running a hardware store and plant nursery in Penrith. He was duly questioned, and a ruby ring, one of the items stolen in 1895, was found to be in his possession — to be precise, it was found on the finger of his wife. Thomas was arrested, tried and convicted, and despite his advanced years (74) was sent to prison for five years. He died within six months of his incarceration.

The jewels were returned to the Pendleton family. Only one piece was never recovered — a butterfly brooch set with precious stones. It can be seen clearly in the portrait of Amelia Pendleton which is on

147

display in the sitting room. By 1935 Amelia Pendleton was dead and her son Sebastian Pendleton, with his wife Alexandria, lived at Brackendale House. They moved to India shortly afterwards, and the house was left empty until, during the war, it was used as a training base for army officers.'

Laura finished reading and looked at Tom. 'So the jewels were discovered in your ancestor's grave, forty years after the robbery?'

'Apparently so! Incredible, isn't it? And I hadn't known that Susie Atkins had Down's Syndrome. I knew she'd never married but that was all I knew about her. Seems she was the key to them discovering the truth — clever woman.'

'I wonder what happened to her, after Brackendale was flooded.'

Tom shrugged. 'Not sure. I only followed up what happened to my direct ancestors — Susie's sister Jane, and then Jane's daughter Maggie who was my great-grandmother.'

'Well, what a story. So this Frederick Thomas must have thought he'd got away with it. Must have been quite a shock to be arrested so many years later. Wonder why he never went back for the stolen jewels?' Laura chuckled. 'Silly place to hide them, really — not easy to recover them once they're six feet under.'

'Yes, and what about this Isaac Walker chap? He said he had nothing to do with it, but I bet he knew what was in the bundle he was burying.'

Laura nodded. 'Yes, it's all very fishy. I bet he was involved all along, just grassed up his mate to get himself off the hook. Nothing like showing a bit of loyalty, eh? Well, if you've seen enough, I reckon it's time for an ice-cream out on the lawns.'

'I reckon it is, too. As long as we can find a shady spot to sit and eat them. Don't want you feeling faint on me again!' Tom gave her a playful nudge on the arm.

'Hey! I'll have you know I brought a hat today. A very fetching one, at that.' Laura pulled the hat out of her bag and rammed it on her head, glaring defiantly at Tom.

'Suits you,' he said with a grin.

They left the museum, and Laura was glad of the hat when she was outside under the blazing sun again. The weather really was very un-English, and most definitely un-Lake District. What would normally be lush green lawns surrounding the house was parched, brown stubble, and the dust from the dry earth quickly coated her feet in their flip-flops. She'd need a shower before she got into her lovely new sleeping bag that night, she thought.

'So, what'll you have?' Tom asked, as they approached the ice-cream hut. 'I'll buy.'

'No, no, let me,' she replied.

'Your round next time,' he said, pulling out his wallet, and ordering two double soft cones with flakes.

Laura smiled. So there was to be a next time. Well, that suited her fine. Tom was good company. So unlike Stuart, and, she was beginning to realise, much more the kind of man she would like to meet. Why were there no men like Tom back home? Or perhaps there were, but she'd spent too many years with Stuart. Perhaps Martine had done her a favour, and released her from a dead-end relationship. Yes, that was a more positive way of looking at it. Perhaps she was finally beginning to get over Stuart, at long last.

They found a picnic bench in the shade of a spreading beech tree, and ate their ice-creams there.

'So,' Tom said, 'what are your plans for the afternoon? Fancy a drive round to Ullswater, and a swim in the lake there? I know a good spot. It'll be lovely to cool off.' He suddenly looked a little worried. 'Or were you joking about wanting a swim?'

'Not at all! I'd love a swim. Not entirely sure I brought a swimsuit on holiday though.'

Tom stared at her wide-eyed. 'You are surely not suggesting skinny-dipping?'

Laura felt herself blush furiously. 'God, no! It'd have to be dark and I would have to be very drunk to do that. And even then . . . no. I'll find something suitable — shorts and a T-shirt or something.'

'Aw, shame.' Tom spoke quietly and turned his face away, so Laura wasn't sure if she'd heard him correctly or not. She could not think what to say next. She found herself, against her will, imagining an after-dark naked swim with Tom. Silky cool water caressing their limbs, silvery moonlight, a bit of playing about and splashing each other and then . . . what? Why was she thinking these things? She had only just met the man. She shook her head slightly and let out an involuntary sigh.

'What's the matter? Everything all right?' Tom asked.

She smiled at him. 'Everything's fine. Yes, let's go for a swim. I'll need to go back to the tent first to find something to wear.'

'No problem, so will I anyway. Come on, then. We can buy something in the campsite shop for an afternoon picnic on the lakeside.'

'Perfect!' With a pang of guilt Laura remembered she really ought to go back to Brackendale Green, call Gran and look for the tea caddy. But the thought of tramping around the hot dry lake-bed that had no shade, in this weather, was not at all appealing. Especially when compared to a swim in the lake with Tom. Looking for the tin could wait another day.

*   *   *

An hour later Laura was equipped with a selection of crisps, dips and biscuits from the campsite shop, her towel and her swimsuit that thankfully she'd discovered she *had* packed after all. It was a longish drive to Ullswater and the little bit of sloping grassy bank that Tom knew was a good place to enter the lake for swimming. One problem with the Lake District, Laura thought, was that distances that looked tiny on the map, and indeed were only a few miles, could take ages to drive as the roads were so twisty and narrow and you had no choice but to keep your speed down. So it was mid-afternoon by the time they arrived. The day was still scorching hot — in fact, she thought, probably hotter now than it had been at midday. Tom parked in a small lay-by off the main road and led her through a little grove of trees to the water's edge.

'This is lovely,' Laura said. 'I am so hot — I can't wait to get in there and cool down.'

'You don't want to eat first, then? We missed lunch!' But Tom was already stripping off, his trunks on under his shorts, and before she could even answer he had run past her, splashing into the shallows of the lake. Once he was thigh deep he dived forward and under the water, emerging a moment later spluttering and gasping.

'It's cold, then?' Laura said, laughing.

'Compared with the air temperature, yes!' But obviously not *that* cold because he immediately lay back in the water, floating. 'Come on in!'

She felt suddenly shy taking off her T-shirt and skirt, exposing her figure. She'd already put her swimsuit on underneath as well. She hadn't a bad body, she knew, although Stuart had always told her that her bum was too big and her breasts too small. Unlike Martine's perfect hourglass figure. She stepped cautiously into the water, and found herself enjoying its coolness on her feet and calves. The lake bottom was a mixture of larger, slippery rocks and sharp smaller stones that hurt her feet, and she understood why Tom had dived in as soon as it was deep enough. He was watching her now, she realised, and suddenly she felt self-conscious. But he was not looking at her body — his eyes were fixed on her face, and he was grinning at her.

Too late she guessed his intentions, and a sheet of water cascaded over her as he flung himself backwards, kicking furiously in her direction. 'Oh, you beast!' she squealed. 'It's freezing!'

'Get in properly, then!' he laughed. She realised there was nothing for it but to submerge herself completely so that his splashes had no effect. The chill took her breath away, but once the initial shock was over she realised it was not that cold. She struck out, swimming a strong crawl out into the lake, glad that she'd taken swimming lessons as a teen and could do a decent stroke, hoping it looked as good as it felt. After twenty metres or so she turned back to face the shore, treading water as she was now out of her depth. But where was Tom? She'd thought he was still back in the shallows, but there was no sign of him. She pivoted but could not see him. Suddenly her ankle was grabbed from beneath and she was yanked under the water, finding herself face to face with a grinning Tom. They surfaced together, Tom spluttering.

'Your face — made me laugh underwater and I've swallowed half the lake!'

'Well, that'll teach you!' she said, laughing herself, realising that he too must be a good swimmer to have got this far out and underneath her in the time it had taken her to swim it. Once again she found herself comparing him with Stuart, who could barely swim and only used his trunks for sunbathing beside the pool on package holidays. Tom really was much more her type. If she ever felt ready for a new relationship, she'd need to find someone like him.

12

JED

Jed stared at Mr and Mrs Pendleton. No! He wouldn't let his father be arrested and imprisoned, at his advanced years. It wasn't fair. All right, Isaac had committed a crime in his youth, but he'd hurt no one and after all these years he didn't deserve to suffer for it. The worry after the jewels were found was punishment enough.

'Jed? That you, son? Need some help in here . . . ' Isaac's quavery voice called from the front room — once Edie's parlour but now a bedroom and sitting room for the old man.

'I'll be with you in a moment,' Jed called back. He turned to Mrs Pendleton. The woman had shown him kindness in the past, and his instincts told him she was the one to appeal to rather than her husband. 'You hear him? I expect he's wet himself again. Beg pardon, ma'am, to speak so bluntly but you must see how it is. He couldn't cope with arrest and trial. It would be the end of him.'

'How is your little girl?' Mrs Pendleton asked suddenly. She had that odd look on her face again, the same one of longing and cunning that he'd seen at the Glydesdale churchyard.

Jed started at the abrupt change of topic. Mr Pendleton, too, stared at his wife with a frown on his face.

'Stella? She's well, thank you for asking. She's taken my little one out to play so that I might work uninterrupted. Although as you see there is still my father to care for.'

As if to back up his words, Isaac called out to him again. 'Jed! I need to use the pot!'

'You have a lot to deal with,' Mrs Pendleton said. There was a touch of compassion in her voice, but something else as well. Something calculating, and Jed did not like it.

'I manage,' he said guardedly.

Mrs Pendleton turned to her husband. 'We should leave him be, Sebastian. He has work to do. We will consider what to do about his father — one way or another it will be resolved before we leave Westmorland, I promise you.'

'Are you changing your mind about pressing charges against Mr Walker, Alexandria?'

'No, I am not. But there may be another way.' She turned back to Jed. 'You need to see to your father's needs now. We will leave you. But this is not over. We must talk it through some more. Come to see us at Brackendale House.' She stood, pulled on her gloves, and beckoned for her husband to follow. He did so, with a confused frown on his face.

Jed showed them out, watching as the chauffeur scrambled out of the Bentley to open the car doors for them. As she climbed in, Mrs Pendleton looked back at him. 'Don't forget to come and see us about this soon, or we will most certainly press charges against your father.'

Jed frowned. 'Not sure quite how I can

manage that, ma'am. I have my little one, and no one to mind her.'

'Bring her with you. I may have something for her.' Mrs Pendleton waved a hand at the chauffeur who closed the car door, got in himself, and drove off.

Jed sighed, and went inside to deal with Isaac's mess.

★   ★   ★

It was a frustrating day. After the interruption by the Pendletons, Jed found it hard to immerse himself in his work. Isaac seemed to be particularly needy as well. Jed had not told him what the Pendletons had wanted — just fobbed the old man off with a story about Sam Wrightson and his wife calling with a child's pram that needed repairing. Isaac's hearing was none too good, and although he'd heard two voices he had not been able to pick out any of the conversation, and seemed satisfied with Jed's lie.

Even his work did not go well. Jed mislaid tools, burned a finger on his soldering iron, stood backwards onto a bicycle wheel and bent it out of shape, dropped a box of assorted nuts and bolts and spent ages crawling around on the floor trying to retrieve them all. He was in a foul mood by the time Stella returned with Jessie. The girls were bright-eyed and excited, chattering about the baby rabbits they'd seen by the lakeside, the kittens old George up at Top Farm had shown them, the den they'd made under the roots of a fallen tree. Jessie was giggling as she so often did, the sound like a babbling brook, but for once it did not make Jed smile. The child was filthy and her dress torn. More work for him then, to bathe the child, wash her clothes and attempt to repair the rip. Women's work, and he with no woman to do it. How he missed Edie!

'Stella, could you not at least try to keep your sister clean and her clothes untorn? This is the second time in a week you've brought her home covered in mud,' he snapped. Jessie stopped giggling and her lower lip quivered. He knew she hated it when he raised his voice. But too bad. She was three now and old enough to understand right from wrong. 'And you, Jessie. Keep out of the mud!'

Jessie began to cry openly.

'Stop that wailing. I can't be dealing with it now. Off with you both.'

'Come on, Jessie. Let's go and see Grandpa,' Stella whispered to her sister.

'Aye, your bloody Grandpa, with his loose bladder, bringing more trouble on us,' Jed grumbled. Stella stared at him, wide-eyed, then grabbed her bawling sister by the hand and pulled her away, into Isaac's room.

Jed sat down at the kitchen table, his head in his hands. How could he cope with it all? He needed a wife, someone to share the workload with, and the girls needed a mother. Perhaps he had been too hasty turning down Maggie. But as soon as this thought entered his mind he chased it away again. If he did ever remarry, it surely wouldn't be her.

* * *

Somehow he got through the evening chores — making dinner and clearing up afterwards, bathing Jessie, washing a tubful of laundry and hanging it on a clothes horse in front of the range to dry. He helped Isaac use the pot and get into bed, and put Jessie to bed too.

'Are you going to the pub tonight, Pa?' Stella asked. 'I'll watch Jessie if you want to go. I'll mend her dress, too.'

'No, lass. I'm too tired tonight, but thank you.' He still felt guilty for snapping at her earlier. She was a good child, the only inhabitant of his cottage who wasn't a burden on him. If it was just the two of them they'd manage easily.

He went to check on Jessie. She was asleep, her blonde curls looking angelic about her face. He sighed. She was no bother when she was asleep. If only she could sleep for ever.

* * *

The following day, Sunday, Jed was trying to work out when and how he should pay a visit to the Pendletons as they had requested. They had not given him a deadline, but he felt he should go within a week, or they might follow up on their threat to press charges against Isaac. How he would get there he wasn't sure, not with little Jessie in tow. If he was on his own or with Stella, he would walk down the valley to the dam, from where a new bus service ran to Penrith. He could get off at a stop near the end of the lane that led to Brackendale House. Jessie could not walk as far as the dam, and she would be difficult to carry. But Mrs Pendleton had said there might be something for her, and he had the impression that pleading Isaac's case would go down better if he did everything she'd asked, including bringing the child. So one way or another he would manage it. He owed it to Isaac. He would do all he could to protect his father.

He was standing outside his front door, gazing up at the surrounding fells and trying to judge what the weather would be that day, when the postman arrived on his motorbike. He pulled up in front of Jed and handed him a letter, which Jed took in surprise. He did not get many letters and this was his second in two days. The first, hand-delivered the previous evening, he was still pondering. It was unusual to have a delivery on a Sunday, but the postman explained that there'd been a delay and he was catching up. For a moment he was fearful it would be from the police, or the Pendletons, or the magistrates, and connected with Isaac's crime, but the envelope was addressed in a hand he vaguely recognised from Christmas cards. It was from Edie's sister, Winnie, and announced that she intended paying him a visit, to 'see how you are getting on'. It would be the first time he'd seen her since Edie's funeral. The date for the visit, he realised, was that very day, which meant he could not go to the Pendletons yet. It was a relief to be able to put it off for a bit longer.

He spent the morning tidying the little cottage, ensuring Isaac was presentable and that the girls were in clean clothes. He wanted everything to look as though he was coping well without Edie. Even though, the Lord knew, he wasn't. Win had a kind heart, like her sister. He didn't want her to be worried about her nieces.

Winnie arrived in the early afternoon, having been given a lift by a Penrith tradesman who had business in Brackendale. She greeted Jed with a warm hug and a kiss. 'My lift back is at five o'clock. I hope you got my letter and that I'm not disturbing you too much?'

'Not at all, lass. It's lovely to see you.' Jed meant it. She was a connection to Edie, someone who had known and loved his wife as much as he did. It was good to have her around. He ushered her through to the kitchen and put the kettle on. Stella was playing with Jessie on the rug on the floor. Isaac was asleep in a chair in his own room. 'We'll have to sit in here, I'm afraid,' he said. 'I've had to move my Pa into the parlour. He's too frail to cope by himself any more. It's easier to care for him here.'

Win's face softened with sympathy. 'Ah, Jed, you have it hard, don't you? I wish I lived nearer and could do more to help you day by day. Where will you move to when the dam is finished? Will you come nearer to Penrith and let me do what I can to help?'

'Aye, I might. I haven't looked into it yet — I've not had time to do so. But it'd be good to be nearer you, Win, and I'd appreciate any help. Are there jobs going in Penrith, do you know?'

She shrugged and gave a small apologetic smile. The area had not recovered fully since the

Great Depression at the start of the decade. 'I'm sure there'll be something for you. I'll ask around.'

'Thank you. I'll need somewhere for us to live, too. There'll be money — the waterworks will pay us for our properties when the dam is complete. But I doubt it'll be enough for a house in town. I'll be renting, I expect.'

'I'll keep an eye out for something suitable.'

'See my picture?' Jessie thrust a piece of paper covered in crayon scribbles in front of Win's nose.

'Did you draw this, Jessie? It's splendid!'

Jed smiled, watching Win examine the scribbles carefully as though it was a detailed work of art. It was just how Edie used to be with the children. Win was unmarried and childless, yet she was totally natural around them. She'd make a good mother.

'Aunt Win, I've drawn something too,' Stella said, and handed over her drawing, which showed a flock of sheep with smiling faces on a hillside.

'Beautiful, Stella dear. You're very talented.' Win turned back to Jed. 'You're doing a good job with the girls. Edie would be so proud of them. I wish I could do more to help you now, before you move.'

A thought occurred to Jed, taking him by surprise. He liked Win. He didn't love her the way he'd loved Edie — no one would ever come close. But he respected her, enjoyed her company, and she was certainly good with the children. Could they . . . would she? It was not a topic he could broach in front of the girls.

'Stella, take your sister outside to play now, would you?'

'But Pa, it's raining a bit,' Stella said. 'And you wanted us to keep clean.'

Jed glanced out of the window. 'It's only drizzle. Put your coats on. Don't go near the lake — stay in the village.'

Stella rolled her eyes but fetched her and Jessie's coats.

'Come on, Jessie. We'll go and look at Mrs Earnshaw's hens. Maybe we can collect some eggs for her.'

When they'd left, Jed turned to Win, who was regarding him with an enquiring look in her eyes. 'Win, it's a lot to ask, but could you . . . do you think . . . is there any way that you would . . . ' He could not seem to find a way to say it.

'What is it, Jed? You know I would do anything in my power for you.'

He sighed, and took her hand across the table. It was cool and smooth. 'I do need help, Win. I'm doing my best, but I'm struggling without a wife. I've got to earn a living to keep us all, and I can't do that with Jessie under my feet and poor old Pa calling out to me every few minutes.'

'What are you asking, Jed?' Win said carefully, a small frown between her eyes. 'If you're asking me to be your wife then I'm sorry, the answer's no. I can't do that.' She gently pulled her hand away and stared out of the window for a moment. 'I've not told you, but I have a gentleman friend. In Penrith. He works in the bank, and we've been stepping out a while now. I

163

know — at my age I thought I'd be a spinster for ever, but perhaps I won't, if Herbert gets up the courage to ask me.' She sighed. 'Besides, I don't think I could in all honesty step into my sister's shoes in that way. I'm sorry, Jed. You're a lovely man. There will be someone else for you.'

'Win, love, I'm so pleased to hear you have a man. You and me — that was just a thought. Forget I ever said anything.'

She laughed. 'I don't think you actually did say anything, did you? Listen, I want to help, I really do. I would take Jessie off your hands if I could, but for the moment I need to be able to work and I don't think I could, with a little one in the house. Perhaps if Herbert does marry me he might agree to us taking her in, as his salary would be enough for the both of us. But we're a little way off that. I could take Stella, if it would help. She's old enough to look after herself when I'm at work.'

Jed shook his head. 'Thank you, Win, but Stella's a big help to me here. She's the only reason I'm coping at all. If you could have taken Jessie for me, just until we moved to Penrith and got settled, that would have helped but I do understand that you can't. We'll manage. Don't worry.'

'Ah, Jed, I do worry, you know. But once you've moved to Penrith I can do more for you. And I'll keep my ears and eyes open for jobs and lodgings for you.'

'You're a good woman, Win. Herbert's a lucky man.' Jed smiled at her.

'Yes, I think he is,' she said, laughing again.

'I'm glad you've not taken this hard, Jed. You're a good man and my sister was lucky to have you. When you've moved nearer to me I'll see a lot more of you and the girls. I'm looking forward to it. I'll do what I can to find job opportunities and lodgings for you, as I promised. Herbert will too. We'll see you right, don't you fret.'

'Thank you, Win,' he said again. He felt a mixture of emotions that she had turned him down. Disappointment, certainly, for had she agreed it could have meant the solution to his problems. But also relief. She might be a lovely woman and Edie's sister, but she was not Edie and he was not ready to take another wife.

Besides, there was no telling what Maggie might do if she heard he was getting wed again. A chill ran through him. His instinct told him she could be dangerous if crossed. She could harm him. Or harm the people he loved. And he had already crossed her, spurning her advances that night after the fight in the pub.

13

LAURA

Returning to the campsite after their swim in the lake, they went their separate ways to have showers and change, having made arrangements to meet up later to walk to the pub. Laura spent a few minutes sprawled on her camping mat outside her tent first, enjoying the shade of the oak. After a little while she thought to check her phone — no missed calls but another two texts from Stuart. The first: Please don't ignore me, Lols. I want to see you. And the second read simply, ominously: I will find you.

Not up here you won't, she thought. She'd have to deal with him when she got back. Perhaps if she met him on some neutral ground — in a pub or a cafe — and let him have his say, she could then explain that no matter what, she wanted nothing more to do with him. He'd been right that they'd drifted apart. And while he'd been with Martine they'd drifted yet further apart. This holiday had shown her that whatever happened, she did not want Stuart back again. They weren't suited, and she would be able to rebuild a life for herself without him. She'd already made an excellent start on that.

★ ★ ★

Later, after a shower, clean and refreshed and wearing her loose cotton skirt and a clean top, she went over to see if Tom was ready yet. She found him lounging outside his tent with a can of beer and a book.

'Hi. I know it's early yet, but if you're ready, I could murder an ice-cold lager,' she said.

'Me too. This is really warm from being in the tent all day, and totally disgusting.' Tom tipped the remains of his can out on the grass and zipped up his tent. 'I'm ready. Shall we go via the old churchyard? We said we might look for graves with our ancestors' names on.'

'Great idea.' Laura had forgotten about that. She felt a tingle of excitement — this genealogy lark was certainly getting to her. Finding out about your ancestors felt as though you were building yourself secure foundations. And after the rug being pulled from under her feet with Stuart, she needed that.

The old church was locked so they could not look around inside. A notice said that services were held there once a month on the second Sunday. The vicar also ran two other parishes nearby. The graveyard was a little overgrown, though due to the drought the grass was brown and withered. So were the weeds — a cluster of thistles and nettles in one corner, some bracken encroaching from the fells along one side.

'I expect someone comes just a couple of times a year to maintain it,' Tom said, as they picked their way along a path that was more ankle-deep brown grass than gravel. Weathered graves lined the path; some were legible while others were too worn for them to be able to make out any words. Partway across the graveyard a low wall divided one section from another. Beyond the wall the graves were not quite as worn — still old but easier to decipher.

Laura bent to read the one nearest her. '*In loving memory of Albert Wrightson, 1845-1903, beloved father and grandfather. His remains reinterred in Glydesdale 1935.* Look! This fellow was reburied here in 1935. Do you think he may have been moved from Brackendale? On the website where I read about the Old Corpse Road it said the graves from Brackendale Church were moved here when the valley was flooded.'

'1935 is about the right date. The village was abandoned by the end of that year as the water levels began to rise.' Tom looked at another nearby grave. 'This one has the same wording at the end. Perhaps this area was put aside for all those moving over from Brackendale.' He began checking each grave in earnest. 'Yes, here's an Atkins grave — one of the names on my family tree. Oh wow — it's Martha Atkins!'

'Who was that?'

'Don't you remember?' Tom's eyes were shining with excitement. 'In the Brackendale House Museum there was that piece about the missing jewels turning up in a grave, and that was Martha Atkins' grave. My great-great-great-grandmother.'

'Oh yes! So this is where she ended up. Without the jewels, I assume.' Laura touched the top of the stone. Odd to think that under here were the remains of Tom's ancestor. Without this

168

woman, he would not be here now. Were there any of her own ancestors? Gran had said her maiden name was Walker. She began scouring the names for any Walker graves.

'*Edith Walker, beloved wife and mother, 1904-1935. Eternally missed.* I wonder if this is one of my ancestors? Gran's name was Walker. It doesn't say this grave was reinterred though.'

Tom came to stand beside her. 'Died 1935. So perhaps they buried her here in the first place as there'd be no point burying her in Brackendale and then moving her soon after. You'll need to ask your gran what her mother's full name was. Maybe this is your great-grandmother.'

Laura knelt beside the grave, her hand resting on the ground, trying to feel a connection with whoever was beneath it. 'I feel stupid that I know so little! But Gran never talked about her early years. Not till now. It's as though she submerged it all in her mind and it's only surfacing now that the old village is exposed again.'

'Nice analogy,' Tom said with a grin. 'What about your gran's little sister? The one who was killed as a child?'

'Gran said they never found her body. So I don't suppose there's a grave for her, the poor little thing.'

'That's so sad. You'd think her name should be engraved somewhere, at least, as a memorial. Perhaps this Edith was her mother too.'

Laura nodded. It was unbearably sad thinking of that small child who had been killed so long ago, who'd never had the chance to fulfil her potential and yet was not remembered by

169

anyone. Except Gran. And when she was gone there'd be no one left to remember her at all. Laura resolved to question Stella more about her sister. It was about time she gave Gran another call. She could note down what she had learned, and perhaps if she did more work on her family tree she could write it all up. Then at least her great-aunt's name would live on in some form.

They poked around the graveyard for a little longer, finding a few more Walker graves and Atkins graves, and an Earnshaw who Tom said was his great-great-grandfather, the father of Maggie Earnshaw. Laura took photos of all the Walker graves to show Gran. She really must record Gran talking about the past, to capture all her memories before it was too late.

At last, hunger pangs made her stop searching the graves and return to Tom. 'Have you seen enough? I'm starving. Shall we go on to the pub now? It's my round, I believe.'

'Ha! Well, in that case, yes, let's go!' Tom laughed and caught hold of her hand for the walk to the pub.

Laura widened her eyes but left her hand in his. It felt cool considering the heat of the evening, and strong. It felt good.

★ ★ ★

They sat outside in the pub garden, at a picnic bench that caught the last of the sunshine. The evening was spent chatting about their day in the hills, what they'd seen at the museum, the family

170

graves they'd found and plans for the rest of the week.

'I definitely must go back to the village tomorrow,' Laura said, 'and have a go at looking for that tin. I'll ring Gran when I'm there and see if she can explain where it is.'

'Is it definitely in the village somewhere? I mean, not hidden up a mountain or something? I'd ring your gran before going, if I were you.'

'Good point.' Laura pulled out her phone and was pleased to see there were a couple of bars of signal. 'I'll try her now.' She made the call, but there was no answer. That was odd. She checked her watch — eight-thirty p.m. Gran should be in, watching TV, doing a bit of knitting. Perhaps the evening carer had come early. Or perhaps she just hadn't reached the phone in time. The answerphone kicked in. 'Gran, it's me. Just checking how you are. I'll try you again tomorrow morning. Hope all's well.' She hung up with a frown.

'No answer?'

'No.'

'Are you worried, Laura?'

She shook her head. 'Not really. I'll try again in the morning. She sometimes forgets to put the phone near to where she's sitting, and can't get to it in time. If there was a real emergency, her care agency would have called me.'

'That's a comfort.'

It was. Laura knew how many of her clients' families appreciated not just the care she gave them, but also the feeling that the frail old people were never left for more than a few hours without someone calling round, even when the relatives themselves were unable to visit often. These days, with families often spread out across the country or beyond, and with women working full-time as well as men, there was a real need for third-party carers. In the past, old people had to rely on their grown sons or daughters to take them in, or if they had no one, they'd have to hope for a kind neighbour or more distant relative. In the days before social security it must have been a real worry. Things were so much better today, and Laura was proud that she played a small part in that.

It was a warm evening, and it passed quickly. All too soon it was closing time. Tom gathered up their last empty glasses to put back on the bar, while Laura used the pub loo. There was better handwash there than in the campsite.

As they left the pub to walk back to the campsite, Tom once more took her hand. It seemed the most natural thing in the world to hold hands with him now. Laura realised she did not want the evening to end.

'I've a bottle of red wine in my car,' she said. 'Fancy sharing it? Or do you think it's too late?'

'I can think of nothing nicer,' he said, with a squeeze of her hand.

Laura felt a little flutter of excitement run through her. She was not imagining this. He liked her as much as she liked him, she was sure of it. She risked a sideways glance at his face, but they were away from the lights of the pub now and it was too dark to make out his expression. There was a half-moon which gave just enough light to see their route along the lane. The mountains on either side of the valley were just black shapes looming against a sky that was almost as dark.

'Check out the stars,' Tom whispered.

Laura looked up to see an incredible display. Away from any light pollution there were an amazing number of stars. The broad sweep of the Milky Way could clearly be seen. She could pick out a couple of constellations she recognised — the huge W of Cassiopeia; the Plough, with its pointers towards the Pole Star; and just visible above a mountain, the three stars of Orion's Belt. 'Beautiful, isn't it?'

'Yes, it's awe-inspiring. I've half a mind to sleep outside tonight, just on my sleeping mat under a blanket of stars.'

That sounds lovely, Laura almost said, but stopped herself. She was picturing herself lying on her own mat beside him, snuggled against him, her head on his shoulder as they both gazed up at the wonders of the cosmos. But maybe he meant he wanted to do this on his own. And she could not imagine waking up in daylight beside him, with early risers already walking past on their way to the shower block. He was a friend, she told herself. They were both too damaged to be able to start a new relationship. It was enough that they enjoyed each other's company.

They reached the campsite and Laura fetched her bottle of wine, her only plastic wine glass and her penknife which had a corkscrew attachment. She hoped Tom had something to drink out of, otherwise one of them would have to use her insulated coffee mug. Thankfully he had a stock of disposable plastic cups and was happy to use one of those. They put their sleeping mats side by side in front of Laura's tent, sat down on them and opened the wine.

'Best keep our voices down,' Tom said quietly. 'The campsite has a 'no noise after eleven' policy. Mind you, there are no kids camping this week so I doubt anyone would complain.'

'Nearest tent is three pitches away in any case,' Laura replied. She poured the wine and gently clinked plastic cups with him. 'It's been a lovely evening. Thank you, Tom.'

'Not sure what I've done, but yes, it's been great.'

Laura sipped her wine, then put it carefully on the ground where she wouldn't knock it over. Turning back to Tom she realised he'd done the same, and in the dim light of the campsite security lights she saw he was looking at her questioningly. She opened her mouth to speak, not entirely sure what she wanted to say, but he leaned forward, cupped her chin with his hand — and kissed her. Gently at first, a mere touch of his lips, but it sent thrills shooting through her. Yes, she wanted this, and more. She responded, and he moved his hand round to the back of her head to pull her closer. She reached up, wrapping her arms around his neck, and leaned into the delicious, warm kiss.

When they finally parted, he stroked her face with his thumb. 'All right?'

'I . . . think so,' she replied, aware that she was probably frowning a little. 'Just . . . that was a little unexpected. Nice, though,' she added with a smile.

He sat back. 'I'm sorry. It's probably too soon after your horrible break-up. I can understand you wanting to keep your distance.' He was smiling at her quizzically. 'I mean, since Sarah I've not wanted to start a new relationship. So I get that you don't, either. But the evening's been so magical it seemed the only way to round things off. A kiss doesn't have to mean more than a kiss, and doesn't have to lead to anything more. We can just enjoy the moment.'

'You're right, we can,' she replied with a smile, and leaned forward to repeat the experience. Enjoy the moment — how wise! And yes, it didn't have to mean anything beyond making the most of the romance of the evening. As she kissed him again, her phone buzzed in her pocket. Another text. This late at night it was bound to be Stuart. She felt an unexpected pang of guilt at kissing another man while Stuart so obviously wanted to talk to her. There was still unresolved business there but right now, she did not want to think about him. Tom's lips were on hers, and the feel of him filled her mind and her soul. There was nothing else, only this moment and this man, and whatever happened after, this was a moment she would never forget.

14

STELLA, JULY 1935

It was the last day of term before the long summer break. Stella dawdled on her way home, enjoying the feel of sunshine on her back. It was nice too to be alone for a short while, with no demands on her time. At school there were always the other children wanting to play, the teachers wanting work done. At home she needed to help Pa, look after Grandpa, take Jessie out to play, help with making the tea. She didn't mind, and she would never complain to Pa as she knew how much he was struggling to cope since Ma died. She knew too that he would never admit it, least of all to her. Anyway, it was good to get a little bit of time for herself now and again. But with the six weeks' break from school ahead of her, she'd have to help a lot more at home, especially with Jessie, and would probably not get any time alone other than the precious couple of hours after Jessie had gone to bed. Those she normally spent reading, escaping into other worlds where for a short while she could live a different life.

Every day as she walked home she passed the dam and checked on progress. It was complete now, but the valves at the bottom were still open so that water could flow through. Stella knew that it would not be long now before they closed the valves, and allowed the water to collect behind the dam, making the existing small lake grow gradually bigger. It would soon burst its banks and flood the low-lying meadows, and then the water would gradually creep near to the village. Stella was dreading that part. She knew they had to move, but Pa had given no indication of where they would move to. She didn't dare ask, knowing Pa had enough on his mind without her pestering him. When Aunt Win had visited and Stella had been sent out to play with Jessie, she'd guessed that maybe the grown-ups were talking about the future and making plans. But Pa had said nothing after Aunt Win left, so Stella wondered whether anything had actually been agreed or not. She supposed she'd find out soon enough, but it was unsettling not knowing where you'd be living by the end of the year.

She kicked a stone along the lane for a little way. Maybe they'd even move out of the village before school restarted in September. Maybe these next few weeks would be her last in the valley where she'd been born. She'd never known anywhere else, although she'd been to Penrith a few times on the bus, visiting Aunt Win and going to the big shops there. Would they end up in Penrith, she wondered? It would make sense for them to be near Aunt Win, who might be able to help a little with Jessie and Grandpa. But then they'd all be living in the big town, away from the fells. Stella sighed and looked around her at the familiar landscape, the twists of the lane that she knew so well, the woodland on the lower slopes and rocky screes further up.

Funny to think it was all going to change so dramatically when the valley was flooded. As she raised her eyes to the mountain tops she saw a bird of prey wheeling around high up in the thermals. There were eagles nesting in one of the side valleys, she knew; she'd seen them a few times but never close up. Maybe it was one of them.

What would she do with Jessie this afternoon when she got home? She knew Pa would want her to take Jessie out, so that he could have a few hours' peace to do some work, as long as Grandpa didn't need him. She daren't take Jessie to the lake in case she got wet and muddy again. Pa had been so cross last time. They could go and see Old George's kittens, but that would not take very long. They could call on Mrs Perkins at the village shop, and see if she had any sweets to spare for them. Sometimes if they were lucky she would give them each a pear drop or a toffee.

As she approached the village she took her customary short-cut through a patch of woodland. The lane twisted around it but there was a path that led straight across, cutting a corner. Sometimes it was too muddy to walk this way in her school shoes, but the weather had been fine for a few days and the path was dry. Stella skipped along this section, enjoying the coolness of the woods. Partway through she noticed a newly fallen tree just off the path. It was an old beech, and had been hollow inside — a favourite place for hide-and-seek. Now the hollow trunk was lying on its side, and the huge root-ball was half in the air. Jessie might like to climb on the trunk amongst the branches. Maybe this was where she could bring her sister this afternoon. As long as she didn't get dirty. Stella knelt down and peered in the hollow. You could no longer get in there yourself to hide, but it would be a good place to put something you wanted kept secret, she thought. If you tucked a box or a tin up inside, no one would spot it and no one would think to look in there. She had nothing that needed hiding right now, but one day she might. Though if they moved to Penrith after the valley was flooded, how on earth would she get back here? And would this tree be underwater then anyway?

Time was getting on, and she felt guilty taking so long to walk home, knowing Pa was relying on her to help with Jessie. She reluctantly left the woods, walked the last part of the lane and entered the village. At the far end of the street, she saw Pa walking towards the Lost Sheep with Sam Wrightson. They were too far ahead to hear her if she called out a hello, so she didn't bother, and instead, went into her home to find Jessie. Presumably Grandpa was minding her.

Inside, Grandpa was asleep on his usual chair in his room. Jessie was nowhere to be seen. Her toys were tidied away in their basket beside the kitchen range.

'Jessie? Where are you?' Stella ran upstairs, checking all the bedrooms, but there was no sign of the child. She went out to Pa's workshop and called again, and looked under the benches in case Jessie was playing an impromptu game of hide-and-seek. Jessie could never keep quiet during these games. She would always give herself away with a giggle. Stella listened, but could hear nothing. She ran back inside to Grandpa's room and shook him awake.

'Grandpa? Sorry to wake you, but do you know where Jessie is?'

'Hmm? What's that?' The old man forced his eyes open and blinked at her.

'Jessie, Grandpa. Where is she?'

'Not here, lass. Your Pa took her off somewhere this morning. Haven't seen her all day. Bring her to me when you find her, will you? I could do with a cuddle from her, the little pet.'

Stella felt a pang of worry at his words. Pa must have left Jessie in Grandpa's care, but he'd fallen asleep and forgotten, and Jessie had wandered off. 'I'll go and find her,' she called over her shoulder, as she hurried out of the cottage.

She ran up the lane and burst into the Lost Sheep, where Jed was at the bar, having just ordered a pint each for himself and Sam. 'Pa! Jessie's missing. Grandpa was asleep and hasn't seen her. I'm off to search — I know all the places where she might go.'

'Little Jessie wandered off? We'll all help search,' Sam said, putting down his tankard.

Pa's eyes opened wide. 'It's all right, she's . . . '

But Stella was already out of the door. Jessie would be in one of the places they went to play, she was sure of it. Outside, she bumped into Maggie Earnshaw.

'Steady on, girl! What's the big rush?'

'Jessie's missing. I have to find her,' Stella said.

'Missing? The poor little love. When did you last see her?' Maggie's eyes glittered and her face was set in a hard expression.

'This morning when I left for school. I helped get her dressed and when I left she was sitting at the kitchen table eating some porridge with Pa. I've got to go, Maggie. Got to find her.'

She ran off, leaving Maggie standing at the door of the pub. Sam Wrightson was on his way out, shrugging on his jacket. Good. At least someone else was going to help search. But it was she, Stella, who'd be most likely to find Jessie. Only she knew the best places to play, and the places where Jessie liked to hide.

Stella first checked Grandpa Isaac's old cottage in case Jessie was there, then retraced the route she'd taken with Jessie the previous evening, when they'd gone out across the fields towards Sam Wrightson's place in search of baby rabbits. Jessie had always loved baby animals of all kinds. The field was full of rabbit holes and maybe she'd tripped and hurt her ankle. Yes, the more she thought about it, the more sure Stella was that she would find her sister hiding in the long grass in one of the low-lying meadows.

She combed the field, walking back and forth, calling Jessie constantly, her shouts becoming more and more frantic. Then she scoured the lower slopes of the nearest hillside. It was covered in bracken — on Stella it came up to her chest so it would easily be taller than Jessie. They'd played hide-and-seek in the bracken a few days ago. Might Jessie have gone there hoping to play some more? But it was a long way from home for Jessie, who was only just three, to have gone by herself.

Stella sat down on a rock in a clearing in the bracken and thought hard. Tears came as she sat there, but she rubbed them away and gritted her teeth. This was no time to be a baby and cry. She needed to be grown up. Her sister needed her.

Where would Jessie go by herself? Suddenly she remembered Old George's barn and the kittens. Jessie might have gone there. There were bales of last year's hay still stacked in it, and lots of places where a small child might hide, or perhaps curl up and fall asleep. Stella was determined to be the one who found her sister. She got up and ran back to the village. The barn was the other side, on the way towards the lake, and she realised she should check with Pa first, in case Jessie had turned up. She was so convinced that Jessie would be in the barn with the kittens and that she, Stella, would be the one to find her, that she almost wished Jessie had not been found yet.

In the cottage, Pa was sitting at the kitchen table, with his head in his hands. Maggie was there too, standing by the door, her expression stern and sharp. Why weren't they out looking?

'Pa, I've checked lots of places and I'm going up to Old George's barn where the kittens . . . '

'There's no need,' said Maggie. 'Your pa says he's taken Jessie away to stay with someone else, so he'll have time to work on finding somewhere else for you to live.'

Stella stared at her father. 'Where, Pa? Where have you taken her?' Why didn't you tell me your plans, she wanted to add.

Pa wouldn't meet her eyes. 'She's with my cousin. In Carlisle. Took her by bus, today. She's safe there.'

'What cousin?' The words were out before she realised she'd said them. Pa's head jerked up to stare at her. There was something in his eyes, something she couldn't quite read.

Maggie's eyes narrowed. 'Jed, I've not heard you talk of a cousin in Carlisle before.'

'Aye, well, that's where she is,' said Jed, but his words carried no conviction.

Stella stared at him. 'Why didn't you say you were taking her away?'

He beckoned her nearer and took hold of her hands. 'Listen, Stella. Our Jessie's all right. She's better off where she is than when she was with us. I can't look after her, and do everything else for you and your grandpa there, and earn a living, and sort out something for our future. Don't you see, something had to give. Jessie's safe and she'll be happy, and she's in a better place now.'

'But where is she?' Stella persisted. Her father's words were frightening her.

He sighed. 'With my cousin in Carlisle.'

Stella pulled her hands away from him. Fear for her sister gripped her like a vice. 'What have you done with her?'

'I told you, she's safe,' was all the response he gave. Stella stared at him in horror. Again, he wouldn't meet her eye. She ran from the cottage, and out of the village towards Old George's barn. It was still worth checking there. Jessie could not have come to harm. Pa was lying but only because he was worried and scared for his daughter. Jessie would be in the barn, curled up asleep behind some hay bales. She *had* to be. Pa wouldn't have done anything to hurt her. He couldn't have. He loved her. Loved them both — she knew that with every inch of her being.

The barn door was open and she charged in, yelling for Jessie. She found the kittens, curled on an old blanket with their mother. She began a systematic search of the barn, into all the corners, behind the hay. She climbed to the top of the highest pile of bales and peered down behind it. There was no sign of her sister anywhere. Eventually, covered in straws and dust, she had to concede defeat. With tears streaming down her face she left the barn and walked slowly back towards the cottage.

Maggie came out of the pub as she passed. 'There you are, Stella. We were wondering where you had got to. God forbid another child should go missing. Now, I want you to go into the Lost Sheep and stay with my mother. John, Sam and I have to go and speak with your father.'

Stella realised that John Teesdale and Sam Wrightson had come out of the pub behind Maggie. All were wearing grim expressions on their faces.

'I've telephoned the police,' Teesdale said. 'They will be here in about half an hour. Sam and I will hold him until then, if force is necessary.' He shook his head. 'Still can't believe it. Jed Walker, of all people.'

'Hold who? Believe what? Why have you called the police?' Stella screamed. 'What's happening?'

'Now, now. Go into the pub like a good girl. My mother is there and she will find you a biscuit and a glass of milk. Run along now.' Maggie gave Stella a push in the direction of the Lost Sheep.

'No. I'm going home. You can't stop me doing that.' Stella turned towards her cottage, just across the lane, but Maggie caught hold of her arm, squeezing it painfully.

'Do as you're told. You're too young to hear what we have to say to your father. And it won't be right to let you see what happens when the police come.'

'Why? What will happen? Let go of me!' Stella pulled hard and managed to free herself. She ran into her cottage before Maggie could catch her again. Maggie and the two men were right behind her. 'Pa! Mr Teesdale says he's called the police! What's happening, Pa? Where's Jessie?'

'Jed, I didn't want to do this, but it's the right thing. I can't sit by and say nothing when I saw what I saw. John has called the police and they will be here soon. You must sit quiet until they get here. No point trying to run.'

'What did you see, Maggie?' Jed's voice was shaky.

Maggie shook her head. 'That can wait until the police get here. I'll say it once, in their hearing.'

Jed's face was ashen. Stella could not believe he had done anything to harm Jessie, but that must be what Maggie was implying. It could not be. She crossed the kitchen to where her father sat and put a hand on his shoulder. 'Pa, is there anything you want to tell us, before the police come? If it's all a big mistake we can put it right, no need for the police . . . '

Though if something had happened to Jessie, how they could put it right she did not know.

'Come away from him, Stella. He . . . he might hurt you.' Maggie stretched out a hand to her.

'No. He's my pa and he wouldn't hurt me. Or Jessie.'

Jed reached a hand up to his shoulder and took hold of hers. 'Aye, lass, you're right. I'd never hurt either of my girls.' He was silent for a moment, looking deep into her eyes as if willing her to read something in his, something he couldn't or wouldn't say aloud. He stood up, and the two men, Teesdale and Wrightson, took a step forward.

'It's all right, lads,' Jed said. 'I don't know what you think I've done or what you think I might do next. Jessie's safe . . . with my cousin in Carlisle, like I already told you. I was just going to offer to put the kettle on and make us all a brew, if we're to sit here and wait for the police to arrive.'

'Aye, a brew would be good,' Sam Wrightson said, as he pulled a chair out from under the table and sat down. 'May as well wait in comfort.'

John Teesdale shrugged, and sat down as well.

Maggie glared at Jed. 'Just don't be getting any ideas, Jed. There's three of us and only one of you.'

186

'Two of us,' Stella said, going over to the stove to help Pa make the tea. Whatever happened, she would stand by him. She was his daughter, and family was family. His eyes had told her to trust him, and trust him she would.

15

LAURA

The next morning Laura awoke, still remembering the delicious taste of Tom's lips on hers. It
had been a magical evening, only ending when
they'd reluctantly parted to go to their own
tents, the bottle of wine half empty and
re-corked to finish another night. She knew she
wasn't ready for a relationship; Tom had made it
quite clear he didn't want one either and that the
kiss was just a kiss, and meant nothing. That
suited her perfectly. Only after he'd gone did
Laura look at her phone to check that latest text
message. It was, as she'd expected, from Stuart.
Saw your Gran today. She told me where you are. Am
coming to see you. Give me another chance. Martine
is moving out.

The words had sent a chill down Laura's spine
at the thought of Stuart going to her gran's.
Gran knew that Laura wanted nothing more to
do with him, so for her to have told him where
she was meant that he must have applied some
pressure. And he was coming up to the Lake
District to find her? She knew she needed to
speak to him to make it clear it was all over and
she would not take him back under any
circumstances, but she did not want to be forced
to have that conversation here, while she was on
holiday. She fervently hoped he'd sent the text

when drunk and was not really on his way.

This morning, however, she made herself put Stuart out of her mind and instead, think about the day's plans. She and Tom had planned today to go back to the ruined village and start looking for this tea caddy Gran had been talking about. First, Laura needed to talk to Gran, and find out more details about exactly where it had been hidden. As soon as she was dressed and out of her tent, gazing around at yet another day that promised glorious sunshine and not a single cloud in the sky, she pulled out her phone and punched in Gran's number. It rang and rang, and eventually the answerphone cut in.

'Gran? If you get this, could you call me back? Or if one of the carers picks up this message, could you call me, it's Laura — my number's in the emergency contacts in Gran's care folder. Just a bit worried I haven't been able to get through to her yesterday or this morning. Hope all's OK. Thanks.'

She frowned, and tried to console herself, again, with the thought that if there had been a real emergency and Gran had been taken to hospital, the care agency would have called her. Or texted if they had not been able to get through.

It was no good. She knew she would worry about it all day. She picked up her phone again and called the agency.

'Stella Braithwaite?' the administrator said, after Laura had explained why she was calling. 'Yes, Sophia was there last night, all was well.'

'What about this morning?'

189

'Sophia's on her rounds still. Don't worry. We'll call you if there's a problem.'

There was nothing more she could do. She looked over to Tom's tent. No sign of life there yet. She decided to go and fetch him a coffee from the campsite shop, but halfway there felt a pang of uncertainty. What if he was embarrassed about last night's intimacy? If she turned up with a coffee for him he might think she was pushing to take it further. But no — surely bringing each other a coffee was simply a friendly thing to do. They were planning on spending the day together again, after all. She quickened her pace towards the shop. White coffee, no sugar, was his favourite. And a bacon butty.

★ ★ ★

'Morning! Breakfast in bed, lazy lump,' she said cheerfully, tapping on the top of his tent. Tom grunted and unzipped it, emerging blinking into the sunlight.

'Cheers. This is a treat!'

'How's your head? Did we drink too much last night?' That would give him a chance to say, yes, we did, and sorry etc., if he really was regretting things.

'No, I think we drank the perfect amount. Don't you?' He smiled up at her. His hair was tousled and a thought flitted through her mind of crawling into the tent alongside him. She quickly dismissed it.

'Oh yes, the perfect amount. Now then, are you coming out? Must be getting hot in there now, you're in full sun.'

'It is a bit,' he said, and began wriggling out of his sleeping bag.

Laura blushed, suddenly wondering if he wore anything to sleep in, but thankfully he was in a pair of boxers. 'I'll leave your coffee and butty here, then, and fetch my deckchair while you sort yourself out.'

An hour later, they were at Brackendale Green, parking Tom's car and preparing to walk across the cracked mud towards the remains of the village. Laura had still not heard from Stella, but she had no reception on her phone now, and knew there'd be none unless she went to the middle of the dried-up reservoir.

'Was it this one, your Gran's cottage?' Tom asked, as they walked along the old village street.

Laura counted, remembering what Gran had said on the phone when they were here before. 'Yes, think so. Now, where might a tin box have been hidden?'

'Under the floorboards? Up the chimney? Buried in the garden?'

Laura stood in the middle of one of the rooms of the cottage and looked at the broken walls, the rubble-strewn floor.

'There's no chance, is there? Of finding it without knowing exactly where it was hidden?'

'Well, we can look in the obvious places,' Tom said. He was on his knees by the remains of the fireplace, reaching up what was left of the chimney, which reached to about chest height. 'Can't feel anything here.' He stood and tried reaching down from the top. 'Nope. But then if

191

the fireplace was in use when it was hidden, I guess this wouldn't be a good hiding place.'

'Are there any nooks and crannies in the walls, I wonder?' Laura said, inspecting the stonework. Some stones were dislodged from their original position but none seemed loose enough to conceal something behind. 'Oh, this is useless. We could be here all day. I'll try once more to phone Gran, if I can get some signal.'

She walked out towards the old stone bridge. She'd been able to get a mobile signal there that first day. But today her phone would not play ball, and the display continued to say 'Emergency calls only'. Must be something to do with weather conditions, she thought, and found herself wanting more than anything to be within range of a signal and able to talk to Gran.

Tom was approaching her. 'Any luck?'

'No. Still no reception.'

'You're worried, aren't you?'

'A bit.'

'Come on then. Let's get out of this valley and find a phone signal. You need to set your mind at rest. Let's go to Penrith, and find a nice cafe for lunch. You'll feel better when you've spoken to her.'

He was right, and she followed him gratefully back to the car. As soon as they were past the dam and out of the valley her phone sprang into life, and before she had a chance to retry Gran's number it rang.

'Gran! Oh, thank goodness. I tried you last night and this morning and couldn't get through.'

'I'm sorry, love. I was invited out last night, would you believe it? My friend Margery asked me round for supper. The carers agreed to come to me last, so I would have plenty of time to spend out. And I'm afraid I slept in a little this morning, as they came to me last again this morning. I've been trying and trying you since I picked up your message.'

'I've had no mobile reception since leaving the campsite this morning. So glad you're all right! What a lovely idea to go round to Margery's for supper.' Laura gave a huge sigh of relief before continuing. 'Listen, Gran, I have a couple of things I need to talk to you about. Firstly — ' Laura glanced at Tom, who was driving, but his concentration seemed to be all on the road ' — did Stuart come to see you? I've had a few texts from him.'

'Yes, he did, love. I must admit I was very surprised to see him. He turned on his charm, but you know, it doesn't work on me. He said he had been trying to contact you and had no response, and I said that's either because she doesn't want to hear from you, or because her telephone isn't properly connected.'

Laura smiled at the way Gran had put that. 'Did you tell him where I was?'

There was a pause, and a sigh, which told her all she needed to know. 'Well, I might have mentioned the Lake District. And camping. And then Brackendale. So it is possible he worked it out. Laura, love, I'm so sorry. I'm not very good at keeping secrets.'

'It's not a problem. I'm going to need to talk

to him some time, to tell him to leave me alone. Don't worry, Gran, you've done nothing wrong.'

'I hope not. What was the other thing you wanted to talk about?'

'This tin box of yours. Can you remember where it was hidden in your cottage?' Next to her, Laura was aware of Tom's ears pricking up. She loved how he was as fascinated by this as she was.

'Yes. My pa told me exactly where he'd put it. In the parlour — the front room — that became my grandpa's bedroom when he moved in with us, there was a loose floorboard just to the right of the fireplace. You could pull it up and tuck something down there. That's where he'd put it.'

'Thanks, Gran. We'll go and look for it.'

'We?'

'Um, yes. I've made a . . . friend. Someone staying in the same campsite as me.'

'*Gentleman* friend?'

'Ye-es.' Laura let out an involuntary giggle.

'Oh Laura, I'm so pleased! You need someone new, after that horrid Stuart. Sorry, love, but I never liked him. Too smooth for my taste. So what's his name, this new chap?'

'Tom. And he's just a friend. Actually, Gran, he's sitting right beside me, driving. So don't ask me too much about him, OK?'

'OK. My lips are sealed. But I am really happy for you, and your *friend*. I shall want to know everything about him when you come home.'

Laura tried, and failed, to imagine telling Gran about how it had felt when Tom had kissed her. Perhaps it was best to just end this conversation now. 'Well, I'll let you go, Gran. I'll ring again tomorrow or when we've had a chance to go back to Brackendale again. I'm so glad you're all right. Love you.'

★ ★ ★

'Another pint?' It was Laura's round. They'd had a quiet lunch, a stroll around Penrith, in and out of the shops, and then had lazed around the campsite for the rest of the afternoon, eating ice-creams from the campsite shop, reading, chatting. As was becoming a habit, they'd gone to the nearby pub for dinner, and were sitting in the pub garden where, once the sun had gone down, the air was refreshingly cool.

'Sure. The last one, though. If I keep drinking at this rate every night, I'll lose all the fitness I've been building up from the walking.'

Laura nodded and went into the bar to order the drinks. There was quite a crowd, it being Saturday, and she had to wait to be served. At the other end of the bar, near the main entrance, there was some commotion.

'You're pissed, mate,' she heard a barman say. 'Can't serve you, sorry.'

'I'm not pissed,' came the reply, noisy and slurred. 'Just a bit loud, ha ha ha. So would you be if you'd driven as far as I have today, all in search of my girl. Need some refreshment before I see her.'

Laura froze. She recognised that voice. Stuart. She ducked behind the nearest person, thankfully a man who was as broad as he was tall.

'All right, pet? You're next to be served,' said the man, stepping aside so that the other barman could see her.

'It's all right,' she began to say, her first thoughts being to abandon the round and go back out to the pub garden to Tom. Maybe they could sneak round the side of the pub without seeing Stuart. But she was too late.

'Lols! There you are! I've driven all the way up the country for you, and this tosser here won't even sell me a pint.'

'Hello, Stuart. I think you'd be better off with water, wouldn't you?' God, how she hated the way he called her Lols, as though she was some kind of a joke.

'Nah. Give us a pint of lager. And a whisky chaser. Lols, they'll serve you. Get it for me?'

'No. And what are you doing here, anyway?' People had moved aside, clearing the area between her and Stuart. He was unsteady on his feet, had clearly already drunk a large quantity of alcohol. Had he driven in this state?

'On me holidays, aren't I? Just like you. Come here, Lols. I've missed you.' He made a lunge towards her and she stepped backwards. He stumbled against a couple of people sitting on bar stools, spilling someone's pint.

'Oy, watch it, mate,' said the man whose beer was now soaking into his clothes.

The barman caught hold of Stuart's arm. 'That's it. I want you outside.'

Stuart seemed to realise he was beaten. 'All right, all right. I'll come quietly, ha ha. Lols'll come with me, won't you, darling? She's my girl, she is. She's gorgeous, isn't she? Bet you wouldn't mind a bit of her, eh?' He said this last to the man whose pint he'd spilled, who looked back at him with disgust.

'Is he with you? Best get him home,' said the barman to Laura, as he escorted him towards the front door of the pub.

'He's my ex,' she said. 'Not my responsibility.'

'Aw, Lols, don't say ex! I'm here to win you back. Come and talk to me.' He called these last words over his shoulder as he was ejected from the pub.

'You'd better go and talk to him,' said the barman. 'He can't come back in here. If there's any trouble, shout and I'll come out if you need any help.'

She gave him a weak but grateful smile, and followed Stuart outside. Part of her wished Tom was beside her, supporting her, but the more rational part knew that would only inflame Stuart, and in this drunken haze he might then turn violent. She'd seen that happen before — like that time in a club in Ibiza, where he'd broken a lad's nose for flirting with Martine. He'd spent a night in a police cell. Not for the first time since she'd come on holiday, she wondered what on earth she'd ever seen in him. His looks, his charm (when sober) and the idea of being in a stable long-term relationship — she supposed that was all she'd been attracted to. The thought crossed her mind that she and Tom had a much deeper connection, even though they'd only shared one kiss. Which had meant nothing.

'Stuart. I think you need to sit down.' She motioned to an unoccupied wooden bench in front of the pub.

'Nah, I'm all right. Good to see you, Lols. I drove all the way up the fucking country to find you, you know?'

'You didn't need to do that. I'll be home in a few days and we could have talked then.' She was keeping her distance from his swaying frame, stepping backwards as he lurched forwards. A few cars were parked on the pub forecourt. One, she noticed, was Stuart's, parked at an angle across two spaces.

'I needed to see you *now*. Martine's gone off with Bazza. She's moved out. I'm free again. You can come back.'

'Stuart, I don't want to come back. You dumped me for Martine. She's dumped you for — whoever it was you said. Doesn't mean I'm coming back to you.'

'But Lols, we were good together. And you've got no one. You must miss me.'

'Who's to say I've got no one?' The words were out before she could stop herself.

'What? You've got a new bloke? Who is he? I'll smash his face in. Not that shit-for-brains you work with, is it? Ian or Ivan or something? What a dick he is. You up here on holiday with him? Where is he?'

'For goodness' sake Stuart, calm down. No, I am not seeing Ewan. No, he is not here. And you're not going to smash anyone's face in. Look, you need to drink some water and then sleep. I can call you a taxi. There are lots of bed-and-breakfast places in Penrith. Bound to be room in one of them.'

'Aw, why can't I sleep with you? Where are you staying, Lols?'

'No room where I'm staying.' She could only hope that he didn't realise she was camping in the site just down the lane.

'Laura? You OK?' Tom had come through the pub, presumably wondering where she'd got to. Again Laura felt that mix of emotions — relief that she had some support but fear for how things might escalate. If Stuart thought there was something going on between her and Tom he might turn nasty.

'Yeah. It's all OK,' she said cautiously.

'Who's this?' Tom asked.

'Um, this is Stuart. He's . . . an old . . . '

'I'm your fucking boyfriend, Lols. Who's this dickhead?'

'Hey, no need for the language,' Tom said, stepping forward. He was taller than Stuart, broader, fitter, and Laura had no doubt who would come off worse in a fight, but she had no desire to see it come to that.

'It's all right, Tom. Stuart just needs to calm down a bit.'

'It's all right, Tom,' Stuart repeated, in a fake high-pitched voice to mock Laura's. 'Who the fuck is Tom then? If this is your new bloke I don't think much of him. Bit posh for you, isn't he? Bit of a prick.' He stepped forward, swaying, and gave Tom a push.

'Watch it, mate.' Tom spoke softly, but there was a definite warning in his voice although he didn't retaliate physically. Laura guessed he'd seen how drunk Stuart was.

Stuart seemed to have picked up on the warning tone. His eyes flicked from Tom to Laura. 'Come on, Lols. Take me home with you. Leave this arsehole here. You know you want to.' He lunged for her again, trying to put his arms around her. She backed away, but was up against a car with nowhere to go. Her patience ran out.

'Get off me, Stuart! Leave me alone. We're over, get it? Over. I'm going. Don't you dare follow me, or I'll call the police.' She tried to slide along the car, keeping her eye on Stuart, but he had an arm either side of her, resting on the car roof.

'You wouldn't do that. Kiss and make up, Lols? Sorry and all that about Martine. Won't happen again, I promise. On me honour.'

He leaned in close to her. She could smell the alcohol on his breath.

And then it all happened at once. Tom grabbed Stuart by the shoulder, trying to spin him round and away from Laura. Stuart lashed out, his arms flailing, and somehow caught Tom around the face. Tom's nose began spurting blood. Laura screamed, and Stuart wheeled back towards her, his head whiplashed forward, making contact with her right between the eyes. There was a burst of pain and light, and then it all went black.

16

STELLA

The kettle was almost boiling when Isaac called out from his bedroom. Stella put down the mugs she'd been taking out of a cupboard so she could go and see what Grandpa wanted, but Jed stopped her.

'It's all right, lass, I'll see to him.' He turned to the others — Sam Wrightson and John Teesdale who were sitting at his kitchen table, and Maggie Earnshaw who was still standing near the cottage door. It looked as though she was on guard in case Pa made a run for it, Stella thought. But of course he wouldn't. He had nothing to be scared of. This was all a terrible, horrible misunderstanding. 'I just need to go into the other room and see to Pa,' Jed said. 'Give me a few minutes.'

'Sam, you go and see what the old man wants,' Maggie said.

Jed shook his head. 'No, let me. He might need — you know — some personal assistance. He'd hate for anyone else to do it. Maggie, I can't escape from that room. Window's too small, even if I wanted to try to climb out.' He rolled his eyes and went through to Isaac's room.

Stella looked at Maggie who was glaring after Pa as though she wanted to run across the room and stop him, but she stayed where she was standing. Stella decided to just carry on with the tea-making, putting two teaspoons of tea in the cracked brown pot, filling it from the kettle, placing it on the table along with the mugs, a jug of milk and the sugar bowl. Acting as though everything was normal, and she was simply helping Pa entertain visitors. As she was doing all this she glanced through the open door to Isaac's room. None of the others could see in, from where they were sitting or standing in the kitchen, but she had a clear view of Pa as he bent over Grandpa. He was whispering something in Grandpa's ear, and the old man was nodding seriously. Then Pa straightened up, and took a tin box out of the drawer where Grandpa's clothes were stored. He put something in it, some papers, from his pocket. Stella tried not to stare. Some instinct told her that Maggie should not see this. Whatever Pa was doing he wanted it kept quiet. Indeed, a moment later he spotted her looking in, and gave the door a gentle push closed with his foot.

What was the tin? What had he put in there? It looked like an old tea caddy, not one that Stella had ever seen before. She resolved to ask him about it later, when they were on their own again.

A few minutes afterwards, as the men were sipping their tea and Maggie was shuffling from foot to foot, clearly anxious that Jed should return to the kitchen where she could keep an eye on him, he finally returned, washed his hands in the deep kitchen sink and sat down at the table. Stella passed him the mug of tea she'd poured.

'Thanks, lass. Well, Maggie, what do we do now?'

'We do what we've been doing this last half-hour. Wait for the police. I've something they'll want to hear. You'll not get away with this, Jed Walker.'

'Get away with what?'

'What you've done to that poor child.'

'I've done nothing. Nothing wrong, at any rate.'

Stella gasped. Pa had as good as admitted he'd done *something* to Jessie. He definitely knew where she was, that much was clear, but for some reason he wouldn't say, other than that lie about the cousin in Carlisle. She glanced at Maggie, whose lips were pinched tightly together, her expression hard.

* * *

It was another hour before the police arrived. An uncomfortable hour, in which they all stayed in the kitchen, with Jed occasionally checking on Isaac. Conversation dried up quickly. Maggie refused to sit down, but continued to hover near the door, shooting hate-filled looks at Jed every so often, and frequently glancing through the kitchen window which looked out onto the street to see if the police had arrived yet. Stella wondered if she should go out and carry on searching for Jessie but it seemed pointless, if Pa was saying she was safe and the other grown-ups seemed to think there was no need to search more. She sat at the table beside Sam Wrightson, chewing at a piece of skin on the side of her thumb, wondering what would happen when the police arrived. She missed Jessie. The cottage seemed empty without her. Oh, where could she be? Why was Pa lying? Her mind went round and round the possibilities — perhaps Pa had left Jessie with someone, perhaps she was sick and in hospital, perhaps she was sleeping, hidden somewhere. He knew, she was sure of it. Yet he wasn't saying anything. If they'd been on their own she'd have shaken his shoulders and screamed at him to tell her, but that wouldn't do, not with Maggie standing sentry and Pa's friends sitting at the table looking confused and concerned. Stella knew she had to keep calm.

'They're here. And not before time,' Maggie said at last. She opened the cottage door and ushered the policemen in. There were two — one in a smart blue uniform with his helmet held under his arm, the other in a brown suit and waistcoat.

The non-uniformed one introduced himself. 'Detective Inspector Parkes. This is Constable Bradley. Now then, a Miss Earnshaw telephoned us, as I understand it. Something about a missing child?'

Stella wanted to speak, and tell them what she knew, but Maggie stepped forward. 'Yes, inspector. I became worried this afternoon when young Stella here told me her little sister was missing. We've all searched the village from top to bottom for the child. The father, Jed Walker, says she's staying with a relative, but I have reason not to believe him. He's proved to me before he can't always be trusted, you see.'

DI Parkes nodded, and waved a hand as though he was trying to speed up Maggie's account. 'Perhaps Mr Walker should tell us what has happened in his own words.'

Stella stared at her father. What would he say? Surely he would not lie to the police as well. Jed seemed stuck for words. He opened and closed his mouth a couple of times, and shook his head sadly.

'You see?' Maggie said. 'He won't say. But I think I know.'

'Then why not enlighten us, Miss Earnshaw.'

She nodded, and Stella noted a strange glint, almost gleeful, in her eye. 'I shall. I didn't think anything of it at the time, but later when Jessie couldn't be found, it made me wonder.'

'Get to the point, Miss Earnshaw.'

Now it was DI Parkes's turn to be on the receiving end of one of Maggie's glares. 'I saw him this morning walking towards the lake with the child — Jessie. It wasn't only me who saw him — my aunt Susie saw him too and she'll swear to that. Then a little later . . . ' She paused and bit her lip briefly as though deciding whether to go on. 'A little later I saw him again when I was on my own. He was in a rowing boat, on the lake. I saw him, clear as day. And I saw him throw something over the side and into the water.'

'I never did! You are making that up!' Jed got to his feet and banged his fist on the table. The constable was immediately at his side, holding his arm, but Jed shook him off.

'Now, now, Mr Walker. Keep calm and let's hear what the lady has to say. Go on, Miss Earnshaw. What was it he threw into the lake, in your opinion?'

'Well, it was a way off, but it was a large bundle, wrapped in some cloth. About the size of a small child.'

'No!' Stella screamed. 'He wouldn't! It couldn't have been Jessie! Pa!'

'Mr Walker?' DI Parkes raised his eyebrows in Jed's direction.

'I was not on the lake today. I don't know what you think you saw, Maggie, but it wasn't me.'

'Oh, it was you all right, Jed. I'd recognise you a mile off. You were in your tweed jacket and cap. That jacket there — ' She pointed to the one hung in its usual spot on the back of the door. 'And you were using Sam's boat, the little green one he keeps tied up on the jetty. At first I assumed you were out fishing and wondered who was looking after your little girl. Then I saw you heave the bundle over the side.'

'What time was this, Miss Earnshaw?' DI Parkes asked.

She frowned. 'Must have been around midday.'

'Mr Walker? Where were you at midday?'

Stella found herself holding her breath. So much depended on whether Pa could give a believable answer to the detective's question.

Jed looked down at the table for a moment before responding. 'I wasn't here. I was on my way back from . . . '

'From where?' DI Parkes was leaning forward, as if he was trying to catch Pa's eye, trying to judge the truth of Pa's words by his expression.

'From some business I had.' Jed looked down again. Stella sighed. Did he not realise how insincere that sounded? Even she was beginning to doubt.

'And where was the little girl at that time?'

Jed sighed, long and deep. 'She was somewhere safe.'

'Mr Walker, you are going to have to tell us where she was. And where she is now. If you are innocent of what Miss Earnshaw says you did, we will need to see the child. Otherwise, I shall have no choice but to arrest you on suspicion of the murder of your daughter.'

'Pa! Tell him where she is! You can't be arrested!' Stella could not help herself. She ran to Jed and flung herself against him, wrapping her arms around his neck as he sat, head in hands, at the table. He made no move to hug her back. She rested her head against his shoulder for a moment, then pulled back, confused and hurt. 'Pa?'

Jed pushed her away and stood abruptly, knocking over his chair. 'For goodness' sake, she's my own child and I know what's best for her. If I say she's safe, that should be good enough for you all! She's with my cousin, in Carlisle, as I already told these good people. Took her there by bus today, to stay for the summer. Maggie, I don't know why you are doing this. Stirring up trouble like this — it's vindictive and uncalled for. These are difficult times for me, I'll not deny that, but to go accusing me of doing away with my own dear child, dear Edie's baby — well, that's a step too far.'

Maggie took a step forward and interrupted him. 'You can't accuse me of lying. Aunt Susie saw you too — you said hello to us both. And you know Susie never lies. She doesn't know how to.'

'You saw me earlier with Jessie — I don't deny that. But you never saw me on the lake. That's a lie.'

'You're the one who's lying,' Maggie spat. 'You've no cousin in Carlisle. We all know that's just made up. You did something to that poor, sweet baby, and you dumped her body in the lake. I saw you!'

Jed ignored her and turned to the policemen. 'Detective, you have had a wasted journey, on account of this woman's desire to see me brought down. I am sorry.'

DI Parkes was on his feet, and the constable had also stepped forward. 'No, Mr Walker, that's not good enough. I cannot simply ignore these allegations. There are two witnesses. As you have provided no adequate explanation of your actions and without sight of the child, I have no choice but to arrest you. If what you say about your Carlisle cousin checks out then you will be released soon, but we must take no chances where a child's safety is concerned. Restrain him, Constable Bradley. You're coming with us, Walker, to the police station in Penrith. Perhaps there you might be a little more forthcoming.'

'Leave off me!' Jed yelled, as he tried to shake off the policeman's grasp. But Bradley had too firm a grip on him.

Sam Wrightson stepped forward too, catching hold of Jed's other arm, holding him firm while Constable Bradley hand-cuffed him. 'Sorry, Jed. But like the detective says, you've not explained things well enough. If you're innocent, tell them the truth, whatever it is.'

Stella stood open-mouthed as Jed was led away. 'But Pa, what about me and Grandpa?'

'Shh, lass. I'll take care of you.' Maggie put an arm around her shoulder, but Stella shrugged it off. It was Maggie's fault all this was happening. Pa said she was stirring up trouble — though why, Stella could not guess. Pa could not have done anything to hurt Jessie, he *couldn't* have. But she knew he had no cousin in Carlisle. That was an outright lie. Why was he not telling the truth about where Jessie was? She refused to consider for a moment that what Maggie was saying was the truth. It couldn't be. It just couldn't be.

She ran out of the cottage after him and the policemen, as they marched him across to the motorcar they'd arrived in. Jed was still shouting his innocence. 'She's safe, I tell you! I'd not hurt her, the precious little thing! Stella, love, trust me!'

Tears were streaming down Stella's face as she watched the police car start to drive away. Her father's face at the window, still shouting, looking back at her in anguish, his face lined and haggard, his eyes staring and wild. 'Pa!' she screamed, running after the motorcar as it sped away down the lane that led out of the valley.

'Hush, lass, there's nothing you can do for him now. 'Tis a sad business this, whatever the outcome.' It was John Teesdale who came to comfort her, and this time she allowed herself to be held while she sobbed, great wracking sobs that shook her entire body. Where was Jessie? What had Pa done? His eyes had told her to trust him; she must hold onto that, and it would all come good in the end. But how, she did not know.

'What's happening? I saw the police car drive off with Jed in the back!' Janie Earnshaw had come running down the lane to the cottage. Maggie quickly explained.

'Well. What a to-do. Isaac must come and stay with us,' Janie said. 'He'll be better off. Poor Stella can't manage by herself. Stella, will you come too? There's space for you, but you'll have to share with Maggie.'

Stella stared at her. Share a house with Maggie — no, share a *room* with her? When it was Maggie's words that made the police arrest Pa? Never.

'Thank you, Mrs Earnshaw, but I'll be all right here on my own,' she replied. 'I know how to cook and clean. Besides, Pa will be back soon, when the police realise what a mistake they have made. And anyway — ' she stifled a sob, not wanting them to see how upset she was — 'I should stay here in case Jessie comes back.'

Maggie laughed. 'You're what, ten years old?'

'Eleven, now.'

'Eleven. Not nearly old enough to live on your own, and your pa won't be coming back any time soon. Neither will your poor sister, who's at the bottom of the lake. You've no choice but to take charity from someone. It may as well be us, so you're with your grandpa.'

John Teesdale had come to stand alongside Stella, a hand on her shoulder. 'There's a room above the pub, lass, if you want it. We get few enough guests these days. You'll pay nowt, of course. Jed was a good friend, and I'll do what I can by his daughter.' Once more she leaned in to him, grateful for the support and the alternative offer of accommodation.

'Thank you, Mr Teesdale. I would like to come to live with you for the moment. But I'm sure it will not be long, and I will help with cleaning the bar or whatever you need, in lieu of rent.'

'That won't be necessary, lass. You're very welcome.'

Anything would be better than moving in with the witch Maggie, she thought. And surely it'd only be for a few days at most, then they'd all be back together in the cottage. All four of them, Jessie included, none the worse for whatever adventure she'd been on.

'I'll pack a bag for Grandpa, then,' she said, and went back inside to get his things.

★   ★   ★

Isaac was shuffling in his chair as if he was trying to get out of it.

'Grandpa? Do you need help?'

'Fetch your pa, lass. I need to use the pot.'

'I'll help you.' She stepped forward to help him stand but he batted her away.

'Nay, lass. You've not to do it. Fetch Jed.'

She bit her lip. How could she explain where her pa was? 'He's not here, Grandpa. He's had to go away for a bit.'

'Away? Where?'

'Come on, let me help you. I don't mind, honest I don't.'

'Pass me my stick. I'll go out to the privy. I can walk that far. You only need hold my other arm to keep me steady, and maybe help with my trouser fastenings.'

She did as he asked, and the mission was accomplished. Stella wondered how he'd cope at Maggie's, when it would have to be Maggie or her mother Janie helping him, dressing him, washing him. All those things Pa had done for him since he'd moved in. Poor Grandpa. He'd have to learn to accept help from people other than Pa. He had no choice. She'd have done it for him, but she couldn't live at Maggie's.

'Put the kettle on, lass. And tell me where your pa is. And the little one. Where's young Jessie, then?'

Stella told him what had happened while she busied herself making tea. That way she didn't need to see the shock and horror in Grandpa's eyes as he listened to her story. She played down what Maggie had said, and tried to make it sound as though it was all a misunderstanding. Which, she hoped fervently, it was.

'What's to become of me?' Isaac asked, when

she'd finished speaking.

'Janie Earnshaw says she'll take you in. She and Maggie will look after you.'

He grunted and nodded acceptance of this plan.

She passed him his tea. 'I'll go and pack some things for you.'

'Right you are, lass. Someone'll need to put me in a wheel-barrow and push me round to Earnshaw's place. I can't walk that far nowadays.'

'Mr Wrightson will do that, I expect.' She went through to his room to pack, realising he had not expressed worry for Pa, or even asked where she, Stella, would be going.

17

LAURA

Her sleeping mat must have sprung a leak and deflated. The ground seemed so much harder than before. And her head hurt. How much had she drunk? Her knee hurt too. Why was that?

There were voices — mumbling, indistinct. She could not make out the words.

She was not on her sleeping mat. She was lying on tarmac, with nothing beneath her and no sleeping bag. Someone was holding her hand. The someone was murmuring to her, but she could not work out what he was saying. Her head was throbbing.

There was a horrible noise, a siren. Through her closed eyes she could see flashing lights, enough to bring on a migraine. She did not get migraines but this flashing, this intense pain in her head — maybe that's what it was. She tried opening her eyes. There was a white blur leaning over her. It was night-time. The flashing lights were blue.

The voices were still mumbling around her, but one was beginning to rise above the others, becoming more distinct. It was closer to her than the others, she thought. Her hand was being squeezed. Her head was pounding.

Words began emerging from the fog, but she could not yet put them in any sequence that made sense. *Laura. Ambulance soon. Safe now. Police here. Stuart.*

Stuart! She'd been talking to Stuart. He was drunk. Something had happened.

Don't try to move. Ambulance will be here soon.

That made some sense. Was someone hurt, then? The voice was familiar, but it wasn't Stuart. Why did her knee hurt?

Further away there was shouting. Arguing. And those blue flashing lights. The shouting was Stuart, she realised. She tried again to open her eyes fully. The pale shape was a face, with little fireworks going off all around it. It was the one talking to her. Tom.

'Wha — what happened?' She tried to form the words, but it made her head hurt even more.

'That bastard Stuart head-butted you. Not sure it was entirely accidental. Lie still, Laura. Don't try to move. The ambulance will be here soon.'

'Stuart did this?'

'Yes.' Tom squeezed her hand again, and she realised he was sitting on the ground with her. 'The police are here. They seem to be having a bit of trouble getting him into the police car though.'

'He's being arrested?'

'Too right he is. He'll be charged with assault, or GBH, I bet. Don't waste time worrying about that insult to humanity. Does your head hurt?'

She tried to nod, but that made it worse, and the fireworks came quicker and faster. 'Yes, it does. And my knee.'

215

He moved to look at it, and she saw he had blood all over his face. 'You're hurt too?'

'Not really. Just a nosebleed. Nothing to worry about. Your knee looks swollen. I think you fell on it hard when you went down.'

'Ugh. Can't decide what hurts more, knee or head.'

Tom didn't answer that, but looked away, his lips pinched tight.

A moment later he spoke again. 'A cop's coming over.'

'Is she awake?' a voice said.

'Yes, but in pain,' Tom replied.

'OK. We'll catch up with her in hospital. The ambulance is only minutes away now. We'll need a statement from each of you. Where will we be able to find you tomorrow?'

'I'm camping down the road,' Tom said, 'but right now I'll go with Laura to the hospital. I'm not leaving her.'

'OK. I'll just take your phone number, if I may.'

Tom gave it to him, and the policeman walked away. She heard a car engine start up, and the crunch of tyres on gravel as it pulled away.

Tom heaved a sigh of relief. 'That's Stuart out of the way, then. The ambulance should be here very soon. In fact — ' he stood up and craned his neck — 'it's here now. I'm coming with you, by the way.'

She smiled weakly at him. She should probably tell him no, she'd be OK, he should go to the campsite and get some sleep, but she realised she would appreciate him staying at her side. God, how her head and knee hurt! At least the flashing fireworks seemed to be subsiding a little.

★   ★   ★

It was a long night, involving a bumpy, painful journey in the ambulance, lots of doctors in white coats and nurses in blue tunics, lots of form-filling, X-rays of her knee, a scan of her head, questions about her medical history, being shunted from pillar to post and finally ending up in a side room off the main accident-and-emergency department. Through it all, Tom stayed by her side, holding her hand if he wasn't in the way, helping provide details for the endless forms, keeping track of her belongings. She slept for a while, once she was settled in the ward, having been given painkillers. When she woke, Tom was still there beside her, sipping a cup of coffee. She suspected he had not slept a wink.

'Morning,' he said. 'How are you feeling?'

'Sore. Better. A bit sick.'

He held a cardboard kidney-shaped dish in front of her while she vomited, and pressed the buzzer for a nurse.

'It's all right. You're concussed, you're bound to feel a bit nauseous. But we've checked your head and no lasting damage done.' The nurse, a well-built middle-aged woman with a badge stating her name was Ayana, smiled broadly at her. 'Feeling any better?'

'A little. Headache's not as bad.'

Ayana nodded, putting the sick bowl to one

side. 'Good, good. Now then, while I'm here I'll just take your pulse and blood pressure.' She did the tests and noted the results on the clipboard that hung on the end of the bed. 'Hungry?'

'A little,' Laura said, though she wasn't sure if she'd be able to eat anything.

'Ha ha, I meant your poor boyfriend here, who's been sitting at your side all night.'

Laura blinked at the word 'boyfriend', momentarily wondering if Stuart was nearby, before realising Ayana was referring to Tom. She began to explain but Ayana was still talking to him.

'Sweetheart, there's a cafe downstairs. It opens for breakfast at seven if you'd like to get yourself something. Just ten minutes to go. Laura here will have something about eight when the trolley comes round.' Ayana smiled again and bustled off back out to the main ward.

'I am a bit hungry. Might go and grab something really quickly, if you're all right on your own for a few minutes?' He looked worried, tired too.

'I won't go anywhere.'

Tom put the call-button on the bed beside her in easy reach and made her promise to buzz a nurse if she felt sick again. 'I won't be long. I promise.'

He was as good as his word. Laura had just about dozed off again when he returned and took up his position on a chair, holding her hand. She had never felt so cared for, not since she'd had chickenpox as a child and her mother had slept in her room for a week, sponging her fevered forehead and applying soothing calamine lotion to the hundreds of spots that had spread across her body.

'The breakfast was good. Probably better than yours will be,' he said, with a rueful smile.

'I don't care. When do you think they'll let me out?'

'In the afternoon, they said, when I asked them earlier. They like to keep concussion cases under observation for twelve to twenty-four hours, but if you're not going to be on your own tonight they'll let you out today.'

She frowned. 'But I will be on my own.'

'No, you won't. You're sharing my tent. I want to keep a close eye on you.' He squeezed her hand. 'And I'll hear no arguments.'

She smiled. He sounded just like her mother had, back in those chickenpox days.

His eyes softened. 'I care about you, you know. That git, Stuart. I can't believe what he did.'

It was on the tip of her tongue to say she couldn't believe it either, but actually, when she thought about it, his actions had probably been wholly in character. It had just taken her a long time to realise it. A long time, and having it rubbed in her face that time she'd found Stuart in bed with Martine. Well, if she hadn't thought herself better off without Stuart before, she most certainly did so now. It was hard to imagine that she'd once thought she would be with Stuart for ever. Difficult to believe she'd spent so many years with him. Despite her fuzzy, concussed head she felt as though she was seeing things clearly now for the first time.

A police sergeant came to talk to them later in the morning, taking detailed statements from both of them. There had been other witnesses to the assault, and Stuart had been charged with Actual Bodily Harm.

'Could be a prison sentence of up to six months,' said the sergeant. 'And it also sounds like you need to get a restraining order against him. He should not be allowed near you after what he's done.'

'He was so drunk,' Laura said, recalling the stink of spirits on his breath.

'Yes, but that's no excuse. We found an empty bottle of vodka in the footwell of his car. He'd probably been knocking it back as he drove up here. Shame he wasn't stopped, and had for that. Would have saved you your injuries.'

Laura shivered at the idea that Stuart could have caused a serious accident, driving in the state he'd been in.

'Tea, folks?' The nurse Ayana poked her head around the door. 'Might be able to rustle up a biscuit or two as well.'

The sergeant grinned and nodded. 'Most kind, thank you.'

Ayana gave a thumbs-up and disappeared.

'They treating you well here?'

'Definitely, especially Ayana.'

'When will you be discharged?'

'This afternoon, I think,' Laura replied, glancing at Tom who nodded. She shifted in bed and winced a bit as the pain from her badly bruised knee flared up.

'Good. Glad there's nothing too serious. And will you be heading home? You're on holiday here as I understand it.'

Laura blinked. She had not thought about that. Going home to Gran made some sense, as she knew she needed some time to recover fully, with her feet up. But going home meant a long uncomfortable drive. Besides, she hadn't had a chance to look for Gran's precious tea caddy. 'Not yet. I've injured my knee as well, and don't think I could drive all that way for a few days. So I'm probably better off sitting on my deckchair at the campsite, while Tom here fetches me cups of tea and bacon butties from the shop.'

'Anything to please her ladyship,' Tom said, with a grin and a roll of his eyes.

'Besides,' Laura said, looking at Tom, 'we've still got to go back to Brackendale and look for Gran's tin box.'

'Not for a day or two. You're in no fit state to go tramping around the reservoir.'

He was right. She wasn't even sure she'd be able to walk at all with her injured knee.

⋆ ⋆ ⋆

She could walk, as she discovered later, after the police sergeant had left and the physiotherapist had been round, but only on crutches. She was issued with a pair, given some painkilling drugs and a warning to take things easy for at least three days, and then around lunchtime Ayana came to her with a discharge paper to sign.

'You can stay and have lunch first, but you might prefer to go to the cafe upstairs for more choice or go someplace else. Up to you. Been lovely having you.' She smiled her broad smile at Laura, who signed the document.

'I think we'll go. Thanks so much for everything.'

'No problem. Come back to A&E if you get any further dizziness or confusion, won't you? I don't think you will, but just in case.'

'We'll need to get a taxi,' Tom said.

'Where are you staying?'

'Glydesdale campsite.'

'Oh, that's a fair old way by taxi. Listen, I'm off shift in twenty minutes. I live out towards Glydesdale. I'll give you a lift. It's not much out of my way.'

'Would you? That's beyond the call of duty. But thank you.'

⋆ ⋆ ⋆

It was early afternoon when they arrived back at the campsite, thanking Ayana profusely for her help as she dropped them off beside Tom's tent.

Tom fussed around, fetching Laura's deck-chair, and making a footstool for her using his cool-box. He bought sandwiches, cakes and two cups of tea from the campsite shop and they picnicked in the sunshine. It wasn't as hot as the previous days — there were wispy clouds in the sky and a light breeze.

'I don't reckon the weather will hold much

longer,' Tom said, gazing up at the sky as he sipped his tea.

'What's the forecast?' Laura asked. Typical, just as she was forced to do nothing but sit and sunbathe for a few days the weather was about to turn.

'Some rain tomorrow. Then it should clear up for a couple of days before a spell of bad weather.'

Laura pulled a face. 'I really want to get back to Brackendale and search for Gran's tea caddy. Hope the rain tomorrow doesn't make it impossible to get to the village ruins.'

'It's due to rain on and off from mid-morning. Won't be enough to fill the reservoir — that'll take months. But it'll make the lake surface pretty muddy. The day after is fine. We could go back there then. Question is, will you be fit enough?'

She nodded. 'Yes, a day's rest will sort out my knee, I'm sure.' A thought had occurred to her. Once the weather turned, Tom would surely pack up and go home. Indeed, she only had a few days left herself before she was due back at work, assuming her knee healed in time. Would they ever see each other again? She'd enjoyed Tom's company so much these last few days. It was hard to believe it was only five days since they'd met — she was already thinking of him as a good friend. And as that kiss had shown, there was a physical attraction there too. Stuart's behaviour had helped her realise she was truly over him, and perhaps ready to begin a tentative new relationship. Could Tom perhaps be feeling the same way? Or was he still too scarred by what his ex, Sarah, had done to him? He'd said the kiss meant nothing; it was only due to the romance of that perfect evening under the stars. But Laura was beginning to realise that for her part, given time, their relationship could develop into something significantly more. If only they had more time to get to know each other slowly. She knew he lived on the western edge of London, about twenty miles from Gran's home. So if he was interested and if she felt ready, it would be possible for them to continue a relationship, albeit one where they'd have to travel at weekends to see each other. A lot of 'ifs', she realised. But who knew? For now, she could only take things one day at a time.

'Penny for them?' Tom said, breaking into her thoughts.

She smiled up at him. 'Just thinking what a fabulous week it's been, up till last night. Shame the weather has to change.'

'Ah, Laura. Nothing lasts for ever.'

That was exactly what she was afraid of.

★ ★ ★

That evening, after a meal of fried sausages and baked beans cooked on their two camping stoves, Tom reorganised his tent to make space for her to share, and fetched her sleeping bag, mat, clothes and wash-things from her own tent. He would not listen to any protestations that she would be all right on her own, and in any case, she rather liked the idea of lying next to him all night.

The sun was just setting as she hobbled over to the facilities block on her crutches, for a shower. Thankfully there was a bench in the shower cubicle so she could sit down rather than try to balance on her bad leg. It was good to feel clean again, and in clean pyjamas. It was early but they were both exhausted after the sleepless night in hospital.

'There's something almost decadent about going to bed before it's completely dark, isn't there?' Tom commented, when she returned from her shower. 'I mean, as a child you hate it, and protest against it in the summer. At least, I did. But as an adult, it's delicious to get to bed so early, knowing you can sleep for the next twelve hours.' His eyes had dark shadows beneath them.

'You need more than twelve hours, by the look of you,' she replied playfully.

'So do you, Ms Concussed Hopalong.'

'Hey, I'd hit you with my crutch for that, only I'd probably fall over if I did,' she laughed.

He helped her into the tent, tucking the crutches under the flysheet alongside the tent when she'd finished with them. She wriggled into her sleeping bag, took her evening painkillers and settled down to wait for him to join her. He seemed to be an age getting ready, and she almost dozed off. At last he crawled in beside her and zipped up the tent. He was still dressed in the jeans and T-shirt he'd been wearing since the previous evening. She debated turning her back while he undressed, but that would mean lying on her bad knee. Instead, she closed her eyes, only opening them again when he'd stopped shuffling around and she calculated he was probably settled in his sleeping bag.

He wasn't. He was sitting up, arms wrapped around his knees, wearing only a pair of boxers. In the light of the head torch he'd hung from the roof of the tent she could see he had a muscular torso, broad hairless chest, well-defined biceps. She closed her eyes again, embarrassed to be caught staring. But he'd been staring at her too, she was sure. He'd obviously noticed her looking as it seemed to spur him into action again, and soon she sensed he was lying down, his face inches from hers.

'Well, goodnight then,' he said, as he clicked off the head torch.

'Night.' She lay quietly, staring into the darkness, waiting for her eyes to adjust.

She felt his breath on her cheek and tensed, wondering if he was going to kiss her. He did — on her forehead. 'So, sleep well. You need it.'

'You too,' she whispered back, and drifted off into a deep, much-needed slumber feeling secure and safe.

18

STELLA

It had been weeks since Pa was taken away and Stella moved into a room above the pub. John Teesdale and his wife were kind to her, giving her little treats of biscuits and sweets now and again as though they were sorry for her, letting her borrow any book she liked from the bookshelf in their sitting room, cooking her dinners. They seemed to have a lot more money than Pa ever had. If it hadn't been for the circumstances that had led to her moving in with them, she thought she might have been very happy. But then she'd remember where Pa was, and miss Jessie with an almost physical pain, and feel tears pricking the backs of her eyes. She would never cry in front of the Teesdales, though. She did her best to seem upbeat and cheerful around them.

Every day during the long school summer holidays she had visited Grandpa Isaac at Maggie's house. The old man was becoming weaker and more confused every day. He could no longer stand at all, and spent almost all his time in bed. Stella was grateful to Maggie and Janie for taking him in. She could not have coped with him by herself, she could see that now. Yet despite this, she still found herself hating Maggie with every fibre of her being. It was Maggie who'd told the police she'd seen Pa dump something in the lake. That was why they had taken him away. She'd questioned Susie, who'd only said she'd seen Pa and Jessie walking down the valley towards the lake, in the morning. That was all. They could have been going anywhere. It was only Maggie who insisted she'd seen Pa in a boat.

One day not long after Pa had gone, the police came back to Brackendale, and went out on the lake. They had long poles with which they poked the bottom of the lake, and a diver who spent hours underwater. 'Searching for your poor little sister,' Maggie Earnshaw told her. 'But it's a big lake and it'll be very hard to find something as small as poor Jessie in there.' Stella felt a shiver run through her at the thought of Jessie lying at the bottom of the lake. And then she remembered Jessie couldn't possibly be there. Pa would not have hurt her. He had told her to trust him. So of course she could not be at the bottom of the lake.

Indeed, the police divers found nothing, and a few days later John Teesdale told her that as Jessie had not been found and Pa's story about a cousin in Carlisle had not checked out, Pa had been charged with child abduction. They could not charge him with murder because they'd found no body. But, Teesdale said, the implication was that they were, pretty sure he had killed her, and disposed of her in the lake as Maggie had said. They just hadn't been able to find her remains. He'd told her gently, his wife sitting beside Stella, holding her hand and passing her a handkerchief to dry her eyes.

After this, Stella spent part of every day at the lakeside, sitting quietly staring out over the water, trying but failing to feel her sister's spirit near her. The dam had been commissioned now, the valves closed and the lake was growing in size daily. It had burst its usual banks and was creeping gradually over the fields. The village was emptying rapidly now, and even the Teesdales were talking about their expected move to take over an empty farmhouse in Glydesdale which they planned to convert to a pub. But they'd promised that the Lost Sheep would stay open for as long as there were people living in Brackendale Green who needed a drink.

Stella had not dared think about where she would go.

She wanted to see her father, talk it over with him, find out how he was and what was happening next. The grown-ups in the village told her so little. She would come across them muttering in the bar of the pub, but as soon as they saw her they'd clam up, put on fake bright smiles and ask her if she was having a lovely break from school, as though this was any other summer holiday. As though nothing had changed.

Halfway through the summer holidays it rained for a week. The lake increased massively in this time — all the water running off the surrounding hills backed up against the dam. It was only a hundred yards or so away from the main street of the village.

'Not long now,' Teesdale said, gazing over the

sodden ground between the village and the lake. 'You coming with us to Glydesdale, young Stella? You're of course most welcome. There's not quite the room in the new place as there is here, but we'll manage somehow.'

'When will Pa come back?' she asked him, not for the first time.

'Ah, lass. He's remanded in custody until his trial. They're worried he'd be a danger to . . . well, to other little children. So they won't let him out.'

He meant they thought Pa would be a danger to her, Stella realised. They thought if he'd killed one daughter he might harm the other one too. He never would hurt either her or Jessie, she thought automatically, but these days with still no alternative explanation of what had happened to Jessie she was not able to tell herself that with quite as much conviction as before.

She walked away from John Teesdale then, aware that he was watching her go. She went to the woods, the ones she'd gone through on her way home from school at the end of the term. The place where there was a hollowed-out fallen tree that she'd wanted to show Jessie. It seemed a lifetime ago, that day, before everything went wrong, before Jessie went missing. The tree had become her thinking spot.

She sat down and considered her options. There might be only a couple of weeks left before the Lost Sheep closed its doors for the last time, and the Teesdales moved to Glydesdale. The Earnshaws were already packing. They had found a house to rent near Keswick. Maggie had told her they were taking Grandpa with them, and would make him as comfortable as possible for as long as he had left. She knew from this that they did not expect him to live much longer. Strangely, this did not upset her as much as she might have thought it would. Perhaps she was numb to heartbreak now: losing Ma, then Jessie, then Pa being taken away had left her unable to feel. Grandpa was old, he'd had his life. But Jessie had been only at the start of hers. Stella still could not believe she was dead. Not Jessie. Not that vibrant, lively little girl who could drive you mad with her demands and tantrums but a minute later melt your heart with her smile and make you laugh at the sound of her giggle.

What would become of her, Stella? She could go with the Teesdales to Glydesdale. But something about the way John Teesdale had made the offer, saying there wasn't as much room at the new place, had made her wonder if they really wanted her. And why should they want her? She was just another mouth to feed. Too young to work in a pub. They'd been kind but she could not continue to impose upon them. Their own sons were full grown and had left Brackendale for jobs in the towns. Why would they want to bring up another child who was no relation of theirs?

Relations, that's what she needed. Of course: Aunt Winnie! Now why hadn't she thought of it before? Her mother's sister in Penrith. Stella liked her — she reminded her of Ma. Aunt Winnie would take her in, she was sure. She had only to write her a letter. And Pa was being held at the police station in Penrith. She'd be able to visit him. She was sure he was allowed visitors. Sam Wrightson had been once, and come back with tales of a pale, shrunken man, insisting on his innocence but coming up with a new story every time he was asked to tell the truth. Stella had overheard all this talk in the bar one night, but when she'd stepped forward out of the shadows to ask Mr Wrightson what exactly Pa had said, the grown-ups had all stopped talking. Maggie had ushered her away, telling her the bar was no place for a child and the talk was not for a child's ears. It happened every time. No one told her anything.

But if she moved to Penrith she might be able to see Pa and ask him herself.

Her decision made, she ran back to the Lost Sheep intending to go straight up to her room to write the letter to Aunt Winnie.

'Whoa, what's the rush?' John Teesdale said as she hurtled through the bar and up the stairs.

'I want to write to my aunt,' Stella said. 'To ask if I can live with her.'

John Teesdale smiled and seemed to relax as though with relief. 'Your ma's sister, do you mean?'

'Yes, Aunt Winnie. Does she know what's happened to Pa?'

He shrugged. 'I've not told her or written to her. I don't know of anyone who has. I suppose we all thought it'd only be a day or so before your pa was released back to us. Good idea to write to her. If you're quick, the post van will be here in an hour — you can send it then.'

She rushed up the stairs and wrote the letter. Having visited a few times with Ma, she knew Aunt Winnie's address. She worked hard to make the letter sound grown up, businesslike and not too needy. She had to make Aunt Winnie think it would be good for both of them if Stella moved in with her.

Ten minutes later she was back downstairs with the letter. John Teesdale gave her a stamp for it, and she put it into the village postbox, in good time for the day's collection.

Her route back to the Lost Sheep passed Pa's cottage. As she had done many times since he'd been taken away, she went inside to look around. Everything looked dusty and uncared for. There was half a loaf of mouldy bread in the kitchen. Drawers in Grandpa's room were left open, where she and Janie had pulled out clothes to stuff into a bag to go with Grandpa to the Earnshaws' house. Jessie's toys were still in a basket in the kitchen. Her own room was neat and tidy — she had packed carefully and left the room with its bed made, ready for when she could move back in. She realised now that would never happen. With a sigh she ran a hand along the back of a chair where she used to leave her folded clothes at night. She gazed out of the bedroom window at the view over their backyard, across to the ever-encroaching lake and beyond, to the mountains. Could you see the mountains from Penrith? She tried to remember. She thought perhaps you could, but only as distant bumps on the horizon. Not like here, where they were all around, dominating the view, crowding the valley, defining her world. At least, her world as it had been, all her life. But soon, not any more. Everything, was changing.

She left the cottage with a sigh, after standing for a moment in Pa's workshop. The broken bicycle he'd been repairing still sat turned upside down on its saddle and handlebars, its cranks and pedals lying on the bench. Pa had explained he needed to replace a spindle in the bottom bracket, and pack ball bearings in grease around it to make it spin freely. Whose bicycle had it been? She wasn't sure. Whoever it was had not come back for it, and probably never would.

Back in the Lost Sheep, people had gathered in the bar. Maggie and Janie were there, Sam Wrightson, the Teesdales of course. As had become her habit, Stella crept through, keeping a low profile, then sat on a bench that was behind a wooden partition. From here she could usually hear what the grown-ups were talking about. She was only visible if someone went to the bar to order drinks.

'I'll be moving out at the end of the week,' said one man, and she recognised Sam Wrightson's voice. 'The water's only forty feet from my house now.'

'A sad day,' said Teesdale.

'Aye. And we'll be off probably next week,' said Maggie.

'Poor old Susie can't understand it,' Janie said. Her voice sounded sad and tired. 'And she'll not understand it any better when we've moved. She's only ever known the valley, never been outside it in all her life.'

'Ah, she's like a child, she'll adapt. Reckon you'll be surprised,' Teesdale replied. 'Anyway, village'll be changing from tomorrow, when the demolitions start.'

Stella gave a stifled gasp. Demolition?

'Aye, it will,' Sam Wrightson said. 'Seems wrong for them to start before we've all left, but I suppose there's a lot to do, and the farms nearest the lake have been empty a while. It's those first, then they'll come to the village.'

'The Lost Sheep'll be last to go,' John Teesdale said. 'Anyhow, the workmen will want some refreshment at the end of their day.'

'You do a good job, John,' said Maggie.

'Aye, we try. It'll be a right shame when it's all over, won't it? And we'll all be spread to the four corners of Westmorland. Even them Pendletons up at the big house have left. Gone to India, I heard, even though their house is not in danger. Ah, well. Nothing ever stays the same, but who'd have thought it? Our proud little community shattered.'

'Stop it. You're too maudlin, John. Let's think no more on it. Well now, I'd best be getting back to Susie and old Isaac. Can't leave either of them too long alone.' There was the sound of a chair pushing back as Janie spoke.

'You're a good woman, Janie. There's not many as would have taken in the old man, and him needing so much care.'

'You're not so bad yourself, John, taking in that poor girl. What's to become of her, when the village empties?'

'She's writing to Edie's sister, in Penrith. Her aunt'll take her in, I hope.'

'Aye. You've done enough for the girl. Terrible business though. I still can't believe it of Jed Walker. That he should harm his own child.'

'I can believe it,' Maggie said. 'I think he always had a vicious streak. Kept it hidden when Edie was alive, but it was there all along. Remember I knew him better than most, when he was young.'

'Think you had a lucky escape there, Maggie,' said Teesdale. 'Who'd have thought he'd turn out so wrong?'

Stella had heard enough. She came out from behind the partition and walked past the group, her head held high. She darted a furious look at Maggie as she went, but said nothing. What could she say, being only a child? But she'd learned enough. The sooner she could get out of Brackendale and never again have to see these people who she'd thought were Pa's friends, the better. Sam Wrightson had been Pa's best mate, but wasn't it him who'd restrained Pa the day the police came? Even John Teesdale, who'd been kind to her, seemed now to be turning against him.

She went up to her room, dragged the suitcase out from under the bed — the one she'd used to bring her things from home — and began flinging her belongings into it. She wouldn't wait to hear back from Aunt Winnie. She'd leave immediately. Aunt Winnie would understand. The letter would arrive before she did, to serve as a warning at least.

Halfway through packing she stopped and lay down on the bed. She couldn't leave without saying goodbye to Grandpa. And how would she even get to Penrith? The bus service only came as far as the dam, and she could not walk that far carrying a suitcase. Besides, there were no more buses today. Tomorrow would be the earliest she could leave, and she'd need someone to give her a lift to the bus stop. Who could do that? She considered all the people in the village who owned a motorcar or tractor. Most had already left. Those remaining — Teesdale, Wrightson — she now considered her enemies.

A thought flashed into her mind. The bicycle, in Pa's workshop. If she could fix it, she could strap the suitcase on the back and make her own way to the bus stop.

She rushed out of her room and down the stairs, almost bumping into John Teesdale as she went.

'Whoa, steady, lass! Are you off out again? I was just coming to talk to you.'

'Got something to do,' she said breathlessly. She didn't want to tell him what she was planning. She'd tell him when she was leaving and not before.

'Don't know what you heard downstairs, but I hope nothing's upset you,' he said, frowning at her.

'No, I'm all right.' She just wanted to go and see if her plan would work, not waste time talking to Teesdale.

'Good girl. We've all got your best interests at heart, lass. You know that, don't you? You're not about to go and do anything silly now, are you?'

'No, Mr Teesdale. Just off to fetch something I need from home.'

'Aye, well, don't be long now. Your tea's in an hour. Mrs T'll be cross if you're late.'

'I won't be.'

Finally he let her go, and she ran across the road to Pa's workshop before anyone else could delay her. There was the bicycle, as she'd seen it earlier. She inspected the tools and parts laid out on the bench. The bicycle cranks with their pedals still attached. A tub of shiny steel ball bearings. Another tub of grease. Two spindles — one old and broken in two, the other new, made by Pa. Thank goodness he'd got that far with the repair. All she needed to do was pack the bearings in grease into each side of the bottom bracket, insert the spindle, and reattach the chain-wheel and cranks. She'd spent enough time watching Pa work on bicycles and handing him tools as he asked for them, to have an idea of what she was doing. Well, there was no time like the present to get started on it.

She soon had the bearings in place. It was fiddly but easy with her small hands. She wondered how Pa managed this kind of job, with his large, rough hands. Thinking of him working here made her choke with emotion. Would he ever work here again? What would happen if he was still in custody when their cottage and the workshop were due for demolition? What would happen to all his tools and furniture? She resolved to ask Aunt Winnie. Perhaps her aunt could arrange for a van to come and collect everything. And take it . . . where? Her head hurt with all these grown-up problems. Her only job, she decided, was to get this bicycle fixed and get herself to Aunt Winnie's.

Had she put enough ball bearings in? There was no room for any more in the grooves either side of the bracket, so she decided she must have. She carefully pushed the new spindle through, taking care not to dislodge any bearings. Once in place, it spun smoothly and freely. That was the first job done. Now to attach the cranks. The chain-wheel was already attached to the right-hand crank. She slotted this one on first, then the other, taking care to set them so that the pedals were opposite each other. They went on easily. But how to stop them falling off? She noticed a hole drilled in each, which lined up with holes through the ends of the spindle. On the bench were a couple of odd-looking pieces of metal, slightly tapered. They looked the right size to fit in the holes. She tried one; it went halfway in before getting stuck. She couldn't get it out again. A thought occurred to her — get a hammer, force it in further. It would stop the crank falling off the spindle. Whether it was the right way to attach it or not she didn't know, but it might work. She found Pa's smallest hammer, the one he used to call 'Stella-sized', and hammered the pins in as far as she could. She spun the cranks and pedals round — they felt firm now.

One thing left — the chain. Where was it? She searched around, and finally found it soaking in a tub of some sort of liquid. Presumably Pa had been cleaning it. She took it out, ran a rag along it a few times, and wrapped it round the chain-wheel and the cog on the hub of the back wheel. Now to join the ends together. There was a small tool she'd seen Pa use before, to open and close links in bicycle chains. She rummaged through his tool box and finally found it, right at the bottom. A minute later, the chain was in place and turning the cranks meant the back wheel also turned perfectly.

'Pa would be proud of me,' she told herself, and it brought a tear to her eye as she imagined telling him all that she'd done. He'd have smiled, ruffled her hair, and said what a grand lass she was to have managed the job by herself. Would she ever hear him say something like that again, she wondered. She had to believe it — had to keep believing that things would work out, Jessie would be found, Pa released and they'd be together again.

With difficulty, she managed to turn the bicycle the right way up. It was too big for her, but the saddle could be lowered. When this was done, she stood the bike beside the workbench and climbed on, holding onto the bench for stability. She could reach the pedals, even at their lowest point, so she knew she'd be able to ride it. Good job she was tall for her age. She could tie her suitcase to the rack over the back wheel.

There was a bus from the dam to Penrith at half past eight each morning. Stella resolved to be on it.

19

LAURA

Laura woke up not entirely sure where she was. In the hospital bed? No. In a tent, but it was unfamiliar. Not her own. Gradually it all came back to her, and she remembered snuggling down next to Tom. She rolled over to look at him, wincing in pain from her knee. But he'd already got up, and there was only an empty sleeping bag next to her. She must have been deeply asleep for him to open the tent and crawl out without disturbing her. She reached over and unzipped the entrance. Tom was just outside, boiling water on his camping stove to make tea.

'Morning! Sleep well?'

'Certainly did,' she said. 'What time is it?'

'Eight-thirty. You've had twelve hours' sleep.'

'Gosh. Well, that's enough, I'd say.' She gingerly began the painful process of extricating herself from her sleeping bag.

Tom rushed over to help. 'How do you feel?'

'Head's better. Knee's killing me.'

He helped her to stand and handed her the crutches. 'Take your painkillers before doing anything else.'

'Can't. Desperate for a wee,' she replied, already hobbling across the campsite.

* * *

When she returned he had made tea, got her painkillers and a glass of water ready, and placed her deckchair beside the tent. She sat down gratefully. 'Where's this rain that was forecast?'

'About half an hour away, I'd say,' he responded, looking at the sky. 'Hope we can finish breakfast and get somewhere sheltered before it reaches us.' He looked at her sideways. 'I don't fancy your chances running for cover.'

'I'd be all right. You'd carry me,' she retorted, and he laughed.

'I probably would and all.'

They ate bread and cheese for breakfast, rather than risk taking ages cooking something or waiting for bacon butties at the campsite shop. The first spots of rain were falling as Tom was finishing clearing up. He pressed the unlock button on his car key fob. 'Go on, get in. I'll tidy up.'

'Cheers.' She hobbled over and waited in the car, watching him quickly stuff everything into the tent and zip it up. By the time he hurled himself into the car beside her the rain was falling heavily, great fat raindrops splashing on the dust-dry earth.

'Well. Just in time. Do you need anything from your tent or are you set to go out for the day?'

'Could do with my mac,' she replied.

'I'll fetch it for you.' He drove the tiny distance across the campsite to park outside her tent, then made a quick dash into it. She suppressed a giggle as he struggled with the zip, the back of his T-shirt growing dark and wet all the while. At last he got it open, reached inside and pulled out her mac, which he held over his head as he rezipped the tent and dashed back to the car. He climbed in and shook his head like a dog, sending droplets flying everywhere.

'Argh, you've made me wet!' she said.

'Serves you right. I saw you laughing at me. Your darned tent zip got caught!'

'I wasn't laughing.' She tried to look solemn and failed. 'Much.'

He regarded her seriously. 'God, Laura, I was so worried about you yesterday. Thank goodness you're getting better. That utter git. Sorry, I know you used to care about him but honestly, how can someone do that to another person?'

Laura shook her head. 'He was pissed.'

'No excuse. Being drunk just brings out a person's true character, I always think. Right then. Let's go somewhere warm, dry and quiet.' Tom put the car into gear and they drove off, along the lane that led out of the valley. They decided not to go to the pub beside the campsite. 'Too many bad associations,' Tom said.

'We'll call in there this evening though,' said Laura. 'Let the bar staff know I'm all right and thank them for helping me.'

★   ★   ★

They ended up driving around to Ullswater, and along the lakeside to Glenridding. Despite the heavy rain the lake and mountain scenery was atmospherically beautiful, in a wholly different way from the brash, bright sunshine of the previous few days. At Glenridding they stopped beside the Inn on the Lake. 'Suitable place for morning coffee?' Tom asked.

'Perfect. Probably about right for lunch as well.'

A few minutes later, and after a hurried hobble across the car park into the pub, Laura was settling down at a table near a window while Tom went to the bar to order the coffees. She pulled out her phone. There was signal here — that was good. It was two days since she'd spoken to Gran. But should she tell her what had happened with Stuart? She was still pondering this when Tom returned.

'You look pensive,' he said.

'I need to phone Gran. She'll want to know if we've had any luck finding the tin yet. But what do I tell her, about all this?' She gestured to her still-swollen knee, which was now a delightful variety of blue and purple shades. 'I mean, it'll still be bruised and sore by the time I go home so I'll have to tell her something.' Driving would be interesting, she thought, but she'd worry about that when the time came.

'Hmm. If it was me, I think I'd make up a little white lie. Tell her you fell over or something. If you tell her the truth, that it was Stuart, she'll only feel really guilty that she told him where you were. If the police get that restraining order in place you shouldn't have any more bother with him anyway.' Tom stopped speaking for a moment while a waitress brought over their coffees.

Laura nodded. It was good advice, as she'd come to expect from Tom. It was still only three months since she'd left Stuart. And given what he had done since, it would be understandable if she found herself unable to trust another man. And yet, she did trust Tom. Implicitly, and instinctively. She just knew that she could. Maybe because they'd spent so much time together this week, maybe because they'd bonded over climbing a mountain, maybe because he'd not left her side in hospital and had supported her ever since. She gazed at him as he sipped the remains of his coffee. His strong jawline, clear eyes, floppy hair and muscular shoulders. He was honest, fun and supportive. They both loved the mountains. She realised he was everything she wanted in a man. Too bad he was not looking for a relationship. And neither should she, yet, she reminded herself.

★ ★ ★

He broke into her thoughts. 'So, your Gran. Are you going to phone her?'

'Do you mind? I won't talk for long.'

'Not at all. You go ahead. They've got WiFi here, so I'll have a poke around on the internet while you're on the phone.'

'Thanks.' She picked up her mobile and punched in Gran's number. Thankfully today Gran answered quickly.

'Laura! How lovely to hear from you again. Is there news? Have you been able to find that tea caddy?'

'Hi, Gran. Sorry, I've not yet been able to go back to Brackendale . . . '

'Oh, what a pity. I thought you were planning to go yesterday? Isn't it raining today? Gosh, I do hope the reservoir doesn't refill before you have a chance to go. Laura, dear, this is so important to me. I realise it's such an odd request and that you may not find it, but I do so want you to have a look . . . so that at least I can go to my grave knowing I did all I could . . .'

'Gran, we will, I mean, I will look, I promise. I wasn't able to go yesterday. I, um, fell over. I've hurt my knee, and I need to rest it for a day or so. I'm all right, though.' She glanced at Tom, who smiled encouragingly at her lie. Yes, it was the right thing to do. No need to upset Gran. She sounded upset enough at the news that Laura had not yet searched for this mysterious tin box.

'Oh love. I'm sorry to hear that. Do be careful up in the mountains, won't you? Is it cut? Did you put a sticky plaster on it?'

Laura smiled. Gran was imagining some sort of playground graze. 'It's more bruised than cut. But it'll heal quickly, I'm sure. I'm hoping we'll go back to Brackendale tomorrow.'

'You and this young man?'

Laura winced at these words. Tom was not, and probably never would be her 'young man'. 'Yes, Tom said he'll come and help search too. Gran, why is this tin so important? You've never really explained it.' Across the table, Tom looked up, clearly wanting to know the answer to this as well.

There was a silence at the other end of the line, and then, with a sigh, Gran spoke. 'I suppose I should tell you it all, as I am asking you to search for it. I told you about my little sister, Jessie, who died when she was three, didn't I?'

'You did, yes.'

'The thing is, the police thought she was perhaps murdered. And . . . '

'Go on.'

'They arrested my father for it. Pa went to prison.'

'Gran, that's awful! But surely he wouldn't have . . . '

'No. Of course he wouldn't. He loved us both. It was hard for him after Ma died. He had two children to bring up by himself, and his business to run, and also his own father to look after. Grandpa moved in with us for a while. Then when Jessie disappeared, and Pa was arrested, Grandpa went to live with a neighbour and I went to live in a room over the Lost Sheep.'

'The pub?'

'Yes, the one in the village. There was a fellow called Tindale, or was it Teedale? Oh, my word. I can't remember. Anyway, he was the landlord there, and when Pa was arrested and taken away, I obviously couldn't stay by myself, so I lived at the pub for a while.'

'So, this tin . . . '

'Pa was put in prison, awaiting trial. I was able to visit him, after I moved to Penrith, when Brackendale was abandoned. He told me to go and look for the tin. He told me where he'd hidden it, under a floorboard on the right of the fireplace in Grandpa's room, what had been our front room.' Gran stifled a sob.

'I don't understand. Sorry, but I've got to ask, why didn't you go and look for it as he'd asked?'

'Oh Laura. I know. I've had to live with that, all my life. Knowing that I failed him. I tried, but wasn't able to retrieve it.'

'What was in the tin?'

'I don't know, love. I only know that he begged me to find it and bring it to him.'

'I promise we will look for it and do our best to find it, Gran.' Laura frowned. What on earth could be in the tea caddy? 'What happened to your father in the end?'

'Oh love, I can't talk about that. Just find the tin for me. I need to know for sure, before I die, that Pa was innocent of murdering my sister. After all these years, I just want the truth. That tin — he wanted it so much. It must be significant. This is my last chance to find out.'

It sounded as though Gran was sobbing openly now. Laura wished she was there, to hug her and comfort her. 'Gran, please, don't upset yourself. We will do everything we can to find it. The rain is due to stop later today, and it'll be fine tomorrow. We'll go to Brackendale first thing to look for it, I promise. Now then, make yourself some tea, put the TV on, and please, Gran, stop worrying about all this. You're making me worried for you.'

'Oh, I'm just a silly old woman, Laura. You're not to fret over me. Very well, I'll have some tea, and I'll think no more about the tin until you telephone me again. But you'll call as soon as you find it, won't you?'

'Of course I will.'

Laura hung up, feeling unnerved by the conversation. What could be in the tea caddy? Why hadn't Gran done more to search for it when her father had asked her to? She looked at Tom. 'I really have to do my utmost to find this thing, you know. It's eating her up. There's still something she isn't telling me, though. I have the feeling it'll all come out if or when we find it.'

20

STELLA

The good thing about living above a pub was that the household were not early risers. Stella woke with the dawn, and was pleased to see it was a fine day. It would have been a miserable cycle ride to the dam if it had been raining. She quietly dressed, dragged the suitcase out from under her bed and put the last few things into it. She crept down to the kitchen and found some bread and cheese for her breakfast. No one else was up yet, and wouldn't be for at least an hour. She had time to get away.

She hauled the suitcase downstairs, trying hard not to let it clatter against the wooden treads of the stairs. At the door she hesitated. The Teesdales would worry, wouldn't they, when they found her gone? Even though she knew they wished now that they could be rid of her, they had been kind, and it wasn't fair to just run away. She left the suitcase by the door, slipped through into the bar area and found a pad of paper and a pencil.

Dear Mr and Mrs Teesdale,
Thank you for all you have done for me since Pa was taken away. I cannot continue staying in your home and eating your food. I have gone to my aunt's in Penrith. I am

sure she will be happy to look after me. Please tell Grandpa I am safe and well and will come to see him whenever I can.

From Stella

Would that do? It would have to. It would stop them worrying, and it told them where she had gone. She'd miss Grandpa but he often didn't seem to know who she was any more. Last night when she'd gone to see him he had called her Jessie and then Edie. She'd not told him where she was going, but had given him an extra hug and a kiss as she left. Who knew when she might see him again?

'Take care, Grandpa,' she'd said.

'Aye, I will. Send Jed in to me, will you, lass?' he'd replied, sending tears springing to her eyes. She'd left quickly before Maggie or Janie noticed.

Now she left the note on the kitchen table, then quietly eased open the front door of the pub, picked up her suitcase and left.

The case was heavy, but she had only to carry it across the lane and into Pa's workshop. The bicycle was where she had left it. She found some rope and with difficulty managed to tie the suitcase to the bicycle's rack. It was a little unsteady but once she had centred it and secured it, pushing the bike out of the workshop was easy enough.

Out in the lane she stopped, looking around her at the familiar cottages and the outside of the workshop, the pub, the church. All she had ever known. She was not sure that she would ever see it again — at least, not like this. From what she had heard the grown-ups saying in the bar yesterday, it would not be long before everyone had moved out and the cottages were demolished before they were flooded. It was to be the end of Brackendale Green. And the end of her childhood, she thought. It was hard to believe she was leaving here for good, on her own. High above, a bird of prey circled over the valley. She couldn't tell if it was one of the eagles. Perhaps it was, and it was watching her leave, saying farewell to her.

She took a deep breath, climbed onto the bicycle and pushed off. Despite the weight on the back it was surprisingly easy to ride. She headed out of the village and onto the road that led along the bottom of the valley towards the dam. This was the old road, the one they had always used, the one she had walked along on her way home from school so many hundreds of times. But as the road neared the lake she realised the floodwater was over the tarmac and she could cycle along it no further. She cut across the fields on a mud track to the new road, the one that had been built just before work began on the dam. This one skirted around the edge of the valley, following its contours. When the valley was flooded, it would follow the edge of the expanded lake, Pa had explained to her.

The going was easy once she was on the new road. From here she could see how much the lake had grown even since the last day of school.

A little further on, she met some traffic. Trucks, and a huge machine painted a dirty yellow that lumbered along the road on caterpillar tracks. She'd seen a picture of something like this in school. It was a bulldozer, and it could knock down walls and flatten buildings. She came to a halt at the side of the road, shuffling the bike onto the grass verge to allow the convoy to pass. So this was it. They really were going to start demolition today. Suddenly she couldn't wait to get away. She was right to leave today. She did not want to see any part of Brackendale Green knocked down. It would break her heart.

As soon as they had passed she got back on the road, and pedalled faster now. The dam came into view as she rounded a corner. As always, she was astounded by its size. So high, so broad at its base! Would the valley really fill with water that high? It was hard to believe, even now that she'd seen how much the lake had expanded in the few weeks since the valves at the base of the dam had been closed.

The road rose slightly as it approached the dam, then skirted around the end of it. Just beyond was a turning circle for the bus, and a small bus shelter. She stopped here, untied the suitcase and then wheeled the bike around the back of the shelter. Someone would find it and probably make good use of it. She whispered an apology to whoever's bicycle it was, but it had done the job.

★ ★ ★

She'd left too early. It was a long wait until the bus came. When it finally arrived, a few dam-workers got off. There was still work to do at the site, it seemed. She was the only passenger to board. The bus driver helped her lift her suitcase onto the luggage rack.

'Where are you off to, all alone?'

'To stay with my aunt in Penrith,' she answered. 'For the summer.'

'That's nice. Which stop do you need, lass?'

Stella gave her aunt's address, and the bus driver promised to tell her where she needed to get off. She settled into a seat near the front of the bus, and stared out of the window as they drove along the road; the valley broadened, the mountains lowered and eventually were left behind. They passed through several villages, and then on to a broader, busier road that led into Penrith itself. Stella had taken this journey a few times before, with Ma, to visit Aunt Winnie. But always those trips had been just for a day's visit. This time it was a one-way journey.

The bus stop was just around the corner from Aunt Winnie's house. Stella recognised the street from her earlier visits — a row of Victorian terraced houses, red brick, all with painted front doors and neat net curtains at their windows. Aunt Winnie's was about halfway along. It had a dark green front door with a shiny brass knocker. Stella put her suitcase down on the step, took a deep breath and rapped the knocker.

Aunt Winnie answered it at once.

'Stella! What are you doing here? Your letter

only arrived this morning, love. I was going to write back to you immediately and tell you to come. What a dreadful situation, with your sister missing and your pa arrested. You should have written to me long before.'

Stella opened her mouth to explain about what she'd overheard, and how she'd just wanted to leave Brackendale as soon as possible now that she'd discovered she was not wanted, but no words would come out. To her embarrassment she began to cry. Great heaving sobs as though she was a five-year-old, not an almost-grown eleven-year-old.

'Oh love. Come inside quickly. Here, let me take your case. I'll make you some hot chocolate and you can tell me all about it. And then I'll sort out my box room for you. It's only tiny, but it's yours for as long as you need it.'

Stella breathed a sigh of relief, and followed Aunt Winnie inside. It was a small but cosy house, with chintzy furnishings and a fully plumbed, indoor bathroom with hot and cold running water. That had always amazed Stella when she'd visited before. No heating up water on the stove and filling a tin bath in the kitchen!

She sat at the table sipping the hot chocolate Aunt Winnie made her, and once her sobs were under control told her everything that had happened since she'd come home from school at the end of the summer term. Jessie's disappearance, the search for her, the visit by the police. Maggie's accusation, Pa's arrest, and the weeks since, waiting and worrying.

'Oh love. Why didn't you contact me before?'

Aunt Winnie stretched out a hand across the table.

Stella shook her head. 'I don't know. I didn't think of it, and no one else did, either. I kept thinking Pa would come back any day, and be pardoned, and Jessie would be found. It was only when Mr Teesdale said about the demolition beginning, and them all moving, and what would become of me, that I realised I could not keep staying with him and Mrs Teesdale. Aunt Winnie, is the prison where Pa is held near here? Will I be able to visit him?'

'I don't know where he'll be held, love. I'll go to the police station this afternoon and find out. Yes, I believe prisons allow visitors at certain hours. We will go together to see him. He must be worried sick about you.'

★ ★ ★

That afternoon, Aunt Winnie went to the police station to find out more about where Pa was being held. While she was gone, Stella set about unpacking her things in the little box room. It contained a narrow iron bed, a chest of drawers, and a tiny bedside table. There was a pink candlewick bedspread, pink and yellow cotton curtains at the window, a rag rug on the floor. Stella thought it was perfect. But as she unpacked, she felt a deep sadness at the circumstances that had brought her here, and the knowledge that things would never go back to how they had been. Even if by some miracle Jessie was found and Pa released, their old cottage and Pa's workshop would be demolished soon. There was no way back.

Aunt Winnie returned looking grave. 'Your father has been put in Preston jail awaiting trial,' she said. 'That is a long distance away. We would have to take a train. Visiting hours are only once a month, and we have missed it for this month. So we will need to wait until September. I am so sorry. But meanwhile, the police sergeant said you may write to your father, and I have the address.'

'I want to do that right away,' Stella said. 'May I borrow some paper and a pen?'

'Of course, poor love,' Aunt Winnie replied, and Stella was shocked to see there were tears in her eyes. She had not considered that people would be pitying her.

Stella felt better once the letter was posted and her room organised. Aunt Winnie had promised to find a new school for her in Penrith. There were still a couple of weeks left before the new term started, so there was time to settle in before making a new start. Aunt Winnie also promised to see what she could do about Pa's furniture and tools. 'You'll meet Herbert at the weekend,' she said, with a little blush. 'He's my . . . gentleman friend. He'll help us find someone with a truck or a cart so we can collect poor Jed's belongings. And we'll find someone with space in a barn to store the things in until . . . well. Until it's all needed again, I suppose, whenever that might be.' Aunt Winnie sighed and looked away. Stella could almost hear the unspoken words: *if* Pa ever needed the things again . . .

Herbert, when Stella met him over Sunday lunch, turned out to be a slightly overweight, affable man in a tweed suit, with thinning hair and a twinkle in his eye. He obviously adored Aunt Winnie and she seemed younger, livelier, happier when he was around. Stella took to him at once. If they married, she realised, Herbert would become her uncle. She thought she would like that very much.

Herbert certainly was able to help with recovering Pa's furniture and tools, and a week later the three of them travelled in a borrowed van to Brackendale. It was strange to see the village again, Stella thought. Demolition had begun of some of the farms that were nearest the lake. Sam Wrightson's farm had gone — only a mound of stone and a half-height chimney breast remained. Old George's barn where Stella had taken Jessie to look at the kittens was just a pile of rubble. She hoped the kittens had been taken somewhere safe. The trucks and bulldozer were working on a row of cottages at the end of the village. With a jolt she realised one of them had been Grandpa's.

While Herbert loaded up the van, Stella took the opportunity to call on the Earnshaws and visit Grandpa.

'Oh, it's you,' Maggie said, when she opened the door. 'After doing a runner like that I'm surprised you've come back.'

'I left a note for Mr Teesdale,' she said. 'He knew where I'd gone. I'd like to see my grandpa, please.'

'Come on in. Though he won't know you, I suspect. I doubt he's got long to go now. The poor man, having to live with the knowledge his own son's a child-murderer!' Maggie shook her head.

Stella gritted her teeth. There was no point arguing with her. She followed Maggie inside, and into the back room where Grandpa had lived since moving in with them. He was in bed, lying on his back, staring at the ceiling. As she approached he turned to look at her and frowned.

'Jessie? You've grown, lass.'

'No, it's me, Stella. How are you, Grandpa?'

'Poorly, Jessie, lass. Your old Grandpa's poorly. But better for seeing you. Will you send your pa in to me? I need to talk to him.'

'Pa's not ... Pa can't come right now, Grandpa. But if you have a message for him I will tell him when I see him.'

'Tell him ... I can't find the tin. The old tea caddy tin. There's something important in it, and it's to be kept hidden. I had it in my room ... ' The old man looked vaguely around the room, with a blank expression as though he didn't recognise anything.

'Which room, Grandpa?'

'My bedroom. Then your pa took it and put it somewhere else. I can't find it. It needs to be kept safe, or they'll take me away. Like they did with Frederick. He died, you know. He went to prison and died. Maggie told me.'

'Who is Frederick?'

'Eh?'

'Grandpa, you were saying something about someone called Frederick?'

'Aye. My old pal. He's dead now. Comes to us all in the end. It'll come to me too, Jessie. You mustn't mind when it does. I've had me days. Not all of 'em good, mind. Done some things in my time, I have.'

The old man shook his head, and stared out of the window. Stella had no idea what he was talking about.

'Should have stayed true to him, I should. Should have kept my promise. You'll do that, lass, won't you?'

'Of course, Grandpa. I always keep my promises.' She held his hand tightly, hoping to reassure him that whatever it was that bothered him didn't matter. Not to him, not now, in what she guessed would be the last months of his life.

'Aye, you're a good girl. Frederick was my friend. Friends and family. 'Tis all we have, in the end. All we have. Tell Pa I can't find the tin, won't you?'

He coughed, a long, rasping cough. Stella could hear it rattle in his chest. She held his hand while he coughed, and when the spasms subsided she stroked his forehead. 'I'll tell Pa. You're right, our family and friends are the most important. You have friends here, don't you? Maggie, and Janie Earnshaw. They're looking after you. I would have, but they said I was too young to do it on my own.'

'Your pa could have helped. But aye, Maggie and Janie are good to me, Jessie. Right good, they are, to an old man.' The cough came again, and then he closed his eyes to sleep.

Stella pulled a cover up over him and tiptoed out of the room. Janie was waiting for her in the passage.

'Maggie said you were here, love. You should know — we're moving in two days. To Keswick. It's all arranged. There's an ambulance coming to fetch your grandpa and take him to our new house. You're very welcome to come and visit us there — look, I've written down the address for you. There's a bus that runs from Penrith to Keswick.' She handed over a slip of paper, then looked at Stella with sympathy. 'I hear you're settling in well at your aunt's. That's good. I reckon it won't be long now for your grandpa. To think there'll be only you left now, of all the Walkers from Brackendale.'

'And Pa,' Stella said.

'Yes, and your pa. For now, at any rate.' Janie put a hand on Stella's shoulder, then pulled her in for a hug. When she finally let go, Stella was surprised to see tears in her eyes.

'Thank you, Mrs Earnshaw, for looking after my grandpa.'

'Brackendale folk, we look after our own,' she replied, and then she turned and hurried back to her kitchen.

Stella let herself out, happy not to bump into Maggie again. At the door she gave a huge sigh. She had the feeling she might never see her grandpa again. At least she knew he was well looked after, even if one of his nurses was Maggie. How someone could be so kind to her grandpa and yet so cruel to her pa she could not understand.

★   ★   ★

Stella called at the Lost Sheep next, to let John Teesdale know she was safe and well. The pub was clearly going to close soon, too. Much of the furniture had gone, and behind the bar were piles of crates, some full, some half empty. Mr Teesdale was there, packing away beer bottles and glasses.

'Ah, the wanderer returns,' he said, and Stella was relieved to see him smile and hear warmth in his voice.

'I'm sorry I left without saying goodbye, Mr Teesdale. But I thought it was for the best.'

'Your aunt can't have replied to your letter before you went to her, surely?'

'No, but I knew she'd be happy to have me. And I knew you needed to be able to get on with your move and not worry about me.'

He nodded slowly. 'Suspect you heard something that wasn't meant for your ears, young Stella. Well, you're settled now and that's good. And as you can see, we'll be gone in a few days too.'

'It's all coming to an end,' she said.

'Aye, lass, it is that.'

★   ★   ★

A couple of hours later, with the cottage and workshop emptied of everything worth keeping and the van packed, Stella, Aunt Winnie and Herbert were almost ready to leave Brackendale. Stella took one last walk around the empty rooms she'd grown up in. This was it. This was the last time she would be here. The last time she would see this cottage, climb these stairs, go through this door, look out of this window at the view across the valley. This was the real farewell. And no Pa to share the moment with. Jessie wouldn't have understood what was happening. Stella could imagine her crying and tantrumming, trying to unpack the crates as fast as they were packed. It was almost a good thing she was not here to see it. But no, Stella stopped herself from continuing along that line of thought. She wished with all her heart Jessie could still be here. For then Pa would be too, and everything would be as it had been. They'd be moving somewhere together, still a family. Even Grandpa.

At the thought of Grandpa, Stella remembered his rambling words about the tin box. Well, if it had been anywhere in the cottage it was surely packed in a crate in the van now. But he hadn't been making any sense. It was probably something from years ago that he was talking about. Not worth worrying about.

She left the cottage, closed the door carefully behind her, and climbed up into the van alongside Aunt Winnie.

'Well, lass? Ready?'

She nodded. Herbert started the engine and they drove out of Brackendale Green. A single tear slid down Stella's cheek as she gazed out of the window at the half-demolished, almost deserted village where she had lived all her life.

21

LAURA

The rain was still hammering down outside. Laura looked gloomily through the window of the pub. Stuart had a lot to answer for. If he hadn't come to find her, hadn't hurt her, she and Tom could have gone to Brackendale yesterday before the rain came and looked for Gran's precious tea caddy. She flexed her injured leg, wincing as pain shot up from her knee. Now it wasn't even certain that she would be able to go tomorrow. And even if she could walk well enough, what state would the village ruins be in after all this rain? Muddy at best, underwater at worst.

'How long do you think it'd take for the reservoir to refill?' she asked Tom.

'Oh, ages. Probably months of normal rainfall to get it up to its usual levels.' He regarded her carefully. 'You're worried we won't be able to look for your gran's tin, aren't you?'

She bit her lip and nodded. 'I don't know what's in it. I don't think Gran knows either, but her father was accused of murdering her sister and sent to prison for it, and begged Gran to find the tin for him. But for some reason she didn't go to look for it, or couldn't find it. She hasn't really explained what happened. I get the feeling that it's been preying on her mind all her life. We've got to do this for her. God, when will this rain stop?'

'In about two hours, according to the weather forecast,' said Tom, consulting a weather page on his phone. 'And it should be fine tomorrow. Even if it's muddy I'll be able to get to your gran's old cottage and search. Even if your knee's not up to it.' He reached for her hand. 'So don't worry. Concentrate on resting and relaxing today.'

She smiled, but pulled her hand away, remembering her promise to herself not to get involved with someone equally as damaged as she was, who was finding it hard to move on and trust someone new. 'There's not much else I can do. Wish there was something, though. Hmm, I suppose we could make use of the internet here, and see if we can find out anything more about Brackendale. Or about Gran's father, and what happened to him . . . '

'If he went to prison, there'd be court records. Not sure if those are accessible online.' Tom peered at his phone, tapping details in. 'Hmm. The National Archives site seems to say many court records are closed for a hundred years.'

Laura frowned, tapping a fingernail against her teeth as she thought hard. 'This kind of case would have been in the newspapers, wouldn't it? Are old newspapers available online?'

'It'd have made local papers at least, if not the nationals. Though a child murder may well have made the national papers.'

'That poor little girl, just three years old. Funny to think of her as my great-aunt.' Laura began searching the internet on her phone, looking for newspaper archive sites, and newspapers from Cumbria, or Westmorland as this part of the county would have been called in the 1930s. She found the *Cumberland and Westmorland Herald*, which covered the area. There was an archive site where papers had been scanned and digitised. She searched for the relevant years in the mid- to late 1930s, not entirely sure exactly when it was that Jessie had gone missing. But she knew it must be after Gran's mother had died, and she had that date from the gravestone in Glydesdale churchyard. And it was before Brackendale had been finally abandoned to the rising reservoir waters, which helped narrow it down.

There were numerous articles mentioning Brackendale and the building of the dam, and the compensation arrangements for the villagers. Laura tried searching using Gran's maiden name of Walker, along with keywords 'missing child'.

'Hey, I've found something,' she said, after checking out a lot of hits and scrolling through an endless list of articles.

'What?' Tom looked up in interest.

'An article about the murder of Jessie Walker. Listen.' She read it out.

'Penrith police, helped by underwater divers, are today searching Bereswater for the remains of a three-year-old child, Jessica Walker, who was last seen five days ago. Jessica lived with her father and older sister in Brackendale Green, the village soon to be demolished to make way for the Bereswater

267

Reservoir. A witness has stated that Jessica's father was seen on a rowing boat on the lake, dumping something over the side, on the day the child went missing. Her father, Mr Jeremiah Walker, has been taken into custody and charged with child abduction. Should a body be found, he will likely be charged with the child's murder.'

Tom stared at her. 'They thought he'd dumped the body in the lake? Good grief. I wonder who the witness was?'

Laura shook her head. 'It doesn't say. But it's, well, suspicious, isn't it? Dumping something into the lake on the day she went missing.'

'Was her body found?'

Laura shook her head. 'Gran said not. But then, it'd be pretty hard to search the whole lake.'

'It was smaller then, before the village was demolished.'

'Still a pretty big area. And they wouldn't have had all the equipment that would be used today, to search for a body underwater. The body could have been there, and the police divers just never found it, if it was weighted down. I'd imagine the lake could have been quite murky and with lots of weeds at the bottom.'

Tom grimaced. 'Horrible to think of a child's body rotting at the bottom of a lake, isn't it?'

She nodded. 'And even more horrible to think it was my ancestor who killed her and dumped her there. His own daughter! A three-year-old! What kind of person does that? And I'm descended from him.' She pulled a face. 'I'm not like that, you know. Whatever this Jed Walker did, it doesn't mean I'm the same kind of person.'

Tom smiled sympathetically. 'Of course it doesn't. I don't believe that kind of thing is passed down the generations. In the nature-versus-nurture argument, I always believe nurture has more influence on who you are and what you make of your life. You inherit things like blue eyes, brown hair and a tendency to get sunburnt et cetera, but not a tendency to murder your offspring. I don't believe that for a second.'

'I hope you're right. Still, it's kind of unnerving. Especially when I think of Gran. Jed Walker's a pretty distant ancestor for me, but he was Gran's father. She knew him and loved him. It must be very hard for her, living all these years not knowing the truth.' Laura shook her head sadly. They *had* to try to find this tea caddy, and discover the truth. She put a tentative hand on her injured knee. Would it hold up to walking out across the lake-bed tomorrow? And would they even be able to get there, or would the mud be too deep after all the rain?

'We'll do what we can,' Tom said. 'Now then, I wonder if we can find any records of the trial online? Or any later newspaper articles covering it?'

Laura watched him stabbing and swiping at his phone as he browsed websites, and felt a pang of longing for what might have been, if only they'd met before Sarah and Stuart damaged them both.

22

STELLA

A few days before the start of term at her new school in Penrith, Stella was finally able to visit her father. Aunt Winnie had written to the prison to book their visit. They travelled by train to Preston, and then walked the final part of the journey. The front of the prison looked like any other whitewashed Victorian building, facing onto the road. It could have been a gentleman's house, Stella thought. Only the sign by the door announced that it was a prison. They entered, gave their names which were checked against the list of expected visitors, and at two o'clock on the dot they were allowed to proceed. There were two locked gates; visitors were allowed through the first which was locked behind them, and then the second was opened. They passed through to a large hall, set with tables and chairs, and were invited to choose one and take a seat. Stella looked around at the other visitors. They were mostly women, some with a child or two in tow. There were a few old couples, who she assumed were parents of younger inmates. Some visitors were cheerful, jolly, bringing with them almost a party atmosphere. Others seemed more like herself and Aunt Winnie, quiet, nervous, worried. Maybe if you knew someone who'd been inside for a long time you got used to the routines of the visiting days and began to look forward to them. Stella knew she would always want to see her father, but not in these surroundings. There was something so bleak and forbidding about the grey-painted room and the functional plain tables and chairs, and the smell of stale cigarette smoke. Even the clock, mounted high on one wall, with its loud ominous ticking counting down the minutes, gave the place an unwelcoming, unnerving atmosphere.

At last a door at the far end of the room opened and a line of prisoners were ushered through. Each peered around the room until they caught sight of their relatives, and with a smile or a wave crossed the room to sit at the appropriate table.

Stella watched each one carefully, wondering when it would be Pa's face that emerged from the doorway. At last it was his turn, second to last. She gasped when she saw him. He looked so much older than she remembered, his hair matted and greying, his face unshaven, his skin mottled and his face drawn.

'Look happy to see him,' Aunt Winnie hissed at her. 'Tell him he looks well. We need to try to make him feel happier.'

Stella fixed a smile on her face as Pa walked over. She wanted to leap up and hug him, feel his arms wrapped around her, breathe in the familiar comforting smell of him, but she'd been told at the prison entrance that they could not touch the prisoner. Not even a hand across the table. So she forced herself to stay sitting as he

271

walked over and took a seat opposite her and Aunt Winnie.

'Stella, lass, it does my heart good to see you again. And Win, I can't thank you enough for taking her on.'

'I stayed with John Teesdale for a while, then wrote to Aunt Winnie,' Stella said.

Pa nodded. 'John's a good man too. But family are best at times like this.'

'Jed, it's good to see you, although the circumstances are, well, not what we would want,' Aunt Winnie said. 'Do you know when the court case will be?'

'Probably not till the New Year,' Jed said, with a shake of his head. 'And meanwhile, they won't let me out. They say I could be a danger. To Stella. As if I'd hurt my girl!' He looked at Stella and reached out a hand. She reached back automatically, but a whistle from a watching guard made her pull back her hand.

'I know you wouldn't hurt me,' she said. 'Or Jessie.' She hoped the last words didn't sound like an afterthought. He wouldn't, couldn't have hurt little Jessie, could he?

'Oh Jed. What are we to do? I mean, of course you are innocent, but what *happened* to Jessie? There must be some explanation! When did you last see the child on that day?'

'Win, I've answered all these questions, a thousand times. Do you not think I've told the police everything, and the barrister they've assigned me?'

'But won't you tell me what happened? And your daughter? Doesn't Stella deserve to know the truth of it?'

Stella watched as Pa looked from her to Aunt Winnie and back again, then shook his head. 'Win, there's nothing to tell. Jessie was there, in the cottage, with my pa. I was working in my workshop. On Bert Rowlstone's bicycle. And then I went to check on them and Pa was asleep, Jessie nowhere to be seen. That's the truth. That's all of it. I swear.'

But as he said these last words, he'd lowered his eyes, to look down at his hands clasped tightly together on the table. Once again Stella had the impression there was something he wasn't telling them. Something he was keeping secret. And this story, of Jessie disappearing from the cottage, was news to her. On the day Jessie had vanished he'd only said that she was safe, and then lied about having taken her to his fictitious cousin in Carlisle.

'Very well. I'll not ask more. I can understand you have had enough of it,' Aunt Winnie replied. Jed gave her a small, grateful smile in return. Stella wished that Aunt Winnie would question him more. Why was he so evasive? It was her sister. She had a right to know what had happened, didn't she?

'Thank you, Win. If I said owt more I'd be breaking a promise, as well as making trouble for someone I care for.' Stella frowned at this. What could he mean? But Jed pressed his lips together as if to signal the end of that topic, then turned to Stella. 'And how is Grandpa, Stella?'

'I saw him a couple of weeks ago. He's staying with the Earnshaws. They've taken him with them to their new house in Keswick. Pa, I said

I'd look after him but Maggie said I couldn't, and took him away. I would have, I could have, I know I could.'

'I know, love. But it's probably better that he is with them. Janie's a good nurse. So's Maggie. And that's what he needs now. How was he when you saw him?'

She wondered how best to answer this. Grandpa had not been well. She'd had the feeling she would never see him again. But Aunt Winnie had said she wasn't to tell Pa anything that might worry him. 'He was well, Pa. He seemed happy. Getting better.'

Pa smiled at this, a sad kind of smile, she thought.

'We've emptied the cottage,' Aunt Winnie said. 'Your furniture and tools are all safe, stowed in a barn that belongs to a friend of Herbert's, ready for when you are released and find somewhere new to live.'

'Thank you, Win.' Again, that sad smile, as though Pa thought he would not be released. 'Come and see me again? You too, Stella.'

'I start a new school next week, Pa. Penrith Girls' Grammar School. But I'll come at half term.'

'Aye. That will be nice. You be sure to work hard at school, lass, make your old pa proud.' Again he reached across the table, only to snatch his hand back when the guard blew his whistle.

'I will.' Stella had to blink to stop tears forming. Under the table Aunt Winnie took her hand and squeezed it.

★ ★ ★

Autumn came, and Jed's trial date was set for mid-January. Stella visited him in prison again during the half-term break, and planned her next visit for when the Christmas holidays started in December. But on the last day of term a letter arrived containing the news she had been expecting but dreading.

The letter was from Janie Earnshaw, and was addressed to Aunt Winnie, who read it out to Stella when she arrived home from school on a wet and windy December day.

'Sit down, love,' she said, pulling out a chair at the kitchen table. Her expression was sombre. 'There's been some bad news. I'll read you Mrs Earnshaw's letter:

> *We have some sad news for you. Isaac Walker took a turn for the worse three days ago. My daughter Maggie sat beside him, sponging his forehead and keeping him as comfortable as possible, but there was nothing that could be done. Yesterday afternoon he finally passed away, and now he is at peace. Please can you pass the news on to Stella in whatever way you think is best. Jed Walker of course must also be informed. Maggie and I do not know where he is being held, and hope that perhaps you do and can arrange for the news to reach him.*
>
> *There are some practicalities we must consider. It is probably simplest if Mr*

275

Walker is buried here in Keswick, rather than have to pay to transport his remains to Penrith or Glydesdale. There will still be funeral expenses of course. It is a delicate question but as we have borne the cost of looking after Isaac these last couple of months we are already out of pocket and cannot afford to give him a decent burial. I am not sure of the state of Jed Walker's finances or whether you have access to his funds to pay for his father's funeral.

Will you and Stella come to the funeral? Please write back by return of post and advise how we should proceed.

Yours,
Janie Earnshaw'

Stella stared at her aunt. Grandpa, gone now. Another member of her family gone. Although she'd expected it, and had seen how frail he was both when she'd seen him on the day they'd gone with Herbert to collect Pa's furniture from Brackendale Green and again when she'd visited him for one last time in Keswick at half term, it was still a shock. A tear ran down her face, but she did nothing to wipe it away, just continued gazing at Aunt Winnie's face.

'Oh love. I am so sorry.' Aunt Winnie came around the table and knelt beside her, wrapping her arms around Stella. 'We'll tell your pa in person. I've booked us a visit to the prison for tomorrow anyway. It'll be better if he hears it from us in person rather than by letter. It'll be hard for him. Your pa worshipped your grandpa, you know. He'd have done anything for him. It'll hurt not having been able to be with his pa at his passing.'

'Poor Pa.' Stella sniffed back her tears. She had to be strong for him. Aunt Winnie was right — it was so much worse for him than for her.

* * *

Snow was falling the next day, when Stella and Aunt Winnie took the now-familiar journey by rail to Preston. Thankfully it was not yet so heavy that the trains were delayed, and their journey passed without incident. Stella was quiet and thoughtful all the way, thinking of the sombre news they were about to impart, wondering how Pa would take it.

It was a strange reaction. Aunt Winnie was the one who broke the news, and as she did so Pa bent his head over, staring down at the table. When he finally looked up, his expression was odd — there was grief, yes, but it was tinged with relief, Stella thought. As though he'd been both dreading and praying for this news.

'Pa, I'm so sorry,' Stella said. This time she did not try to stop herself from crying. If you couldn't weep when telling your father about his father's death, when could you?

'It's all right, lass. I knew he wouldn't live much longer,' Pa said. 'Even though you told me he was well enough, I knew how sick he'd been back in the summer. His ailments were not ones a man can recover from. It was only a matter of time. I am glad that Maggie and Janie made sure he was comfortable in the end.'

'Jed, I'm so sorry for your loss.' Aunt Winnie was crying too, dabbing at her face with a handkerchief. 'If you'll excuse me, I had better go and freshen up. I shan't be long, Stella.' Aunt Winnie stood up, had a word with one of the guards and was escorted out to the entrance to use the visitors' toilet.

Jed watched her go and then leaned across the table, speaking urgently to Stella in a whisper, his face just inches from hers. 'When you fetched all the furniture and things from home, was there a tin? An old tea caddy? It would have been in your grandpa's room.'

'I don't know, Pa. Aunt Winnie and Herbert did most of the clearing of the cottage. I was visiting Grandpa.' A memory came to her — hadn't Grandpa been gabbling something about a tin as well? She frowned. 'Where was it in his room?'

'Unless Grandpa had taken it out for some reason, it would have been hidden. On the right-hand side of the fireplace there is a loose floorboard. Lift that up, and underneath is a hiding place. The tin was wrapped in some oilcloth and tucked in there, the last time I saw it. I put it there the day the police arrested me.'

'Why was it hidden?'

Pa paused a moment before answering. His gaze flicked over to the door that Aunt Winnie had left by. 'Because there was something in it that would have meant trouble for Grandpa, if it had been found by the police. I promised him

I'd never let it see the light of day. He's gone now, and it can't hurt him any more. But it can help me. There's something else in it, Stella, lass. Something that could help get me out of here. Can you go back to Brackendale and find it? If it's not in Herbert's friend's barn, can you go to the cottage and search for it, for me, please, lass?'

'Of course I can. It's the Christmas holidays now. I can get a bus up to the dam and walk from there.' Or ride that bicycle I borrowed, if it's still behind the bus stop, she thought.

'Good girl. What would I do without you, eh?' Pa's eyes were shining with hope.

'I don't really understand though, Pa. If you can prove your innocence, why haven't you told the police about this tin? They could have gone to fetch it, or I could have . . . '

Pa shook his head. 'It was because of your grandpa. He was too old to face what I've been through. I knew he wouldn't last long, and I wanted the tin kept hidden while he still lived. I'd promised him. He was a good father to me. I owed him that much, at the end of his life. It's not been too bad in here, and better that I suffer than him.' He took a deep, shuddering breath. 'But now he's gone I need that tin, lass. It'll prove what I told the police — that I didn't kill Jessie, and that they need to talk to the Pendletons, up at the big house.'

'What did happen to Jessie, Pa?' Stella asked quietly. Surely now he could tell her the truth. She was about to ask what was in the tin and what on earth the Pendletons had to do with it all, when she spotted Aunt Winnie returning to the visitors' hall.

'Not a word to your aunt, now. She wouldn't understand. This has to be between us. When you find the tea caddy, write and tell me, and I'll write back and tell you what to do.'

'All right.' Stella didn't understand why Aunt Winnie wasn't to know or why the tin was so important. But Pa seemed to think it would save him, and that was enough for her. She resolved to go to Brackendale the very next day. She could tell Aunt Winnie she was spending the day with a school friend. If Pa needed the tin she would find it for him.

★ ★ ★

But the snow continued all that day and all night, and Stella awoke the next day to two feet of it covering the street outside, drifts against Aunt Winnie's front door, and the wireless news announcing that all bus services from Penrith were suspended. She spent the day sitting in the front room, reading, and every now and again glancing out of the window to see if the snow had begun to thaw. Aunt Winnie tried to persuade her to go out to play, digging out an old toboggan from the cellar, but Stella did not want to. It felt wrong to be out enjoying the snow, when the snow was stopping her from doing what Pa had asked, no, begged her to do for him.

There was more snow during the day, and the next night. Herbert visited, tramping through the deep snow with bread, pork chops and milk for them. He ended up staying the night as the snow worsened and Aunt Winnie would not let him go out again.

Stella remembered how she had always loved snow in the Brackendale valley. The way it made the mountains sparkle. There'd never been any hope of getting to school when it snowed heavily, so she'd stayed home, playing out in it as much as possible, loving the feeling of her little village being cut off from the outside world yet still managing to be self-sufficient. Everyone had looked after everyone else. Farmers with dairy cattle had called round, delivering their milk to everyone in the village as there was no hope of getting it out of the valley to the usual markets. The chickens had continued laying, and there were fresh eggs each day. There'd be meat enough, hung in the outhouses, which would last. And the villagers were in the habit of buying flour and potatoes by the sack-load, so there were plenty of stores. Not like here in the town, where Aunt Winnie usually went every day to the shops to buy food in small amounts for that day and the next.

But now she resented the snow. Hated it. As the days wore on and it showed no sign of melting, she grew more and more restless. The streets of Penrith had been cleared enough to allow people to get around locally, but bus services further afield were still suspended.

It was not until after Christmas, a subdued affair with just Aunt Winnie, Herbert and herself sitting around the little table in Aunt Winnie's kitchen, that the thaw set in at last. As soon as the buses began running once more, Stella announced to Aunt Winnie that she was going to visit a school friend, who lived in a village outside Penrith. She got the feeling Aunt Winnie was only too glad to see her get out of the house at long last. She knew she'd been morose since the last visit to Preston, but she had not been able to make herself snap out of it.

★   ★   ★

It had been months since she had last made the journey to Brackendale, and she gazed out of the bus window with interest, noting everything that was different. Her last visit had been in late summer, in the borrowed van with Aunt Winnie and Herbert, when the leaves on the trees had been just beginning to turn to golden yellow and orange. Today, with the trees bare of leaves, snow still piled along the sides of the road, and grey, overcast weather, it was all very different. At last the bus reached the turning circle beside the dam, and Stella got off, checking with the driver the times for the return trip.

As soon as the bus was out of sight she checked behind the shelter, but the bicycle she had dumped there so long ago was gone. There was no choice but to walk, though without a heavy suitcase it would be easy enough. Anyway, she reminded herself, she had always walked in the past, from her primary school at Beresford in the valley just downstream of the dam. Today would be the first time she had walked this route since that fateful day at the end of the summer term, the day Jessie had gone missing and Pa had been arrested. That day felt as though it belonged to another lifetime.

As she set off, she could see the dam was doing its job. The water level on the upstream side was surprisingly high — so much higher than the last time she had been here. The old road, in the valley bottom, was completely submerged so she had no choice but to use the new road. Across the valley she could see a couple of demolished farm buildings, the lake now almost reaching to the ruins. What would Brackendale Green be like? The shape of the valley and the twists of the road kept it hidden from her until she reached the crest of a little rise in the road. From there, she knew, she would be able to see the whole village laid out before her. She steeled herself to be prepared for the sight — the demolition crew had already begun work when she had last visited, so she knew the whole village would have been knocked down by now. She had been praying that she would still be able to reach the fireplace in Grandpa's room, and that it would not be covered with rubble.

When she reached this spot she gasped, and clapped a hand over her mouth. The scene before her was not at all what she had imagined — never had she thought it would look like this. The entire village was underwater. Here and there the tops of broken-down walls or remains of chimney breasts could be seen just poking above the water level. The lane leading from the new road into the village only reached about thirty feet before disappearing underwater.

Stella slumped down onto the wet earth at the side of the road, and stared at the grey, forbidding waters of the lake. There was no way she would be able to reach her old cottage. She couldn't even tell where it was. And even if she could reach it, the tin box Pa wanted was hidden under the floorboards, under at least three or four feet of freezing water, and possibly covered by rubble as well. He'd said it contained something that would prove his innocence. But she could not get it for him. She could not help him. She could not save him. Her tears fell unchecked. It was the end of everything. She had failed him, and what that would mean for their future she could not tell.

23

LAURA

As Tom drove along the road towards the dam, Laura wondered what state the lake would be in after all the downpour of the previous day. Thankfully the forecast had been correct, and the rain had stopped overnight. The morning had dawned grey and overcast, but the clouds were high and no rain was forecast.

They passed the dam, and could see that the reservoir was still very much depleted.

'Thank goodness for that,' Laura said.

Tom smiled. 'You didn't think it would refill after a day's rain, did you?'

'Not completely, obviously, but enough to make things hard for us. We won't know the state of it until a bit further along the road anyway.'

They fell silent as they negotiated the twisting road, and then finally, as it crested a small rise, there was a view across to the old village.

'Oh my God,' Laura said, as she stared at the sight laid out before her.

'Hmm,' was Tom's only comment.

The village was still exposed, but in places the lake had encroached on it once more. Everywhere there were puddles and ponds. Gone was the dried, cracked earth of their previous visits, and in its place was a sea of mud.

'Will we be able to get across?' Laura said. As

they drove on she was trying to pick out Gran's cottage, but from the road it was hard to work it out.

'We can have a go. At least, I can, even if you find it too hard with your bad knee.'

'I'll try.' She had to try. She owed it to Gran.

★ ★ ★

They parked the car, and Tom helped Laura get out. She debated using her crutches, but in the end left them in the car and used a pair of walking poles instead. She was able to put weight on her bad leg today, and just needed a little extra support. They had the valley to themselves — the car park was deserted.

It was easy enough walking back along the road, but as she left it and crossed the line of shingle that marked the reservoir's usual high point, she found the going much harder on the lake-bed. The mud was slippery and sucked at her boots and sticks with every step.

'Follow my footprints,' Tom said. He carefully picked a route, trying to keep to the firmest-looking ground, skirting around the sizeable puddles, and gradually they made their way across to the nearest end of the village.

Laura found it hard going but she got into a rhythm and the pain from her knee was just about bearable. She would not let this defeat her.

'Can you remember which cottage it was?' Tom had stopped in what had once been the lane through the centre of the village.

'Further up. Near the other end,' she replied.

Some cottages' remains had what looked like several inches of water on their floors. She hoped Gran's was still dry enough. There was a loose floorboard by the fireplace, Gran had said. It would be one thing to dig through mud, but if it was also underwater that would make the search very difficult.

'Watch yourself here,' Tom said, skirting round a particularly deep puddle in the middle of the lane. Laura inched along beside what was left of a wall, one stick in the water to steady herself.

At that moment she felt a drop of rain. And another, and another. She looked up. The sky had darkened and the clouds lowered since they'd left the campsite, and now it was obvious that more rain would fall, despite the forecast. Tom turned to look at her.

'Hopefully only a short shower,' he said, but his worried tone told her he didn't really think so, and indeed, the rain quickly began to fall steadily. Laura cursed herself for not bringing a mac. Her clothes were soon sodden and her hair plastered to her head.

'We should go back,' Tom said.

'No. I must at least try,' she said, pushing a strand of wet hair out of her eyes. 'This is our last chance. If the rain continues it'll only get worse and the village will flood again. You go back if you want.'

'No chance. I'm staying with you,' Tom replied, and she nodded her thanks.

Laura continued picking her way through the mud, along what had once been the main street of the village. At last she reached the right cottage, with the workshop behind.

'It's this one,' she called out, and Tom lent her a steadying hand while she negotiated a large puddle in the doorway. Her trainers were soaked through. Should have put walking boots on, she thought.

'I think you're right. Where did your gran say the tin was?'

'Through there, in that back room. Right-hand side of the fireplace, under a loose floorboard.' Laura followed him through, and perched herself on a piece of wall. The rain was beginning to fall heavily now. Shame the cottage had no roof, she thought, flicking a wet strand of hair out of her eyes.

Tom knelt down in the mud and began investigating the ground beside the remains of the fireplace. He grunted as he shifted a few loose stones that had once been part of the wall of the house. Thankfully here there was not too much rubble. In other corners it was piled high. It was obvious that bulldozers had simply pushed down walls, allowing roofs to collapse, and had stopped as soon as everything was no more than about waist or chest high.

The rain was coming down in sheets now. Tom stopped scrabbling at the rubble and tugged a mac out of his day sack. 'Bit late I suppose but do you want to put this on?'

She shook her head. 'No point. Let me help.' She eased herself down to the ground, wincing at the pain in her knee. She couldn't kneel but could sit in the mud and help move rubble from there.

Tom shook his head but didn't try to stop her. The rain was growing heavier by the second and the floor of the cottage was almost entirely underwater.

Laura scrabbled at the mud and stones, pushing them out of the way. 'I can feel floorboards. You'd think the wood might have rotted after all this time.'

'Depends how much oxygen was in the water here. Being under a layer of stones and mud would have preserved it.' Tom reached into the hole she'd made and felt around. 'Definitely floorboards. We need to move a few more stones before we can see if any are loose.' They kept working, and a little while later Laura was able to get her fingers through a gap in the boards and tug. 'It's coming . . . it's coming up . . . '

'Let me,' Tom said, and Laura moved aside so he could pull at the floorboard with all his strength.

The board suddenly gave way, sending Tom crashing backwards, slipping in the mud. 'Now my bum matches my knees, in a fetching shade of mud,' he commented, as he hauled himself back to his feet. 'Anything in there?'

Laura was bending over the gap he'd exposed. 'Yes, there's something, in the mud.' She ignored the screaming pain in her knee and reached into the hole, pulling out a package wrapped in tarpaulin. 'This must be it!' Tom grinned at her, rain dripping off the end of his nose.

Laura could barely breathe as she unwrapped it. The oilcloth was stiff with age and caked with mud but came away easily enough even though it had been tightly folded at the ends and twisted back on itself. Inside was a tin — and she gasped to see it was indeed a tea caddy, decorated with images of women in saris picking tea. It seemed undamaged from being underwater for eighty years. The tarpaulin had been wrapped tightly enough to make a waterproof seal.

'Go on then, open it,' Tom said. 'I *have* to know what's in it.'

'Not in this rain!' Laura said. 'Whatever it is has survived this long. I'm not risking ruining it now. Maybe I should take it home so Gran can be the first to open it?'

'I'd bloody murder you if you did that,' he said. 'The suspense is killing me. Let's get back to the car and you can open it there. Depending on what's inside, you can work out how best to tell her about it.'

'You're right. It might not provide the answers she wants.'

Laura wrapped the tea caddy back in its tarpaulin, and with Tom's help hauled herself to her feet. Just the small matter of getting back across the mud to the road now.

It was a long and painful hobble through deepening mud, with the rainwater soaking through to her skin and running down her back, but finally they reached Tom's car. He threw an old blanket across the seats and gestured for her to get in. They used a sweatshirt that had been left on the back seat to dry themselves off a little.

At last Laura was able to unwrap the tin again. She shook it experimentally. Something moved around inside. It was definitely not empty. She dried her hands on a corner of the blanket, carefully prised off the lid with her fingernails and looked inside. There were a number of folded pieces of paper, and a small leather box. She took out the little box, and opened it. Inside was a sparkling butterfly brooch, made of gold and set with stones in many colours — sapphires, emeralds, rubies and diamonds.

'Bloody hell,' said Tom, as she held it up to him. 'That is some piece of jewellery.' He frowned. 'Where have I heard something about a butterfly brooch before? Recently, I mean . . . '

Laura thought, and then it came to her. 'At the museum. That robbery, where a load of jewellery was taken and then found years later in your ancestor's grave, when they exhumed it from here. It said just one piece was never recovered — a butterfly brooch.'

'And this could be it. In *your* ancestor's cottage.'

Laura remembered something else from the museum visit. An Isaac Walker had admitted to putting the jewels in the grave. She had not made the connection at the time — but Walker was Gran's maiden name. Isaac must have been Stella's grandfather. 'I think it was Gran's grandpa who was the gravedigger and had been questioned about the robbery. Oh God. Looks like he was definitely involved somehow, then, if he not only put the jewels in the grave but also kept one of the pieces.'

'Is this what your gran was hoping we'd find?'

Laura shook her head. 'No, it can't be. She's

hoping there's something that would prove her father's innocence regarding the murder of her little sister. I mean, this is fascinating stuff but looks to be the solution to a different mystery, not the one we're investigating.'

'What are those papers?' Tom said, gesturing to the bundle of documents.

She began to pull the papers from the tin but a drip of water from her hair fell on them, and she quickly put the lid back on, shivering. 'I think we need to be warm and dry before we go any further with this.'

'You're right,' he said. 'Come on then, let's go back to the campsite, change, and then go to the pub to investigate them properly. It's almost lunchtime anyway.'

Laura nodded, holding the precious tin on her lap. Her knee was throbbing. She'd probably overdone it, but at least they had found the tin. She took out the brooch again and inspected it closely. 'If this really is the one from the Brackendale House burglary, does that mean we would need to hand it in to the police?'

Tom glanced sideways briefly as he negotiated the twisting road along the lakeside. 'Wouldn't have thought so. Not after so many years. That burglary was in what, eighteen ninety-something? There'd be no one left alive who was even a *child* of the victims. It probably counts as treasure trove. I think you can keep it. It was in your ancestors' cottage, anyway.'

'Hmm. Well, I'll give it to Gran.' Had Gran known it was there? Was it what she'd really wanted Laura to find? As soon as she'd gone through the documents in the tin, she'd ring Gran and find out.

★   ★   ★

A little later, in dry clothes and with the rain easing off once more, they were back in the pub near the campsite. Laura felt strange going in there, for the first time since being assaulted by Stuart. One of the bar staff recognised her and Tom, was delighted to see her up on her feet and insisted they have their first drinks on the house.

'Well, that was a result,' Tom said with a grin, as they settled themselves at a table near the window.

'Don't expect me to get beaten up every time you want a free drink,' Laura replied, laughing. She put the tin on the table and once more opened it up, pulling out the little bundle of papers which she laid on the table between them. Tom moved their drinks well out of the way.

'Well, here goes,' she said, taking the first one and carefully unfolding it. She felt shaky at revealing the secrets that had been hidden so long. If she felt this nervous, how on earth must Gran feel about it? The paper was yellowed and brittle, covered in faded lettering in a spidery hand. She frowned as she read it aloud.

'This paper makes an agreement between myself, Frederick Thomas, and my friend Isaac Walker. All we had from Brackendale House to be buried in the open grave that is

293

ready for Martha Atkins, God rest her soul. Excepting one ruby ring to be kept and hidden by Frederick Thomas. The rest to be buried, and not to be retrieved until two years hence, when the hue and cry have died down. Thereafter the goods to be divided evenly, and taken afar from here, Carlisle or beyond, to be sold. And here we sign our names. Neither one of us shall ever betray the other.'

Tom listened carefully, his mouth agape. 'Wow. I seem to remember it was a Frederick Thomas who was imprisoned for the robbery when they found his wife was wearing a ring that matched the description of one of the missing pieces. And yes, Isaac Walker was questioned, wasn't he, and his cottage searched. But they didn't find this tin — that paper together with the butterfly brooch is so incriminating!'

'I suppose if it was hidden under the floorboards and covered with a rug or furniture it could easily have been overlooked by the police. But didn't Isaac tell the police the bundle in the grave had been given to him by Frederick Thomas? So he did betray him, years later, despite this agreement!'

Tom nodded. 'And he'd kept a piece back.'

'I suppose he thought that as Thomas had kept a piece so might he. Well, I'm descended from a jewel thief, it seems. One who was disloyal to his accomplice, despite their written agreement saying neither would betray the other. And I'm possibly descended from a murderer.

And here's me thinking my family were boring.'
Laura laughed aloud.

'Your great-grandfather might not be a murderer. Come on. What are these other pieces of paper?'

Laura picked up the next one and carefully unfolded, it. 'It's a letter. To Jed Walker — that's my great-grandfather. And it's from — ' she turned the letter over to see the signature — 'someone called Alexandria Pendleton. Hmm. No one we've heard of.'

'Yes, we have. Pendleton was the name of the family that owned Brackendale House. The victims of the jewellery theft. Wonder why this woman was writing to Jed Walker?'

Laura didn't answer. She was reading the letter, struggling to interpret the loopy copperplate writing. 'Seems to be connected with that burglary. Oh God. I think this Pendleton woman knew it was Jed's father who had stolen the jewels. She's threatening him with exposure. Listen:

'*You know, and I know, that your father is lying. He lied to the police forty years ago and he's lying now. I could press charges against him, but you tell me he's too old and sick to be able to face trial. You tell me it would finish him off. I commend you for your loyalty to him, but, Mr Walker, we are therefore going to have to reach some other arrangement. Something that is of benefit to us both. And of benefit as well to your children. I do see a way forward. As I suggested when I called on you earlier today, come to see me, at Brackendale House, as soon as possible. Bring your little girl.'*

Tom stared at her. 'Why did she want him to bring the child?'

Laura shrugged. 'I don't know. But there's something unnerving and a little spooky about the tone of that letter. There was something going on. Hold on, what's the date on it?' She flipped it back over. 'July the fifteenth, 1935. That's right around the time Jessie went missing.'

'Did this Alexandria Pendleton have something to do with it then, I wonder?'

Laura was already opening out the final piece of paper from the bundle. It was in the same handwriting as the previous letter. She felt a shiver run down her spine as she scanned its contents.

'Yes, Tom. She did. Read this.' She handed the paper over to him, and watched his eyes widening as he read it. 'I think it's time I phoned Gran, don't you?'

24

JED, JULY 1935

It was the last day of the school summer term. Jessie was being a nightmare of a child — touching everything in the workshop, refusing to do as she was told, giggling infuriatingly every time Jed scolded her. It was impossible to work with her around. She wouldn't stay in the cottage with Isaac either, and besides, he was asleep most of the time and no use at all as a babysitter. Jed was at his wits' end as to what to do. He had work piling up. Bert Rowlstone had brought an old bicycle in that wanted repairing. It was making a clanking sound from the bottom bracket and probably needed a new spindle. Jed had promised him it'd be done within a couple of days, but there were several other jobs half started that he needed to finish first. Thankfully, from tomorrow, Stella would be at home and could look after Jessie, before he was driven completely mad by the child. He loved her, the Lord knew he did, but he had so much else to do and to worry about.

He watched her emptying a box of screws all over the floor, and then made a grab for her as she picked up a handful of them and tried to put them in her mouth. 'Oh no, you don't, young lady. They're for fixing, not for eating.'

A thought occurred to him. He still had not

gone to see Mrs Pendleton at the big house, as she'd asked. The note, hand-delivered on the evening of her visit, had unnerved him. It reiterated what she'd said about Isaac's guilt, stating again that he should visit and that they might come to an arrangement that was of mutual benefit. He'd hidden that note. It wouldn't do to have it fall into the wrong hands. What she meant by mutual benefit he could not tell. But today, as he was clearly not going to be able to get any work done, seemed like a good day to go and find out. It couldn't hurt. And maybe it could help.

'Come on, lass. We're off for a walk. We'll go and see the big dam, shall we?'

Jessie leapt to her feet. 'Yes, let's see the big dam! Big dam!'

She had no idea what he was talking about, he realised, but no matter. As long as she behaved on the way to Brackendale House. It was a long walk, and he'd have to carry her. Unless . . . he eyed up Bert Rowlstone's bicycle. It was usable in its current state. He could sit Jessie on the crossbar. But he shook his head. She could not be trusted to hold on, or sit still, and all in all it'd be harder work by bicycle than if he carried her on his shoulders.

'Right then, let's go and tell Grandpa we're off out, and be on our way. You and me, lass, going on an adventure, eh?'

'Adventure, adventure!' Jessie squealed, jumping up and down in excitement. Jed felt a pang of guilt. He'd not been able to spend as much time with her or Stella as he should have, lately. Not since Edie had died. Well, that might all change over the summer. With Stella at home to help with the chores, perhaps he'd be able to spare some time to play with his children, the way he used to. But no. That was all a pipe-dream. Any spare time he had after working, looking after the children and Isaac, would have to be spent on finding them somewhere else to live once the valley was flooded. There were only a couple of months left before demolition was due to begin, and he still had no idea where to go or how he'd earn his living.

'Pa? I'm taking Jessie out for a bit. You'll be all right on your own?'

'Bye-bye Grandpa. Bye-bye, be good.' Jessie climbed onto her grandfather's lap and wrapped her little arms around his neck. Jed smiled as she kissed the old man's grizzled face over and over, as though she was saying goodbye to him for ever.

'Come on now, Jessie. You'll see Grandpa again at teatime. We must go or there'll be no time for our adventure.'

'Where are you taking the lass?' Isaac asked.

'Just . . . out for a jaunt. We'll be back to do your lunch.' Jed lifted Jessie off Isaac's lap and set her on the floor, to wrestle her into her coat. It might be July but there was a chill wind in the air. He did not want Mrs Pendleton thinking he didn't look after his daughter properly.

'Don't want coat!' Jessie yelled, as he tried to thread her arms into the sleeves.

'You'll wear your coat and like it,' he growled at her.

It took a while but in the end they were on their way, Jessie sitting on Jed's shoulders, her coat held under his arm. She'd won the fight. He had not the mental energy to battle her over it any longer. He headed along the old road, the one that led along the bottom of the valley. Soon, when they closed off the valves at the bottom of the dam, this road would become impassable. He wanted to use it, for old times' sake, while he still could.

Just out of the village he came across Maggie and Susie. They were walking hand in hand, Susie carrying a bunch of buttercups.

'How do, Maggie,' he said. 'Hello, Susie.'

'How do, Jed. Fine day,' Maggie responded, without a smile.

'Aye, 'tis.'

He walked on by, Jessie on his shoulders twisting to look back at them. He was glad that Maggie hadn't asked him where he was going.

★ ★ ★

Further along, a track joined the old road to the new, under the shadow of the now-completed dam. Looking up at its enormity brought it home to Jed how soon it would be before the valley had to be evacuated. This place where he'd lived all his adult life. Where he'd married and had children and lived a happy life until Edie died. Funny to think it would all be gone soon, underwater, with only fading memories remaining.

'Look, Jessie. See the big dam? When they close it off the lake will get bigger and the water will reach right to the top.' That was hard to believe too.

Jessie did not seem much interested in the dam. He lifted her down from his shoulders for a while, to give himself a rest. The child almost immediately began running off, wanting to hide in the bushes and scramble down the bank to the base of the dam.

'Jessie, come back here. It's not safe.' He ran after her, scooped up the giggling girl and put her back on his shoulders. 'Come on. We're going to take the bus now.' He had just spotted it approaching up the lane. He knew it turned around beside the dam and then headed back towards Penrith. There was a stop near the turn to Brackendale House, so it would save him about a mile's walk.

'Bus, bus!' Jessie squealed. She was so easily excited. She could be quite wearing.

It was all he could do to control her. She wanted to run up and down the aisle, climb over the seats, make faces at the driver. Thankfully at last the bus stopped beside the turning to Brackendale House and Jed left, lifting Jessie down. The driver looked relieved to see the back of them. Jed could not blame him.

What sort of reception would await them at the big house? Jed still could not fathom out why he had been invited to visit. Perhaps Mrs Pendleton had a job for him. Perhaps she wanted once more to question him about Isaac's involvement in the jewellery robbery of forty years ago. Whatever it was, she had made it quite clear to him that he should come.

As they approached the front door to the big house, Jed stopped, put Jessie down, straightened her frock and attempted once more to make her put her coat on.

'No coat!' she screamed, and Jed quickly gave up, reckoning that a calm, coatless child would be more acceptable as a visitor than a tantrumming one.

He knocked on the door of the house, wondering whether Mrs Pendleton herself would open it or whether they employed many staff. There'd been a time, before the Great War, when a house such as this would have had a full complement of servants but that war had changed everything. Isaac had been one of two gardeners here. Jed gazed around at the neatly tended shrubs and weed-free driveway and wondered who the gardener was nowadays. No one he knew, that was for certain.

The door was opened by a maid in a black dress and starched white apron and cap, but just as Jed began to introduce himself Mrs Pendleton emerged from one of the rooms off the hallway. 'Ah, Mr Walker. You have come as I asked. Please, go through to the sitting room. Polly, bring us tea and cakes. And some lemonade for the little one to drink.'

'She's never had lemonade,' Jed said.

'What would she like to drink then?'

'Milk, perhaps, if it's not too much trouble.'

Mrs Pendleton smiled indulgently and nodded. 'Of course. Milk for the child then, Polly, please.'

The maid curtseyed and scurried off towards the kitchens. Jed followed Mrs Pendleton into a large room, with dark wood-panelled walls, lined with portraits of Victorians, one woman painted dripping with jewels. A huge glass door stood open, leading out to the garden. As soon as Jessie saw it she ran out before Jed could stop her.

'Jessie, come back here now, child!' Jed called after her but Mrs Pendleton placed a restraining hand on his arm.

'It's all right. Let her run around. She cannot come to any harm out there. The garden is secure. I'm glad you have come to visit.'

'You asked me to, and said I could bring Jessie,' Jed reminded her.

'Yes, that's right. Now then, do sit down. What I have to say to you is perhaps a little delicate. I have, Mr Walker, a proposition for you. Mr Pendleton is at present in London, but he knows my mind and I have his full support.' She sat down opposite him and swallowed before continuing. 'You are struggling, I believe? You have your two daughters, you've lost your wife, and your father needs constant care and attention, as I have seen for myself. And you must surely be worried for your family's future. There is not much longer before the valley must be evacuated. Have you made any plans as to where you will live?'

'Not as yet, ma'am.' Jed was confused. Where was she going with this line of questioning?

'And I suppose it must be almost impossible

for you to travel away from Brackendale Green in order to look for lodgings, as you cannot leave either your sick father or your little girl.'

'It will be easier when school finishes for the summer,' he replied. 'Stella — my older daughter — will be home and able to take care of Jessie for me.'

'You would leave the little one in the care of a ten-year-old?' Mrs Pendleton gasped.

'Eleven. And my Stella's a responsible lass.'

'Hmm. But not a suitable person to be left in charge of a small child. Why, I witnessed for myself an accident, when your Stella allowed the child to fall into the lake. She could so nearly have been drowned! I am afraid you are guilty of neglect, Mr Walker.' She cleared her throat before continuing, holding up a hand to prevent Jed from speaking. 'Which brings me to my proposition, and the reason I summoned you here. Mr Pendleton and I were never blessed with children. And yet we would have made such good parents. The very best. I would like, Mr Walker, to have the experience of mothering, for a little while. It occurs to me that we could come to some mutually beneficial arrangement. I could care for your little girl — Jessie, you call her? — for a short while. For the summer, perhaps. While you find some-where else to live and work, and get your family organised.'

'You want to mind Jessie for me?' Jed frowned.

'I want to . . . foster her.'

'And then she'd come back to me, once I have found somewhere else for us to live?'

'Yes. The arrangement need not be permanent. Assuming, of course, that you are then in a position to be able to care for her properly.'

Jed shook his head. 'I couldn't do it. It's a kind offer, Mrs Pendleton, but I can't send my little Jessie to live with strangers, begging your pardon, ma'am.'

Mrs Pendleton stared at him, her eyes blue and cold. 'I don't think you fully understand me. I need to experience being a mother. I *have* to do this. If you do not agree, then I am afraid I shall have no choice but to press charges against your father, for his part in the burglary.'

'You are blackmailing me?'

She smiled waspishly. 'I prefer to think of it as a mutually beneficial arrangement. You get the freedom to search for a new home, unencumbered by a demanding three-year-old. You also get my assurance that we will never press charges against your father, so he can live the remainder of his life in peace. And I am given the chance to test my mothering instincts. We all win, Mr Walker.'

'Except Jessie,' Jed said quietly. He could not believe what she was proposing.

'Jessie wins too, Mr Walker. She will be safer with me, and she shall want for nothing. My husband and I will be able to provide her with so much more than you can. She shall have new clothes, a room full of toys, the best food, a nursemaid to see to her every need.'

'But she will not be with her pa, her sister and her grandpa who all love her dearly.'

'I shall love her too, Mr Walker. Don't you see,

I have so much love to give!' With these words she reached across to him and took his hand, squeezing it as if this would lend weight to her words. Her eyes glinted with unshed tears.

He believed her. She would do her best for Jessie. But could he give her up? 'And when I have a place to live, then you will bring Jessie back to me?'

'Yes, if that's what we deem is best for her at that time.'

Jed frowned again. 'Why might it not be best?'

She sighed. 'I'm just saying, things might change. We don't know what the future might hold. We might decide, at that time, that Jessie's well-being is best served by her remaining with my husband and me.'

'You mean you might keep her?'

'Only if that's what we all agreed was for the best when that time comes, Mr Walker. I am not trying to cheat you out of your child. I will write up our agreement and we shall both sign it. Now come on, Mr Walker. This is for the best for everyone, isn't it? You must see that.'

'When would you want to take her?' Jed's mind was reeling.

'There would be no point you taking her home again today, would there? So she may as well stay here now. I already have a room ready for her.'

'You planned this?'

'You know I did. I'd hardly propose such a thing on the spur of the moment. I asked you to come here with her, didn't I? And I am glad you did so. Going to the police with evidence of your father's crimes would have been a very uncomfortable thing to do.'

'But I need to fetch all her things, her clothes and such-like . . . '

Mrs Pendleton waved an elegant hand. 'No need. As I said, she shall have everything new. I shall take her to London very soon and kit her out in the finest children's clothes available.'

'London! So far! I would not be able to see her if you took her to London!'

'It may seem far to you, Mr Walker. I imagine you have not travelled much outside of Westmorland. But it is possible to reach London by train in just a few hours. My husband has an apartment there where we can live perfectly comfortably. And I do think that it would be less confusing for Jessie if we made a clean break of it, and moved her away from the surroundings she's grown up with so far. It'll be easier for her to accept the changes if they all come at once, as it were.'

'Mrs Pendleton, are you saying I would not be able to visit Jessie?'

'I think that would be for the best, don't you? It would only distress the child if she were to see you and then you were to go away again. Better that you keep away during the period of the fostering. For the summer. In any case — ' she looked away, and coughed slightly — 'we are likely to spend much of the summer away from Westmorland.'

Jed glanced out of the French doors, where he could see Jessie lying on the neatly manicured lawn, rolling down the gentle slope, giggling as she did so. Could he do it? Could he leave her here now, with people she did not know, and then not see her again for weeks, perhaps even months, until he, Pa and Stella were settled in some new lodgings, and he had set himself up with a new job? It seemed impossible. But then again, sorting out a future for his family seemed impossible too, especially with Jessie around. Maybe it would be for the best. It'd be like a holiday for her. A break from the hardships of her usual life. Who was he to deny her this chance? And if he did say no, then what would it mean for Pa? He was too old and frail to cope with being arrested and tried. It would kill him.

Jessie was skipping around the garden now, stopping here and there to pick a flower. She was not even glancing back at the house. She was happy. Every day could be like this for her, this summer, if he were to leave her here. Stella could then look after Isaac, while he, Jed, began the search for a new home and job. Yes. It would all work out perfectly.

'You agree, then?' Mrs Pendleton said, as he turned back to face her.

'You leave me little choice, ma'am. But if you will promise to love her and cherish her, the way I always have and always will, then yes, I agree to it.'

'Good. I will draw up our agreement, then. You must promise me something first, however.'

'What?'

'You will not tell anyone where Jessie is. I do not want people coming here and disturbing her, poking their noses in.'

'But folk will wonder where she is. We are a

close community in Brackendale Green. They will ask.'

'And you will not tell. You will say that she is safe, and perhaps that she has gone to live with some relative or other, while you find new accommodation. That is near enough the truth, in any case. And I will tell my staff she is an orphan I have taken under my wing.'

'But Stella . . . '

'Your other daughter? You will not even tell her the truth. That child is old enough to take it into her head to come searching for her sister herself. No, you must keep the secret. If you do not, I need hardly warn you what will happen. This will form part of our written agreement.'

Jed gazed out of the window again. Jessie was sitting on the lawn now, picking daisies and making them into a little pile. He could see she was chattering away to herself, giggling now and again. She was happy in her own little world. If he left now, she wouldn't even notice. He sighed. 'All right. I'll not say anything.'

'Good. Then I can set to work on our agreement.' Mrs Pendleton crossed the room and sat down at a walnut writing desk. As she began writing, Jed went to stand near the French windows. He wanted to go outside, gather Jessie up into his arms, breathe in the scent of her hair, tell her she was loved and that he would come back for her. But he knew that would anger Mrs Pendleton, and would only serve to confuse and upset Jessie. Instead he just stood and watched her, imprinting every last detail of her onto his memory. It would only be a couple of months. Maybe only weeks. A summer apart, and then they'd be a family again, somewhere new. And Jessie would have benefited from her time living with the rich Pendletons. Perhaps they'd stay in touch, as benefactors, sending her gifts in the future. Perhaps she might spend a couple of weeks every summer with them. Yes, he could see a good future ahead for the child. This was the right thing to do.

'Mr Walker? Perhaps you could cast your eye over this agreement which I have written out twice, and then sign both copies at the bottom. I shall sign them too, and you will keep your copy safe.'

He crossed the room to the desk and took the piece of paper she held out.

'*This is an agreement between Alexandria Pendleton of Brackendale House and Jeremiah Walker of Brackendale Green. Jessica Walker, known as Jessie and currently three years old, is to come to live at Brackendale House for the summer months, under the care of Alexandria and Sebastian Pendleton. There are to be no visits or any contact by Mr Walker or any member of his family. Mr Walker is not to tell anyone of the whereabouts of Jessie. When Mr Walker has made alternative housing arrangements for his family, and is in suitable employment, then discussions will be held to determine future arrangements for the well-being of the child.*'

Jed read the paper in silence, then gritted his teeth as he signed and dated both copies at the bottom, where Mrs Pendleton indicated. He felt as though he was signing away his own child. But it was only for a short period, and it would be beneficial for all.

Mrs Pendleton signed too, folded one paper and handed it to him with a smile, tucking the other copy away in her writing bureau. 'Well done. This is the best thing for your dear little daughter, you do realise that. She shall be well cared for, I assure you. And now, perhaps you should leave. It is almost time for luncheon.'

'I must say goodbye to her,' Jed said, walking towards the French windows.

Mrs Pendleton stepped in front of him and placed a restraining hand on his arm. 'I think not. She won't understand if you go to say farewell. When she realises you have gone and asks for you, I will distract her with toys and books and sweet things.' She smiled. 'I will tell her every day that you love her, and she will remember you and her sister in her prayers every night. Go now, before she grows bored of her games.'

She was right, he knew, but as he turned away from the windows and left the room it felt as though his heart was being torn from his chest. From the door he looked back for one last sight of Jessie. She was lying down now, on her back, throwing her collection of daisies up in the air and giggling as they fell on her in a cloud of petals. He smiled at the sight, and pushed back a tear. He could not trust himself to say anything more to Mrs Pendleton. The signed agreement was safe in his pocket, and he clutched it tightly as though it was Jessie herself.

'Write to me here when you have found a place to live, and are in a position to be able to take her back again,' Mrs Pendleton called after him.

Jed nodded. 'Aye. I will. It may only need a week or two.' If he put his mind to it, and asked Stella to care for her grandpa, maybe it would be as short a time as that until he could have Jessie back again.

'I doubt that, Mr Walker, but we'll see. Meanwhile, do not worry about her. She will be well cared for here.' She was gazing out at Jessie, her face bearing an expression of intense longing mingled with satisfaction.

★　★　★

Jed saw himself out, and walked quickly away from the house. At the turn in the driveway he stopped and looked back, but Jessie was presumably still in the back garden, and could not be seen from where he stood. To think, his daughter, living in the big house! And to think, he'd signed an agreement that said he would not see her or tell anyone where she was, all to save his own father from prison. Had he done the right thing? It was all he could do to stop himself running back to the house, hammering on the door, insisting on taking Jessie away with him again and to hell with what Mrs Pendleton might do in retaliation! But it was done now, and Jessie would be well looked after. And it wouldn't be for long.

He walked home slowly, considering what he would tell people who asked where Jessie was. He'd invent a cousin, perhaps, in Carlisle, who'd agreed to take her. Far enough away to deter people from wanting to go and check. Near enough to be a believable solution.

Stella would know it to be a lie, he realised. She'd go searching for her sister, and would be heartbroken when she couldn't find her. She'd turn against him. He'd have to find some way to tell her that Jessie was safe, and she wasn't to worry. He pictured sitting by the kitchen range with her that evening, explaining without telling her exactly where Jessie was, helping her to understand that in the long run it would all turn out for the best for their little family.

He would have to hide the agreement, he realised. As soon as he got home. Somewhere safe. The tea caddy — the same one in which Pa had hidden the butterfly brooch and his own incriminating agreement with Frederick Thomas. Yes, that was the place.

25

LAURA

Gran answered the phone quickly, thankfully. Laura could not imagine having to wait to tell her what she had found out, all that the documents said.

'Gran, we found the tea caddy,' she said, as soon as Stella had picked up.

'Oh my goodness. You really found it?' Gran's voice was shaky. 'After all this time. I never dared hope you really would . . . '

'There were some documents in it,' Laura said cautiously. 'They explain what happened to your little sister.'

Stella gasped. 'Oh . . . oh my goodness . . . my goodness . . . '

'Gran? Are you OK?' Laura was worried. Perhaps this should not be done at a distance. Perhaps it would be better if she was sitting with Gran, keeping a close eye on her, as she revealed what was in the tea caddy.

Stella answered in a shaky voice. 'Yes, dear, I'm all right. It's just, after all this time, I'm finally going to know the truth. It's a big moment. I've spent eighty years wondering about it. Knowing the truth might change everything. I'm not sure . . . '

'Gran, if you'd rather wait till I'm home, that's OK. But let me just tell you that it's not bad news. Your father definitely did not kill Jessie.'

There was a sob at the end of the phone. 'Oh, thank God. I don't think I could have borne it if he had. All these years thinking maybe he had but hoping he was innocent. And now you're telling me he was?'

'Yes, Gran. He was innocent. Do you want to hear it all?'

Laura listened as Gran took a few deep breaths and finally replied, 'Yes, love. I'm ready to hear it now.'

Laura read out the two papers relating to Jessie — the letter from Alexandria Pendleton and the 'adoption' agreement. 'You see? Your father agreed that these Pendleton people would look after Jessie for the summer, while he searched for a job and somewhere new to live.'

'He never told me where she was,' Gran whispered.

'He'd agreed not to. He kept his word. I wonder why he didn't speak up after he was accused of murder and arrested though.'

'I do remember hearing something about the Pendletons from the big house that summer. That they'd left and gone to India, I think it was. Oh — perhaps they took Jessie with them!'

'They must have planned it,' Laura said. 'They must have known they were going to India when they took Jessie, but there's nothing in the document about it, and I'm sure your father wouldn't have agreed to them taking her so far away. This agreement makes it sound like it's only a short-term arrangement.'

'They must have cheated him,' Gran said.

'He'd not have given her up for good. I can understand him agreeing to her being fostered for a short while. It would have given him time to find us a new house, and for him to get work. It was all so difficult for him at that time. But he'd never have agreed to them taking her so far away, and for good.'

'Unless they were putting some sort of pressure on him. Did you know these people well?'

'No, love. I think I may have seen them once or twice but we certainly didn't know them well. At least, I didn't. Maybe Pa knew them better.'

'There was something else, Gran, in the tin. It relates to your grandfather. It's, well, it's not such good news. Do you want to hear it?'

Gran sighed. 'Yes, love. I might as well hear everything now, and have time to think about it all before you come home. I wasn't that close to Grandpa, so I don't think bad news about him would upset me too much.'

'All right then, here goes.' Laura read out the other agreement, the one between Isaac Walker and Frederick Thomas. There was a long pause when she had finished.

'I loved Grandpa, in the way one is supposed to love a grandparent. But there was always something selfish about him. So he was a thief. And he'd robbed Brackendale House! Seems my family's history is rather tied up with that place.'

'Yes. And I wonder if the two events are connected in some way,' Laura said. 'I don't know — I'm guessing here — but what if this Alexandria Pendleton knew something about

316

your grandpa being involved in that robbery, and was using it as leverage over your pa? That seems to be what she was saying in that letter to your pa about knowing Isaac was lying.'

'Why would she have wanted Jessie?'

'Perhaps she couldn't have children of her own. It does seem suspicious — the way they disappeared off to India so soon after setting up this agreement with your father.'

'And poor Pa — he kept his word about not saying anything, even though he was arrested. I remember him saying something about Jessie having gone to live with a cousin in Carlisle. I knew he had no cousin in Carlisle. But he told me to trust him, and I did, although it was very hard when I knew he was lying and he wouldn't say anything more. The police soon found out that part was a lie, and it can't have helped his case. I knew he wouldn't have hurt Jessie, no matter what that woman was saying she'd seen.'

'What woman?' Laura asked.

'The one who said she had seen Pa dump something from a boat into the lake, on the day Jessie went missing. The assumption was that he'd been dumping her body. I knew he couldn't have hurt her! And now you have proved it! Oh Laura, thank you! I knew he was innocent!'

'Gran, what happened to him?' Laura asked gently. Last time she'd asked, Gran had refused to say.

There was a pause before the answer came in a whisper. 'He died, in prison. I can't . . . don't ask me how. I'm sorry. If I'd been able to find the tea caddy, when he asked me to, then

317

perhaps he wouldn't have . . . '

'Gran, don't blame yourself. You can't. It wasn't your fault. Your pa should have told the truth, when he was arrested. No matter what his agreement with Alexandria Pendleton was. He was . . . well . . . pretty stupid really, to allow himself to be imprisoned when he had a perfectly legitimate explanation for where his daughter was.' Jed Walker should have considered his *other* daughter, Laura thought. Letting Stella think her sister was dead. Allowing himself to be arrested and imprisoned, leaving Stella alone at such a young age! 'Gran, where did you go after your pa was put in prison? Who looked after you? Was it your grandpa?'

'Oh no. He was too frail and ill at that time. He couldn't even look after himself. I said I'd care for him but they all thought I was too young. And I was. I was only eleven. So Grandpa went to . . . oh yes, that's right. He went to live with the Earnshaws. With Maggie Earnshaw — the same woman whose evidence had put Pa in prison. She lived with her mother and her aunt. They looked after him until he died, which wasn't all that long after. I went to my aunt — my mother's sister — in Penrith. Dear old Aunt Winnie. I stayed with her right through until I was grown up and moved to London.'

'Maggie Earnshaw?' Laura had heard that name before. Tom glanced up at her, frowning.

'Yes. I didn't like her. Not just because of what she accused Pa of doing. I'd never got along with her before then either. Her mother was a kind woman — it was she who insisted they would

318

take in Grandpa. She didn't have to do that for him. And if she hadn't, who knows where he would have gone. Aunt Winnie couldn't have taken him in as well as me. She was my mother's sister. Grandpa was no relation of hers. Maggie Earnshaw had no choice but to help nurse him along with her mother. I was grateful for it at the time.' She sighed. 'Now, it makes me think, it's like divine retribution. Maggie had to atone for her sins lying about my pa, by having to look after Grandpa.'

'Well, I think our next step is to try to find out what happened to Jessie after she went to live with the Pendletons,' Laura said. A thought occurred to her. Might it be possible that Jessie was still alive? She'd have been eight years younger than Gran, so yes, theoretically it was possible.

'Oh, I would love to know what became of her,' Gran said. 'Now that I know she didn't die when she was three. I would really love to know.'

'I'll do my best to find out,' Laura said. 'But I can't promise anything.'

'Of course not. But thank you. I can rest easy now I know Pa was not a murderer.' Laura heard Gran give a huge sigh — one of relief and satisfaction.

★ ★ ★

After she'd hung up, Laura looked at Tom. 'Maggie Earnshaw. Wasn't she some relation of yours?'

He nodded. 'My great-grandmother. Did your

gran mention her? In what context?'

'Two things. Firstly, it seems that after Jed Walker was arrested, it was Maggie Earnshaw and her mother who took in Gran's grandpa — my great-great-grandfather. He was old and frail and needed nursing by that time.'

'That was good of her. I met her, you know. When I was very little, she was still alive. I remember being taken to see this very old lady, who scared me somehow. I don't know if it was just because she seemed so very old, or if it was her attitude. I have this impression she was the kind of person you wouldn't want to upset. That doesn't tally with what you've said about her looking after your ancestor. What was the other thing?'

Laura bit her lip, wondering how to tell him. She sighed. 'It seems it was the same person, Maggie Earnshaw, who gave evidence against Gran's father. It was she who said she'd seen him dump something in the lake, that the police assumed was little Jessie's body.'

'Christ. My great-grandmother dropped your great-grandfather right in it.' Tom looked down at his hands. When he raised his eyes again he looked stricken. 'God, I can't believe it. Why would she have done something like that? I mean, I had the impression as a child she could be vindictive — I remember her pinching me when no one was looking, because I'd accidentally spilled my orange squash over the table. But she must have lied about what she saw, as we know now what really happened to Jessie.'

'Perhaps though, she did see him on the lake, just doing something else. Fishing, perhaps. And she thought she'd seen him dump something.' Laura reached across the table to take Tom's hand. 'It could all be a mistake. She must have thought she was doing the right thing.'

'I feel awful. Your great-grandfather went to prison because of something my ancestor said. How long was he in prison for?'

'I don't know. Long enough. Gran said he died in prison.'

Tom shook his head. 'Tragic. How did he die?'

'Gran won't talk about that. She still feels guilty that she wasn't able to get the tea caddy from the cottage, discover its contents and prove his innocence.'

'Oh, the poor woman. I wish there was something we could do.'

'Yes. So do I.' Laura took a sip of her coffee and grimaced. It was stone cold. 'All we could try to do is find out what happened to Jessie after she went to live with the Pendletons. Gran never saw her again.'

'Hey, she could be still alive!' Tom said. 'Imagine if she was, and we could find her, and . . . '

Laura grinned. 'I don't want to dare imagine that. But yes, that would be quite something.'

'What are we waiting for, then? Get googling!'

'Let me get us some fresh coffees first,' Laura said, hauling herself to her feet to go to the bar.

'Oh no, you don't. You need to rest that leg. I'll get them.'

While he was placing the order, Laura pulled out her phone, went online and began searching. She tried searching for 'Jessie Walker', 'Jessie Pendleton', 'Jessica Pendleton' and various other combinations. Of course, they might have changed her name, she realised. She then tried 'Alexandria Pendleton', which threw up the Brackendale House website among a few other references.

'Tom, we should go back to the Brackendale House Museum,' she said, when he returned with the coffees. 'They might have more information on the Pendletons. We weren't really interested in them when we were there before. But we could go back and have a better look, and maybe even ask to see any archives they have . . . '

'Great idea!'

'You don't mind? I mean, if you'd rather do something else I could go by myself . . . '

He shook his head. 'Firstly, you're in no fit state to drive yourself with that injured knee. And secondly, if it was my great-grandmother who put your great-grandfather in prison, then I owe it to your family to help find Jessie at long last.'

She smiled. He seemed such a lovely man. What a pity the holiday was nearly over. She would miss his company.

★ ★ ★

They decided to have a quick lunch in the pub, and then head out to Brackendale House. It was raining lightly. The long hot summer seemed to be well and truly over. Laura called the museum while they waited for their food, to explain their interest in the Pendletons and to ask if there was perhaps any additional material in the archives that they might be able to see. The person who took the call sounded elderly, a National Trust volunteer, Laura guessed. His name was Frank Lowbottom, and he agreed to meet them later that afternoon.

'Well, that's us sorted for the rest of the day then!' said Tom, when she'd told him of the arrangements. 'It'll be like a bit of detective work. A cold case. I can't wait!'

Laura grinned at him. She was looking forward to it too.

* * *

They arrived at the museum around three o'clock, and were met at the front desk by Frank Lowbottom. He turned out to be exactly as he'd sounded on the phone — elderly, wearing a worn tweed suit and a mustard yellow tie, of upright bearing and with a twinkle in his eye.

'Lovely to meet you both,' he said, after Laura introduced herself and Tom. 'I must admit I do enjoy it when someone comes here with a research query. Properly gets my blood flowing, you know. So, you want to know more about the people who lived here before the war?'

'Yes, please. I have a name — Alexandria Pendleton. I think she was here in the mid-1930s and wonder what happened to her after that. She may have gone to India.'

Frank smiled and rubbed his hands. 'I can certainly help. Come this way, please.' He ushered them through to an office, which was lined with shelves holding old ledgers, books and boxes. 'We are very lucky in that the paperwork was left here. During the Second World War the house was used as billets for army officers in training. All the documents, silver and valuables were put in this room and locked away. After the war the house was left empty but with a caretaker, and then in 1973 it was gifted to the National Trust, along with its remaining furniture and archives. Now then. Alexandria Pendleton, you say?' He took a box down from a shelf and began rummaging through, then pulled out an address book. 'Now then. Here we are. This has forwarding addresses, from when the house was left empty in 1935 onwards. The caretaker kept it. It seems the Pendletons moved around a bit.'

He flicked through, and then stabbed at a page with his finger. 'Here. They went to India in the summer of 1935. They split their time between Agra and a hill station near Darjeeling. There was a Sebastian Pendleton, who worked for the civil service, his wife Alexandria, and their daughter Clara.' He flicked over another page. 'Then in 1947, after India gained independence, the family moved to London. There's an address in Kensington.'

Laura was barely listening. She was staring at Tom. 'Clara,' she whispered.

'Yes, the daughter. Are you particularly interested in her?'

'I don't know — possibly,' Laura said. 'How old was she, in 1935?'

Frank rubbed his chin and frowned. 'Well now, I have the family bible here. All the births and deaths were listed.' He pulled out an enormous leather-bound bible, opened it up and peered at the inscriptions. 'Hmm. Here's Sebastian, born 1887, but no sign of the birth of Clara. Perhaps Sebastian's generation were the last to be written in here. What a pity.'

'At least we have a name. We could try it in Google,' Tom said. 'Something might come up.'

'Ah-ha.' Frank had pulled out a sheaf of papers. 'Now then, I would photocopy these for you if I had the facilities. Lists of people — the family and staff — who lived here each year. Goes back to the mid-1800s and right through to the late 1930s. But we have no photocopier and I can't let you take them away, I'm afraid.'

'May I take a photo of them on my phone?' Laura asked. 'Should be able to zoom in and scroll around and read them then.'

Frank smiled. 'The wonders of modern technology, eh? I'd never have thought of that. Of course you may.' He laid down the documents and Laura flicked through to find relevant pages, taking snaps on her phone. She copied the pages from 1935 and 1936, then went back to the 1890s where she found mentions of Isaac Walker and Frederick Thomas in the lists of staff members. She took photos of those pages as well.

'I'm not sure what else we have here. It'd take weeks to sort through. But I hope what you have will help. I'm afraid I really must be going now. I'm due to cover the front desk in five minutes.' Frank crossed the room to the door and held it open.

Laura realised they needed to leave. She was vaguely disappointed — she could happily have spent the rest of the day going through the archives but she had a good feeling about this Clara Pendleton lead.

'Is there any Wi-Fi we can use in the museum?' Tom asked Frank.

'Oh, yes. Sit in the coffee shop, and hold on, let me jot down the password for you.' Frank handed Tom a slip of paper.

'Perfect! Coffee, Laura?'

She grinned. 'Tea and cake, please. Thank you, Frank. You've been so helpful.'

'I hope you find what you're looking for,' he replied with a warm smile, as they made their way back to the museum entrance.

⋆ ⋆ ⋆

In the coffee shop Laura connected her phone to the Wi-Fi while Tom went to order tea and cakes. She immediately began searching for 'Clara Pendleton'. Google returned several pages of hits. Laura began checking each one out. There was someone by that name on Facebook, but the photos showed a blonde woman in her twenties, partying, on holiday in Tenerife, as bridesmaid at a wedding. There was another Clara Pendleton on LinkedIn — an IT professional with experience designing point-of-sale systems. And there was a reference to the name on someone's blog about their genealogy research. Laura read this last one with interest, but this Clara had lived from 1834 to 1876, in Pennsylvania.

She realised that Clara, if it was the right person, could have married and changed her name. Her next stop was a website that listed births, marriages and deaths. She entered the name Clara Pendleton and a date range — 1950 to 1970 — but found nothing. She was on the point of giving up when she tried yet another Google search, clicked on a link to Amazon, and found a second-hand children's book, entitled *Impish Ivy and the Reluctant Rose*, written by Clara Pendleton. The date of publication was 1962. Further searches on both 'Clara Pendleton' and 'Impish Ivy' showed the book was part of a series which could be bought second-hand on various sites. 'This is promising,' she said to Tom, who'd returned with a tray of coffee and cake. 'There's a children's author from the 1960s by the name of Clara Pendleton.' She noted down the name of the publisher. The books had been out of print for well over forty years, but would the publisher still have contact details for the author? It was worth a try.

'You can buy these Impish Ivy books second-hand. And I have the name of the publisher. Would be worth contacting them, I guess.' She scrolled through the other search results. 'Oh, here's a link to an interview with Clara Pendleton!'

'That'll be interesting.'

'It's part of a series about children's authors

from the 1960s. The gist of the article seems to be that there were more authors than just Enid Blyton writing at that time, even though she's the only one most people still remember. It's dated — ' she scrolled to find the date — 'oh, just last year! And the journalist interviewed Clara Pendleton. So she might be alive still.'

'And you think she could be our Jessie?'

'It's possible — hold on.' Laura was skim-reading the article. Her heart gave a leap at what she saw. 'Wow. Yes, I do. Listen: *Clara Pendleton was born in the Lake District in 1932, and was adopted as a young child. She spent twelve years in India with her adoptive parents, before moving to London where she still lives.* The age is right. And it states that she was adopted. Yes, I think this is her.' Laura scrolled on through, then stopped suddenly, her mouth open. Silently she passed her phone to Tom so he could see too.

'*As well as the better-known Impish Ivy books,*' he read out, '*Clara Pendleton also wrote a series about a fairy godmother character called Stella. These were less popular, but Ms Pendleton said she always liked them best. 'They were based on an imaginary friend I had when I was young. Dear Stella, who was always there to look after me and with whom I had so many adventures. I was very proud of those books.''*

'It's definitely her,' Laura said. 'And now I have to find her.'

26

STELLA, JANUARY 1936

It was three days after her visit to flooded Brackendale before Stella could bring herself to write to Pa and tell him she'd been unable to reach the cottage and retrieve the tea caddy. Three days, and three sleepless nights in which she tossed and turned, trying to work out whether it would be better to write to him about it, or wait until she and Aunt Win could visit him again and she could tell him in person. Trying to decide the best way to word a letter. Whatever was in that tin was so important to him. It would prove his innocence, he'd said. But she'd failed to reach it. When she had managed to sleep at last, she'd dreamed of rising water, of reaching for something that was just beyond her grasp, her father's face looming over her telling her to reach further, stretch harder, and never mind the water. She'd wake each time just as the water went over her head, panicking, heart pounding, palms sweating. She'd never get the tea caddy now. It had rained almost constantly for the last few days and that, added to the meltwater from the snows, meant the reservoir would be filling up fast. And it would never empty again. The village, their cottage and the tin with it were submerged for ever.

Finally, one cold Sunday afternoon, Stella

forced herself to take some writing paper up to her room at Aunt Win's, and sit down to write the letter. He'd be waiting to hear from her. His future was at stake. It was the hardest letter she had ever written; it took several attempts to get it right, and as she posted it the next day she felt as though she was imposing a death sentence on him.

She had an answer within a few days.

Dear Stella,

Thank you so much for going to Brackendale Green and trying to find the thing I asked for. I have such a wonderful daughter, to do this for me. I really do think that, and appreciate all you have done.

It doesn't matter that you couldn't reach it. My case is coming to trial next month and I am sure all will be well, although my barrister says Maggie still insists she saw me that day, on the lake. Why she would say this I don't know. Truth is, Alexandria Pendleton knows where Jessie is. There was something in the tin that would prove that. I told it all to the police, but Mrs Pendleton it seems is on her way to India with her husband, taking in a tour of South Africa on the way. She never said anything about India to me. She lied to me, by omission. The police say they can't contact her until she reaches her destination in India. I can only hope she arrives there and they can get in touch with her before my trial. Don't tell your Aunt Win this. No need for her to worry any more about all this. She's good to be looking after you. It's a comfort to know you are safe there with her.

I am keeping well, and look forward to seeing you at your next half term if you are able to come then. Or if the trial is over quickly and I am found innocent, I will see you before then.

Be brave my girl, and it will soon be all over.

Pa

Stella read the letter several times trying to understand it. What did Pa mean that Mrs Pendleton knew where Jessie was? Had Mrs Pendleton taken her? Or, for some unfathomable reason, killed her? None of it made any sense.

It was only a few weeks until Pa's trial was scheduled. Stella had been pleading with Aunt Win to let her stay off school and attend the trial every day, but Aunt Win said it was no place for a child, and anyway children couldn't be present, nor must she miss her schoolwork. What would her pa think if she fell behind at school? She owed it to him to attend every lesson, learn as much as she could, and whatever happened in the future, lead a good and useful life.

Could she go and see Maggie, and convince her not to testify against Pa? Stella investigated bus times to Keswick. It was possible. She could go after school, call on Maggie, tell her what she knew from Pa's letter, plead with her to withdraw her evidence. It was only Maggie's witness statement that had made the police arrest Pa. If she withdrew it, then surely there was no case against him? Susie had only seen Pa and Jessie walking along the lane; Maggie was the only one who'd seen anything more, or at least said she had. And when the police were able to contact Mrs Pendleton in India, the truth, whatever it was, would come out. It was a plan. A good one. She resolved to put it into practice the very next week. She could tell Aunt Win she was having tea with a friend after school. Aunt Win, if she knew the truth, would be bound to stop her, saying they must let the court do its job.

* * *

It was two days later that the accident happened. She was on her way home from school, skipping alongside her friend Ada, when somehow she missed her footing, stepped on the very edge of the kerb, twisted an ankle and fell heavily. A sharp pain shot up from her foot. Ada tried to pull Stella up, away from the road, but Stella could not put any weight at all on her injured foot.

'Put your arm around my neck, I'll help you up,' Ada said, and Stella did so. Somehow they managed to get off the road and across the pavement, and Stella sat down on a garden wall. She looked at her ankle. It was horribly swollen, and the strap of her school shoe was cutting into her foot. She tried to reach down to remove the shoe, but a wave of dizziness washed over her and she almost fell. 'Hold still,' Ada said. 'I'll sort it out.'

The pain as Ada undid the buckle and gently eased the shoe off her foot was almost unbearable, and Stella had to bite her tongue to stop herself screaming out. Released from the shoe, her foot immediately swelled further.

'Oh Lord. I think you've broken something,' Ada said. 'I'll fetch help. You sit there.' She went to knock on the door of the house whose garden wall Stella was sitting on. A few moments later she returned, along with a matronly-looking woman wearing an apron.

'Aw, duckie, let's have a look at your poor foot, shall we? Can you hop along inside, if your friend helps you?' With Ada on one side and the woman on the other, Stella managed to get inside the house where the woman made her sit on a chair in the kitchen.

'Hmm. That looks nasty. You'll need to go to the hospital. Does your ma have a telephone in her house?'

'I live with my aunt. No, there's no telephone there.'

'Where do you live, duckie? I can send my Alfie round to find your aunt.'

Stella gave Aunt Win's address, and the woman went to the foot of the stairs and hollered for Alfie, who turned out to be a boy a year or so younger than Stella, wearing school shorts beneath which were a pair of dirty knees. He widened his eyes to see the two girls in the kitchen, then raced off on his errand.

Alfie's mum made sweet tea for Stella, but she

could barely drink it. She was afraid of vomiting, as her ankle was throbbing horribly. The woman had fetched a footstool and a cushion, to try to raise the ankle a little. It was all Stella could do to keep herself upright and stop herself from wailing. If only Pa wasn't in prison! Oh, to have Pa's strong arms wrapped around her now, Pa's shoulder to cry on, Pa's words of comfort in her ear!

It wasn't long before Aunt Win arrived, followed shortly afterwards by Herbert in a borrowed motorcar. He drove Stella to the hospital and a few hours later, once the swelling had subsided, a huge plaster cast was put on her leg and she was issued with a pair of wooden crutches. She and Aunt Win were given strict instructions that she must rest; there was to be no school for two weeks, no unnecessary walking on the leg — only what she had to do to get around the house.

It was when Stella returned home with Aunt Win and Herbert that she realised this meant she would not be able to go to plead with Maggie to retract her witness statement. Then, finally, she could no longer hold back the tears, and she sobbed uncontrollably while Aunt Win held her.

★   ★   ★

Before the two weeks of enforced rest were up, Jed's trial began. He was being tried for child abduction, as despite searching the lake, the village and the entire valley no body had been found. Herbert attended the trial, and brought back the news that Maggie had indeed testified, saying that she had definitely seen Jed, in a rowing boat on the lake, dumping something overboard on the day Jessie had gone missing. The bundle was wrapped in a blanket. No, she could not say what the bundle was. Yes, it was about the size that a child Jessie's age wrapped in a blanket would be.

Maggie had been smartly dressed and had spoken clearly and calmly, and the jury had nodded seriously as she gave her account. They'd believed her, Herbert thought. Aunt Win sighed, and turned away to put the kettle on.

Stella hobbled upstairs to her room, cursing her broken leg. Once again, she had failed her father. If only she could have gone to Keswick and talked Maggie out of testifying!

*   *   *

The trial was expected to last a week, and those next few days were some of the longest Stella had ever experienced. Herbert went to the courtroom each day, saying it was the least he could do, to ensure Aunt Win and Stella were kept up to date with what was happening. Aunt Win herself had not wanted to go, and besides, said she needed to look after poor Stella whose leg was healing only very slowly.

And then, three days after the trial began, in the evening after Herbert had called to give them an update on what had happened that day, they were sitting in the front room, reading quietly and drinking cocoa before bedtime, when there

335

was a knock on the door.

Aunt Win got up, smoothed her skirt and patted her hair. 'Who can that be at this time of night?' she said, as she went out to the hallway to answer the door.

She was back a moment later, her face ashen white, followed by two police officers. Stella recognised one of them — DI Parkes. He was the one who'd come to Brackendale when Jessie first went missing. It was he who'd arrested Pa and taken him away.

'Stella, love. The policemen have some bad news for us.' Aunt Win bade the police sit down, and they chose the sofa, sitting awkwardly side by side.

Stella was still sitting in the armchair by the fire, with her bad leg up on a footstool. Surely the trial couldn't be over, and Pa found guilty? Herbert had called on his way home, and told them the case for the defence would start the next day, and Pa would get to tell his side of the story at last.

'What is it?' She set her mouth into a firm line. Whatever he had come to say to them, nothing could hurt as much as when he had taken Pa away. She steeled herself to be brave.

DI Parkes cleared his throat. He looked extremely uncomfortable. 'Your father, Mr Jeremiah Walker, has, I am sorry to say, met with a spot of trouble in prison this evening. He was taken back to Preston prison after the proceedings in court today, and was returned to his cell. The trouble happened as the prisoners were on their way to the refectory for their evening meal.'

DI Parkes ran a finger around his collar.

'What happened?' If only he would just come out with it. What kind of trouble was Pa in? Had he been hurt?

The detective swallowed, his Adam's apple bobbing up and down. 'Word had got out that Mr Walker was being tried for abduction, and that his little daughter was missing, presumed dead. The prisoners, I'm afraid, made up their minds that whatever the outcome of the trial, your father was guilty of murder. Child-killers are not popular in prisons.'

Aunt Win, who had remained standing while the policeman spoke, sat down heavily in the remaining chair in the room, on the opposite side of the fireplace to Stella. She was staring at the floor, and would not raise her eyes to Stella.

'What are you saying?' Stella whispered. Not Pa hurt. After everything that had happened already, it could not be that.

'Half a dozen men, who I must make clear have all been put into solitary confinement, and will all be charged with their crime, set upon Mr Walker. He was very badly beaten and kicked, before the prison staff were able to intervene and stop the attack.'

'Oh Pa! Is he very badly hurt? Will the trial have to be halted? He was supposed to be giving his defence tomorrow, I think.'

DI Parkes shook his head sadly. 'The trial will not continue.' For one brief, glorious moment Stella thought that meant Pa would be released, proclaimed innocent, all charges dropped, and then she saw the look on the policeman's face.

'I'm very sorry to have to inform you, Miss Walker, but your father passed away from the injuries sustained in this attack. It was a vicious assault, and although the warders were very quickly able to break it up and remove Mr Walker to the sickbay, he died within minutes, and was . . . '

Stella had stopped listening. Pa, dead? Pa, murdered in prison by other inmates? It couldn't be! Not her lovely, strong pa, who could always put everything right, whose arms wrapped round her made everything better.

'Miss Walker? Do you understand what I have told you? I am extremely sorry for your loss . . . '

She nodded numbly. Her tummy felt as though a block of ice had begun forming inside it.

Aunt Win got up and crossed the room to kneel beside her. 'Stella, dear, you must be strong. This is a terrible, awful thing to happen. I can't . . . I just can't believe it.' She put an arm around Stella and tried to pull her close for a hug, but Stella felt too shocked to respond. It couldn't have happened. It just couldn't. Her pa, gone from her — she'd never see him again!

If she had been able to go to Brackendale before the snow came, and reach the tin, its contents would have proved his innocence and he'd have been released. If she had been able to follow up on her plan to go to Maggie, and convince her not to testify, the charge would have been dropped and he'd have been released. It was her fault Pa was dead. She'd had the power to save him, but she'd failed. Twice.

An enormous sob bubbled up inside her. She tried to swallow it down, and made a choking noise as she struggled to her feet, out of the room and up the stairs. Aunt Win called after her but she did not reply. She could hear DI Parkes beginning to discuss practical arrangements regarding undertakers, funerals and moving 'the body'. He wasn't a body. He was her pa. She was halfway up the stairs when she heard this, and she turned and made her way back down again, back into the sitting room.

'I-I want to see him, Aunt Win. Before we b-bury him. I want to see him.'

'Oh love.' Aunt Win held out her arms, and Stella hobbled forward and into them, and this time let herself cry, huge heaving sobs. She was vaguely aware of the policemen shuffling awkwardly out of the room behind her, but Aunt Win did not let her go, just held her tight, pressing her head against her breast, her arms holding her tightly.

'You will always have a home with me, Stella love. You know that, don't you?' she whispered. 'We'll get through this. Together.'

And Stella realised that Aunt Win was now all the family she had left.

27

LAURA

It was time to go home. Thankfully the weather had improved a little so it wasn't raining in the morning when Laura took down her tent and packed everything into her car. There was nothing worse than having to pack up camp in the rain. Tom was leaving on the same day, and they'd agreed on a couple of service stations to meet up at on the long journey back to London. Once they reached the M25 they'd go their separate ways. But they'd swapped phone numbers and email addresses, and arranged to get together the following weekend in central London to discuss progress on finding Clara Pendleton.

'I'm looking forward to seeing you again next week,' said Tom, as he helped her roll up the tent so that it fitted into its bag. He stood up and gave her a hug. 'This week's been amazing. Meeting you, following up on your gran's mystery. Just a pity the middle of the week was spoiled by your ex paying you a visit. How is your knee feeling today — you're sure you're up for driving? Because I can give you a lift, and . . . '

'And I'd have to come back up here by train some time to collect my car? No, it's fine. I'll be OK to drive. It's mostly motorway. But thanks for the offer.' She hugged him briefly back. In another life, they might perhaps have been able to turn their friendship into a relationship. But Tom had made it clear he wasn't looking for one, after Sarah, and Laura knew she should give herself more time too, after Stuart. A shame, but there it was.

And then it was time to go, and they got in their separate cars and drove out of the campsite, out of the valley that had been home for the last week, out towards Penrith, via the hospital to return the crutches she no longer needed, and onto the motorway heading south. Pressing the clutch pedal to change gear was a little uncomfortable, but once she was on the motorway Laura could stretch out her bad leg and it was easy enough. She felt lonely in the car, and switched the radio on, wondering if Tom was perhaps tuning in to the same station, listening to the same music and banter as she was . . . She shook the thought out of her head. He was a mate — that was all. That was all he ever could be, despite that delicious kiss on that romantic starlit night outside her tent. It felt like a lifetime ago.

★ ★ ★

Six hours and two stops later, she arrived outside Gran's house. Home at last! At least, the only home she had right now.

Gran must have seen her pull up outside, for she was already opening the door, Jasper the cat streaking out between her legs. Laura climbed out of the car, wincing a little as she put weight on her stiffened knee. Thank goodness she did not need crutches any more.

'Laura! Welcome home, love. How was your holiday? Have you not brought your new young man to meet me?' Gran chuckled as she stood on the doorstep with her arms held wide for a hug.

Laura tried not to limp as she walked up the garden path and into her grandmother's embrace. 'It was wonderful. And sorry, Tom's not my young man. We're just friends.'

Gran smiled. 'I've heard that one before — just friends. Maybe it'll progress to something more in time. You deserve it, after all that nastiness with Stuart. And once again, I am really sorry I let on to him where you were.'

'It's not a problem, Gran. All sorted.'

'Is it? Good. You probably needed to have a talk.'

'Er, yes. I suppose we did. But more importantly, I have that tea caddy. Let's go inside and I'll show you.' Laura quickly changed the subject. She knew she would never tell Gran about Stuart's assault on her. The police had told her that if Stuart ever harassed her in any way again she would have good grounds for taking out a restraining order on him. She'd agreed to drop charges against him and he'd been released with a stern warning.

'Oh yes, the tea caddy!' Gran turned and went inside. Laura returned to the car to fetch the carrier bag containing the tin, then followed Gran inside, pulling the front door closed behind her. Unpacking her car could wait till later.

'I'll make tea. Then I'll go through it all and tell you what we've discovered.' Laura went to the kitchen, put the tea caddy on the table and filled the kettle. She looked around. Everything was tidy and clean, dishes on the drainer, the table wiped and the floor mopped. She opened the fridge. A stack of ready meals, fresh milk, a half-dozen eggs. And bread in the bread bin. She smiled. The carers had done a good job while she'd been away.

Gran had come into the kitchen too and sat down at the table. 'It's Sophia who's been in most days to look after me,' she said, as though she'd read Laura's mind. 'We've been getting on like a house on fire. It's lovely to have you back again, but you mustn't ever worry about me, you know. If you ever want to move out and live somewhere else, I shan't mind at all.'

'Aw, thanks, Gran. But I'd like to stay here longer, if that's all right with you.' Where else could she go anyway?

'Of course it is, love. This can be your home for as long as you want it to be. You know that. Come on then, this tea caddy. I've been waiting over eighty years to see it. Show me!'

Laura placed two mugs of tea on the table, then pulled the tin out of the carrier bag and passed it to Gran. The old lady's eyes filled up as she reached out tentatively to touch it. Her hand was shaking, and she let out a deep sigh. 'All these years. I've dreamed of finding this tin but it was always just out of reach. And here it is now, sitting on my kitchen table, and my fingers are touching it at last.'

'Shall I open it for you, Gran?'

Stella didn't answer immediately. She pulled the tin closer and ran her trembling hands over the outside, tracing the faded lettering advertising Twinings tea, leaning in close to sniff at it, as though she was trying to imprint every detail on her memory. At last she pushed it back towards Laura, and nodded. 'Yes, go on then.'

'I've already described what's inside, on the phone. But good for you to see it all for yourself.' First Laura handed over the butterfly brooch and the paper documenting the agreement between Isaac and Frederick.

Gran turned the brooch over in her hands. 'This is beautiful. But it's not mine, is it? It belongs to the Pendleton family. To think of my old grandpa being a house-burglar!' She shook her head in disbelief.

'And here's the letter and the agreement about Jessie,' Laura said, handing those over for Gran to read for herself. She sipped her tea, watching as Stella's eyes travelled over the papers.

'So Pa agreed for her to be adopted,' Gran said, when she'd finished.

'I suspect he thought he was agreeing to fostering for a short period. I suspect also, judging by the tone of that letter, that Alexandria Pendleton was threatening to expose Isaac's guilt, if your pa did not agree. She must have been desperate for a child.'

'All this time, I've wondered if perhaps she or her husband killed Jessie. I knew they had something to do with it. In prison, Pa had told me that the police needed to speak to them. But they'd gone to India, and the police couldn't contact them.'

Laura stared at her grandmother. 'I don't understand that. Why couldn't the police contact them in India? Surely they could have telegraphed or written a letter?'

'Not while they were en route. I believe the police did find out the Pendletons' destination in India, and wrote to them care of the British Consul of the town, but they had no reply before . . . '

'Before what, Gran?' Laura frowned. Her grandmother's eyes had misted over.

'Before Pa died.' Stella swallowed, then reached for Laura's hand. 'I never told you what happened to him. It was halfway through the trial. That Maggie Earnshaw had already testified, saying she had seen him drop something from a boat into the lake the day Jessie disappeared. She was making it all up, but the jury believed her.'

'Were you at the trial?' Laura wondered when or if she should tell Gran that Tom was Maggie's descendant. Perhaps that was a detail that should be left out.

'No, but my aunt's gentleman friend was there, and he reported back to us each evening. It was the day before Pa was due to take the stand, when he'd been taken back to prison, that it happened.' Stella took a deep breath, then turned tear-filled eyes to Laura. 'He was attacked by other inmates, and they . . . they killed him.'

'Oh God. How horrible.' Laura was shocked.

For it to happen during the trial too — when possibly he might have been found not guilty. 'Why?'

'They thought he was a child-killer.'

'But he hadn't been convicted!'

'He wasn't even on trial for murder. It was for abduction. There was no body, so they couldn't charge him with murder. But the police told Aunt Win and me that the other inmates decided he was guilty of child-murder anyway and dished out their own punishment. I'm not sure if they meant to kill him or just give him a beating. But he died almost immediately.'

'Gran, I'm so sorry.' Laura stood, went around the table and leaned over her grandmother from behind to give her a hug. 'That's so tragic.'

'And the thing is . . . the awful thing is . . . it's my fault. If I could have found the tin, or persuaded Maggie not to lie in court . . . I could have stopped it all. I could have saved him, Laura! It's all my fault!'

'Shh, Gran. No, of course it's not your fault. You were a child. It wasn't up to you. Someone else could have found the tea caddy. He could have told the police about the agreement with Alexandria Pendleton. He chose not to, for his father's sake, but he didn't have to. And Maggie made her own decision too, though God knows why. None of it is your fault.'

'All these years. All these long years.' Gran shook her head. 'I've gone from thinking perhaps Pa did do what Maggie said, to knowing he couldn't have, to imagining reaching the tin and opening it, and discovering — who knew? And

346

the dreams, the dreams.'

'What dreams, Gran?' Laura sat down again, in the chair beside Stella, and kept hold of her hand.

'Silly ones, really. Endless dreams of trying to reach the tin, but the water rising and stopping me, and Pa shouting that I have to get to it . . . '

'And now you have.'

'Thank you, love. Maybe those dreams will stop now.' Gran patted Laura's hand, then dabbed at her eyes with a tissue she'd tucked inside her sleeve. 'The police dropped the case after Pa died. With no body and no suspect there was nothing further they could do. She was just one more missing person. I wonder though, is there any way of finding out what happened to Jessie after she went away to India with the Pendletons?'

Laura smiled. 'I'm working on that, Gran. I'll find out whatever I can, I promise.' She did not want to say too much, until she knew whether Jessie, or Clara as she was now known, was still alive. It would be awful to raise Gran's hopes only to then have to tell her that her sister was dead.

*   *   *

The days seemed to drag by as Laura waited till the weekend, when she was due to see Tom again. She'd returned to work and been greeted enthusiastically by her clients, especially Bert Williamson, who'd saved up a dozen terrible jokes to regale her with. She'd also resumed most of Gran's care duties although Gran insisted on still having Sophia come several times a week. 'Must keep in with her, for when you move out,' she said, whenever Laura protested that it was no bother for her to handle all Gran's care needs.

Whenever she had free time, Laura was searching online for news of Clara Pendleton. She discovered that Clara's publisher had been taken over years before, by HarperCollins, and contacted them to find out if they kept contact details for authors. The books were all out of print so no more royalties would be paid, but even so, perhaps they'd know something. Unfortunately though, Clara's books had been published long before the publisher was taken over, and HarperCollins were unable to help.

She turned back to the internet, and tried various searches. But she found nothing more than the hits she'd already seen — links to Clara's books, and that interview with her. Of course she'd be in her eighties and unlikely to be a user of social media, but Laura dutifully checked every possible Facebook profile and Twitter handle, with no success.

In desperation she typed into Google, 'How to find someone online in UK', and read through various articles, some offering detective services, some links to dodgy-looking software at extortionate cost. But one article suggested using the electoral roll, and gave a link.

'Why didn't I think of that?' she muttered to herself. She bet Tom would have known. Following the link she put the name Clara

Pendleton into the search box. 'No free results found' was the outcome, but further down the page a couple of Clara Pendletons were listed, the records being accessible only if she bought some credits. She sighed, but went ahead, bought the credits, and set about checking each one. The first was a young woman in Leeds, probably the same person whose Facebook photos she'd seen.

But further down the list was a Clara Pendleton, of the right age range, living in Shepherd's Bush. The record was a few years old, so it still wasn't definitive, but it was a promising lead. Laura had to stop herself from rushing through to where Gran was sitting watching TV, to tell her what she'd found. The woman still might not be alive and even if she was, might not be the right person. Laura knew she must contact her on her own first, before telling Stella anything. But how exactly would she do that? Phone her and say, 'Sorry, you don't know me but I think I may be the granddaughter of your long-lost older sister, the one you probably never knew you had? Oh, and by the way your name's not Clara Pendleton, it's Jessie Walker, and you were illegally adopted . . . ' It was a tricky situation. Not one Laura felt she could resolve herself.

There was, of course, only one thing to do. She closed the kitchen door so that Gran wouldn't overhear, and called Tom. She hoped he wouldn't mind the intrusion.

'Bloody hell, you've found her!' was his initial reaction.

Laura laughed. 'Possibly. But how can I be sure?'

'Saturday. We'll go over to Shepherd's Bush and call on her, together.'

'But . . . are you sure you want to come with me? Could be a wasted journey . . . '

'No buts. We were going to meet up anyway, might as well go to Shepherd's Bush. We can visit the market after, if you like. Besides, I was in at the start of this journey. You're not leaving me out at this exciting stage!'

'All right then. Actually, it'll be a lot easier with two of us. Of course, she might not be living there any more.'

'We'll find out on Saturday, won't we?'

'I hope so.' Laura felt her pulse race at the thought of seeing Tom again, and told herself sternly for the hundredth time that he could only ever be a friend.

28

STELLA, 1956

As she drove along the winding lane leading towards the dam, Stella found herself gradually recognising more and more of the scenery. She passed the turn-off to the old primary school, now a private home. How many times had she walked this stretch of road, firstly with her mother when she was very young, and then on her own? The last time, of course, had been on that terrible day at the end of the summer term. The day Jessie went missing. The day her life had turned upside down. She remembered how the sun had shone that day, and she'd taken a detour through the woods, and made plans for all the things she'd do with Jessie over the summer. Today, a bright, colourful day in late April, the sun shone too but from lower in the sky. The woods were an eye-watering shade of green, the sky a stunning clear blue. The meadows on the valley floor sported grass of a colour to rival the new-season leaves, and the Herdwick sheep in the fields had all lambed. Everywhere Stella looked there was new life, new growth, a future.

And yet she was driving towards her past.

At last she reached the dam, and pulled into the small car park beside it. There was an information board, displaying a few photographs of the dam under construction, and a brief mention of Brackendale Green, the village that had been demolished to make way for the dam. She counted up the words related to it. Seventeen. Just seventeen words to tell the story of the death of a community.

There was a fine view down the valley from here. Stella stood for a moment, picking out buildings she recognised — the old schoolhouse, a couple of farms, and further afield but just visible, a larger house — Brackendale House. She'd never been there, but knew it belonged to the Pendletons, although it had stood empty for many years, since they went to India before the war. What was their part in the disappearance of Jessie? Had Pa just been rambling when he'd mentioned their name in his letter from prison? She sighed, supposing she would never know.

She turned away from this view, crossed the car park and gazed over the reservoir that filled the valley above the dam. It was the first time she had come back since that terrible day when she had failed to reach their cottage and retrieve the tin Pa had wanted. Another day she hated to bring to mind. She'd lived with good old Aunt Win, and later with Herbert too after they married — a joyous occasion when she was thirteen — until she reached the age of twenty-one, after the war. She'd moved to London, attended drama school and then found theatre work in the West End, taking chorus or small parts in numerous plays and musicals. And then, in a Lyons Corner House one Tuesday afternoon between the matinee finishing and the evening show starting, she'd met Robert. Once again, her life turned upside down but this time in a good way. The best way. To think that was seven years ago and now they had two beautiful children together. Stella smiled at the memory.

But in all that time she had never been back here, to Brackendale. She'd been to Penrith many a time, of course, visiting Win and Herbert, and had always paid her respects at her mother's grave in Glydesdale and her father's in Preston, but she'd never ventured into the valley where she'd been born. Until today. She couldn't say why she'd wanted to come today, the day after poor Herbert's funeral, but it had seemed right. She'd wanted to come alone, and had left Robert looking after the children, promising them a boat trip on the *Lady of the Lake* on Ullswater the next day.

She returned to the car. Time to drive along what she still thought of as the 'new road', even though it had been here for over twenty years and the old road was deep underwater. The road hugged the shores of the lake, twisting and winding its way along. As she was driving, it was hard to look at the view — all her concentration was on the road — but she could glimpse enough to see that it was still very beautiful. Perhaps even more so with the lake filling the valley. Eventually, at the end, she reached a small, empty car park. She got out, locked the car, and stood for a moment, gazing around. The mountains were so familiar, like old friends she'd grown up with and would never forget. But the rest of the view was so different from how she remembered it. The reservoir was completely still, its surface reflecting the mountains perfectly. There was a small island a little way out in the lake — Stella tried to work out whose land that would have been. Probably part of Sam Wrightson's farm. She vaguely remembered a little hillock in his winter paddocks.

She walked towards the lakeside, back along the road a little way, and then spotted a footpath leading off to the right, up the hillside. It was signposted, 'To Glydesdale 2 miles'. It was the Old Corpse Road, she realised. The path she had last walked on the day of her mother's funeral, all those years ago.

On a whim she decided to walk it now, at least to the top of the hill. She had all day, and it was a beautiful one. Why not do it?

It was a strenuous climb. She realised that years living in London, on flat land, had made her unfit. As a child she'd have run up here. The path was well trodden. It was clear that it was a popular route with tourists. With a start she realised that she too was a tourist here, and yet she'd once been a part of this valley.

She reached the first lych-stone, situated at a bend in the path, and sat upon it to rest a while. Raising her eyes she saw the beauty of the Brackendale valley spread out before her. It was truly glorious, framed all around by the mountains, Bracken Fell soaring magnificently at its head, the lower slopes covered with last year's bracken, mostly brown but with patches here and there of the new growth in a luminous green. It was beautiful, she thought. Truly spectacular. In many ways, the lake had improved the look of the valley. No wonder many people came to visit here, to stroll along the lakeside or to climb the mountains. How many, she wondered, had any idea what lay beneath the still waters? How many had ever seen the valley as it used to be, when it was filled with fields and farms, a working community, a village at its centre and a pub, church, shop and her father's workshop at the heart of that village? So much had changed, so much had been lost, never to be recovered.

Across the valley she could see a couple of birds wheeling in the thermals. Were they the eagles, perhaps? The same ones she had known as a child or descendants of that pair, perhaps? She smiled. At least some things never changed.

29

LAURA

At last Saturday came. Laura felt like a teenager on a first date as she got ready to meet Tom, though why, she couldn't say. This wasn't a date, after all. In the Lake District her wardrobe had been limited to shorts and T-shirts, walking trousers and fleeces. But here, in cosmopolitan London, on her way to trendy Shepherd's Bush, what would she wear? What would he wear? In the end she chose a pair of ripped jeans, a loose shirt and a battered brown leather jacket she'd bought in a charity shop.

She met Tom outside Shepherd's Bush tube station as agreed. Her tummy flipped over as he walked towards her, grinning broadly, holding out his arms to give her a hug.

'Great to see you again!' He pulled her close and kissed her cheek.

It was a friendly kiss only. She forced herself to read nothing into it. Neither of them were looking for a new relationship, were they?

'How was your week?' she asked.

'Lonely. Boring, being back at work, chained to my desk. Missing the mountains. How's your gran?'

'Coming to terms with the idea that her father more or less gave her little sister away to strangers. Beginning to believe that it's not her

356

fault her father died in prison.'

'What? Why would it be?'

Laura explained about the attack, and Stella's feelings of guilt that she hadn't been able to find the tea caddy. 'She also thought she should have gone to see Maggie Earnshaw and persuaded her to retract her witness statement.'

'Aw. But she was only a child.'

Laura nodded. 'Yes, that's what I told her. It'll take time to process all she's learned but she'll get there, and find peace at last.'

Tom looked thoughtful. 'I still feel rubbish that it was my ancestor who put your ancestor in prison. Especially now we know that Maggie Earnshaw lied. It's she who was to blame for your great-grandfather's death, if anyone. I always felt she had a vindictive streak, when I met her as a kid, but I do wonder what on earth drove her to do that?'

Laura squeezed his arm. 'Don't feel bad. We're not responsible for the actions of our ancestors, are we?'

'No, I suppose not. Right then, where does this Clara Pendleton live? I can't wait to solve this mystery!'

Laura told him the address, and he opened up a map on his phone. It was only a few streets away. They began walking, past shops and cafes, then turned off the main road and along leafy streets lined with fine three-storey Victorian houses that in many cases had been split up into flats. The address Laura had for Clara turned out to be one of these, but with only one doorbell, indicating that it was still a single residence.

'Well, here we are. Number eighty-seven,' Tom said. 'Go on, ring the doorbell.'

'I'm suddenly too scared!' Laura said, with a nervous laugh. 'I mean, what will I say if she answers?'

Tom squeezed her hand. 'Just start with a smile and a 'hello', and I'm sure it'll all flow from there.'

She took a deep breath and pressed on the doorbell. Time slowed down while they waited for an answer, but finally the door was opened by a smartly dressed, middle-aged woman.

'Ah, hello, we were looking for Clara Pendleton,' Laura said.

The woman frowned. 'Sorry, I don't know anyone of that name.'

Laura felt a wave of disappointment. The electoral roll was a few years out of date but she'd hoped Clara would still be here. 'I'm sorry. I believe she used to live here. Perhaps she moved out, or . . . '

'Wait a moment. What was the name again?' the woman said.

'Pendleton. Clara Pendleton.'

'Is she old?'

'In her eighties.'

The woman frowned. 'I have a memory like a sieve, I'm afraid, but we did buy this house from an old lady, and that might have been her name. It was four years ago. She moved, now let me think, to a retirement flat. Oh! I have the address. She left a note in case any mail needed forwarding. Hold on.' She ducked back inside and a moment later returned holding an address book. 'Yes, here we are. That's her.'

Laura grinned at Tom who was waiting on the pavement, and pulled out her phone to note down the address. Still in Shepherd's Bush, she was pleased to see, so not too far away. 'Thank you. You've been so helpful.'

'Oh, good. Though I suppose I'm irresponsible, really. I should have checked what business you had with her before giving out her address?'

'She's — well, I think she may be a long-lost relative,' Laura said.

'Well, how lovely! Best of luck, then.' The woman smiled and gently closed the door.

Laura returned to Tom and showed him the address. He found it quickly on his phone's map. 'About fifteen minutes' walk away. Shall we?'

She nodded and they set off.

*   *   *

The retirement flat was one of many in a modern block a few streets away. It was conveniently situated near shops and cafes, and had its own gardens liberally sprinkled with benches and bird baths. A nice place to live at the end of your life, Laura thought. She'd been to many, many such developments. Half her clients lived in them. Their quality varied considerably and this one, she thought, was one of the better ones.

She pressed on the buzzer for flat four, before she had time to think too much about it. An answer came quickly. 'Yes?'

'Hello, is that Clara Pendleton?'

'Who's asking?' The accent was clipped, brisk.

'My name is Laura Braithwaite. I think
... that you might know my grandmother.'
Laura grimaced. Explaining the connection via
the entrance intercom system would be impossible, but thankfully at that moment a buzzer
sounded and the door was released. She smiled
at Tom and they went inside, following signs to
flat four past a communal lounge and along
corridors carpeted in beige. The door to the flat
was already open, and a petite woman wearing
tailored jeans and a pale blue cashmere sweater
was standing waiting for them. Her hair, Laura
noted, was a cloud of white, just like Gran's. Her
nose, too, had the same upturned end as Gran's
and her own.

'Miss Pendleton? It's lovely to meet you.'
Laura held out her hand, and the old lady shook
it. Her grasp was remarkably firm.

'Nice to meet you too, Miss Braithwaite. Now
then, I know a lot of people. Who is your
grandmother?'

'Her name is Stella Braithwaite. Her maiden
name was Walker. It's kind of a long story. May
we come in for a moment?'

★ ★ ★

'What time is she coming, did you say?'

'Half past three, Gran. Go and sit down,
please. Have a little rest. I'll get everything
ready.' Laura ushered Stella out of the kitchen
and into the sitting room, where Jasper was
prowling, waiting for Gran to sit down and
cuddle him. She was, understandably, nervous. It

was only to be expected. It wasn't every day you met your long-lost sister. 'Sit down, Gran. I'll show her in as soon as she arrives. Tom will be here soon as well.'

'All right, if you're sure you don't need my help. What about that cake? Have you put it out on a plate?'

'Just about to do that, Gran. Don't worry, it'll all be ready for her.'

Stella gave her a worried look but did as she'd been told, seating herself at one end of the sofa, twisting her fingers together. Jasper made himself comfortable on her lap. Laura smiled to see her reach for yet another tissue and tuck it up her sleeve, in readiness. There must be at least four up there by now.

Laura returned to the kitchen and completed the preparations. She was as nervous as her grandmother, but did not want to let on that she was. Not just about how the reunion between the sisters would go, but also about seeing Tom. Now that the mystery was solved, would this be the last time she saw him? There'd be no reason to meet up again. Perhaps they'd keep in touch for a while on social media but that wouldn't be the same. The feeling of his lips on hers, on that perfect romantic evening under the stars, came unbidden to her mind. And that night after she was discharged from hospital, lying close to Tom in his tent. There had been a spark between them, she was sure of it. She could not have imagined it. She asked herself again if she felt ready for another relationship, after Stuart. Perhaps, just perhaps she could, if it was with

Tom. But he'd said he was keeping clear of matters of the heart, since Sarah's betrayal. If only they were both unscarred, they could have had a future together.

Just as she was thinking this, the doorbell rang. She glanced in the hall mirror on her way to the door, and pushed back a stray strand of hair before opening it to Tom.

'Hi, Laura,' he said, giving her a quick peck on the cheek. 'How's your gran? She must be very excited.'

'She is. Nervous and excited. Come and meet her.' Laura showed him into the sitting room and made the introductions.

Gran's eyes sparkled as she reached up and shook Tom's hand. 'Lovely to meet you. I hear you were very helpful to Laura in the Lake District. Thank you very much.' Laura winced as she noticed Gran wink at Tom. 'I hope we'll be seeing a lot of you.'

Tom smiled. 'Yes, I hope so too.'

He was being polite, Laura could see. Before she could say anything more, the doorbell rang once more. This was it. This would be Clara Pendleton. Gran looked suddenly stricken.

'I'll get it,' Laura said, and Tom began making small talk with Stella. Calming her down, giving her something else to think about. Laura was hugely grateful to him for his sensitivity.

Clara was dressed today in a neat navy trouser suit with a pale pink blouse. She looked as though she had taken great care over her appearance. As had Stella. A taxi pulled away as Laura welcomed Clara into the hallway. 'I've asked him to come back again at five. I hope that's all right?' Clara said. Her voice sounded a little wobbly.

'Of course it is,' Laura said. Impulsively she took hold of Clara's hand and squeezed it. 'She can't wait to meet you, you know.'

Clara smiled nervously in response, and with her free hand patted her hair. 'I can't wait either.'

'Come on, then.' Laura gently pulled her towards the sitting-room doorway, and then stood aside to let her enter first.

Gran had got to her feet. Tom was standing at her side, ready, Laura thought, to support her if she needed it.

'Jessie?' Gran said, her eyes wide and glistening.

'Clara, these days,' Clara smiled. 'And you are Stella?' She took a step forward.

'Yes, Stella Braithwaite. Stella Walker as was. You were Jessie Walker. My little sister.' Gran held out her hands.

Laura realised she was holding her breath as Clara took another step forward and then took hold of both of Gran's hands.

'When I was very young, in India,' Clara whispered, 'I had an imaginary friend. She was older than me. Her name was Stella and I loved her very much.'

'Oh, my . . . my dear sister!' There were tears running down Gran's face. Laura felt her own eyes welling up and rubbed the back of her hand across them.

'Stella . . . my sister! I always wished I had one. And all along, I did!' Clara hugged Stella tightly, her diminutive figure reaching only to Gran's shoulder.

'Please, sit down, will you? I'll go and put the kettle on in a moment,' Laura said.

Both women sat on the sofa, not letting go of each other's hands, and not taking their gaze from each other's eyes.

'I would have known you, you know,' Gran said. 'You look just the same.'

'Eighty years older!' laughed Clara. 'But I suppose I never really grew up. Still tiny.'

'So tell me all about your life, Jessie — I mean, Clara! I'm sorry, but all my life you've been Jessie. It'll take me a while to remember to call you Clara.'

'That's perfectly all right. I rather like the name Jessie. And if it's what our parents named me, then of course I don't mind at all. You must tell me all about our parents. Laura didn't say very much yesterday. I always knew I was adopted, that I'd been born in Brackendale and that my real parents had died when I was very young, but that's all I knew, really.' Clara looked expectantly at Stella.

'Well, yes, that's all there is to it, really,' Gran said hesitantly. Laura had advised her not to tell all the detail of exactly how Clara had been adopted or how Jed had died. She wondered now how Gran would explain it. 'Our ma died, and Pa struggled for a while to look after us both, as well as looking after our grandpa. You were Grandpa's favourite, you know. The dam had been built and Pa was trying to find somewhere else for us to live before the village was flooded.

364

Mr and Mrs Pendleton, um, kindly offered to look after you while Pa searched for a house, but then he died suddenly, so the Pendletons adopted you and took you to India. I went to live with an aunt, Ma's sister Winnie.'

Nicely done, Gran, Laura thought, catching Gran's eye and giving a slight nod of approval.

'How did our father die?' Clara tilted her head on one side, her eyes full of sympathy for Stella.

'Um, well, it was an accident. Terrible. I don't like to . . . think about it.'

'I'm so sorry. I shouldn't have asked. I suppose I was too young to be affected by it but you, of course — it must have been so hard for you, at such a young age.' Clara leaned over to hug Stella again. 'I am glad you had an aunt to look after you. I wish, though, that Mama and Papa had adopted you as well as me.'

'I wish we'd been able to stay together too. We were far apart in age but best of friends nonetheless,' Stella said, and both women were silent for a while, just drinking in the sight of each other. 'Oh, I have something for you.' Stella reached into a pocket and pulled out the butterfly brooch.

'That's beautiful! But I couldn't possibly . . . ' Clara began, but Stella waved a hand to cut her off.

'It's nothing. It's just something I feel belongs more to you than to me. Please take it.'

* * *

Laura quietly left the room then, to make the tea. Let the sisters get to know each other again.

365

After eighty years apart, it would not be easy. She'd had a hard time yesterday initially, explaining to Clara who she really was and how she'd tracked her down. Thankfully, as Clara had known she was adopted and came from Brackendale, she was more willing to listen than Laura had feared.

Tom had followed Laura out. 'Well, that seems to have gone well,' he said. 'Can't be easy after eighty years. I had a tear in my eye then, when Clara said about her imaginary friend.'

'Me too,' Laura said. There'd be a tear in her own eye again before the end of the day, she was sure, after she'd said goodbye to Tom. As long as she managed to hold it together until he'd left. She filled the kettle and switched it on, and began putting teacups and saucers on a tray.

'What can I do to help?' Tom asked.

'Nothing, it's all right. You're a guest here too.' Laura filled a sugar bowl and added it to the tray.

'Ah, don't treat me as a guest, Laura. I'm more than that, aren't I?'

She turned to smile at him. 'You're a good friend.'

He frowned slightly, and seemed to slump a little. She crossed the kitchen to the fridge, took out a milk carton and filled a dainty jug with it.

'Should I go?' Tom said suddenly. 'I feel I'm in the way, not being part of the family. I'm glad I've seen your gran reunited with her sister, but now that's over, I probably shouldn't stay.'

Laura bit her lip. It looked as though the farewell was coming sooner than expected. 'If you like. It's up to you. I imagine you've got lots to do today.'

He stared at her, and she had to look away. She didn't want him to see that her eyes were brimming with tears.

'All right, then. I'll, um, be off. Say goodbye to your gran for me. I don't want to interrupt them.' He left the kitchen.

Laura scurried after him. 'So, well, I guess I'll see you on Facebook, then. Thanks for everything.'

Tom opened the front door, then paused. 'You don't want to get together again, perhaps, I don't know, next weekend? I was thinking of getting out of the city, maybe a walk on the South Downs or something?'

God, that was a tempting offer. But being with Tom and not being able to be *with* him would just be too difficult to bear. Better a clean break. She gave him a tight smile.

'It sounds lovely, but I'll have to say no. I think I'm working all next weekend.'

'Oh. Some other time then, perhaps.'

He turned to go, his hand on the door, one foot already over the threshold, and then she couldn't help herself. She couldn't just let him go. Not like this. One more hug, one more kiss, and then. She reached out a hand to his arm, pulled him back, and before she was fully aware of what she was doing her arms were around his neck, her body was pressed against him and her lips were upon his. This was no chaste friendly hug and kiss. This was full on, and she felt her body respond. It felt so good, it had to be right.

As she kissed him she realised two things simultaneously. One, that he was kissing her back just as fervently, and two, that enough time had passed since Stuart. She was ready, if only Tom was!

At last the kiss ended and they both came up for air.

'God, that was good,' Tom said, still holding her, stroking her hair.

'I'm sorry,' she said. 'I know you're not, well, not looking for anyone but . . . '

'Oh Christ, I did say that, didn't I? Halfway up Bracken Fell as I recall.'

'Yes, after you'd told me about what Sarah did . . . ' And she'd told him about Stuart.

He pulled her close again. 'So . . . Sarah was two years ago. I think I'm over her now, but the question is . . . '

' . . . am I over Stuart?' she finished for him. She looked up at him, at the question in his eyes, and smiled. 'Yes, I think I am. Shall we give it a go then, and see where it leads us?'

'Oh God, yes! Whoop!' Tom lifted her off her feet, and began kissing her before he put her down.

★ ★ ★

'Well, now I can see why our tea hasn't arrived yet!' Gran was standing in the doorway to the sitting room, grinning broadly. 'Look, Jess-Clara, what the young people get up to as soon as our backs are turned!'

'Shocking, isn't it?' Clara was chuckling. An

infectious, bubbling giggle.

Gran laughed too. 'Clara, you have the exact same laugh you had as a child! Like a babbling brook, Pa always said.'

'A silly, childish laugh, I always thought,' Clara replied, smiling. She fingered the butterfly brooch that was now pinned to her lapel. 'Stella, dear, shall I fetch the tea things then?'

'Oh Clara, it's all right, I'll do it!' Laura reluctantly disentangled herself from Tom. 'Give me one minute and I'll bring it in.' She closed the front door, went to the kitchen and this time allowed Tom to help.

A few minutes later, back in the sitting room and having handed everyone tea and cake, Laura settled down beside Tom on the small sofa. Gran and Clara were deep in conversation again. Tom slipped an arm around her, and whispered in her ear.

'Are you really working next weekend?'

'No, don't think so,' she replied.

'Want to do a bit of the South Downs Way, then? We could stay over in a B&B, if you like, if your gran can spare you . . . '

'Oh, of course I can spare her!' Stella interrupted. 'Sophia can come instead. You two go off and do your own thing. Clara, would you perhaps like to come to tea again next weekend?'

'With my big sister? Of course I would!' The two ladies caught at each other's hands again. Laura smiled to see them so happy, reunited at last, and then turned back to Tom.

'I'd love to spend more time with you. A walking weekend sounds perfect.'

He grinned, and she felt happier than she had ever been. A bright future shone before her, and she was looking forward to every minute of it.

Author's Note

Readers who are well acquainted with the Lake District in north-west England might recognise the real-life valley of Mardale and reservoir of Haweswater in my descriptions of Brackendale and Bereswater, and they are absolutely what this novel is based on.

A couple of years ago, having parked in the Mardale Head car park, a friend and I stood reading an information board that told the story of the destruction of Mardale Green to make way for the Haweswater reservoir. 'Here, Kath,' said my friend, 'you could write a novel about this.' And that comment is all it took — I was immediately hooked on the idea and could think of nothing else.

We climbed that day up the Riggindale Ridge and on to High Street, then over Mardale Ill Bell and down via Mardale Beck — a walk repeated by Laura and Tom in my novel albeit over renamed mountains. Until 2016 golden eagles did indeed nest in this area, the only ones in England, but it is thought the last one has now sadly died of old age.

Haweswater has dried out on a few occasions over the years, revealing the remains of Mardale Green. I was able to find photos and video footage online, all of which helped inspire the novel.

The Old Corpse Road exists, running from

Mardale Head over the fells into Swindale and was used as described in the novel to carry coffins to the mother church at Shap, before a burial ground in Mardale was consecrated.

While researching for this novel I came across a lovely account of a boy's summers in Mardale in the early years of the twentieth century. The authors, David and Joan Hay, will be long gone by now, but I owe them a debt of gratitude for their beautiful, descriptive prose which brought the drowned village to life for me.

Acknowledgements

Three editors provided input into this novel, and my heartfelt thanks go to all of them — Victoria Oundjian, Kate Mills and Celia Lomas. As always, your comments and thoughts were invaluable and helped make the book the best it could be. Thanks too to the copy-editor, proofreader, fabulous cover designers and marketing team at HQ — so many people involved in getting this book out to its readers.

I'd also like to thank my husband Ignatius and son Fionn, who both read an early version of this novel and provided useful feedback. It's so good to have the unquestioning support of my family. 'Mum, it's OK, you got this,' says my other son, Connor, whenever I have a wobble. It's much appreciated.

As always, thanks to my many writing friends — fellow HQ authors and RNA members. It's always great to be in touch with people who really understand this writing lark, and can help with encouragement, sympathy or celebration depending on what's needed.

Finally, my thanks to Pete Leeming, whose comment as we stood reading an information board in Mardale planted the seed for this novel in my head. I said at the time I'd put you in the acknowledgements, so here you are.

We do hope that you have enjoyed reading
this large print book.

Did you know that all of our titles
are available for purchase?

We publish a wide range of high quality
large print books including:
Romances, Mysteries, Classics
General Fiction
Non Fiction and Westerns

Special interest titles available in
large print are:
The Little Oxford Dictionary
Music Book
Song Book
Hymn Book
Service Book

Also available from us courtesy of
Oxford University Press:
Young Readers' Dictionary
(large print edition)
Young Readers' Thesaurus
(large print edition)

For further information or a free
brochure, please contact us at:
Ulverscroft Large Print Books Ltd.,
The Green, Bradgate Road, Anstey,
Leicester, LE7 7FU, England.
Tel: (00 44) 0116 236 4325
Fax: (00 44) 0116 234 0205